HOW DEAR IS LIFE

" How dear life is to all men ".

>Admiral Lord Nelson, dying in the cockpit of
>H.M.S. *Victory* (from *The Life of Nelson* by
>Capt. A. T. Mahan D.C.L., LLD., United
>States Navy).

HOW DEAR IS LIFE

by

HENRY WILLIAMSON

MACDONALD : LONDON

First published in 1954 by
Macdonald & Co. (Publishers), Ltd.
16 Maddox Street, W.1
Made and printed in Great Britain by
Purnell and Sons, Ltd.
Paulton (Somerset) and London

TO

C. M. D. W.

without whose help these novels

might have remained

unwritten

The characters in this book are imagined, although several of them had an existence, for one man at least, in a world which has passed away. Most of the events, including the scenes in France and Belgium, are based on actuality but are not to be attributed to any particular unit of the British Army.

For some of the details of scenes in war-time London, the author gratefully acknowledges his debt to the authors of two books:—*The Home Front* (by E. Sylvia Pankhurst), and *In London During the Great War* (by Michael Mac-Donagh).

CONTENTS

PART ONE

WINE VAULTS LANE

PART TWO

"THE GREAT ADVENTURE"

CONTENTS

Part Three

"THE RED LITTLE, DEAD LITTLE ARMY"

PART ONE

WINE VAULTS LANE

"And Summer's lease hath all too short a date."

W. Shakespeare.

Chapter 1

BOY IN THE MOON

JUST before Ladyday he bought a third-class monthly ticket from Wakenham Station to London Bridge. His father had advanced him money for this, also for luncheon tickets, since he would not be paid his first salary until half-quarter day, in the second week of May.

"At Head Office Luncheon Club, there are two kinds of luncheons available, one for a shilling and a penny, the other for ninepence. You will soon find out what proportion you will be able to afford during each half-quarter. Go steady at first, old chap, and feel your way. Experience teaches us all how to cut our coat according to our cloth."

"Yes, Father," said Phillip, thinking that his was ready-made.

"Well, don't look so doleful, my boy! A City life is not exactly the prison that you seem to think it will be. Why, bless my soul, the hours of the Moon Fire Office are considerably shorter now, than when I first went to work there in the 'nineties."

Richard went on to say that Phillip was also fortunate in the fact that he had been taken on at a Branch Office. He would find Mr. Howlett a decent manager; and if he did what he was told, and proved reliable, there were good opportunities for advancement. The office hours were now from a quarter to ten until a quarter to five, a period which gave plenty of time for long summer evenings; while six Saturday mornings a year, together with Bank Holidays, and a fortnight's summer holiday, were not to be sneezed at.

"No, Father."

Richard explained that he had made it a point for the past twenty years of leaving for the office earlier than he need, to allow for eventualities and to avoid undue hurry; he liked to walk on the far-side pavement over London Bridge, to be away from the crowd. The rush-hour was more intense now, than in his young days.

"Yes, Father."

"It will take all of twelve minutes to get to the station, Phillip."

"Yes, Father."

"Well, I hope you will not live to regret that you decided against an open-air life in Australia."

"So do I, Father."

Suspecting irony in his son—a curious boy, taken all round—Richard said no more, except, as he opened the front door, "Now mind you are not late!"

"No, Father."

The next train left Wakenham station twelve minutes after Father's, so Phillip had a little time to wait. He went into the front room, to think of old times, to enjoy the pang of reverie. Never again would he wear his school-cap, or free-wheel down the hill from school, or feel the rush of wind in his ears as the hard tyres hummed on the cobbled High Street, as in top-gear he overtook horse drays, carts, motorbuses, trams,—flying past Clock Tower and Roman Catholic church, market stalls and Electric Palace, Gild Hall and Public Baths—over Randiswell Bridge and through Randiswell; then, in bottom gear at last, up the curving avenue of chestnut trees lining Charlotte Road, past Aunt Dorrie's and Mrs. Neville's, up Hillside Road, and home. Never again to the woods in the spring—*his* woods, *his* preserves, *his* warblers and woodpeckers and nightingales.

"Phillip dear, shouldn't you be starting?"

His mother had come into the room—her room, containing her 'treasures' on the Sheraton side-table: beaded moccasins and necklaces from Canada; miniature Zulu shield, a native knee-band, an ostrich's egg, relics from South Africa brought home by her brother; little pieces of china and silver left her by Mamma; bowl of rose-leaves, its twin of lavender—this and other objects were almost as dear as life itself to Hetty, to whom the past was as real, sometimes more so indeed, as the present. Her son was her dearest possession, though never would she admit it even to herself. Had she not, when he was a baby, very nearly lost him?

He was still a child, she thought, though often wilful, even strange. For a rare moment their feelings met and mingled. Usually his feelings were concealed, for he was afraid of his family, with whom he did not share his feelings. Now on impulse he kissed his mother hurriedly, cried out "Feed Timmy Rat for me, won't you?" as he threw on new raincoat, and dobbed bowler hat on head; then snatching walking-stick and gloves, ran out of the door and down the path to the gate, while making sure of money in trouser pocket, handkerchief in breast pocket, gun-metal watch on plaited horse-hair cord across waistcoat. Why did Mother have to wave and smile by the fern in the middle window of the front room, as though he was going away for good? He waved slightly, and then heard the front door of Mrs. Bigge's house below opening, and Mrs. Bigge's voice saying, as she too waved a hand,

"Good luck, Phillip! Don't let me stop you, dear! I just wanted to wish you luck!"

"Thank you, and the same to you, Mrs. Bigge."

Then of course as he passed Gran'pa's house there was rattle of knuckles on glass, and Gran'pa and Miss Rooney, his house-keeper, smiling and nodding.

Waving perfunctorily, he hurried on, before they could stop him. Eyes on asphalt path he passed the top house—to dare to look for Helena Rolls was like daring to look at the sun—and strode fast up the gully to the crest of the Hill. He was across it and had left behind the old, pale-brown flag-stones, haunt of many idle dogs let out from the early Victorian houses, and was crossing the High Road to Wakenham station, in just over seven minutes since leaving home.

In Railway Approach he bought a ha'penny newspaper from a man with a wooden leg standing at a trestle table covered with piles of newspapers. He took *The Daily Chronicle*, the first one to hand, for the man was busy with many people, tossing coppers into a tin plate, whipping off papers with both hands, some-times putting sixpences between his lips while giving change.

Phillip went away with it under his arm, feeling rather daring that he had bought a Liberal paper, the one Uncle Jim Pickering took, when he was Unionist, like Father. He showed his clean new season-ticket, a little surprised that the collector did not appear to notice that it was his first day. He went up the wooden steps and over the covered bridge to the far platform. There he waited with others for the up train.

No one spoke. There was a push for carriages when the train came in. Not wanting to be one of the pushers, he hung back and managed to get into a crowded smoker just as the guard

waved his green flag and the whistle blew. The engine starting
jerked him against someone's bowler hat: he apologised, but
received only a semi-indignant glance as the owner, puffing a
pipe with a cracked, coke-like rim, opened a newspaper and hid
his face from further sight.

He opened the *Chronicle*. Imagining Uncle Jim Pickering on
his face, he tried to read while he swayed, throat and eyes
irritated by blue tobacco smoke arising from five bowler hats
on one side and five on the other, and three in front of him.
The windows were closed. The only human sounds were occasional coughing, rustling of paper, gurgling and puffing of pipes.
Now and then an eye regarded him covertly. He moved his feet,
to get a better balance. He trod on someone's toe, and apologised. Again there was no reply.

It was impossible to read, so he made a game of trying to
balance with only one finger on the bar of the luggage rack.
The train rattled and swayed over points, rushed momentarily
into dark tunnels. Its speed increased past the familiar red-brick
Mazawattee Tea factory, and now it was on the embankment
above the low cottages of Bermondsey. There was a stir, folding
of newspapers, pressing of bodies, as London Bridge approached.
In turn he squeezed his way out, relieved to breathe cold fresh
air again, and went along in the dark streams slowing by the
ticket barrier. Out of the station, at last he could lengthen his
stride and find his own way past and between slower, older men.

Upon London Bridge bowler hats bobbled away as far as he
could see, right up to the buildings on the other side. As he
crossed over the Thames he marvelled at the roar of continuous
wheeled traffic arising from the granite roadway. Red motor
omnibuses were passing and repassing on solid rubber tyres.
Drays, drawn by great Clydesdale and grey Percheron horses,
and piled high with beer barrels, bales of straw and hay, coal,
or great white rolls of paper, had the iron rims of their wheels
polished bright. Among them cabs, carts, taxicabs passed end-
lessly, in the dull roar of iron on sett-stone. Gulls screamed just
over the parapet, adding to the lesser continuous noise of
leather soles upon the big square flag-stones. The entire bridge
was a-roar with wheels. It was all rather thrilling.

He kept beside the parapet, to see the river below. The Pool
to the Tower Bridge was crowded with all kinds of shipping;
sails, masts, smoke-stacks, barges. Perhaps cousin Gerry was,

at that moment, steaming up from beyond Gravesend and Rochester. He stared for a while, watching a tug with brown fenders on its high black bows pushing yellow-white waves before it. Behind it was a steam-pinnace, its brass-bound smoke-stack being lowered on a wire rope, to pass under the bridge. A man on the bridge was drinking an enamel mug of tea. How lovely to own a pinnace!

Then, looking at his watch, he began to hurry onwards, seeing the Monument in front of him, a tall stone column with brassy flames at its top—one of the few sights of London he knew; pointed out by Mother as the place where the Great Fire had started in sixteen sixty-six. He smelt a distinctly fishy smell coming from the slopes by the grey base. Surely down there was Billingsgate, where the swearing came from? He went down to have a look. Porters, with thick flat leather hats on their heads covered with fish-scales, wearing dirty white overalls and enormous boots, stood about, unswearing.

At the junction of several streets beyond the Monument he stopped, bewildered by clack of hoofs and noise of motor engines. He decided to ask a policeman, directing traffic, the way to No. 42 Wine Vaults Lane. With arms extended, chest out, size 13 boots planted well apart, red-and-white duty-band on left cuff, the immense City of London constable said, without a glance at his questioner, "Over East Cheap up Gracechurch Street first right up Fenchurch Street third right again and you're there." Then moving his arms like railway signals he blew a whistle, at which one lot of traffic stopped and another began to cross over.

Phillip hesitated on the pavement. He had not listened to the directions. When the traffic stopped he crossed over, not liking to ask the same policeman again, and went on until a dreadful feeling of being in the wrong direction arose in him. He was in what seemed a different human stream, among many silk hats on both sides of a narrow street under tall dark buildings, some with signs hanging above their doors. One was a gilt grass-hopper on a green field. From the lettering on the wall he saw he was in Lombard Street. Surely the policeman had not mentioned that name?

Dread of being lost, of being late, nearly became panic. He was looking for another policeman when he saw a brown face which seemed familiar. At the same time the face, under a silk hat, looked at him. Then the face smiled.

"Aren't you Phillip?"

"Yes! And aren't you Uncle George Lemon?"

"Yes, my dear boy. I remembered you by your eyes. 'Mr. Cornflower'. Do you remember that name you gave yourself, when you ran away to the Derby, and met the gipsy woman? You were staying with us, and your baby sister, let me see, it must be thirteen years ago this year. It was about the time of Mafeking—yes, I remember now, your Uncle Hilary came down, to see Beatrice—do you remember Aunt Bee?—it was when they became engaged. You ran off with a dog, didn't you, to the races, by yourself? How you have grown! I heard from Hilary that he had seen you."

Phillip was relieved that his uncle by marriage seemed to have forgotten the last time he had seen him, when Father had taken him over to Epsom, to tell Aunt Vicky what a beastly little coward he was, getting Peter Wallace to fight his quarrels for him on the Hill. Ever since, he had squirmed whenever he thought of it.

"Which way are you going, Phillip?"

"I'm trying to find Wine Vaults Lane, Uncle George. It's my first day at the Moon Fire Office. I—I'm rather late, I'm afraid. I have to be there at a quarter to ten. Oh lor', it's twenty to, now!"

"We'll soon put that right. Taxi!" said George Lemon, seeing the anxiety on his nephew's face. Phillip had time to notice that it was a Belsize before the door opened, and Uncle George told him to jump in. "I'm going your way, Phillip, so can drop you almost at your door. I know your office, it's only a few steps back from Fenchurch Street. We'll have you there in a jiffy."

It was the first time Phillip had been in a taxicab, but he could not fully enjoy the experience, owing to anxiety. George Lemon tried to put him at ease by telling him that they were a thoroughly decent lot of fellows in the Moon, and that he did a certain amount of business with the Chancery Lane branch, insuring clients' properties against fire and burglary.

As Phillip did not respond, George Lemon tried another line.

"Your Aunt Dora's living not far from your office, you know—doing good works among the poor, east of Aldgate, somewhere. Do you see anything of her?"

"Yes, Uncle George," said Phillip.

"You two are much alike in temperament, I fancy. Well, here we are. You must come and have luncheon with me one day. I'm thinking of leaving the City, and going to farm in Cornwall. But you don't like farming, I understand."

Phillip got out of the taxi at the corner of a narrow street enclosed by tall dark buildings, and with relief saw the white letters WINE VAULTS LANE. He was too disturbed by all the strangeness to remember to thank his uncle for the ride; but George Lemon understood. With a wave of his hand he said goodbye, then told the driver to return to where he had picked him up.

George Lemon had been about to enter the bank with the grasshopper sign when he had met Phillip.

Phillip saw the sign of the Moon hanging above the door of a building only a few yards away. Brown mottled marble pillars stood on either side of the door. Electric light was burning behind the windows. As he hesitated by the door, about to enter, an athletic-looking man with a red face and thin beaked nose, in blue serge suit and polished brown shoes, wearing a bowler rather low over his red ears and carrying a silk umbrella, passed him and went inside. Phillip followed.

The room, or office, was empty of people. He saw three desks with frosted glass screens in front of them, one on the left side, two on the right. There was a mahogany counter between the two right-hand desks, which were set at an angle to the small square room. In front, a staircase led up through a gap in the ceiling. The walls were bare except for a large rolled-down calendar, with particulars of the Directors, Branches, Capital, and Establishment of the Moon Fire Office, above a low table in the corner. An electric light with a green shade burned over this table, revealing, plastered on the wall under the calendar, many pictures of boxers, cut out of newspapers and magazines.

While he was standing there, an extremely small boy, with an alert face, and hair plastered down with water, pushed open the door, let it close of itself behind him, and, passing Phillip with a grin, sat down at the table.

He was about to ask the boy where everybody was, when rapid footfalls came up from an open door beyond the two right-hand desks, and the athletic man who had entered before him reappeared.

"Good morning," he said genially, as he laid his newspaper beside the single desk on the left. "You're Maddison, aren't you?" He smiled and held out his hand. "I'm Downham."

Phillip shook the hand, receiving a keen grip which was just not painful. "I'll give Edgar the post, then I'll show you the basement where we keep our coats."

He went to the front door, opened the letter box with a key, and laid a heap of letters on the low table. Then crossing to the door he had just come through, he pointed downwards into a basement, and switching on the light, said, "You lead on." Phillip descended in front of him.

"Here we are. The lavatory's over there."

Downham pointed to a table on which a screwed iron frame stood, painted black with florid gold lettering on its cross beam. "That's the letter book. It will be your job to press copies of the letters each afternoon. Your predecessor, Smithy, did it for the last three years. Now he's gone to our Shanghai branch, where he'll live on the fat of the land, and get all the shooting and sailing he wants. We used to go down to the Thames estuary together, duck shooting Ever done any?"

"Oh yes," said Phillip, nervous lest he be thought insufficient. "With my cousin, this last winter."

"Really? Where?" asked Downham, interested.

He thought rapidly of what cousin Bertie had told him. "Oh, down in the Blackwater estuary, by Goldhanger Creek."

"Then you must know the Heybridge Basin! Did you use a punt, or pattens?"

"No, oh no, I don't think I did," stammered Phillip, beginning to feel hot. What were pattens? Or was it patterns? Copies? Bertie had never mentioned them. They must be decoys. "No, we did not use decoys," he said, feeling himself flush.

Downham looked at him. "But pattens aren't decoys! They're the wooden frames you strap on your boots, to prevent sinking into the mud. Do you know 'The Sailor' at Heybridge?"

"Not by name," said Phillip, feeling he was floundering. He stared at the concrete floor.

"'The Sailor' is a pub!" retorted Downham, with a laugh. "What did you think of the Basin?"

All Phillip could think of were the wash-basins in the lavatory of the Voyagers' Club. He was saved from a reply by someone clumping down the stairs rapidly. An older man, with a brown lean face, and smoking a pipe, looked keenly at him. Then he smiled, held out his hand, and said, "You must be Maddison!"

Before Phillip could take the hand it was withdrawn as the newcomer began to cough violently. He bent double, shouting "Hell and the Devil!" in intervals of coughing. He stood up, breathed in, took a handkerchief from his pocket and blew his nose with a loud trumpet note. "Blast this damned March wind!" A smell of camphorated oil spread in the basement.

He adjusted his face to a smile again, and said winsomely, "My name is Hollis." Once more he held out his hand, but pulled it back as he shut his eyes, wavered, and then plunged to an enormous sneeze.

"Do forgive me," he lamented, as he wiped his eyes. "I hope I haven't got this damned 'flu that's going about. Well, young feller, how are you?" Free at last, he shot out his hand.

"Very well, thank you, sir," said Phillip, shaking it.

"Don't you go sir'ing me, young feller! I'm Mr. Hollis to you, and Hollis to Downham here. You can sir Mr. Howlett, the branch manager, if you like, as indeed you should. After all, you are only a damned junior!"

Mr. Hollis smiled in the friendliest way at Phillip. Then his expression changed.

"Well, there's work to be done. Someone in this Branch has to do it. Downham will show you your post-book."

Phillip knew he was dismissed, and in some elation went sedately up the stairs. He was in time to see the remembered figure of Mr. Howlett entering the door, while the boy in the corner stood up.

"Ah, Maddison," said Mr. Howlett, in his soft voice. "Welcome to Wine Vaults Lane!" He held out a soft hand, which did not have the decisive clasp of Downham or the firm grip of Mr. Hollis. He looked most kindly at Phillip.

"I expect Downham, when he comes upstairs, will show you what to do in a moment," he said as, puffing his pipe, he walked slowly and quietly up the stairs. They were covered with lead, Phillip noticed through the banister rails when the door above had closed.

The extremely small boy in the corner was still standing up. He grinned at Phillip, and said, "I'm Edgar."

"Hullo, Edgar," said Phillip, wondering if he should shake hands. He decided he might, as none of the others were there. "You work here, too, Edgar?"

"I'm the Messenger," said Edgar, with another grin. On his table was a pile of slit envelopes. His work apparently done, Edgar opened a magazine, arranged a pair of scissors and a bottle of Gloy beside him, and began to cut out a picture of Bombardier Billy Wells.

"Oh, you take messages, do you, in your spare time?" asked Phillip.

"Well, sort of, but not exackly, sir," said Edgar. The 'sir' pleased Phillip. "I folds up the renewal notices, see, and sticks up the envelopes and puts on the stamps. And I answers the telephone from Head Office."

"You're a pretty important person here, I can see. Do you box, too?"

"Yes," said Edgar, shyly. "Down our club nights. Do you like boxing?"

"Rather! Though I'm a rabbit. I see you've got Jack Johnson, Bombardier Billy Wells, Pat O'Keefe, Jimmy Wilde, Gunner Moir, Gunboat Smith, Carpentier—I have a cousin called Hubert Cakebread, who used to be one of the best boxers at Dulwich College. He is going to teach me one day."

"I bet you're really hot stuff," said Edgar, admiringly; and Phillip thought it best to leave it at that. Shades of Peter Wallace, and the cowardly self of his young days! Oh, and his wildfowling fib. *Be sure your sin will find you out.* He felt himself going hot.

Thus Phillip began City life.

First impressions of a happy family remained. Neither Mr. Hollis, Mr. Howlett, nor Downham showed any other sides to their characters. The work was easy, though without real interest to Phillip. He did it much as he had worked at school, lacking ambition to get on. His first job after arrival was to enter into the Post Book particulars—date, name, address, subject—of the letters passed to him by Mr. Hollis, after that gentleman, a pair of pince-nez glasses perpetuating a red mark on the bridge of his nose, had taken them out of the envelopes slit by Edgar.

Remittances of renewal and other premiums were not entered in the Post Book, but in the counterfoils of the Receipt Book, at the time of filling in and signing the receipts and addressing the envelopes. Mr. Hollis kept the cheques and postal orders in his desk; while the addressed envelopes passed from Phillip, in due course, to Edgar in the corner, who placed them in a pile ready for stamping in the afternoon, together with the rest of the outward post. After this, Phillip had to enter up the details in the Stamp Book; finally Edgar took the piles in a wicker tray to the pillar-box on the corner. Phillip was responsible for Edgar's Stamp Book.

As the fourteen days of grace for renewal premiums came to an end, there were second notices to be made out, to remind the careless or forgetful that their policies had lapsed. For each notice Phillip made a tick in the record book; later a second tick denoted that the third notice had been sent off. When this final demand for premium had been ignored for a further fortnight, he was instructed by Mr. Hollis to write *lapsed* against the name in the ledger. There were variations in the manner of recording a dead policy.

Someone from Billericay wrote to say that he was not continuing. "Ah, one of the marks of a gentleman, Maddison!" said Mr. Hollis, "is that he takes trouble beyond the ordinary. Write WNR against his name—Will Not Renew."

Phillip's other work was making-out policies from proposal forms given him by Downham. This was fairly simple. Most of the policies were for Household Goods in Slated or Tiled Houses, Brick or Stone built. The rate was 2s. per £100 per annum, while the buildings themselves were 1s. 6d. Many of the two-shilling policies were for properties in East London, and were brought in by agents, of which there seemed to be a great number. When they came in, they were seen by Downham, who took their money, often in florins, this being the minimum premium. For each florin received, Downham from the mahogany cups inside one of his drawers took four pennies, the commission due.

"Hm!" Downham would ejaculate, as the door closed behind Mr. L. Dicks, or Mr. S. Levi, or Mr. N. Moses, or Mr. J. Morris. "Phew! Fiss-an'-sipps! Do they ever eat anything else in Whitechapel?"

Certainly the cash, which Phillip had to take every afternoon at half-past three to the Westminster Bank on the other side of the Lane, and pay in with postal orders and cheques, seemed to be saturated with the smell of frying grease. But that was nothing to the whiff he got from Mr. L. Dicks, a saturnine individual with faded yellow teeth and a faded yellow straw-yard with a black band round it greenish with age and London air, one afternoon while he wrote a receipt for him, as he stood by his desk. The whiff was a concentration of stable ammonia, sweat on linen so long unwashed that it smelt *black*: a whiff coming in rings of invisible smoke every time Mr. L. Dicks moved, his dark clothes seemingly saturated in the vapours of the East End.

Of all the little agents from the East End the most industrious, as he was the most polite, was Mr. J. Konigswinter. This spare, aloof person would come into the office, almost without visible motion, like a partial animation of frost and bone, and wait quietly until someone spoke to him. Mr. Konigswinter always wore a collar and tie, whether his overcoat was buttoned to the neck or not. Mr. J. Konigswinter, grey-haired, grey-faced, grey-celluloid-collar'd, always raised his straw-yard to Mr. Hollis, and gave a bleak, wintry smile as he did so. He spoke in a very soft voice, he appeared and disappeared soundlessly, leaving without trace after another lift of the straw hat.

No one spoke of Mr. Konigswinter when he had gone. He left behind no whiff, no echo of personality. Mr. Konigswinter had hundreds of £100 Domestic Goods policies ('*in the event of loss by fire no one item is to be deemed of greater value than £5*') under his agency.

Not all the agents were seedy, smelly, small, or bleak of face. Some were very splendid people, he thought. One morning a smiling young man with dark hair and dark-brown eyes came in, to be greeted very affably by Mr. Hollis. The young man, obviously rich and high in the social scale by his clothes, was dressed in a brown bowler hat, brown jacket and fawn trousers, with yellow gloves. He carried a clouded cane with a large gold top on it. He talked very politely to Mr. Hollis, smiling a lot. Mr. Hollis was also very polite and smiling; for, as he explained to Phillip when the visitor had gone, that was young Roy Cohen, a broker with an office in Piccadilly, whose father bought up all the old uniforms of the City of London Police Force, as well as many military uniforms. Roy Cohen, declared Mr. Hollis, had come out of his way to the Branch to see him, when he might easily have gone to the Charing Cross Branch, for all

that complacent old owl upstairs cared about new business.
Mr. Hollis waved a proposal form.

"Six thousand pounds of stock and utensils in trade in a
warehouse in Aldgate! It will be a fairly high rate, but young
Roy Cohen told me he only places his insurances with tariff
companies. Edgar, get me on to the Guarantee Department of
Head Office!"

The Guarantee Department, Phillip had already learned, was
where the 'risks were spread', or re-insured with other companies.

"Yessir!" said Edgar, springing up. Edgar had been snipping
with scissors a photograph of Zena Dare, to add to his new
spring series of actresses, which was replacing his winter interest
in boxers. Edgar went to the private line to Head Office. The
handle of the dynamo whirred.

"I hope his Yiddisher Pappy isn't on the Black List," laughed
Downham. Phillip thought of the Black Line at his second
school, and with head held down, went on with a short-period
policy of Merchandise at Bellamy's Wharf.

"Guarantee Department on the line, sir."

"Thank you, Edgar," said Mr. Hollis, springing off his stool,
and saying as he hurried behind Phillip: "Good God no!
Old Moses Cohen's as honest as the day! He doesn't need fire
to purify spurious figures in his ledgers. Good morning, is that
Guarantee? Get me Mr. Ironside, will you, please. Wine
Vaults Lane speaking. Hullo, is that you, Ironside? I want to
spread a risk, six thousand on contents of Moses Cohen's clothing
factory in Aldgate. Right. My thanks to you!" He hung the
receiver on the brass bracket.

"Yes, young Roy Cohen should bring us some useful business,"
he said, smiling at Phillip as he passed his desk again. The smile
encouraged Phillip to say,

"What is a broker, sir?"

"A broker, my lad, is a superior form of commission agent.
Just as an Esquire, so described on a domestic policy, is a superior
form of the general description, Gentleman. Now don't you go
and call Mr. Tate, when you make out the policy for the new
country house he is building for sixty thousand pounds, a Gentleman. He's an Esquire. He wouldn't like it if he found himself
among the sort of people, worthy folk as no doubt they are,
insured under the agency of Mr. L. Dicks or even of the good
grey Konigswinter! If in any doubt, ask me. See?"

"Yes, Mr. Hollis."

Mr. Tate had recently come into the office. He was a beefy man with a very big red face, and a genial, hearty manner. He wore, Phillip noticed, a short vicuna jacket like his own, and with it the shiniest and biggest silk hat he had seen in the Lane so far. Indeed, he had been so impressed by the shininess of the hat of what Mr. Hollis called the Sugar King, that an idea had come to him as exciting as it was tempting: he would buy for himself such a hat when he got his first salary cheque. Why not? It was obviously correct, with vicuna jacket and striped trousers. Mr. Hollis sometimes came into the office so dressed, but with a morning tail-coat; so did Downham. They came through the door seemingly a little faster on these occasions, and certainly looking taller. On the other hand, Mr. Howlett always wore a lounge suit and a bowler, entering slowly, in his usual strolling walk. Mr. Howlett lived in Highgate, where, he told Phillip, were big carp in the ponds near his house. However, none of the fishermen on the banks ever seemed to catch them, he said, with a short laugh.

"Well you know, it largely depends on the bait, sir," said Phillip. "If they used aniseed on dough, well kneaded with cotton wool, the carp would not be able to suck it off. I got a fairly big carp like that, one day, in one of my uncle's ponds in the country."

"Where was that, in the Heybridge Basin?" asked Downham, with a laugh.

"No," said Phillip. "As a matter'r fact, it was at a place called Brickhill. The ponds there swarm with perch and roach, too. *And* duck, in season, flight there from the Duke's moors."

Phillip wondered if he could get Uncle Jim Pickering to transfer his insurance policy to the Moon. That would show Downham! Would he be an Esquire? Probably not; all the same, he was a seed merchant, and secretary of the local gas company.

Out of curiosity, when he was alone for a few minutes, he looked up Hollis' policy. It was for £300, Household Goods, at a house at Woking in Surrey. Hollis had written it out himself, *Harold Fazackerley Hollis, Esquire*! There it was, in his galloping writing, with a Waverley nib. Then he looked up Mr. Howlett's policy. He was for £450 Domestic Goods, and £850 the brick built and slated house. Mr. Howlett was only a Gentleman. Mr. Howlett had also made out his own policy.

However, Mr. Hollis had a very distinguished father-in-law.

Mr. Hollis had told him that he was Carlton Turnham, the famous civil engineer who had been responsible for the new kind of sewerage plant of a big town in Surrey, a new and epoch-making design. The effluent, said Mr. Hollis, was spread over six hundred acres of specially planted rye-grass. The area was divided so that the grass was fertilised one year, and left for hay the next. The bumper hay crop every year paid most of the urban district council's sanitary department's wages. "There's economy for you, and a useful distribution of waste products!" Phillip was duly impressed.

Very important men, he learned from Mr. Hollis, had offices in the Lane. They were Household Names in sugar, tea, and coffee. Had he been to see the Cloth Hall? Then he should. The Corn Exchange in Mark Lane, nearby, was worth visiting, too. All the corn that fed London and the barleys that supplied the great breweries passed through a few hands there, in samples only of course, he said. At times Mr. Hollis was almost an enthusiastic as Gran'pa and Mother were, about the City. Fancy preferring that sort of thing to birds and fish! He dared to say so, one day. Mr. Hollis looked at him intently.

"I yield to no one in my love of Outdoors, my young would-be Waterton, but do you realize that in the City, in which you are privileged to earn your bread and butter, nearly three quarters of a million workers run almost the entire country? Think a moment what that means, my lad! Approximately seven hundred and fifty thousand toiling souls—less you and Edgar over there, of course—Edgar, get on with your work!—seriously, Maddison, it is a fact that approximately three-quarters of a million people, all more or less experts in the various branches of commerce, banking, and insurance, arrive in this square mile every morning, and depart again in the afternoon, more rather than less to the suburbs, most of them—again excepting you and Edgar—stop grinning, Edgar!—as I was saying, seriously, Maddison—all joking apart—what the hell are *you* smirking at?—shipping clerks, insurance men, typists, shop-keepers, bank-clerks, and many other decent and respectable people with inherited skills and techniques of a thousand years—since the Romans left, in fact, and the Danes and Saxons were absorbed, and one of my ancestors, Baron Holles—spelt with an 'e' and not an 'i', according to the family records—Ah, hullo, Thistlethwaite! And a good day to you, too!"

Phillip was beginning to recognise many of the regular callers. Mr. Thistlethwaite was one of them. He was a Broker. He always wore a top hat, an old-fashioned frock coat, and new-fashioned dark-pearl button boots with fawn cloth sides. Mr. Thistlethwaite had a very big moustache, which looked as though it had been waxed at one time, but the wax had never been properly washed out. Mr. Thistlethwaite always greeted Mr. Hollis in a loud, hearty voice, which dropped, as though it belonged to a bass-viol, to a gutty sort of grumble as Mr. Thistlethwaite leaned over Mr. Hollis' desk and recounted his grievance against the Metropolitan Insurance Company, which had dismissed him, for some reason or other, Phillip gathered, with an offer of six months salary as an *ex gratia* payment. Mr. Thistlethwaite, who had started an agency in Crutched Friars, was going to fight them, he said. What did Hollis think?

Mr. Hollis demurred. He said that he was not really competent to give advice. But he knew all about the case, insisted Mr. Thistlethwaite. It was rather complicated, said Mr. Hollis. Anyway, he wished him good luck. Phillip signed a receipt for a new £2,400 Domestic policy, made out to an Esquire, and waited quietly to give it to the tall top-hatted figure, who took it without glance or word, Mr. Thistlethwaite being too intent on watching Mr. Hollis' brown, studious face.

As soon as Mr. Thistlethwaite had gone out of the glass-panelled door, Mr. Hollis let fly with his real opinion.

"Thistlethwaite's a first-class bloody fool, Downham! How can the great ass fight the Metropolitan in the courts for wrongful dismissal, since they've given him the excuse of reorganisation and redundancy, and offered him six months' screw? Well, I tried to tell the silly blighter many times, but he won't listen. What the devil are you beaming at me for, young Maddison? Get on with your work, you look like one of your own stuffed birds, you horrible taxidermist, you!"

Phillip had been unconscious of beaming at Mr. Hollis: he liked Mr. Hollis' face, and was always interested in what he said. Mr. Hollis was already frowning over his own work, so he went on preparing his policy, after a glance at the clock. His time of leaving for Head Office first luncheon was ten minutes to twelve; he had to be back again by half-past.

Downham left for his luncheon at a quarter-past twelve. He was supposed to be back by ten-past one, but he usually arrived

back any time up to half-past one, the time when Mr. Howlett
came down the leaden stairs, smoking his pipe; and, after an
amiable word to Phillip, and smiling talk with Downham, went
to his luncheon, usually at the London Tavern. Mr. Howlett's
time of returning, smoking the same pipe, was between a quarter
to three and three o'clock.

"Lazy blighter," remarked Mr. Hollis once, to Phillip. "If I
didn't stir my stumps and do most of his work for him, this
branch would have to close down." Downham, on the other
hand, never criticised Mr. Howlett, but treated him like a
favourite uncle, always careful to call him "sir".

"Hollis is jealous of Howlett," said Downham once, quietly,
to Phillip, with a kind of satisfaction. The two were alone,
Edgar having gone to a sandwich shop in Leadenhall Market
for his twopenny meal—cheese sandwich and cup of Camp
coffee. "Hollis likes to please himself, so Howlett gives him his
head. On the other hand, Hollis thinks that Howlett ought to
go out more after new business. I say, look at this! How dare
you! Why in the name of all that's not insane did you sign this
endorsement like that?"

Looking angry suddenly, Downham brought over two policies,
both with printed change-of-address labels stuck on the back—
*notwithstanding anything herein contained to the contrary, it is hereby
agreed and allowed that the Insured's address shall be deemed to be as
hereinunder stated.* The first endorsement was signed by Phillip
with an enormous scrawled signature six inches long, in letters
an inch high. "Is this your idea of a joke?" He pointed to the
second endorsement, signed with extreme neatness in minute
letters barely one-eighth of an inch high, and three-quarters of
an inch in length. The first policy was one of Mr. L. Dicks,
the fish-and-chips smeller; the second for the neat Mr. J.
Konigswinter.

After Downham's complaint, he put on a subdued expression
and went on with his work. When Mr. Howlett came in, Downham showed him the two endorsements.

"Look at this, sir, did you ever see such asinine behaviour?"
Mr. Howlett appeared to be highly amused. "I've ticked him
off, sir," said Downham, in lowered voice.

"I see," replied Mr. Howlett, nodding to Phillip, as he went
up the leaden stairs to his room. This was a dark place, being
lit from the Lane outside only along the floor by the top

arc of the bow window below. When Mr. Howlett was there, the electric light was always switched on.

Mr. Hollis wrote three of the letters which had to be copied by Phillip every afternoon for Mr. Howlett's one. All were in copying ink, from which an impression was taken when they were laid between damped flimsy sheets in the big leather-bound book and screwed down in the basement press. The letters were then taken out, and when dried, folded by Phillip and put in their envelopes, for Edgar to stamp. There were big sheets of penny and halfpenny stamps in Edgar's drawer, which once a week Phillip was supposed to check.

Downham sometimes wrote letters on the Branch Office writing paper, which Phillip copied. They were about his own insurances, for which he received the usual fifteen per cent commission. Mr. Hollis explained that members of the staff were not allowed to be agents for the Moon Fire Office; so they put them through Mr. Potts, of the Accident Department, on the top floor of Head Office. The Accident Department was a recent addition, and the clerks there were not on the staff, so they could be agents for fire business. The commissions on premiums therefore were paid through F. Potts, who obligingly signed the receipts.

One day Phillip had an ambition to write a letter on Branch Office paper, sign it, press it in the Copy Book, and have it stamped and posted by Edgar. He wrote to T. W. Turney, Esq., of Wespalaer, Hillside Road, Wakenham, Kent, beginning *Dear Sir*, and suggesting that he should transfer both business and domestic insurances to the Wine Vaults Branch of the above Office, at the same rates of premium as he paid now. He assumed that his present insurance was with a tariff company, and therefore the rate would be the same. But, added the writer, chuckling as he wrote, should it so happen that the firm of Messrs. Carter, Mallard & Turney, Ltd., was on the Black List of the Tariff Companies, then notwithstanding anything herein contained to the contrary, it was hereby understood and agreed that the offer was deemed to be cancelled.

The letter was duly posted, and Phillip awaited results from his joke.

They were not long in coming. Downham, who had gone to the basement to wash his hands, came leaping up the stairs again three at a time, Copy Book under an arm. He banged it down beside Phillip, who was making out a short-period policy for merchandise at the Free Trade Wharf.

"You've done it this time, my wildfowling young Christian friend of a first-class bloody fool! What in the name of all that's holy do you think you are doing?" At that moment the door above opened, as Mr. Howlett prepared to descend. "If this is your idea of a joke, Maddison, all I can say is that you've missed your vocation. You should be on the Halls! Here, Hollis, I leave you to deal with our comic genius!" He showed Mr. Hollis the copy of the letter.

Mr. Hollis exploded. "Who in the name of the devil do you think *you* are? The Deputy Assistant Undeveloped Moon Calf of Wine Vaults Lane? And take that grin off your face, and that damned pen from behind your ear! What do you think this Office is? A basement bucket shop, run on half commission? And who the hell are you anyway to sign letters on behalf of the Branch?" The explosion ended abruptly: a smile broke over Mr. Hollis' face as he said, "Don't look at me like Tiny Tim Cratchit."

Almost eagerly Mr. Howlett was descending the leaden stairs to enjoy the latest perturbation of H. Fazackerley Hollis, of whose occasional criticisms of himself he was well aware. He regarded them with tolerance, since he fully appreciated his right-hand man's ability and drive for new business. There was a difference of eight years in seniority between them.

Downham placed the open Copy Book on the mahogany slab between Phillip's desk and that of Mr. Hollis in the corner by the window. Then in his rich baritone voice, with its usual friendly deference whenever he was speaking to the manager, he read aloud the letter. Mr. Howlett listened, looking over Downham's shoulder, while one wing of his high starched collar stuck in the loose fold of his neck, Phillip noticed. Mr. Howlett seemed to be amused.

When he had finished reading, Downham turned to Phillip his lean rugger-red face (he played on Saturday afternoons for the Old Merchant Taylor's first fifteen) and said with slight viciousness, "I don't think this is at all funny! Do you want to let the Moon Fire Office in for an action for libel-in-trade? Really, you know sir——" he turned complainingly to Mr. Howlett, with an addition of blandness to his tone. "This is the

limit!" Then to Phillip, "Whatever made you do it? It's like
your damned cheek, to write a letter, on Office Paper, too!
What is the idea?"

"I thought it might get some new business."

Mr. Howlett, with a smile, had gone to the telephone. This
was a single line only, to Head Office. He turned the ringing
handle. "Give me the Town Department, will you?" he asked
the exchange girl, quietly.

Phillip felt his insides go black. Mr. Howlett was going to
tell Father. So far, he had avoided Father at Head Office.
He sat at his desk, listening to Mr. Howlett's voice.

"Hullo, is that you, Journend? I say, a little matter of territory
has arisen. I wonder if you would confirm that Head Office
is on the risk of Mallard, Carter & Turney, of Sparhawk Street,
Holborn, manufacturing stationers and printers. Oh they are,
are they? Yes, I thought so. What? Oh, is he? Ha ha ha!
Oh, nothing, nothing. Most interesting! Oh no, I'll explain
sometime, when I see you. Goodbye."

He hung up the black trumpet-like receiver, and turned round
with an amused expression on his face.

"Oh that reminds me, Hollis," he said. "Head Office has
approved your idea that we should get Edgar here into uniform.
I've arranged with Church the tailor, to get him measured up.
Edgar," said Mr. Howlett, turning to the boy in the corner,
"Don't you go and sprout up suddenly, whatever you do! You're
going to have a messenger's livery specially made for you."

Edgar looked extremely pleased. He smoothed back his half-dry
hair with a palm, then swung his legs on his chair, boots rubbing
together as though enjoying this reward to the rest of the body.

Mr. Hollis was writing rapidly. His pen scratched as it
travelled decisively. With an extra spurt of scratching, he signed
his name with a flourish. Phillip always knew when Mr. Hollis
was endorsing a cheque, by the sound it made on paper, *H.
Fazackerley Hollis*, followed by a swift squiggle underneath the
name, like a whip cracking, or a snake striking, or a cock
pheasant crowing at the moment it drummed its wings. Having
signed his name, Mr. Hollis usually sniffed. He could not
realise, Phillip thought, that he sniffed, for once he had jumped
on him for doing the same thing.

"We use handkerchiefs in this office," he had said, shortly,
and Phillip had felt inferior.

Mr. Hollis finished his signature, sniffed, and then, deciding
not to pretend indifference at his senior's exasperating slowness
any longer, demanded to know what Journend had said.

"Oh that. As I thought, Mallard, Carter & Turney already
have a policy with Head Office."

"I fail to see why that should be amusing," retorted Mr.
Hollis, thumping another cheque with the office rubber stamp,
and endorsing it.

Mr. Howlett came over to Phillip and said, softly, "That's
your grandfather's firm, isn't it, Maddison?"

"Yes, sir."

An expression of pure pleasure crossed Mr. Howlett's face.
He turned to Mr. Hollis and said, "Apparently our young
colleague was trying to get some new business. Maddison's
grandfather is chairman of the firm!"

Mr. Hollis did not reply, but went on stamping and endorsing
cheques until, suddenly looking up, he said in a terse voice,
"In my opinion, Howlett, for what it is worth, of course, I think
that you and I should continue to run this Branch as we did
on lines approved and laid down before our young genius arrived."

With a wink, and sudden smile at Phillip, he said in a lowered,
confidential voice, "By all means, Maddison, continue to get
all the new business for the Branch that you can. If you care
to ask me for advice on any point, I shall always be most pleased
to give it, in so far as my limited experience of twenty-eight years
in insurance, permits. Furthermore, and without equivocation,
lest there be any possible doubt in the matter, I now state
definitely that in all such matters you will come to me, as I am
the Head Clerk here, Mr. Howlett is the Manager, Downham
is your Immediate Senior, and you are still only a Bloody Boy!"

Mr. Hollis said this in a very dry, comical manner, which made
Phillip like him more than he did already.

"Thank you, Mr. Hollis," he said.

"You see, my lad," said Mr. Hollis, very quietly, "in this
office we work as a team."

Shortly afterwards the door opened and a man slipped in,
deferentially, and with a silent rapid movement closed the door
behind him, as though it were his chief care that no cold air
from outside should enter. He had a thin grey moustache, waxed
to fine points, on a thin almost anxious face. He wore the usual
yellow straw-hat and carried a leather bag in one hand.

"Ah!" exclaimed Mr. Howlett, his eyes almost goggling with pleasure. "The very man I wanted to see! I am down to my last half-ounce!"

Mr. Hollis looked up from the paying-in book, and said briskly to the newcomer, "A good day to you!"

The newcomer hesitated a bare moment before opening his bag and putting on the counter, in two separate piles, a number of packets in lead-foil, each partly covered with the picture of a Jacobean horseman in gay colours.

"There you are gentlemen! Sixteen one-ounce packets of 'Hignett's Cavalier', as usual; thank you very much indeed."

Mr. Hollis produced a half-crown and fourpence; so did Mr. Howlett. Pocketing the money, the little man vanished as swiftly and silently as he had entered.

Mr. Howlett and Mr. Hollis each took eight packages.

"You haven't yet come to the fragrant weed, I suppose, Maddison?" asked Mr. Howlett.

"No, sir," said Phillip, hoping that Downham would not say anything to make him feel ridiculous.

"Plenty of time, my boy," beamed Mr. Howlett, going up the stairs, his tobacco nursed in his arms; while Mr. Hollis, having made out the paying-in book, said to Phillip with a smile, "Here you are, you Mercantile Wonder. I suppose after what Mr. Howlett said to you just now, this Branch will soon be too small to hold you, what?" And handing over the cheques and postal-orders, Mr. Hollis gave Phillip's forearm a friendly squeeze.

Chapter 2

A MAN OF MEANS

THE DAY which he had been eagerly looking forward to came at last: half-quarter day. Many times he had imagined himself going to the grill of the cashier in the Westminster Bank, presenting his cheque, hearing the cashier say, "How would you like this?" as he had heard him ask others, while he waited to pay in the Branch's money. Many times had he imagined the joy of being able to jingle golden sovereigns of his own in his pocket, as he walked across the Hill, later to show Mother and Mrs. Neville.

This was the moment. His heart beat faster as Mr. Howlett
came down the stairs with three pink cheques in his hand. He
placed one on Phillip's desk, saying, "Here you are, my boy,"
and paused a moment to enjoy the light in his junior's face.

Phillip thanked him, before gazing at the magic piece of
paper. *Pay to Mr. P. S. T. Maddison the sum of Five pounds!*
Every stroke and curl of the letters of his name, the date of
6 May 1913, the signature of E. Rob Howlett, thin and twirly,
the figure of £5 and the written words, the water-mark on the
cheque, the myriads of little teeny-weeny lines of joined-up
words *thewestminsterbankthewestminsterbankthe* right across and down
the background of the pink paper—every detail was fresh, vivid,
and wonderful. So was the moment when, having presented the
cheque, he received a glance from the bald-headed cashier
behind the grill and heard him say "How would you like this?
Gold?"

"Oh," said Phillip, as he had rehearsed several times. "Three
sovereigns, three half-sovereigns, and ten shillings in silver,
please."

The gold was weighed on the polished copper scales, and then
shovelled in a little copper shovel through the small hole.
Three sovereigns, each with naked St. George on a rearing horse
spiking the dragon; three smaller gold circles with milled edges;
two half-crowns, one florin, two shillings, two sixpences—all
new and bright. They jingled in his pocket, as he walked the
few steps down the narrow Lane—just wide enough for one
horse-dray loaded with crates of wine to pass at a time—away
from the office. It was a great moment. Five pounds, earned by
himself, in his pocket!

The narrow gorge between the tall and sombre office buildings
was now filled with light. Sooted blocks of stone, glass windows,
even the boot-smoothed iron-grills above basement and cellar
seemed to be insubstantial, to be dissolved in a dust of soft
radiance from the sun standing high in the south-west over the
street which was a fen when the Romans came, and still a fen
when they had gone, to march no more through their walled
city, by the old gate: the Aldgate beyond which, unthought
of and unrealised by Phillip on that bright afternoon of a world
that was accepted unconsciously as one that would exist as it
was for evermore, in streets of tenements and dark courts and

blackened slums lived "the insured" of L. Dicks and J. Konigswinter and their like, to whom an annual premium of two
shillings was a considerable sum of money, to be saved in pennies
and ha'pennies, not all smelling of fish-and-chips—as Theodora
Maddison, servant of the poor among whom she now lived,
knew daily, almost hourly.

At Lunn's the hatters in Fenchurch Street, Phillip bought a
cork-lined silk hat for 12s. 6d. about twenty minutes later that
afternoon; and the shop assistant, with delicate fingers, put his
straw-yard in a cardboard box for him to carry home. Then
he bowed Phillip out of the shop. A hundred yards or so from
Mr. Lunn's, was Daniel's, the watch and clock shop on the corner
of Gracechurch Street. There Phillip purchased a tenpenny
ha'penny safety razor; a fourpenny ha'penny shaving brush
with imitation badger-hair bound by painted string to a brown-
painted wooden handle; a twopenny stick of shaving soap; a
one-and-threepenny nickel silver watch-chain to replace the
plaited horse-hair "tether" which great-uncle Charley Turney
had given him at Beau Brickhill; and with his purchases, turned
to the south, feet firm upon pavement and cobble, waiting for
the moment of Mother's face when he arrived home.

Silk hat on the back of his head, in imitation of Mr. F. E.
Smith in a cartoon, Phillip walked past the Monument and over
London Bridge with an expression of inhibited superiority on his
face, while inwardly thrilling at the sight of white fleecy clouds
floating high in the blue sky. He carried his dark-grey raincoat
folded on his arm; and entering No. 4 platform, sought an
empty carriage, placed the new hat with great care upon the
luggage rack, and opening *The Globe*, feet on cushions opposite,
began to read. He had observed that several men who wore
silk hats bought this evening paper. Very soon the paper was
put aside, it was more interesting to look out of the window. Far
away he heard the urgent clanging of the Fire Brigade bell.

Walking up Foxfield Road from the station, he decided that
his black vicuna jacket might be too short for the tall hat, so he
put on his raincoat, which reached below his knees. Though of
dark grey mixed woollen and cotton material, this coat, with its
raglan sleeves, did not really go with a topper, he felt. Mr. Tate
wore his in the Lane with only a short jacket; still, Mr. Tate
was big and hearty, looking as though he had had nothing but

the biggest beef steaks for luncheon in the London Tavern for many many years. Some of the men in the Lane wore blue serge suits with top hats, but Mr. Hollis had explained that they put on their silk hats only when calling on one another in their offices, or meeting to do business in vault or exchange. They would not wear them with a blue serge suit outside the City. The silk hat was a compliment to the other fellow, as well as to the tradition of the City, said Mr. Hollis, in a tone that made Phillip feel that he too was of the City.

The silk hat survived its first crossing of the Hill. No small boys jeered. Indeed, no one appeared to notice it, to his relief. As he went down the gully, and approached the top of Hillside Road, his features became set, a little strained, his upper lip stiff, as he tried to think that there was nothing unusual in wearing such headgear, should he be seen by Helena, or Mr. and Mrs. Rolls, as he passed their house. After all, he was entitled to wear a silk hat; he was a man of the Lane; and one of the seven hundred and fifty thousand who kept the country going, as Mr. Hollis had said.

To his mingled relief and disappointment, none of the Rolls family were visible. Old Pye, in the next house lower down, was not in evidence, either, thank God. Now he was safe, opposite Gran'pa's gate. He looked in, and waved. Gran'pa saw him through the window, and beckoned him in. Phillip mouthed through the glass that he would see him later: his purpose was achieved. Gran'pa had seen him in the hat, and so had Aunt Marian, who had come because of the departure of Miss Rooney, the housekeeper. He lifted it, feeling like Mr. Tate, and setting it at a slightly forward tilt, again like Mr. Tate, walked on down behind the privet hedge.

Mrs. Bigge was at her gate. He bowed, and raised what he felt was the equivalent of that splendid headgear of magazine stories, a "faultless Lincoln Bennett", even if it was only a Lunn.

"Goodness me, Phillip, I thought for a moment you were your Father! Though you haven't got a beard yet. My eyes are not what they were. Just come back from London Town?"

"Yes, Mrs. Bigge," he said, disappointed that she had not remarked on his distinguished appearance. "There's been a slight fire in the East India Docks this afternoon, and we are on several risks there. However, we always spread risks by guarantee."

"Fancy that."

"Do you like my new headgear?"

"So that's what it is about you that was puzzling me! I knew somehow it wasn't you, Phillip. My, you are quite a swell!"

He swept off his hat to her with a bow, and went in his gate, the hat now slightly over one brow, like Mr. Thistlethwaite wore his. He left his raincoat behind him on the wall of the porch. He rang the bell.

Mother came. She stared. He waited. Then a smile came upon her face.

"How do you do," he said, lifting his hat slightly.

The sight of her little son, as Hetty still thought of him, standing there, so serious of face, made her laugh. Her laugh was of tenderness, of pathos, of a sense of childlike fun that her experience had not yet turned to despair and acceptance of defeat. Standing before her, he looked so comic, so much a slender, young-faced edition of Dickie, that she could not restrain her feelings. And knowing Phillip's sense of humour at times, she felt he was giving a little parody of his father. To her dismay his expression changed.

"Well, you needn't laugh! I don't think it's so funny, anyway. May I come in? Thank you." He hung the hat on the top of the newel post and without further word went into the scullery. He always went to Timmy Rat when he felt upset, she knew.

Hearing his footfall, Timmy Rat dashed through its fretwork hole, tail knocking on box in its eagerness to be scratched. Nose pointed, whiskers trembling, pink raindrops of eyes glistening, it waited to dream as finger-tips gently rubbed its ears.

"At any rate, you don't laugh at me," said Phillip, loud enough for his mother to hear.

"I'm very sorry, dear, but I was not really laughing *at* you, you know. I was really so taken by surprise that——"

"There is really no need to explain, thank you all the same. You weren't laughing at me, only at my hat. Personally, I always thought you tried, not always successfully, I admit, to impress on me that it was rather bad manners to take any notice of other people's appearances. At least, that is what you and Father were always trying to drum into me when I was young!"

She was shocked by his tone of voice. "Really, Phillip, if anyone else heard you speaking like that, they might think you were serious."

"I *am* serious."

Could this be her own son speaking? Could it mean that he had *really* taken her expression amiss, in the manner of his father? Must she then in future guard all her feelings with her own son? *Her* son—he who, only a little while ago, almost a terrifyingly short while ago, had been entirely hers to confide in, trusting in her for everything. She sighed; and as he remained with his back to her, unspeaking, she went away, and sat in the front room, to be beside the aspidistra fern she had tended, and even confided in, from almost the very beginning of her married life with Dickie, in the little house in Comfort Road, before her little boy was born.

She felt suddenly overcome. She told herself that it was foolish to let her imagination carry her away; that she was probably exaggerating a molehill into a mountain; but all the same, the feeling persisted that he no longer had the same affection for her as before. Could it be that he had never had any real feeling for her, apart from his need of her in the matter of protection, food, and the necessities of life? Was she going to be Dickie all over again? Oh, please God, spare him from an unhappy life. That tone of voice! If she had shut her eyes, it might almost have been Dickie speaking, in the days when the children were small.

Ah well, it was done now. She saw it clearly—she had made the mistake of giving up her entire life to her children, and they —or at least Phillip and Mavis—had grown up selfish, taking all for granted, as her husband had from the very beginning. The more one did for others, the more they expected; the more they demanded. She felt like weeping, for a moment; then telling herself not to exaggerate things, not to be silly—all that fuss over a hat!—O, why had she laughed—she got up, thinking that Phillip would be hungry, and wanting his tea.

This was more the case than Hetty realised. For the past fortnight Phillip had had nothing to eat in the middle day. His tickets had run out for the Head Office club, and he had not been able to ask father for a further loan, in case Father said something.

As the rule about juniors not going out to luncheon applied to Head Office only, nobody knew that Phillip had spent his forty minutes each day in wandering about Leadenhall Market, watching the porters and poultry-salesmen, staring at windows with plates of cheese-cakes, ham- and cheese-rolls, tomatoes on plates, and large glass containers of lemonade with lemons stuck in their necks. He had gone several times on London Bridge and watched the shipping in the Pool. Once or twice he had sat in the Churchyard of St. Botolph, at the corner of Houndsditch and Aldgate, and in other City churchyards, small dank places where soot-spotted tombs were splashed with pigeon-droppings from the plane trees above, where poor-looking office-boys and other workers sat on the seats eating sandwiches, or walking slowly on paths confined between half-dead patches of grass. Once beside him sat a pale-faced girl with no expression in her eyes as she waited there, not eating, like himself. He wished he had sixpence, to press it into her hand, and then to leave her—his intentions strictly honourable in every way. Alas, he had not even a penny for a cheesecake, which was a nourishing thing.

For himself, in a remote sort of way, he had enjoyed the feeling of having nothing to eat. It was rather like the feeling when in the past he had run away from Mother. Self-imposed suffering made you feel very clear and simple, somehow.

Hetty went into the kitchen.

"Are you hungry, Phillip?"

"No thank you. I think I'll go out on my Swift."

"Well, you ought to have something, dear. It's a long time since twelve o'clock."

He did not reply.

"Will you let me boil you an egg, Phillip?"

He turned an anguished face upon her.

"Why can't you let me alone? You don't like me spending so much time with Mrs. Neville, but at least she doesn't laugh at me, or worry me about this or that!"

She felt the shock right through her. She strove to hide her feelings. She, too, ate little in the middle day: a cup of tea, some scraps of left-over dishes, or a slice of white bread and butter. She was alone in the house, except when Mrs. Feeney came, or she went up to London with Papa, on a 'stolen' visit to the Tower, one of the picture galleries, perhaps Westminster Cathedral, or the Abbey and St. James's Park with its water-fowl. Sometimes they went to a *matinée* in a theatre in the Waterloo Road, which Thomas Turney and his wife, before their children

came, used to go to in the early Camberwell days. Then, said
Papa, it was called the Royal Coburg Theatre; but later it
changed its name to the Royal Victoria Coffee Music Hall,
where lectures and penny readings were held. Now it was the
Royal Victoria Hall, and gave an occasional play by Shakespeare.

"Well dear, have a cup of tea with me before you go out,
do! Won't you let me boil you an egg? I do so look forward
to everyone coming home, you know. It's a little lonely sometimes, with everyone away all day. If it were not for Gran'pa,
I should feel quite lost! Of course, dear, I don't mind in the
least you spending any of your time with Mrs. Neville! I am
only too glad that you find her such good company. Well, I'm
going to make some tea, anyway."

He jingled the coins in his pocket. Then she remembered
what he had told her that morning. Of course, his first salary!

"It must be a very satisfactory feeling, Phillip, to have your
own money."

"Oh, I don't know. In a way, I suppose it is. Look."

He put the coins in a neat row along the edge of the kitchen
table.

"Aren't the sovereigns lovely? They feel so heavy, but if they
were lead, it would not be the same feeling. These kind-of
know they're gold. I suppose they will soon be gone. I've got
to pay back Father quite a lot. Then there's what I've got to
give you for my keep. How much is that?"

"Well, your Father and I have discussed it, Phillip, and we
thought half-a-crown a week, if you could manage it, dear."

"That's fifteen shillings out of one sovereign. Then my
monthly season ticket, nine and fourpence. Luncheon tickets,
twenty-five bob, for thirty meals. Pay back Father, two pounds."
He calculated. "Four pounds nine and fourpence. What have
I got here? Four pounds six and six. H'm. I owe two shillings
and tenpence, and have to pay one pound to Mr. Howlett for
my Fidelity Guarantee. So I shall have exactly nothing for the
next six weeks except luncheon and train tickets. Well, all of
you can take this!" he cried, sweeping the handful of coins on
the floor. "Take the lot, all of you," and ran out of the house.

Less than a minute later, he returned. "I am sorry, Mum,"
he said, and burst into tears.

"I know how you feel, dear," said Hetty afterwards. "But
why didn't you tell me you weren't having any food in London?

Of course, you are wrought up. I'll soon have two boiled eggs, they are new laid, and such lovely brown shells. Mrs. Feeney brought them today. I'll just put them on to boil, then I'll help you find the rest of the money."

It was picked up, except one sixpence, which had rolled down the mouse-hole beside the gas-pipe.

"No, dear, for goodness gracious sake don't go digging under the floor for it! I am sure Father won't expect the two pounds returned, but he would be pleased if you were to offer to do so. But you do what you think is best. Now you're grown up, and come to manhood, you must decide things for yourself."

"Of course I'll do what you say, Mum," he said, after his tea, optimistic once more. And when Richard came home, he found two sovereigns under his plate. He saw also the silk hat in the hall, but said nothing about that. About the money he said, "Look, old chap, I really don't want this returned, but thank you for thinking of it. You keep it. Put it in the bank is my advice, for what it is worth. Did you see the smoke as you walked over the Hill? Or did you come home by taxi?" he said, lightly.

"What smoke, Father?"

"In the East India Docks. As I was leaving the City all the Outer London fire-engines were clanging their bells as they rushed east through the streets. It must be a big fire, judging by the smoke to be seen from the Hill."

"Good Lord!" said Phillip. He had made it up to Mrs. Bigge, and it was true after all! But what Phillip had forgotten, as he had 'invented' the news to Mrs. Bigge, was his idle glance at the stop-press column of *The Globe*, while his thoughts had been all on the gloss of his hat.

Phillip went down to show his golden sovereigns to Mrs. Neville, and to tell her the latest news about everything, including the abrupt departure of Miss Rooney, Gran'pa's housekeeper. Walking down the road, in tweed cap and old school jacket, rather tight and short in the sleeve, and Timmy Rat on his shoulder, he crossed over to the flat, waving to Mrs. Neville sitting at her open window.

"I've had to close the door, dear," she called down, "as it's catsmeat day. Here's the key." She threw it on the grass.

He opened the door, and having closed it, walked upstairs, hiding his white rat under his jacket. On the landing, front paws over the top step, sat Mrs. Neville's huge cat, Mazeppa, who, according to Mrs. Neville, had second-sight. Mazeppa could see ghosts; most animals could, the fat woman often declared.

Mazeppa's yellow eyes were fixed on its second-sight dinner now, thought Phillip. He knew the cat had been crouching there for hours, awaiting the well-known Tuesday miracle of the brass letter-box turning into horse-flesh. The catsmeat man was young Soal, the coalman's son, who went his rounds on his bicycle after hours.

Mrs. Neville was telling Phillip that she was sure some human beings as well as animals—"After all, the same God made us all!"—were gifted with second-sight, and illustrating this with a story of her journalistic friends at Highgate, when a dull noise, a prolonged thudding, seemed faintly to be shaking the room. It was about sixteen pounds of Mazeppa hurtling down the stairs. The catsmeat man had arrived, to slip the weekly twopenn'oth of skewered horse-flesh through the letter-box. Up the stairs the grey cat bounded, to enter the drawing-room growling; and then from under the sofa came a steady noise of sideway chewing.

"Mazeppa knows the day and time all right, Phillip. He never makes a mistake in the calendar. Every Tuesday, as soon as he's had his lunch and washed himself, he takes up his position at the top of the stairs."

"Second-sight!" laughed Phillip; then over another cup of tea went on to tell her about Gran'pa.

"Don't tell me, dear, if you think it is a family matter," said Mrs. Neville, in the creamy voice she assumed sometimes, particularly when pouring from her silver teapot. "I don't want your Mother to think that you come here only to tell me things which perhaps, after all, are not my concern. But I must confess that I thought something was in the air when I saw Miss Rooney following the outside porter from Randiswell wheeling her black corded box down Hillside Road this afternoon."

"She came in this morning, just as Father left, and seemed a bit agitated, Mrs. Neville. She said nothing while I was there, but went into the front room with Mother. Then at tea tonight Mother mentioned that Great-Aunt Marian was going to keep house for Gran'pa for the time-being."

"Do tell me, dear, how old is your grandfather?"

"Seventy-three, I think."

Mrs. Neville's society manner disappeared as she cried, "The old roué!" with a shriek, and put down the teapot. The shriek always detonated laughter between them. "Ah, a woman is never safe when alone in a house with a man, Phillip! Why, your grandfather has tried more than once to come up and see me!" and they both shook with laughter again. "Ah, the old dog! Now not a word to your Mother, Phillip, promise me? I don't want her to think——"

"You can rely on me, Mrs. Neville," said Phillip, munching his second doughnut; and thus dismissing all thought of it from his head, asked after Desmond, his great friend, who was at boarding-school near Chelmsford in Essex.

Chapter 3

SPARE TIME

"Tell me, my lad," said Mr. Hollis, soon after noon on the Saturday, "what do you do with yourself in your spare time? Tennis, I suppose, or is it cricket?" He lit his pipe.

"Well, just at the moment, Mr. Hollis, I go after birds."

Mr. Hollis threw back his head and roared with laughter. Mr. Howlett smiled, as he lit his pipe; while Downham, tanned of face, looked sardonically across from his desk. Phillip knew the implication, of course, but pretended to innocence.

"By birds, I take you to mean our feathered friends?" enquired Mr. Hollis, with sudden assumption of courtesy towards his junior. "And not what the term apparently means in vulgar parlance?"

"Yes, Mr. Hollis. This afternoon I'm going past the Salt Box, beyond Reynard's Common, and I shall either go down into the valley below Biggin Hill, and look for woodpeckers in the beeches there, or continue onwards into Westerham, where I have permission from the châtelaine to roam all over the estate, and to fish after hay-cutting."

Mr. Hollis stared at him. "Where did you get that high-falutin' word 'châtelaine' from?"

"My father, Mr. Hollis, said it was the right term."

"Who are they, family friends? Wasn't your grandfather a military man?"

"Yes, Mr. Hollis, but I don't really know them. I just wrote for permission to study and photograph wild birds."

"Westerham, did you say? Isn't that where General Wolfe, of Quebec fame, was born?"

"Yes, Mr. Hollis. There's a statue of him in the village. But perhaps you know it? There's a terrific hill before you get to the village."

"No, I can't say I do, Maddison. How do you get there? Bicycle?"

"Well, I walk part of the way now, Mr. Hollis, until I am round the bend, anyway."

"Round the bend? What bend?" asked Downham.

"Round the bend of the terrific hill. Crikey, the first time I and my friend Desmond biked to Westerham, a year ago, we didn't know what was coming, as we free-wheeled faster and faster, until we came to a right-hand bend too late to stop. I was in front, slewing about in the thick dust, and knew it would be fatal to put on the brakes. I had no idea it was such a dangerous hill, until I saw the country laid out below me like a sort of map. Golly, I went faster and faster, feeling like a bony skeleton out of the chalk suddenly fixed on a bike! I couldn't steer, only hold the shuddering handlebars rigid and pray that the wheel-spokes wouldn't bust. I felt I had no hair, only a skull. The bike felt thin as a knife rushing down before a white furrow of dust. You may not believe it, but my eye-lashes were actually turned in upon my eyeballs. Near the bottom, by some farm buildings, I saw a cross-roads. Phew! If a cart appeared——! I reckon I was doing quite sixty miles an hour by that time!"

"Why bless my soul," said Mr. Howlett, when Phillip had stopped talking. "I've let my pipe go out, listening to you."

"Well my lad," remarked Mr. Hollis briskly. "I've a train to catch, so tell us quickly what happened at the cross-roads."

"We got over, just in time. A May Day procession of kids in white, and Boy Scouts, was about to cross as we hurtled by."

"You've missed your vocation, my lad," remarked Mr. Hollis, putting on his straw-yard. "You should be in Fleet Street! Well, I must be off. Good-day to you all!"

"I did think of going to Fleet Street, as a matter of fact," said Phillip, when Mr. Hollis had gone. "I met Castleton some years ago, when I was still at school, and he asked me to call and see him when I left. But I never went."

"Where did you meet him?" asked Downham, sardonically.
"Down by the Heybridge Basin, when you were wildfowling?"

"No, as a matter-of-fact it was at Brighton. He was in a Rolls-
Royce landaulette. What's more, I can give you the number!"

Phillip was telling the truth, but he felt guilty all the same.

"Brighton!" remarked Downham. "Don't tell us you were
there with a bird!"

Fool, thought Phillip; and assumed the false amiable smile he
wore whenever Downham was chipping him.

When he arrived at the lake in front of a yellow house half-a-
mile below the big red-brick Court, he saw thousands of mayflies
lying on the surface of the water and fluttering in the air, while
all over the lake big rainbow trout were rolling up and splashing
to take the white flies. Sitting down on the stone-built edge, he
watched shrimp-like insects crawling up the stones and the
sedges by the verge, and knew from his reading that these were
the mayfly *imagines*, their skins soon to split and a fly to crawl forth.
The big trout, some nearly a foot and a half long, did not seem
afraid of his presence; they came to within arm's-length, showing
their black spots, and when they rolled to take a fly, the pinky
green sheen, as on boiled salt beef, was visible on the lateral line.

This lake was private, of course, like the larger lake in front of
the Court up the valley; his permit to fish was in the pond by
the road, opposite the brewery; but watching fish was the next
best thing to fishing. As the hay in the meadow was not cut,
he did not cross over to look at the pond, which held coarse
fish, and a legendary monster pike, but wandered off, along his
usual round. The chain of small lakes up the valley, feeding the
water-mill under the trees, were made by the damming of a water-
thread, which was the beginning of the river Darent. The tiny
brook ran at the foot of the beech wood, opposite the rabbit
warrens. The trout in these smaller ponds were not so large,
but they, too, were rising all over the clouded surface of the
chalky water after mayfly. He sat and watched them, warm and
happy to be in the sunshine, with a feeling of intense joy in being
alive with so much beauty around him.

A pair of sparrowhawks had a nest in the high top of one of
the spruces in a plantation beyond the hill above the valley.
The nest had been shot at by the keeper, several times, but it
was built on an old crow's nest, and the twigs were thick.

Walking there, he longed to be able to climb up, and get one of the fledglings. He could hear them faintly mewing as he lay on the ivy under the tall spruce poles, shadowed below except where little freckles of sunlight came down in shafts. They would be flying, very soon now. Woodpigeons were cooing far away. The cries of jackdaws came from far up in the blue beyond the sighing canopies of the spruces. It was pure happiness to lie there, feeling himself to be part of England. He closed his eyes, he felt as though little golden bubbles were arising through him; and when he opened his eyes again, he saw a robin looking at him from a twig, not twelve inches away.

His packet of sandwiches lay beside him. He put some crumbs on his open palm, and sat up. The robin flew to his knee, eyeing the out-held hand; then jumped upon it, seized a crumb, and flew away. The bird came back again, showing no fear.

There was peace in the plantation. Shafts of sunlight speckled the ivy on the ground, growing over fallen limbs of the firs. The wind sighing in the tall tops of the spruces was like the sound of the sea, far away. The mewing of the young hawks was remote, too. The parent birds did not hunt in the plantation, but away in the beech woods, and along the hedgerows of the cornfields. The robin, perhaps, had not seen a man before.

From the plantation, he walked to the keeper's cottage. Near it stood an ash with a broken limb. In this stump of a branch was a hole where a white owl nested. He had taken one of the eggs in April, and now the young were hatched, squatting among many dead mice and voles which were left from the old birds' dawn hunting. He wanted one of the owls later on. How lovely to see it, quartering the grasses of the Backfield, and perhaps on the Hill at twilight—his white owl, returning to sleep during the day in a special box in the elm!

The keeper showed him a kestrel sitting in a disused ferret cage in his garden. It was an adult bird, with a broken wing. Would he like it? Phillip said, "Rather!" Into his haversack it went, a tightly compressed small falcon, with yellow legs and black claws, large liquid brown eyes. It was bluish grey on its back, its breast plumage being chestnut streaked with black. Its yellow scaley feet were clenched tight. The hawk's beak could give a sharp cut, so take care, said the keeper. Fortunately in his pocket was a present for the keeper—a sixpenny packet of yellow perils, twenty Gold Flakes.

With the kestrel in his bag, he set out for home. He would be able to shoot sparrows for it with his saloon gun, in the elm thicket behind the garden fence. Perhaps he could put the broken wing in a splint, and mend it; then the kestrel might fly wild, and return to him for food. It might even attract a mate, and nest among the chimney pots on his house. What fun that would be! With the kestrels, and an owl, he would bring wild life back to what Father called the lost province of Kent, now officially part of London.

Dreaming thus, he pushed his cycle up the steep and lonely hill, his back hot in the ardent sun of young summer. On the summit of the Downs he rested, watching the swifts racing over green fields of hay and corn. The only sounds were their shrill whistling, the trilling of larks, a faraway cracked cuckoo-voice, and the burring of bees on hedgerow flowers. Far below lay woods and cornfields and meadows, in shadow and sunshine, extending to the Weald of Kent. How glad he was that he had not gone to Australia! Office life wasn't so bad after all, with plenty of time in the evenings for tennis, and rides like this into the country. He liked being alone in the country best of all.

Still, the fellows on the Hillies were fun to be with, the little band he went with sometimes, sky-larking after tennis, a grass court for which could be hired for twopence an hour. Helena Rolls sometimes played there in white clothes and shoes and stockings, with her friends from Twistleton Road, but of course he did not stare, or hang about; but passed on quickly when he saw them, as though bent on going somewhere. If she smiled when he raised his hat—as she always did—he was at once filled with elation, which lasted for days—until, suddenly, a lead weight dropped inside him, and there was nothing to be done about it; except to hope.

With a sigh, he got on his bicycle again, and headed home, the kestrel in the haversack crouched taut, alive to every movement, thrilling and starting with shock of every sound, its wingless life burning away, burning, burning, burning, as it passed the lonely fields of corn and pasture on top of Biggin Hill.

Thursday night was the great weekly occasion on the Hill. The band played; then fireworks from the Crystal Palace, on Sydenham ridge to the south, arose into the summer's soft darkness. While the band played, ere it was twilight, small boys stopped

Phillip for cigarette cards of boxers and musical comedy beauties, motorcars and flowers, as once he had stopped what had seemed to be tall men for similar clean, radiant, coloured wonders— faintly smelling of delicious tobacco threads—depicting the series of Birds and Their Eggs, Fish, and Flying Machines. These tall men were still about, but looking quite different: they seemed to have shrunk, and many had pimply faces, barber's rash, which he had not noticed before. He heard one of them, standing by the bandstand, straw hat tilted on back of head, say to another fellow leaning on his stick, "God, what a poxy hole! Look at all these snotty-nosed kids, like a lot o' spadgers' crap!"

Phillip was hurt by the remark. Hitherto he had regarded the Hill as rather a good place to live beside. The two men looked a poor sort themselves; weedy. The one that had spoken had a face yellow-spotted with barber's rash. Why then had he spoken like that about poor children? After all, it wasn't their fault that they had been born where they were. Take Cranmer, for example. Cranmer, although poor, was at least a thoroughly decent chap. What fun they had had together, as Boy Scouts. It was sad how you seemed to drift apart from your old friends when you grew up. Cranmer, what days they had had together, in the old Bloodhound patrol! Cranmer was a sort of sparrow, a spadger.

He wandered on the Hill, feeling lonesome. The cuckoo's voice had cracked; another spring had gone. He was glad to meet some of the fellows of the band he belonged to, despite the fact that Tom Ching usually attached himself to them. Phillip knew that he was after his sister Mavis, and so trying to court favour with himself. Mavis was still at the convent in Belgium.

Jack Hart, the bold bad Jack Hart who had been expelled from school, sometimes was to be seen, in Merchant Service uniform, his arm in his regular girl's. If only he could be bold, like Jack Hart! Phillip still felt a mixture of admiration and fear for Jack Hart. Fancy blacking his father's eye, when still at school, when he had been thrashed for taking girls into the sheepfold at night!

Phillip still felt slight horror, mingled with envy, that Jack Hart had had carnal knowledge of eight High School girls before he was fourteen. Jack Hart was a black sheep; and yet he never told smutty stories, like Tom Ching did; he just pleased himself, and went his own way, always laughing.

Phillip was glad that Jack now had a regular girl. It made him feel that he himself was not such a weakling, somehow, for not wanting to lie down on the grass with any girl. He was quite happy to be one of a skittling band, in the twilight, talking and joking, and having badinage with occasional couples of young girls. The girls on the Hill always seemed to go in couples, while the youths roved in a loose pack, sometimes, in the safety of dusk, singing songs in harmony. Phillip thought singing in the open air rather vulgar, until one moonlit June night he joined in. It was lovely to feel yourself only a voice in the timeless warm dusk, the evening star shining in the sky, the elms beginning to blacken against the sunset. Life seemed to be eternal, in such moments.

Cousin Bertie sometimes came on the Hill. He never could make out what Bertie thought of him. Did he *really* think he was a bit of a tyke, as once he had called him? Bertie had never been, even in his young days, a "hooligan of the Hillies", as he himself had been. Bertie played tennis, but with his own set, two of whom were the sort who were genuinely entitled to wear silk hats to church on Sundays, with morning suits, for they worked in the Bank of England. Bertie, who was a terrier in the London Highlanders, and a keen athlete, practised running on the Hill after dark twice a week—crunch of plimsolls on gravel, dim ghost suddenly appearing, scarce-audible panting, then fading away. Bertie also spent an evening a week at headquarters, boxing and bayonet-fighting in the School of Arms. He had wonderful muscles.

Phillip had thought of joining to increase his muscles. Many of the men at Head Office were in the London Highlanders. Downham was. So, among the Hill-ites, were Peter Wallace, and Mr. Bolton's son. Peter's father, Mr. Wallace, had been in them too, a sergeant in the days of the Volunteers.

"Why don't you come along with me, as my guest, to a canteen sing-song, young Phil?" said Bertie, one evening, when Phillip, to his surprise, had been asked to make a fourth at tennis. "We want recruits, and apart from all else, it's a top-hole club, with no subscription."

Phillip was much exhilarated that Bertie didn't really look down on him. The two Bank of England men were awfully decent.

"Yes, I'll think about it, after my holiday."

"When are you going?"

"In September."

"Any idea where you're going?"

"Not yet, Bertie. But it may be to Devon. Mother's written to Aunt Dora, to ask if I can go to her cottage." His voice dropped. "The trouble is, only don't mention it to your friends, will you, we don't know whether Aunt Dora was mixed up in that race-horse business, yesterday. So she may be back in prison again."

"All the best people are, anyway, young Phil! Well, so long!"

"So long! And thanks for the game, Bertie."

"Delighted, old thing!"

It was wonderful to be called "old thing" by Cousin Bertie, and in the hearing of the two Bank of England men.

"Well, you know where good intentions lead to, don't you, Hetty?" Phillip heard Father's voice saying to Mother (it was always to Mother when he used that forceful tone of voice). "And that is putting it at its most charitable aspect. The real trouble with Dora is that she has too much spare time on her hands—you know the proverb, I dare say, about Satan and idle hands. Well, this Epsom business is the last straw. As *The Trident* says——"

Phillip hesitated: if Father were in grumbling mood he would slip away, and see Mrs. Neville.

"It's about the Suffragettes," Doris whispered to him, as he hesitated on the mat.

"I know."

"Ah well," said Mother's voice, "it is all very sad. I think I shall write to Dora and urge her to give up her activities for her own sake. But perhaps it will sound ungracious if I do it at the same time that I inquire about Phillip's holiday."

"Well, you must decide for yourself," said Father; and his newspaper rustled.

Phillip went down into the sitting-room.

The letter was posted that night to Dora's address in Old Ford, where she was helping to run the East London Suffragettes Federation. Before a reply could come, the very next day in fact, Hetty heard from Miss Martinant, a suffragette living in Charlotte Road, whose daughter was friendly with Doris (the daughter was, well—no matter, it would be wrong to allow it to make any difference) that Theodora Maddison would be carrying a banner at the funeral of Emily Davidson, who had seized the bridle of the king's colt Amna, at Tattenham Corner, and been trampled on. Whereupon Hetty returned home at once to ask Aunt Marian to go with her to London, to see the funeral procession. Perhaps she might have a chance to talk to Dora afterwards.

Hetty walked beside Aunt Marian to the 'bus with some trepidation: for the outrage had caused much angry comment. They took a 36 to Vauxhall, and walked from there, in beautiful summer weather, to Hyde Park corner, where a crowd was already gathered.

Hetty was afraid of crowds, and fearing for Aunt Marian, who was nearly eighty, she suggested crossing over to the park railings, to be near several policemen standing there, in case there was a crush.

After waiting awhile, they heard in the distance the music of the *Dead March in Saul*. It was very solemn and sad; deeply, deeply sad. She thought of Mamma, of Hugh, of Jennie, of Mr. Newman—the dead in her life who lived with her yet, who now seemed to be faces watching, not in sorrow, but with happy gentleness.

The leaves of the plane tree rustled overhead, so green, so lightly in the warm summer day; then as the procession came nearer, they seemed to be shaking with the heavy beats of the funeral music, the thuddings of the muffled drums. Glancing at Aunt Marian's face, she saw tears running down her cheeks. But Aunt Marian held herself upright, her shoulders squared.

She noticed in the waiting crowd banners and placards bearing slogans hostile to the procession. Quite near a lady in a big hat, expensively dressed, was giving away handbills. Hetty took one from her. It was headed *Woman's League Against the Suffrage*. Aunt Marian said that she resembled the photographs of Mrs. Humphrey Ward, the great novelist. Hetty had read *Robert Elsmere*, and had been much impressed. She and Dora had read the book together, in the days at Cross Aulton. It seemed strange that the authoress should be against the Movement, which was really so idealistic. But Mrs. Humphrey Ward was rich, and probably knew little about the sufferings of the poor. In this thought, Hetty needlessly hurt herself: for Mrs. Ward was, and had been, actively engaged in creating rest rooms and play rooms for children among the poor. It was the methods of the militant suffragettes (who went to the root of the matter, rather than a branch) that the famous novelist objected to.

Hetty took Aunt Marian's arm; Aunt Marian took her hand, and squeezed it.

The coffin, drawn by black horses, and covered with a purple pall on which three laurel leaves were resting, followed behind the band now playing the beautiful uplifting passage of resurrection. But what was happening? She was startled to hear people in the crowd shouting out in anger. With relief she saw that the procession was accompanied by policemen walking on either side. The crowd booed when the banner was carried past.

FIGHT ON AND GOD WILL GIVE THE VICTORY

Then she saw Dora. She was walking with other women, some carrying posies of purple irises in their hands, and red peonies, and bunches of white violets for woman's purity. She gave, without thinking, a little wave of her hand; then she was glad she had not attracted Dora's attention. Dora looked straight ahead. There followed a banner of the Woman's Social and Political Union, with the purple, green and white colours.

The booing was very loud. As Dora passed, she inclined her head slightly, but did not smile. She had seen them! Perhaps Dora considered it advisable not to recognise anyone at that juncture.

On the other hand, she thought, perhaps Dora was a little hurt by what she had written in her letter, begging her to give up the hopeless struggle, which Dickie had said was directed by mad women who in the old days would have been burned at the stake as witches. Windows of London houses had been smashed by stones covered with paper; empty mansions burned down; vitriol poured into pillar-boxes, destroying hundreds of letters; Cabinet Ministers had been assaulted; dynamite bombs placed in public buildings. Property to the value of over half a million pounds had been destroyed.

She held Aunt Marian's arm tightly. How calm, how self-possessed Aunt Marian always was! What a splendid character! How glad she was to be beside her. Oh dear, more angry shouting!

"What about the King's jockey? Three cheers for 'im, boys!"

Mingled cheers and boos arose. Mounted policemen were now pressing their chargers against the edge of the crowd.

"Smash up the coffin! What right has the likes o' 'er for Christian burial?"

A ragged man was trying to pull a policeman off his horse. An inspector, in blue pill-box hat and tight jacket, trotted up. A terrible harsh noise from the crowd arose.

She began to feel terror. Her children, her children! What would happen to them, who would look after them, and Dickie, if the crowd got out of hand, and anything happened to her? She felt she could not breathe. Her high collar, with its whale-bone stiffeners that constricted breathing, her high straw hat covered with artificial flowers and tilted downwards from her piled hair, the sleeves of her blouse fastened at the wrist, her heavy dragging skirt, her boots so hot round the ankles—she thought that if she did not have air she would faint. She tried to tell Aunt Marian that she must get away.

Marian Turney held her up when she fainted. With the help of policemen clearing a way, she was carried into the Park; and after recovery, and a long wait on a seat, with Aunt Marian's arm round her shoulders, in the shade of a tall tree with a vista of mown grass before her, she was saying that she felt much better, and perhaps it would be wiser to return home, when she saw Dora coming towards her—a Dora whose face shocked her, it was so sallow, so lined, so dreadfully thin.

"Hetty, my dear friend! How very dear of you to have come! And how are you, dearest Aunt Marian? You must tell me all your news. How is Dickie, and Phillip, and Mavis, and little Doris? Why, you look pale, Hetty, are you feeling unwell, dear?"

"Oh, it is nothing really, Dora. Very foolishly, I fainted earlier on."

"Hetty, my dear dear girl——" Dora sat beside her, took her hand. "You are too sensitive, you should not have come."

Pigeons were cooing in the trees, and flying down to the grass, to strut and feed, to pursue and be pursued. Young ladies, habited and riding side-saddle, followed by grooms, cantered sedately down Rotten Row. It was the height of the season. Children followed, in basket-seats strapped to Shetland ponies, accompanied by nurses in uniforms of grey bonnets and capes, while under-grooms, or stable boys in livery, held the bridles.

Carriages passed, open landaus and victorias wherein sun-shaded dowagers taking the air of the London season and beautiful prim women in wide hats sat and bowed to their friends in passing. Among the equipages was the yellow landau of Lord and Lady Lonsdale, which Dora recognised.

"Just think of the contrast, Hetty. I suppose that splendid English family receives one hundred thousand a year in royalties from coal alone. Yet how many realise the other side? Do you know, two million, eight hundred thousand people, no less, sleep out, homeless, in our cities every night of the year—in darkest England? Lord Lonsdale is a worthy man, a great sportsman, a landlord of the best type; it is the dark forces of the System which are to blame. It cannot go on much longer. A crisis is very near, all the signs point to it. There is violence everywhere, at home and abroad—gun-running in Ulster— Labour violence, violence at the docks—violence in the House of Commons. Violence in our Movement, yes, yes, you deplore it, I know; but a cauterising violence, Hetty, to cure the proud flesh from becoming gangrenous, and killing the body. Women must save the children, which are England's future. Either there must be a better future, or no future at all. It is we women who must help, in the direction of the new earth which is to be, a nation based on truth; but if we do not come to power *now*, all will be lost. Our violence is deliberate, Hetty, to prevent great catastrophe, perhaps the final catastrophe of the West. It is the same in Germany, another nation possessed by the hubris of industrial power, for the sake of money. In the end such men say, ' We are the nation'. Such men are uncertain of their true strength, Hetty; their 'national' violence is of their true nature thwarted, and too often darkened for ever, in the gehenna of the little helpless child's mind, in its very soul, shut up as in a dark cupboard, suffering nightmares which are but writhings of a soul in darkness to find the light—to find the truth—to be saved from fear by love. This, my dear friend, is the only reply I can make to your most kind letter."

Tears ran down Dora's face; she sought Hetty's hand. Aunt Marian sat between them, a protecting arm given to each.

"The truth will prevail, the truth will prevail," she said stalwartly.

"If only all English people, in the more comfortable classes, could but see what I have seen, what I see daily, hourly, what I know is waiting to leap forth from the maimed minds of children, now grown-up, everywhere, in all classes—but most of all in the poverty classes, since they are most numerous—O, we are doing the Lord's work, we are, we are."

After this confession, uttered in a voice that was so sweetly reasonable that Hetty wondered how anyone could ever gainsay what her dear friend ever said, Dora looked up, and blinking away her tears, saw those in the eyes of her friend, and bending down her head, kissed the hand she held between her own. Then she touched with her lips the reticulated cheek of the old woman beside her.

"And now," she said, with a smile, meeting Hetty's smile, " before I forget—I am not always a wild and wilful woman, you know!—about my little cottage in Lynmouth—how well I remember our wonderful holiday together when my god-son was only three months old!—well, Hetty, my dear, it is for you or Phillip or Dickie to visit and stay in so long as you like, and at any time any of you care to go there. Just send me a line at any time, with a few days' notice if possible, so that I can be sure of having the place ready for you."

"Thank you, Dora dear, thank you very much, it is most kind of you I am sure," said Hetty, still unhappy that her letter had caused a restraint between them, despite Dora's gracious manner.

Hardly had she spoken when two brown-moustached men in straw-yards, jackets and trousers of dark material, and big black boots, got out of a taxicab which had stopped on the drive opposite the seat, and walked to the seat.

"Are you Theodora Maddison? I have a warrant for your arrest under the Prisoners Temporary Discharge for Ill-health Act, Section 1, subsection 12a. Now then, no trouble, miss, be reasonable, and come along quietly."

Hetty and her Aunt Marian were left on the seat.

Phillip hoped that by the time his friend Desmond Neville came home for the summer holidays the kestrel would be tame and they could take it on the Hill and fly it; but the bird proved intractable. Whenever he opened its cage, it ran out and squatted on the lawn; soon it attracted spadgers, the sooty little cockney sparrows, always quarrelling and chittering, always scrapping for their rights. The spadgers hopped around it, scolding. The kestrel appeared to shrink into its shoulders. The sparrows hopped nearer. Phillip, like the kestrel, remained absolutely still. Then running sideways with unbelievable speed, the fierce, brown-eyed falcon managed to snatch a spadger before it could fly up with the others. Yet this did not, apparently, warn the others; back they came, sooner rather than later, to mob the kestrel. Again the sudden dash on yellow feet, feathered thighs like little pantaloons moving so swiftly that the broken wing had not appeared even to drag. The snatch, the crushing power of a yellow foot with its black claws of sharpest horn, had to be felt on your forearm, through your jacket sleeve, to be realized. The falcon stood on the spadger, squeezed its life out as it crouched there, all the bird's life and cockiness turned to an escaping scream of terror as it lay gripped shapeless under black claws.

One evening the kestrel got through the fence, at the end where the post had rotted, and the boards leaned outwards. Phillip let it go—it would not accept him as a friend. He hoped it would manage to live in the long grass, on mice and birds in the Backfield. But that was its own look out.

The August sun burned down, the tennis courts on the Hill showed worn patches, the band played on Thursdays to thousands of shrill sparrow-like children come up from the old-time marshes around the great ox-bend and eyot in the Thames, called the Isle of Dogs: an area long since covered with rows and terraces of cottage-like dwellings with tiled roofs darkened by soot, their brick walls saturated with the odours of leather, vinegar, hops, sulphur, and glue: while beyond the dark low clusters, seen under their haze of smoke from the Hill, stood up the red and yellow funnels of liners, the masts and spars of sailing ships which crossed the seas with their cargoes to and from the docks and basins of London river.

Phillip was to take his holidays in September. Where, he could not decide. Mavis and Cousin Petal, home from the convent in Belgium, sang at the piano the song Phillip had heard on the concert platform of Hayling Island, in those family holidays which now seemed so far away.

Phillip's holidays are in Septem-bah!
He's been saving up since last Novem-bah!

Richard had cycled to the Norfolk Broads for his holiday, having taken it in the last fortnight in June, and the first week of July. In early manhood, in the days of butterfly collecting, he had dreamed of visiting that remote and mysterious place, with its fabulous bitterns, harriers, and bearded titmice; great shoals of bream, rudd, pike and tench, brown-sailed wherries and windmills rising above the reeds vibrating with the thousand tongues of the wind ruffling watery solitude; and, most wonderful of all, Large Copper and Swallowtail butterflies, extinct elsewhere in Britain. His collecting days were over; an elderly man went to the Broads, to make real a boyhood dream, from which he returned bronzed and happy; but it was not the West Country.

"I hope you two will be all right while we are away," said Hetty, on the eve of her departure with Mavis and Doris to Beau Brickhill, to stay with Aunt Liz and Polly.

"Rather!" cried Phillip. "Give my love to old Percy!"

Percy Pickering had left school and gone to work in Uncle Jim's firm of corn and seed merchants.

It was rather nice and quiet to be alone in the house. He seldom saw Father. He had his breakfast next door with Aunt Marian, and his supper, when he returned in the evening, with Desmond and Mrs. Neville. Desmond had another three years at school before going to the University, then into his Uncle's lace business in Nottingham. Of Desmond's father Phillip knew nothing beyond that he was still alive; he had not the least curiosity, nor did Desmond ever speak of him.

What was there to do in the evenings, and at week-ends? The nests in his preserves were long since forsaken; a spirit had departed. And Desmond nowadays seemed to have no interest in birds. He cared more for fishing. It was no good going any more to the round-ponds in Whitefoot Lane woods, or the dewponds in the Seven Fields of Shrofften, where once they had caught roach. Old cans and bits of broken carts lay in those little ponds now that the houses were creeping up in long red and yellow rows. The woods themselves were bare, threaded with broad paths where hundreds of strange feet had trodden.

It was a fashion that year to wear in the buttonhole a little German silver tube, holding water, and flowers—perhaps a rose and maidenhair fern. All the youths on the Hill sported them. Phillip wore a white carnation—for Helena.

Sometimes, if it looked like rain, the boys went together to the

Electric Palace in the High Street to see Nazimova, Mary Pick-
ford, Theda Bara, or a Mack Sennett film, which was always
screamingly funny. Once a week they had a sixpenny seat in
the dress circle of the first house of the Hippodrome, where
strange new music called rag-time was to be heard. A little
brown-faced man—"All handsome men are slightly sunburnt,"
laughed Phillip, quoting the oft-seen advertisement, to Desmond
—came on with a violin and sang wheezily,

> *Yiddle, on your fiddle,*
> *Won't you please to play some rag-time?*

while his violin went sort of scrittchy scratch and there was not
a lot of clapping afterwards. He was one of the first turns, of
course. Phillip thought that Uncle Hugh could have done ever
so much better, if he had lived. But there he was, in the cemetery
beside Grannie: two white tombstones.

> *In the evening, in the moonlight, you can hear those darkies singing—*

Harmony floated through the warm summer twilight on the
Hill; laughing girls passed; sudden feet running over dusky
grass, shouts and more laughter, as youth wrestled and ragged
in fun. Cries in the gloaming; the near double-warble of some
sweet whistler, feeling grand in a new pair of peg-topped
trousers, all the rage among the sort of chaps who "warbled";
two-fingered screech of Cranmer leaving for home, a salute for
his admired, his beloved Phillip—an attitude of which the re-
cipient was entirely unconscious. Phillip wished he wouldn't do
it, but, of course, didn't like to tell old Horace.

The harvest moon rose over the Thames estuary, casting long
shadows: and among the shadows, fancy might have seen one
of the wraiths of the Hill, the ghost of Hugh Turney swaying
in the mist of light between two dark hawthorn patches, and re-
marking in a whisper of his old ironic self, *Keep it going boys—
your race is nearly run.*

> *You have stolen my heart, my heart away—*

The high moon shone on *her* house, dark and with drawn
blinds, and glistened on the little turret that was her bedroom.
Standing in the blackness of the hawthorns across the road,

merging his own darkness with the shadows of the moon, he dreamed of a face there, a smile, of white arms held out to him below, all his spirit like a nightingale singing. It was safe to stand there and dream: for she was with her people in the Isle of Wight. Alas, that his holidays began before they were due to return! Ah, he was glad, for might she not then miss him? When the moon shone down upon the Hill, all fancies seemed possible. Ghosts walked, dreams became truth.

Night by night the moon rose later, to slant in gold upon the singing, the playing, and the fun. *Keep it going, boys——*

"Well, old chap—if I might make a suggestion for your holiday next week—you could join the Cyclists' Touring Club, you know. They provide one, on request, with a list of suitable lodgings for the night. Why not go awheel down to the West Country? It is a wonderful journey, across the Plain—though I fancy it is too late to hear the quails——"

"I was wondering, Father—do you think I might pay Uncle John and Willie a visit, at Rookhurst? Of course, I don't want to be in the way."

"Well, you might call at Uncle John's on the way down, Phillip. Then he might invite you to stay. A postcard to your Cousin Willie, say three days in advance, would be the thing, I think."

So with rod and saloon gun strapped to cross-bar of the Swift, Phillip cycled away very early one morning, to cross the Thames by Kingston Bridge; and by way of Staines, Bagshot Common, and Andover, to Salisbury for the night in an eighteen-penny bed-and-breakfast C.T.C.-recommended lodging; then onwards across the Great Plain, in heat radiating from white dust and stubble field of that chalk country where he lingered throughout a summer day, dreaming of the ventriloquial notes of quails; and at owl-light he came to the thatched village of Rookhurst, and the stone house of Willie and Uncle John under the downs.

Chapter 4

LAST WINTER OF THE OLD WORLD

ON THE first day of October the coal fire was lit in the office. The Michaelmas renewals were now coming in. They were

connected, in Phillip's eyes, with a most desirable thing: overtime. This began after five o'clock, and was paid for at the
wonderful rate of one shilling and sixpence an hour for a junior
of under ten years' service. He worked out that this was slightly
more than thrice the rate of his day work. The Overtime Book
was a big black-covered one, and the entries had to be counter-
signed by E.R.H.—except Mr. Hollis', Phillip noticed: he
counter-signed his own. Mr. Hollis worked alone, too—never
when he ordered Phillip to remain. He got half a crown an
hour; Downham got two shillings. Downham seldom did any
overtime, nor did E. Rob Howlett.

Phillip liked to be alone with Edgar on the occasions when
Mr. Hollis suggested that he should stay. Then he and Edgar
had some fun. The occasions when he stayed were the addressing
of the first renewal reminder notices. Edgar had to stay in order
to stamp them. Bouts of work were interrupted by bouts of
boxing and football in the basement. Phillip was now six feet
tall, though very thin; he weighed, according to the machine
on London Bridge station, nine stone ten pounds with top hat,
raincoat, and umbrella.

That silk hat had drawn some remarks at first.

"Here, what the devil have you got on your head?" Mr.
Hollis demanded, when he appeared in his topper. "Who the
blazes do you think you are? No, no, don't take it off, keep
it on! Look at this, Howlett, what do you think of your
junior?"

Downham looked sardonic. Phillip thought that he was rather
despised by Downham.

"Well, Maddison," gurgled Mr. Howlett, pipe hanging from
mouth, its rim oily black with Hignett's Cavalier. "Didn't
recognise you at first, I must say."

"Young monkey, apeing his seniors," laughed Hollis. "Get
on with the post book, you lamp-post."

Phillip hastily disappeared into the basement, to hang up
coat and hat, then to leap up the stairs again. When Mr. Hollis
came to him with the post he whispered, "Don't mind my
fooling, Maddison. I appreciate that you are trying to keep up
the traditions of the Lane."

The hat was an old story by October, not so shiny as when
new. Mid-day sittings in the churchyard of St. Botolph at the
corner of Houndsditch and Aldgate, when money for lunches

had run out, had exposed it to more than one pigeon. In places it looked as though it had been licked by a cat.

If Phillip was a lamp-post, Edgar was still a little tich, with treble voice and child face free of the quick cunning of Cockney van or newspaper boy. Unknown to Phillip, Edgar had a hero upon whom to model his mind. In his messenger's uniform, with silver-gilt buttons, he looked a happy mite beside his mural display of boxers and beauties.

At football in the basement Edgar was very quick, and scored more goals with the string-tied ball of brown-paper, against Phillip's wall, than Phillip did against Edgar's wall. Edgar butted a lot; an act impossible to Phillip, since not only was Edgar never there when he charged, but he had to bend down to meet Edgar shoulder to shoulder. This made the breaks in clerical work all the more hilarious.

As for the boxing, with towels wrapped round fists, Edgar invariably scored more blows, or light taps, than Phillip. Edgar's head was never there when Phillip launched his gentle straight lefts. More than once Edgar got under his guard, and a series of left-right-lefts on his ribs and solar-plexus made him aware that he ought to do something about his total ignorance of the art of self-defence.

The directors of the Moon Fire Office made a grant of four pounds to every clerk who joined the territorials. Phillip wanted a new suit; there was Church the tailor in Fenchurch Street who advertised a thick, dark-grey herring-bone all-wool suit, made to measure, for fifty shillings. Cheaper suits were thirty-five bob. The four pounds grant was therefore attractive. Also, said Downham, there was the camp every year, near the sea, in addition to the annual two weeks' holiday. A whole month in the open air, with full salary; and the second fortnight under canvas without cost, and a shilling a day soldier's pay as well! Phillip decided to join the territorials.

There were many battalions in the London Regiment, twenty-eight in fact, he learned from Downham. Then there was the Honourable Artillery Company, a corps apart. Most of the fellows at Head Office were in one or the other of the crack battalions—the Inns of Court, London Rifles, Queen's West-minsters, Artists' Rifles, London Highlanders, and one or two more. But for the Highlanders you not only had to have Scottish blood, declared Downham: you had to be first-class socially. They would not take any old rag-tag or bobtail who presented himself.

"The battalion for the bobtails is the Tower Hamlets, down the river, the Shiny Old Seventh, the louts from Leytonstone," pointing with his pen to a map of London on the wall.

Phillip was somewhat subdued by what he considered to be a reference to himself as a supposed bobtail. Pype, who had been one of the Bagmen in his last term at school, had recently got a post at Head Office. Phillip had not forgotten how Downham had spoken rather slightingly about Pype.

"Fancy a chap like that being admitted on the staff!" were his words to Mr. Hollis. "Why, he was a scholarship boy at some suburban grammar school!"

Pype certainly was small, and rather sallow; but surely Heath's was a pretty good school, being founded in Elizabethan times? Both Downham and Mr. Hollis were proud of the fact that they had gone to public schools, Merchant Taylors and St. Paul's respectively.

At Head Office luncheon that day Phillip thought he would ask Costello, who was an Old Heathian, and in the London Highlanders, pretending that the idea had only just come into his head. He waited until Costello, opposite him at table, had finished his lunch.

Wielding a quill toothpick, Costello said, "Oh, we're pretty well full up I think. Why not try the Twentieth, they're your way, aren't they," and then turned to talk to some others at the next table. So that was it! Costello knew Downham, and they thought him not good enough for the Highlanders.

Going downstairs, on impulse he went into the telephone box, and asked for Wine Vaults Lane. Downham answered. Putting on an assumed voice, Phillip asked for himself. Downham replied that he was out to lunch, so Phillip said, "Oh, I see. Well, I'm his uncle, and I was going to ask him to luncheon, so I'll ring up another day. Good day to you."

When he got back to the office Downham was furious. "Why the hell do you ring yourself up from Head Office, saying you were your uncle? What's the game? Don't you know this is a private line? The telephone girl asked me as soon as you hung up, 'Is his uncle at Head Office, as well as his father?', and then she rang the Town Department, who said you'd just left the box. You young idiot, why do you do such damn silly things?"

Later in the afternoon Phillip assembled himself sufficiently to say, "Oh, about the London Highlanders, I have a cousin in them, you know."

"What's his name?"

"Hubert Cakebread."

"Why, Bertie Cakebread is a corporal in my company!" exclaimed Downham. "He's one of the best bayonet fighters in the School of Arms."

Phillip kept his eyes modestly on his work, writing his neatest hand. He was glad when Mr. Hollis returned, top-hatted and in morning coat, from inspecting a Moses Cohen factory at Leytonstone, where a new fire-sprinkler system had been installed.

Then Downham told him about the ringing-up. Mr. Hollis made no comment, as he drew off his gloves.

"What a frightful neighbourhood," he said. "Young Roy Cohen tells me that ass's milk has a large sale down there, from the costers' mokes. Isn't that what you were brought up on as a brat, Maddison, what?"

Phillip noticed that Mr. Hollis always said *What?*, instead of *Eh?*, when he wore his tail coat with the black braid around the hem, his highly-creased morning trousers, ironed top-hat, chamois-leather gloves, gold-banded umbrella, and rose-bud or other flower in his button-hole. He went on writing, face held low.

"I say, Maddison, I do apologise for my extremely rude remark! But you are a bit of a donkey, you know."

In gratitude for the great man's kindness, Phillip smiled, and said, "Oh, that's quite all right, thank you, Mr. Hollis."

He felt that it was almost a case of second sight when, the next morning, Uncle George Lemon came into the office; but he kept his face hidden, in case Uncle did not want to recognise him.

"Good morning, good morning to you, Mr. Lemon!" cried Mr. Hollis, affably. "To what do I owe this unexpected pleasure?"

Phillip went on with his work, after a faint smile at Uncle George's small brown face. He listened. It was something to do with a house Uncle said he was going to have rebuilt in Cornwall. He unrolled a lot of crinkling plans.

"Quite a mansion, Mr. Lemon," said Mr. Hollis. "By Lutyens, what? What are there, twenty bedrooms? Let me see.

H'm. The cubic footage must run to well over a million—at sixpence a cubic foot, this is going to be in the neighbourhood of twenty-five thousand pounds, at a very rough estimate! Then there is Lutyen's fee—what is that?—two thousand guineas?"

"I am going to chuck this unnatural City life," said Uncle George, as though he had not heard. "I want to farm land owned by m'forebears. I am going to bring back the Longhorn. I want to breed a winter-wheat that will ripen in July, to defeat the old swampy harvests of the past. Two out of every three Cornish Augusts are swampy, as you know. I have just bought a thousand acres in a ring fence, for a start, land once belonging to m'family."

"Well, it's extremely good of you to think of us, Mr. Lemon! I don't know what our Chancery Lane Branch will say about it, but healthy rivalry, you know, stimulates, what?"

Uncle Lemon rolled up the plans, and put them in their long tube. Then he went to Phillip's desk and said quietly, "How are you, Phil? When are you coming out to luncheon with me, as you promised? Hilary's back from Sydney, did you know? We must foregather. How is your father? And your mother? Do give them both my kind regards. And your sisters. Come over and see us one Sunday, before we leave Epsom. Are you still keen on fishing? If all goes well, I shall be able to offer you some real good salmon fishing in Cornwall in the course of a year or two. One of my plans is to change the late-running fish in the Camel to springers, by introducing, by way of Khashmir boxes, early-running eyed-ova from the Tay. Don't forget—write to me. Goodbye," and Uncle Lemon held out his hand.

When he had gone, leaving Phillip in a daze of glory, Mr. Hollis said, "How did you come to know Mr. George Lemon?"

"He's my uncle, Mr. Hollis."

"George Lemon your uncle?" cried Mr. Hollis, in surprise. "Why, he is the senior partner in Wilton, Lemon and Co., since old Wilton died. They act for my father-in-law's firm, Carlton Turnham and Co., you know, the Civil Engineers."

That evening, when he told his father about Uncle George's visit, Richard showed surprise, too; but a different kind of surprise.

"I refuse to believe it! He was spoofing you, my boy."

"But I saw the plans of the mansion, truly, Father!"

The next night Father said, "Well, Hollis confirms your story,
I must admit that. But whatever does George Lemon think he's
doing, to want to rebuild a house of that kind? Has he come
into a fortune? Or gone out of his mind? A house of twenty
bedrooms, to be redesigned internally by one of the most expensive architects in England! And at a time when taxation is
already making many owners of such houses feel the pinch! You
mark my words, there is something fishy about it all."

Richard took up the *Trident* again, and said no more.

"At any rate, dear," said Hetty, "Phillip was quite right in
what he said."

There was no reply from behind the newspaper.

Mr. Hollis' attitude to Phillip became mellower. He brought
up a basket of apples from his Woking garden, and gave two
yellow-red ones to Phillip, two to Downham, one to Edgar, and
the rest to Mr. Howlett. They were Cox's orange pippins, not
yet ripe, he said; they should be kept until they became mellow.

Mellowness was in the air, in the attitude of Mr. Hollis particularly: the ripe mellowness of St. Martin's Little Summer,
of dwarf-yellow sun shining upon apples, peaches, and sunflowers
in his garden, the working of which, Mr. Hollis often declared,
provided him with the only true antidote to a damned office life
lived eighty per cent in electric light.

To Phillip, office life did not feel to be so damned. As the
days shortened there was overtime for the Michaelmas second
and third renewal notices. Edgar took them in batches, folded
and stamped them, carried them in wicker tray to the pillar-
box in Fenchurch Street.

It was wonderful to have the office key in his charge. When
the others had left, with blinds drawn Phillip sat and wrote
with feelings of adventure. When should he go to tea? He was
his own master. Then there was Edgar to think of. What time
should he send him to tea tonight? Five-fifteen, or five-thirty?

"You go to tea at half-past five, will you, Edgar?"

"Yessir!"

"Back at six, my lad!"

"Yessir!"

At 5.28 p.m., to show his power, Edgar slipped out. Five
minutes later the man-in-charge got up, locked the door, strolled
round the corner to his usual A.B.C. shop, and ordered his

favourite meal of boiled country egg (as the menu described it), portion of cottage loaf, pat of butter, pot of tea, and penny pot of jam.

"I think I'll have apricot tonight."

"Yes, sir."

The pot of jam was all the more attractive as it was only about two inches high, and little more than one in diameter. There were many kinds to choose from: cherry, quince, plum, greengage, apricot, damson, apple jelly, marmalade, raspberry, and strawberry. Tea, which cost sevenpence, was eaten slowly, to relish every mouthful, while he read in *The London Magazine* one of those thrilling nature stories by F. St. Mars, illustrated by Warwick Reynolds. This month's was about a buzzard.

There was a magazine club in the Branch: Mr. Howlett bought *Nash's*, Mr. Hollis *The Royal*, Downham *The London*, and he bought *Pearson's*. When they had read them for a week, they passed them round. Then Edgar bore them home.

The London was Phillip's favourite; it usually had an F. St. Mars story.

He read, oblivious of cabs and buses and drays outside, while munching slowly to make the portion of crusty cottage loaf last, magazine propped against tea-pot. He was on his own; he could return when he wanted to; even so, Edgar would be back at six, so he must not linger. After all, he was now in charge of the Branch. It was seven minutes to six. He had six and a half more minutes.

The story finished, he took out his diary, and gloated upon the amount of overtime already due to him, £2 5s. 6d. Riches indeed! By working from five o'clock until nine that evening, he would make a further six shillings: more than he earned in nearly three ordinary days. From this diary, given him by Mr. Hollis—one of scores sent to the Branch every New Year, from other firms and companies—he learned from the *Table of Income or Wages* that his £40 per year was £3 6s. 8d. per month, 15s. 4½d. per week, or 2s. 2½d. per day. After Christmas he would buy a Belgian double-barrel gun, and go with Bertie down to the Blackwater estuary wildfowling during the week-ends!

Having scraped the pot of apricot jam clean, and picked off his plate the last group of crumbs, he sipped his third cup of tea, and regarded further information in the *North British and Mercantile Diary* about the population of the United Kingdom at the last census, two years previously; and reflected that, had he died before donkey's milk had saved his life as a baby, the number of people in England would now be 34,047, 658. "Donkey Boy", his old nickname. "Worry Guts", Father had sometimes called him. Was that because he had thread-worms all the time, and had been ashamed to tell Mother how they had itched so? After his scholarship exam, he had told her; and kept in bed, starved, medicine had killed them all.

He asked for the bill. He liked the waitress who usually served him; she always smiled at him, she was plump and pink-faced, unlike most of the pale thin waitresses in black clothes and white caps and aprons.

Four minutes left. He read the *Table of Inhabited House Duty*, and wondered why anyone had to pay tax. Father often grumbled about income tax. What would Father have to pay? He had been in the M.F.O. for nearly twenty years, and Mother said he had started, coming from Doggett's Bank, at £120 per annum, so now he would be earning in the neighbourhood of £320. The first £160 was abated, which meant it didn't count; so he would have to pay 160 lots of 9*d*., or 160 @ 6*d*. equalled £8, plus £4, total £12. But there was an allowance for every child under 16. Mavis was just 16, so Father would have to pay ten more ninepences than last year; more than that, for with his £10 annual rise it would mean twenty ninepences more, or 15*s*. Twelve pounds fifteen shillings a year! What a swizz! Hard cheese, Pater old Man, you should have gone to Australia when you had the chance!

Three minutes left. How long before he would have to pay income tax? By £10 annual rises, including the £20 rise from £50 to £70 during his third year, it would take him—he counted on his fingers—eleven more years before he reached £160. He would be Downham's age by then!

Lips and fingers working, he reckoned it would take him fifteen and a half years to reach £200, twenty-five to £300, thirty-five to £400, fifty-five to £500, sixty-five to £600, seventy-five to £700, eighty-five to £800, ninety-five to £900, a hundred and five to £1,000. By that time he would be like Old Parr! Then looking at his watch, he saw with slight alarm that he ought to be going.

The waitress who took an interest in what she thought of as the tall Irish boy with the dark blue eyes and lovely shy smile wondered if he was hard-up, and reckoning how far his money would go. So when he rose and offered her his usual twopence she said quickly, with a sudden full look into his eyes, "No dear, that's quite all right, really, you keep it. I know what it is to be hard up."

He felt shame that twopence was not enough. He had a thr'penny bit in his pocket, too. It was too late to offer it now. He said, "Oh, I see, well, thank you, good evening," and in confusion went out of the door, feeling that he could never go there again. Was he mean? Grandfather Maddison, who had died of drink, used to tip porters half-a-sovereign sometimes, when they opened carriage doors for him. And Gran'pa Turney once had given only a cigar-stub to a poor man who had carried his bag from Liverpool Street to London Bridge Station. He hurried down the street and turned into Wine Vaults Lane, to see Edgar approaching, whistling loudly *Oh, oh, that Gaby Gaby Glide.*

A few evenings later, still thinking of the £4 grant in terms of new suit and Belgian double-barrel for wildfowling down by the Heybridge Basin (which, he had learned from Bertie, was the end of a canal, where it joined the Blackwater estuary by means of big wooden lock-gates) Phillip went to the Headquarters of the London Highlanders. There he declared a Scottish great-great-grandfather (of which Richard had informed him) and was accepted, sworn in by the Adjutant while holding a Bible and standing to attention; and posted to "B" Company.

Bertie took him to the School of Arms. Here amidst other activities men in flannel trousers, plimsolls, and singlets were bayonet-fighting, wearing wire masks and a sort of leather armour in front. He watched two at it. Long dummy rifles clashed, they ran in and out; suddenly one hurled his rifle forward with the full length of his arm and his body with it. The heavy iron button on the extended rod which took the place of the bayonet struck the other man on his leather chest-guard. The weight of the thrust drove the iron rod back against its spring. It shot out again with a snap. The umpire declared that Wallace had driven the bayonet through his opponent's ribs.

Wallace! When the wire mask was removed, he saw Peter's bespectacled face. He moved away, not wanting to meet Peter. He was still ashamed of having got Peter to fight for him on the Hill, although it was six years ago now. He still winced whenever he recalled how Peter had come up to call him a coward, after Mr. Pye next door to the Rolls had complained to Father, and Father had told Uncle Hilary and Aunt Viccy at Epsom about it, to his utter shame. O, why had he not joined the Twentieth County of London, at Blackheath? He was forever branded a coward.

Self-critical, envious, haunted, hopeless (he had had no lunch and no tea), he watched Bertie in a bout with Peter. Others came to watch. Bertie was very agile and quick, he had a different manner of fighting. He ran in under Peter's guard, and holding his rifle short, made the button spring against his chest. Phillip heard the staff-sergeant say, "Unorthodox, Corporal Cakebread, but I must admit you pinked your opponent."

Elsewhere in the large drill hall, lit by electric globes hanging from the roof, men were boxing. The instructor, in dirty white jersey and grey flannel trousers, had a grinning scarred face, few teeth, and conglomerated ears. Beyond was a vaulting horse, parallel and horizontal bars. Phillip realised that everyone there was ever so much better than himself.

A recruit had to attend three drills a month, he learned. School of Arms was voluntary. Next week, said the storeman, he would have his uniform and equipment ready, stamped 9689 Pte. P. S. T. Maddison.

On the following Thursday he collected his kilt of hodden grey, purse or sporran, hose or stockings, spats, khaki jacket, and blue glengarry with the white-metal badge of the Scottish lion held by St. Andrew's Cross. These went into a grey canvas kit-bag. With this equipment he went by omnibus to London Bridge, feeling that he was now really in the grown-up world.

During the walk over the Hill in the darkness he met the band with whom he sometimes wandered and played, and told them about his enlistment. They accompanied him down the gully, Ching insisting on carrying the kit-bag.

"Well, I'd like to ask you in," said Phillip, to the four youths, to impress them further, "but I expect they will be in the middle of dinner."

"Oh, it's quite all right, Phil. Good night!"

He had told Mother he would be late that evening. There was a tray laid for him; bread, brawn, a slice of mince pie.

Would he like tea or cocoa with his supper? Richard looked up from the *Trident*.

"How about a plate of oatmeal for our soldier boy? You can't produce a haggis, I suppose, Hetty?"

"I'm not really hungry, thank you."

"Perhaps you would care for a glass of whusky?"

"Really, Dickie!" said Hetty, pleased with his amiability.

"Well, it is an occasion, your best boy joining the Army, surely? And I thought all Scotsmen lived on oatmeal and whiskey. Well, old chap, so you're a territorial! What make of rifle did they issue you with?"

Phillip said he didn't know, it was still in the armoury. He took his kit-bag up to his bedroom. He was not going to be persuaded to try on the kilt, and risk possible remarks about his "sparrow knees", as once Mr. Swinerd, the assistant scoutmaster of the old North-west Kent Troop, had referred to them. Mr. Swinerd with his loose lips, and so-called jokes about orange juice swelling up bread in a boy's stomach and stopping his heart, the silly rotter!

Richard would not have made such a remark to his grown son: but in the past, he had sometimes spoken of his "weepy" face, his "creepy-crawly" ways, his "throw-back" behaviour; and the son had not forgotten, even if the parent had.

At his first School of Arms night, in singlet, white flannel trousers and plimsolls, Phillip felt, at least at first, that he was a man among men. The boxing lesson convinced him that he wasn't. Two punches, like two fireworks in the streets outside exploding on his face, removed all desire to continue. The comic-paper drawings of a splosh with stars exactly described the feeling; the first crashed like a jumping cracker on his mouth, the second darkened all his head, spreading to his eyes with flashy darkness.

"Come on, lad, open yer peepers! Where's that guard? Go on, after him! Up you get! That warn't nothin'! Up you get! Nah then, watch 'im! Where's yer guard? Use yer elbows! Never mind that one, 'e ain't got no hoss-shoe in 'is glove! You ain't goin' to let no one do that to you! Cross with yer right! Where's that straight left? What are yer feet doin', tryin' ter grow through the floor? Batter 'is gums! Change that smile on 'is dial! 'It *'im*, not the air, lad! 'Ere, 'alf a mo', I'll show yer."

After leaving the ring to wash his face free of blood, he decided to join the group for the vaulting horse. But he could only do simple exercises; no hand-springs. So he did a bit of rope-climbing on his own. He could do that, anyway.

On his first drill night he went on parade holding rifle at the half-trail, like a scout's pole. He saluted the man in charge, the butt meanwhile resting on the floor. Downham was there, laughing.

"Don't salute me, lad, I'm not an orficer!" growled the staff-sergeant. "And keep that butt from dragging on the floor, it ain't a broom. Fall in and dress by the right."

He learned to form fours, to slope arms, to turn left and right, to stand to attention, to ground arms, to port arms for inspection with breech and cut-off open, to present arms, to fix and unfix bayonet; and most welcome of all, to dismiss—and so to the canteen.

"Cheerio!"

"Here's the skin off your nose."

"Thanks."

One evening he went to call on Mr. Graham, who was president of the Old Boys' Club, and tell him his news. Mr. Graham spoke of a reunion at the school on the following Saturday evening, and said he looked forward to meeting him there. In due course, wearing his new made-to-measure dark grey herring-bone woollen suit, bought for fifty shillings at Church the tailor's, Phillip walked over the Hill, down into the murky High Street glowing in a pool of electric light, and up towards the dark levels of the Heath.

Outside the school he hesitated; then assembling himself against old feelings of magisterial apprehension, went through the iron gates, past the chemistry laboratory and so to the entrance. Opening the door slightly, the first face he saw, in the rings of flickering gas-light under the high beams and rafters, was the Magister's. There it was, pink and big, smiling among a group of old boys. Awaiting a chance to slip in unobserved, he darted into a cloak-room until the Magister was on the other side of Hall, before strolling out to talk to Tom Cundall and others he knew. He avoided the Magister: too many times had those icy Viking eyes looked into his inner self, and seen nothing there, for all Celtic personality had taken flight in fear.

An extraordinary thing happened later, when the Magister had left. Mr. Graham suggested his name to Fitcheyson, president of the Old Heathians Football Club, as captain of the new fourth team being formed!

He was amazed. He was no good at footer. He had been one of the worst boys in the school—not really bad, of course, like Jack Hart—but still, all the same, not much good: and here was Gildart Fitcheyson asking him if he would captain the Fourth Eleven!

Fitcheyson said he would arrange the fixtures. What about it? He agreed, with some wonder and more self-doubt; and in due course the matches were made, the cards printed. *Captain*, P. S. T. Maddison!

Phillip determined to do his best with the football team. He was a useful outside-left on occasion, with a good lifting kick from the side-line to the goal's mouth.

At first it seemed that the Fourth Eleven as a team would never materialise. Only odd members turned up. The greatest number was six, when the match was on the Heath. Usually the game had to be started with four or five, more usually four. Phillip did his best to make his men keen, sometimes calling on them on Friday night, to ensure a full turn-out. Game after game was lost.

However, he kept on hoping that one afternoon a full team would take the field, and then the Old Heathians Fourth might win a match. He travelled by omnibus and train and cycle to the various local grounds and fields where the matches were to be played; and when yet once again it was obvious that most of the chaps were not coming, he went round asking strangers, of all sorts and sizes, to make up his team.

One Saturday by the Obelisk he met Cranmer, to their mutual delight, and on impulse took him along, to play against the Old Shootershillians Third. It proved a happy combination, himself on the left wing, and Cranmer at centre-forward. Nothing could stop Cranmer's dash, or his own racing along the line, to lift the ball over the goal's mouth for Cranmer to head into the net. It was a dry day, the ball light; and the lifting kick at right angles, with his left boot, the "pill" smote by the side of the foot, was the one kick that Phillip could always bring off. Cranmer's cropped and bullet head did the rest. It was the first match the Old Heathians Fourth had not lost. A draw, seven all! Up the old Bloodhounds!

"It's absolutely topping meeting you again, Horace. Can you play next week?"

"Sure it's all right, Phil? I ain't——"

"Of course you are! I hereby make you an honorary Old Fourthian!"

Phillip found an old and discarded torn shirt in one corner of the pavilion, and took it home, for his mother to repair. It would do for Cranmer. Hetty washed, patched, and ironed it, ready for Phillip to take with him the following Saturday. It was a most important match, said Phillip; they were playing the London Highlanders "C" on the home ground, at Colt Park.

Meanwhile there was a football supper to be held at the Rose of Lee, at the beginning of the second week in December: a date of double importance to Phillip: for that night at the Holborn Stadium, Bombardier Billy Wells was to fight Georges Carpentier for the heavyweight championship of Europe.

In Wine Vaults Lane, the Bombardier was the favourite of both Phillip and Edgar. Three pictures of the tall, handsome, curly-haired, broad-shouldered, slender-waisted hero were stuck up in Edgar's corner, with only one of the clean-shaven Frenchman in his white shorts, long hair brushed back, and deadly serious face. There had been a previous fight at Ghent, when the Bombardier had been knocked out, due to under-training, and unguarded stomach-muscles; this would not happen again, declared Edgar, when questioned that afternoon about the forthcoming fight by Mr. Hollis. One wallop of the Bombardier's left, and Carp'n'teer would be sent flying back again over the Channel, prophesied Edgar from his corner, with a demonstration against the waste-paper basket.

Phillip left the office that afternoon with a feeling of double anticipation. There was the Big Fight; and the Football Supper. It was the first of its kind he had been to. He walked over the Hill, following the old way down through Mill Lane, past Obelisk and Clock Tower, and so to the Rose of Lee.

There already about three dozen men had foregathered, including Milton. Phillip had a glass of beer with them. The talk was mainly about the fight that night. It was agreed by all that the Bombardier was properly trained this time, his solar plexus covered by powerful muscles!

After the roast mutton and red-currant jelly, followed by apple dumplings and cream, and when songs were being sung and from pipes was issuing companionable tobacco smoke, the landlord came in and said to Gildart Fitcheyson, the Football Club Chairman, that the news had just arrived, by someone on a motorcycle who had been to the first house at the New Cross Empire, where it had been given out from the stage, that Bombardier Billy Wells had been knocked out in the first round, in seventy-three seconds!

It was unbelievable. That sun-burned torso, that great chest and narrow waist, that handsome face and fair curly hair of the Bombardier training on Beachy Head in the open air—had gone down with a solar-plexus punch followed by a crashing right to the point from the pale ex-pit boy from Lille, in seventy-three seconds!

The rich baritone of Milton singing *Drake Goes West* afterwards was not so inspiring as it might have been to Phillip, thinking of England's fallen hero.

"'O lachrymae, lachrymae, ubi estis?'" remarked Tom Cundall.

"What does that mean?" asked Phillip.

"It was the cry of our young Founder, for his hero Essex, after three slashes had been taken at the poor bloke's neck on the block. Surely you've read your 'History of the School'?"

Phillip could never be sure whether Cundall was ragging, or not. "Well, not all of it, yet."

"Actually, that bit is frightfully interesting. Our illustrious Founder was pinched for his seditious but laudatory speech in the Common Room at Christ Church, in praise of his hero Essex, and on being sent to bed, wrote out another speech, in favour of ye late Earle's decapitation, more or less. After that, he went to quod for a bit, and came out a wiser and better man, and founded our school. What more could you ask of any man? That is how every politician has ever kept his place, by keeping his trousers creased and his coat turned on the appropriate occasion."

Cundall was a bit of a brainy bird, Phillip could see. He had been one of his friends among the Bagmen, and was in the secret about Cranmer. Cundall had promised to say, if asked, that he remembered Cranmer in 3a, for one term, under Mr. Davenport. Mr. Davenport had left the school after one term, remarked Cundall: so it evened things up nicely. No evidence!

"I shall say that when Cranmer left to join his parents in China, I remember the firework display in his honour."

"I say, don't rot too much, Tom, will you?"

"Rot?" said Cundall. "I am merely manufacturing circumstantial evidence. It was Cranmer's Chinese *ayah* who let off the fireworks!"

For the match with the London Highlanders "C" team, Cranmer wore the orange, red, and black striped shirt of the Old Heathians. It was a fine, dry afternoon. The ball was light, not of a soggy foot-breaking weight. Phillip, tall and thin, sped along the left wing, passing and repassing with Cundall at inside-left; up rose the ball, up rose Cranmer's bullet head; the Highlanders' full backs charged, the ball was rooted down the field, and a scrimmage went on at the home goal. Then the race back again, the lifting kick, the leap and the bob, the ball headed in. Goal!

At half-time the score was 3—1 in favour of the home team; then, after sucking lemons, the Highlanders seemed to have found new life. As the red-smoky sunset diminished behind the roof-tops and leafless elms around Colt Park, the touch-lines became crowded with spectators; for the game had started ten minutes late, and by this time the First Eleven had won their game against the Old Haberdashers. Five minutes to go, and the score 3 all! Then Phillip made a mistake; he felt they could not win, but they must not lose. He put Cranmer at centre-half, to stop the Highland forwards. He put Cundall at centre-forward; but Cundall was blown, pale of face. Up the Bagmen! cried Phillip.

Then as the referee, whistle in mouth, was looking at his watch, Cranmer in a mêlée round their goal leapt to head away a ball and the ball, glancing off the back of his skull, went into the Heathians' net. A roar went up; the whistle blew; the London Highlanders had won 4—3.

"Cranmer," said Phillip. "You are a cuckoo. But you deserve to be an honorary Old Heathian all the same."

"Sorry, Phil," moaned Cranmer. "I wor dizzy. I ain't had no dinner." He looked unhappy.

"I think you ought to sling your hook, Horace," said Phillip, out of the side of his mouth. Mr. Graham, camera slung on shoulder, was coming towards them. Head down, Cranmer broke into a run.

"See you later," Phillip called out, not loudly, lest Mr. Graham hear. "At the pease-puddin' shop. My treat, remember."

Mr. Graham congratulated Phillip on a splendid effort; and asked him as they walked towards the pavilion what was the name of the centre-forward.

Phillip replied, before he could think what to say, that he was Horace Cuck—here he coughed—who had left some years before.

"How interesting," said Mr. Graham. "I must have a word with him. Cook, did you say, Phillip? The ordinary spelling, or C-O-K-E? We had a Coke, about forty years ago, I recall——"

"I think he spells his with a 'u', Mr. Graham."

Before Mr. Graham could reply, Cundall, with a most innocent expression, offered the information that Cuck had had to hurry away to meet an important relation who had just returned from Hong Kong.

"I think he is part Chinese, or something, Mr. Graham."

"Oh," said Mr. Graham. Then, "Well, I look forward to meeting him some other time. Cuck—an unusual spelling. Of course all names were originally phonetic—the spelling came later. C-U-C-K—most unusual. I thought I knew every old boy in the register, too, but Horace Cuck escapes me. How is Timmy, your white rat, by the way, Phillip? He can almost be regarded as an honorary Old Boy, don't you think?"

"Yes, Mr. Graham. He's quite well, thank you."

What did Mr. Graham mean? Had he smelled a rat about Cranmer, and then, thinking about it, remembered Timmy Rat? For that was how people thought, he had discovered—one picture in the mind led to another. If you wanted to hide your real thoughts, you had to be careful what you said.

Feeling rather ashamed at the way he had ragged the decent Old Boy, he went with Tom Cundall to join Cranmer down by the pease-pudding shop at Lee Green. But Cranmer was not there—nor did Phillip see his old friend again until the following summer, in different circumstances.

Very soon, the team seemed to disintegrate. The last match was at Dulwich. To the captain's unhappiness, only four turned up; even Cundall seemed to have got tired. The match with the Old Alleynians "C" was scratched. Gildart Fitcheyson, who had come over on his N.U.T. motor-bike to see them, said that perhaps they would have better luck next season, when the Old Boys' Club would have had new entries from the school.

"Thank you for the keenness you have shown, old man," he said, reversing his cap as he prepared to push off his 10-h.p. twin-cylinder J.A.P. engine. "I think, if you agree, we'd better scratch the remaining fixtures. Don't let's lose touch, though. We started the team rather late in the season, perhaps. Next year we'll have more chaps to reinforce us. You'll be keen, will you?"

Phillip said he would.

"Right-o! If I don't see you at the club-house or the school before then, we'll meet next year, about the middle of September, for the nineteen-fourteen season."

Then the great man, hand on valve-lifter, shoved his dark brown machine until abruptly it roared into life. Vaulting into the saddle, he disappeared in a clatter of blue smoke.

Chapter 5

PATTERNS

ON THE last Sunday before Desmond went back to school, Phillip asked his mother if he might invite him to tea in the front room, by themselves.

"Will Father mind?"

"I don't see why not," replied Hetty, "if you are quiet. You know he always goes to sleep on Sunday afternoon."

Phillip and Desmond went for a walk, returning with muddy shoes, after a farewell expedition to Whitefoot Lane Woods, now nearly part of the spreading suburbs.

Pleasantly tired, they reclined on the small of their backs before the fire, feet up. Desmond smoked a Marsuma cigarette, Phillip his new and "splendiferous" Artist's Pipe.

He had recently bought this heavy curved object from a shop under the arches of London Bridge station. It was his first pipe. It held nearly half an ounce of tobacco and weighed nearly half a pound. It was a bargain at ninepence, marked down to half-price after Christmas, he told Desmond. The first pipeful had made him feel faint; so he had changed from St. Bruno Flake, which was dark, to Hignett's Cavalier, which was fair. With this Virginian leaf he hoped to season the huge bowl. He had rubbed the bowl beside his nose as recommended by Bertie, in order to give it a gloss. The trouble was that the bowl was far too big for the grease to go round. And grease or no grease, the Artist's Pipe remained very much unseasoned.

Despite pipeful after pipeful of Hignett's Cavalier being pushed in, lighted, sucked at, relit, blown upon to keep alight, before being tapped out and a fresh start made, the desired maturity or seasoning did not come about. Doubting that it was real briar, and suspecting paint, Phillip had boiled it on the kitchen gas, afterwards scrubbing it with soda and nail-brush. Ah! it was a fraud. Bits of putty in a pale-pink bowl lay disclosed. He picked them out with nail-scissors; dried the bowl in the oven; started the seasoning afresh, and hoped meanwhile to improve its appearance with sandpaper. After that, the Artist's Pipe seemed little more than scratched wood so he recoloured it with brown boot polish. Would it never become seasoned?

"It will take a dam' long time whichever way I try, Des. This bowl is fake, I am sure. You can taste pine-wood burning, when you smoke it." He blew through it: smoke rose vertical, with a spark or two.

"I know, why not season it with a bicycle pump? That will prevent the rank taste while it's new."

Thereafter the front room began to fill with smoke, as the bowl became a kiln. As each packing of tobacco was blasted away, the bowl was refilled. Soon tiny brown beads were bubbling in the grain; and it cracked.

"I told you so, it's a swizz! Look, it's *glue* bubbling! Anyway, no decent briar would ever crack. God, it doesn't half stink! Damned swindle, to sell a pipe like that as a French briar. I've a good mind to take it back, only it's too far gone now." Indeed, the Artist's Pipe was blazing, so it went into the fire.

O, it was wonderful to be with Desmond: what fun life was: as Mrs. Neville said, they were like David and Jonathan. Never, never, never would they cease to be friends.

The next day Phillip bought a half-crown Civic, which the salesman said was a very sound pipe. It had a silver band. It was a beauty. It had little burrs all over the bowl. "Don't pack it too tight, sir, if you don't mind me telling you," said the salesman. So the Civic consumed Hignett's fair threads in cool fragrance; and every day was a day nearer that blissful time when it would have a little charred crater, surrounded by tar and carbon, like all Mr. Hollis' pipes had.

What happened in the big world outside his private world, Phillip little knew nor cared. He never read the main items of news in his ha'penny paper, now a picture one. Father, with his snortings, protests, and *Daily Trident* readings-out-loud to Mother in the evenings at home was just part of the half-fossilised world of grown-ups who had forgotten their own youth. What did it matter about politics, whether Lloyd George said this, or Asquith that, when soon the chiffchaff, the sand-martin, and the willow wren would be returning? He avoided whenever he could the sitting-room where Father everlastingly rustled the paper before saying, "Listen to this, Hetty——" If it wasn't the Germans dumping their goods in England under a rotten Liberal Government it was Carson and Irish Home Rule, the Suffragettes, Income Tax, or the Socialists—all the same to him. The coming of Spring was the only thing that really mattered—and Helena Rolls.

Pale green and white luncheon tickets ran out a fortnight before Ladyday; he ate cheaply in refreshment shops in Leadenhall Market. It was an adventure, exploring little streets and alleys during the luncheon forty minutes. It was fun to imagine himself very poor, to economise, like Father did after he was born, Mother had told him, to pay the doctor's bill. Penny salmon-roll, penny cup of coffee, penny cheese-cake with head like a white chrysanthemum made of coconut shavings, eaten to the last crumb pressed on finger-tip—then a stroll around the poulterer shops, where wildfowl hung on hooks, tier upon tier reaching high up under the glass roof, lifted down on long poles. A salesman told him they came from Holland. He wore, like all the others, white apron, and jacket, and straw-yard. Tier upon tier of mallard, pochard, teal, widgeon, golden-eye, pintail, under electric lights, on foggy days, with figure-of-eight carbon filaments. O leaf-mottled woodcock, bog-haunting snipe, wild geese and swans, from polar regions, and—could it be? it was—it *was*—a bittern!

As soon as he saw the long sharp beak, the yellow-black-brown-reedy plumage, he bought it for half a crown. It would mean no more salmon-rolls or cheese-cakes for ten days, but what

was that beside a bittern? With pride and suppressed importance
he carried it back to the office, showing it with glee to Edgar,
and asking him to deliver it that evening to Watkins and Don-
caster, the taxidermists in the Strand, to be stuffed and mounted.
He gave Edgar his last sixpence for bus fare, telling him to keep
the change. He was a sportsman who had shot the bittern by
mistake for a goose in the Blackwater estuary! Edgar was his
man, his ghillie.

Edgar hung the bird by its lanky legs, tied together, on a nail
in the wall above his picture gallery. Its shady wings fell open.
And there it remained, to draw varying comments from some of
the better-dressed visitors to the office that afternoon.

"My junior is equipping a natural-history museum in his spare
time," said Mr. Hollis to a short, chubby-faced man with a little
black moustache whose scented personality, left in the air behind
him, always excited in Mr. Howlett a sort of glee when he had
gone. The visitor was "Little Freddy" Fanlight, an inspector of
the Fenchurch Street branch of the Moon Life Insurance Company. The Moon Life had no official connexion with the Moon
Fire, beyond name and device of the lunar face; but the officials,
as Mr. Hollis told Phillip, of each company were "automatically"
agents for the other, on the basis of usual commission.

It was, Mr. Hollis had explained further, Little Freddy's job
to visit agents, stimulate them to acquire new business, and to
inspect proposals.

"H'm, what is it?" remarked Little Freddy Fanlight, in his
tenor voice, as he gave a glance at the bittern. "An oof bird?"
Thereupon he swung round on the heel of fawn cloth-topped
boots, brushed up ends of moustaches first with one forefinger-
back, then the other, and disregarding Phillip, began to talk to
Mr. Hollis about the insurance of a sports-club pavilion at Mill
Hill. As he talked, he moved about the confined space of the
office as though he were on the stage of the pavilion, in the
annual Gilbert and Sullivan production of his club. He was a
dapper little man, almost a fop. Phillip thought he looked conceited, strutting there in his bowler with very curly brim and
red satin lining.

He went on filling in a policy form, until something Little
Freddy said made him listen intently.

"By the way, Hollis, have you had a proposal recently from a
George Lemon, solicitor of Lincoln's Inn? He has two pretty

big endowments with us, and from his recent behaviour it might
well be a case of——"

"Hi, my lad! You! Maddison!!" exclaimed Mr. Hollis.
While Little Freddy paused, Mr. Hollis said in an even voice,
"Maddison, would you be so good as to go out and get me a
Star evening paper? I don't want any other kind. You'll get one
from the boy standing outside the London Tavern."

"I'll go, sir, shall I?" volunteered Edgar.

"No, Edgar, I want you for something else in a moment,"
replied Mr. Hollis in an even voice.

Phillip knew Mr. Hollis wanted to get rid of him. He would
ask Edgar what was said, later. But while he was going out of
the door, he heard Mr. Howlett say, "Come on upstairs to my
office, Freddy. There's a little matter I would like your opinion
on, if you can spare a moment."

Phillip arrived back with the evening paper as Little Freddy
Fanlight and Mr. Howlett came downstairs. When he had gone,
Mr. Howlett described to Mr. Hollis how he had seen Little
Freddy, at three o'clock that afternoon, lying back in the
barber's shop in Crutched Friars, stretched out full length in a
chair, hot towel swathing his entire face and head, only his up-
curled moustaches in their regulating cup strapped round his
head being visible, while a manicurist held one hand as she
worked at his nails.

"I suppose Little Freddy gets his work done somehow," said
Mr. Howlett, amiably. "Oh by the way, Hollis, I'm just going
down to see Vandenberg's man about that guarantee risk at
Ohlenschlager's Wharf. In case anyone rings up in my absence,
I'll be back in about ten minutes."

Mr. Hollis looked across at Downham as the manager went
out. "What the devil was Howlett doing in a barber's shop at
three o'clock in the afternoon I should like to know?"

"Getting his hair cut and singed, I should imagine," replied
Downham, airily.

"H'm," grunted Mr. Hollis. "Where would this Branch be, if
it wasn't for me?" He looked at Phillip. "And for our taxidermist here, or should it be Sportsman of Leadenhall Market?"
Seeing his junior's eyes wince, he added, "Don't mind my joking,
Maddison. Thank God you show keenness about something,
unlike most of the youth of this generation! And thank you for
the paper, my lad."

Phillip murmured gratefully that it was quite all right.

The next visitor was Mr. Thistlethwaite, familiar in curly-crowned silk hat and frock-coat. At once he began to talk in a low, bass voice to Mr. Hollis. Phillip listened. Mr. Thistle-thwaite told a story of how the powers-that-be stick together; there was a conspiracy against him: for he had not only lost his action against Metropolitan Assurance for wrongful dismissal, but his ex-gratia payment as well.

"Entre nous, Hollis, I am convinced, Hollis, that my lawyer was in with the other side," said Mr. Thistlethwaite before opening the glass door.

"I told the idiot often enough that he could not possibly win his case," remarked Mr. Hollis, after Mr. Thistlethwaite had gone. "So did his attorneys, but he is so damned conceited, he's impervious to any ideas except his own. His mind still exists in the easy, early years of the century, before the Boer War. Just like Howlett." He looked severely at Phillip. "What you hear in this office, my lad, is on no account to be repeated, mind!"

"It's all the same to me, Mr. Hollis."

"I don't want things to get around to Head Office. What is said here is purely private to this Branch, remember! Although from what I know of your respected parent, he is the last man to talk about other people."

Mr. Hollis obviously said this as a question, so Phillip replied that his father never said anything to him.

"Nothing at all? Joking apart, aren't you and your father on good terms?"

"I don't know," muttered Phillip, getting on with his work.

Mr. Hollis screwed up an envelope into a ball, and threw it at him. Phillip went on with his policy, saying loud enough for Mr. Hollis to hear, "Somebody's got to do the work in this Branch."

"Ha ha! Good for you, my boy!"

"Come and check some figures with me, Maddison, will you?" said Downham, a minute later. Phillip went over to his desk. Downham whispered, "Go and clip Hollis' ear with the tongs, not hard, just a slight nip."

Phillip entered into the joke. The steel tongs, kept bright in the fire-place by the early-morning charwoman, lay in the hearth. Picking them up silently, he hid them behind him, watched by grinning Edgar, and Downham ostensibly opening a ledger; and

passing behind his stool, pretended to be going to take down one
of the big black policy record books beside Mr. Hollis.

The unsuspecting chief clerk, frowning through *pince-nez* as he
worked out a short-time premium for a £30,000 risk on Merchandise at the Surrey Commercial Docks, felt the lobe of his
right ear touched, and looking up, saw the tongs extended in his
direction.

He dropped his pen and shouted, "Blast your donkey soul to
hell!" Seeing him pick up a round ebony ruler, Phillip dodged
away. It whirled past his head and struck the wall between the
bittern and Edgar, who stared open-mouthed with a green halfpenny stamp on his tongue as Mr. Hollis, leaping off his stool,
started in pursuit of his junior now darting through the door.

Scared by his anger, still holding the steel tongs, Phillip fled up
the Lane. He ran on until, looking back, he saw Mr. Hollis
shaking his fist at him in the doorway under the hanging sign of
the Moon.

When after a minute he returned ready to apologise, he saw
Mr. Howlett, standing back to fire, apparently enjoying Downham's account of what had happened.

"Hullo," said Mr. Howlett. "You passed me just now, with
the office tongs. I thought perhaps your precious bittern had
escaped."

Mr. Hollis went on writing as though nothing had happened;
so Phillip did the same.

"Well, you March Hare," he said, when handing over the
paying-in book, "how I wish I could feel the Spring in my blood
at eighteen, again!"

Richard Maddison had a visit from his brother one afternoon
at Head Office in Haybundle Street. From Hilary he learned of
the plight of their sister Victoria, and that steps were being considered to certify George Lemon insane. Apparently, in addition
to buying back an old family property in Cornwall, he had
asked Knight, Frank, and Rutley to find him a steward, ordered
a Rolls-Royce landaulette from Barkers in St. James Street, and
arranged with Tattersalls to purchase bloodstock. Two Harley
Street specialists, after Wasserman blood-tests, had diagnosed
G.P.I., a tertiary stage of infection by *spirella spirocheta*.

"That's the aftermath of syphilis, as you know, Dick. Apparently
he got it when Viccy was pregnant, in the time of the Boer War."

"Hush, Hilary—not so loud, my dear fellow."

Startled, shocked, repelled, Richard recalled the red-haired demi-mondaine in Leicester Square who had said to him, as she passed, *My word if I catch you bending;* with horror he relived his temptation to reply. Thank the Lord he had not given way to erotic impulse! A few moments afterwards he had watched George Lemon raise his hat to her, and the two had gone off together. Syphilis! And now, General Paralysis of the Insane!

"Just like Hugh Turney, Dick old man," said Hilary, and stopped, surprised at the expression on his brother's face. "Why didn't they take precautions, that's what beats me. Viccy is shattered, as you can well imagine."

"What is her position, Hilary?"

"None too good, I fear. George's financial affairs are in a mess. He went to a quack, instead of telling a proper doctor, when he first got it. Well, Viccy's the one to be considered now. She'll have to leave Epsom, of course, and find a smaller house elsewhere. At her age, it's not easy to have to give up the friend-ships of a lifetime. Rotten bad luck for George, too——"

"I call it worse than that, Hilary!" replied Richard. Hilary saw, for the first time, the resemblance between his brother and his sister Victoria. He had been perturbed at her attitude towards her husband: she had refused to see him, saying she was done with him, he had disgraced her, he had disgraced the family. And now, in Dick's face, he saw the same expression. Richard was pale. He recovered himself, and said with a show of affability, "Well, I shall say no more, Hilary. Thanks for looking in, old chap. Give my kind regards to your lady wife, won't you?"

With a hesitant half-wave of his hand, he turned away towards his desk, his mind forming the word *blackguard* as Hugh Turney's abhorred image replaced that of brown-faced George Lemon. He deserves what he has brought upon himself, that's all I can say, he thought, with a kind of petrific glee, as he got, rather shakily, upon his stool.

That night Hetty had to pretend to listen to the danger of the Germans building Dreadnoughts as a direct challenge to British Naval Supremacy, and the Idiocy of the Liberal Government in reducing the Army Estimates. Then, looking at his watch, "Where is your best boy tonight, I wonder? Gadding about on the Hill, as usual? I consider that he should be in by half-past

nine every night—the Hill after dark is no place for a young chap,
you know. I smelt a whiff of drink in his breath the other night—
although I did not say anything at the time. I shall have to
speak firmly to Master Phillip."

"Oh no, Dickie, he is not on the Hill. He went out on his
bicycle to the woods, with Desmond."

"H'mph. That's what *he* says."

But Phillip had two proofs of his visit to the bluebell woods,
when he returned home, *viz.*, a black eye and a fat lip. Desmond,
too, showed damage. They were jubilant as they reviewed their
fight with the louts who had been stripping the woods around
Cutler's Pond of wild hyacinth and pussy willow.

For it was once again the time of renewal of the "Mother" of
the western hemisphere, the earth, the soil, and in response to
Spring the human tide was flowing from the darkness of the town
to the countryside, eager for light and beauty. Wheels hummed
over drying sett-stones, woods were invaded. Hundreds of
thousands of white stalks left their bulbs with sappy squeaks,
hundreds of blue armfuls quivered by bending backs.

"Why don't you leave them where they are? Soon there won't
be a bluebell left! Anyway, who gave you permission to come
into these woods?"

"If I don't take'm, someone else'll, so why shouldn't I?
What's it got to do with you? Mind yer own biz!"

"You vulgar cads, it is my business! These woods are private!"

"They aren't your'n, you can't kid us!"

"They belong to the Cator Estate, if you want to know.
You've no right here."

"No more'v you, you sprucer! Fancy yourself, don't you, as
the owner? Well, you ain't, see? You're only a nosey parker."

"You clear off!"

"I knows 'im! 'Is ole man flies kites on the Hillies! Slosh 'im,
boys!"

After the Battle of the Bluebells Phillip swore to Desmond that
he would learn to box, without fail, at the School of Arms after
Easter. He gave away his tobacco pouch and pipe to a tramp,
as a preliminary to hard training, but took back the Civic, on
second thoughts. It had been a glorious fight, before they were
forced to retreat before superior numbers.

Chapter 6

THE CLOBSTER

SINCE Phillip had been going to the City, Hetty to her happiness had observed that he was becoming kinder to his younger sister, giving her butter-scotch, and once inviting her to the Hippodrome.

"How kind of you, dear. Of course Doris will be quite safe with you to look after her."

Hetty had heard stories, from Mrs. Feeney, of occasional rowdiness outside the new, red-brick music-hall. Hughie had frequented such places, in the Strand and elsewhere.

"You won't get into any more fights, will you, dear, or go through the Recreation Ground, but come straight home afterwards."

"If I came straight home, it would mean knocking down houses, trams, and wading the Randisbourne."

Phillip, after several occasions at the School of Arms, felt equal to any roughs who might be lurking in the Rec.

He and Doris sat in sixpenny seats of red plush in the upper circle. He explained the turns to her, as befitted his rôle of habitué. The stars were David Devant the Magician, Fred Karno's Mumming Birds, an American comedienne who sang *The Broken Doll* and *You made me Love you*, and a long-haired musician in a black velvet suit called Van Diene who played on the 'cello what Phillip thought was the most hauntingly beautiful and sad *Broken Melody*.

Doris, fourteen, sedate in uniform of the Grey Ladies, responded to her big brother's friendliness rather shyly; she could not get over a feeling that she was unwanted by everyone, except her mother.

Delighted with the new kindness between her children, Hetty arranged with her cousin Liz Pickering for the two to spend the Whitsun holidays at Beau Brickhill. Mr. Howlett agreed to let Phillip have the Saturday morning as one of the six due to him in the year. He told Phillip that, as Hollis always took the Saturday before Whitsun, he and Downham would take care of the office on that morning. When later Downham asked for the Saturday, he was furious, after Mr. Howlett had gone upstairs, with Phillip for getting leave first.

"It's like your damned cheek to ask behind my back! Who the hell d'you think you are?"

Beau Brickhill had always been a lovely place. It was so free and easy, never any cross words in Uncle Jim's house. There were lots of interesting things to do; the billiard table for competitions; duets with cousin Percy; the walk to church on Sunday was an adventure, the service with harmonium, the old fat beadle in his uniform.

Doris was staying on after Whit Monday. Phillip had intended to leave on the night of Bank Holiday, but he did not do so, owing to an attraction to Polly, which led to a private agreement with her during the return from a long walk over the fields in the afternoon to visit Great-aunt Hepzibiah Turney.

The four cousins, Percy and Doris, Phillip and Polly, had looked for nests on the way there. A white owl had flown from a hollow hedgerow elm, but the hole was too high up to be climbed. O, for a young white owl to take home and tame! More excitement—out of another elm a kestrel had flown, uttering its plaintive cry as it soared in circles above. There was an old carrion crow's nest high in the crown, obviously in use by the hawk. He climbed up, despite his fear, and tremblingly saw four white-fluffy eyesses staring at him with full brown eyes that held an expression between anguish and decrepit fear, behind which burned the spirit of ageless blood. Should he have one? Would it pine, away from its wild sky? Quivering because of the height, and remembering tales of talon-strikes at eyes, he decided not to risk it.

He felt quite pleased with himself after the climb, as they walked on to the village of Conquest Moretaine. Aunt Hepzibiah lived in a very old cottage, and made lace on a pillow for a living. After tea they said goodbye, Phillip's mind on the 7 o'clock to London. Time was short: it was several miles to Brickhill. Polly strode on in front beside him. He thought she was a sport. Seeing her red cheeks, so pretty with her black curls, he decided to forego the evening train and catch the early one in the morning, if she— would she? Polly would.

Thereafter they strolled home, Polly and Phillip well in front, Percy and Doris following a field behind. Free of time, they went a longer way round, and as a memento of the walk put some oak-apple sprays, tied to brass wire, in the Satchville brook, whose waters after a year or so would turn the sprays to stone.

There was an exciting event in the water-meadow: a stoat running with a missel-thrush in its mouth, bounding along, head high, long body rippling, tail like a bit of frayed rope with a black tip. Phillip chased it. The stoat chattered, and turned at last to run at him. He kicked it with a lucky kick and broke its neck. It took some time to die. The missel-thrush was dead.

"A clobster!" said Percy. Phillip wrapped it in his handkerchief, with the bird, intending to skin them both when he got home. He intended also to wake up in time to catch the early train in the morning, but slept on; and when eventually he turned into Wine Vaults Lane, the face of the office clock showed the frightful hour of a quarter to eleven. Four other faces confronted him—Mr. Howlett, Mr. Hollis, Downham, and Edgar.

"Good morning, gentlemen," he said to all the faces at once. He took the stoat from his pocket, with the bird, and put them on the counter. Then, as though in explanation of the corpses lying there, he said to Mr. Howlett, "My train was late, sir."

"We were beginning to give you up for lost, Maddison."

Phillip saw with a sinking feeling that Mr. Howlett did not smile. Downham had his eyes fixed upon him. Mr. Hollis said, "Where the devil d'you think you've been?"

Phillip looked on the ground, waiting. The musky smell of the stoat began to steal into the air. Edgar grinned from the corner, where the stuffed bittern, on stiff varnished legs, stood with a ticket marked 10/6d. round its neck. Edgar had collected it from the taxidermist's in the Strand.

"What the blazes do you think this place is, the Natural History Museum?" said Mr. Hollis. Phillip lifted the stoat to stand on its hind legs, hoping the sight would change the subject.

"Well, don't let it happen again," said Mr. Howlett, quietly, as he went upstairs.

Hardly had the door shut when Downham said, suppressed violence in his voice, "It's like your blasted nerve! And you had Saturday extra, too! Haven't you the decency even to apologise to Mr. Howlett? You take advantage of his generosity! You're nothing but a cheap skunk yourself! And there's another thing! You've been helping yourself to the tablets of Pears Soap in the basement, haven't you?"

"Steady on, Downham," said Mr. Hollis. "All the same, my lad, let me tell you that it is hardly cricket to impose on Mr. Howlett's good nature. If there were anyone else here, you would not get off so easily, I can assure you! They are not so easy-going, you know, at Head Office. There, you'd be right up on the carpet before the General Manager."

Phillip tried to look humble, as he put stoat and missel-thrush in his desk. After skinning the bird, he might fry it with bacon, and offer it to Mother. Zippy the cat could have the stoat, when skinned. He had a book on how to stuff and mount birds and animals.

Edgar winked at him. He did not wink back; better to look chastened. Would he be sent to Head Office? What a fool he had been, not to return the night before—it hadn't been any good, anyway, with Polly. Head Office would be awful, men working silently in big rooms, nothing free and easy, as in Wine Vaults Lane, no going out to lunch in the Market, and looking at the wildfowl in the poulterers' tiers. If you did anything wrong at H.O. you were liable to be sacked at once. There was the case of Joe Flack, who had been summarily dismissed with six weeks salary for coming back half an hour late from outside lunch only the week before Easter. And he had had only a little bit extra to drink, Mr. Hollis had told him. Joe Flack had a wife and three children. Because he had passed forty, he had little hope of another job, Mr. Hollis said, and in any case nobody would employ a man without a reference.

"You watch your step, my lad!"

"Yes, Mr. Hollis, I will."

"Take my advice, and don't mix big-game hunting and business another time."

Phillip laughed at this sally, hoping thereby to keep Mr. Hollis on his side, in case the matter of his lateness was not yet settled.

"What are you, setting up a taxidermist's shop, or one of those gamekeeper's gibbets you told me about?"

"Both, Mr. Hollis. Would you like this clobster when I've stuffed it?"

"Good God, no!" cried Mr. Hollis. "It smells like—well, never mind what it smells like."

When he came back from Head Office luncheon that day, Phillip hung the stoat from the map above Edgar's gallery of portraits. His vermin pole!

The thought of leaving Wine Vaults Lane kept recurring: and when, about four o'clock that afternoon, Mr. Howlett opened his door and asked him to come up, Phillip went up as though his heart were of the same lead as the stairs. He must keep a stiff upper lip. Be like the Spartan boy, with a fox under his cloak.

Mr. Howlett sat at his desk. There were photographs of his family on it, in silver frames, among them a girl in white, with long hair, playing the 'cello.

"I had a conversation with Head Office today," began Mr. Howlett; "apparently all policies will have to be made out in future on the typewriting machine. Would you object to such work, or rather, machine?"

Phillip thought, with sinking heart, that this was Mr. Howlett's way of getting rid of him. To be a typist was much lower than being an Insurance Official. Yes, Mr. Howlett must have given Head Office a bad report on himself.

"To work a typewriter, sir? I have never done any before."

"You may have noticed the small room, or rather compartment, beyond the glass screen behind you, as you came in. I was thinking we might have our new machine, when it comes, on the table in there. I expect you'll soon pick it up. The other companies are all installing them, I understand. By the way, when would you like to take your holiday this year? I shall be away during August, Hollis wants the first three weeks in September, and Downham is having the first fortnight in July. Any other time you may care for is yours. We choose in order of seniority, of course. Well, let me know when you have decided."

"Yes, sir!"

He was not to be sent away from the Branch after all! In future he would go entirely straight. How had Downham known he had helped himself to a packet of Pears Soap from the shelf in the basement? Then there were the brass ash-trays which had remained over, gifts to agents and others, at the bi-centenary of the Moon Fire Office. After all, he had sort of used them to get new business, in a way, by giving them as Christmas presents to Mrs. Neville, Gran'pa, Uncle Jim Pickering, and Great-aunt Marian. This last he had taken away again and given to Bertie, without Aunt Marian knowing.

Going downstairs with his new resolutions, Phillip was a little relieved to be accused of something he had not done, by Mr. Hollis, who had just come up from the basement.

"Now look here, my lad, this is a respectable office! We don't leave plugs unpulled in the Moon Fire Office!"

"I haven't been there today, Mr. Hollis, really."

"Then it must have been your damned bittern."

The door above the leaden stairs opened.

"Oh, Maddison. Just a moment."

Once more his heart bumped with apprehension.

"I'm sorry to keep you so on the move," said the manager, in an affable voice. "I meant to ask you just now if you were any relation to the Theodora Maddison who is prominent in the Suffragette Movement? You read the paper, I suppose?"

"Yes, I do sometimes, sir."

Lloyd George's new house on Walton Heath had been partly burned down; the portrait by Sargent of Henry James, the novelist, hacked by a meat-chopper in the Academy; the Rokesby Venus similarly damaged in the National Gallery—but these details had meant little or nothing to Phillip. It was his Aunt's name that mattered.

Seeing the pink colour rising in his junior's cheeks, Mr. Howlett hastened to say, "My dear boy, please do not think, for one moment, that I am suggesting the least reflection on yourself! Nothing is farther from my mind! In fact, I should not really be asking such a question, my only excuse is my interest in you. Of course all families are made up of diverse temperaments. Personally, I believe in certain responsible women being given the vote, though present ways and means are bound to antagonise many who otherwise might be sympathisers. I won't, of course, repeat anything you may care to tell me. It is only curiosity on my part, and I should not really ask the question."

Phillip thought that Mr. Howlett would regard him in a better light if he told the truth in this case.

"Yes, she's my aunt, sir. I was hoping to spend my holiday in Lynmouth in her cottage, but I don't know if she will be there."

"Ah, the Cat and Mouse business!" Mr. Howlett's tone became very friendly. "If I remember rightly, didn't your father spend his holiday at Lynmouth during his first year at Head Office? I was in the Town Department when he came to us from Doggett's Bank, you know. You were born just about that time, weren't you? When did you think of going?"

"In the second fortnight of July, sir, if that is convenient to everyone, sir?"

"That will be all right with me. And I hope you find all

well by that time! Apart from the deplorable tactics, one can't help admiring the courage of those women. But they are going a little too far, don't you think?"

Phillip replied in what he hoped was a manly voice, "Yes, sir, I do."

"Now about the question of typing. Will you be willing to learn?"

"Yes, Mr. Howlett. I will do my best, sir."

"I'll tell them at Head Office, then."

"Please sir, may I ask a question?"

"Certainly, my dear boy."

"Does it mean—the typewriter I mean—that you will have another junior?"

Mr. Howlett laughed. "God bless me soul no! I think one donkey boy is quite sufficient! Now, don't mistake me, my dear boy! I did not mean it unkindly, not in the very least! I have had an interest in you since you were born, you know. Yes, your father and I sat in the same department at Head Office in the 'nineties. My little girl, born about the same time, was delicate too. That is she, in the photograph there. Fortunately we, too, found the right food. So do not look so worried."

Jubilantly Phillip left the room, with its low arc of window on the floor facing the dark stone wall of the building across the narrow lane, and so far forgot himself that he plunged down the leaden steps two at a time, to smell the musky smell of the stoat in his nostrils. At the bottom, Downham was talking to Little Freddy Fanlight, who with boater tilted over his round forehead was resting back on his rolled umbrella. Downham was saying,

"She was slightly spotty in front between her breasts, and on the back of her shoulders, and hadn't made any effort to cover them with powder. She pressed herself against me, as she squirted Furrow with scent."

To which Little Freddy replied, in his tenor voice, "Seems you brought another of her—ahem!—scents with you."

Phillip knew what Downham was talking about; he had already heard during Mr. Hollis' absence at luncheon how he and some friends of the London Rowing Club had "dined up west in tails", and afterwards gone to the Palace Theatre to see the celebrated French actress. After the show, three of them had gone round to the stage-door, and so to the dressing-room of

Gaby Deslys; and how she had taken a fancy to him, stroking his hand and saying, "You—ni-i-ice boy!"

"Are you sure she only stroked your hand?" enquired Little Freddy, in his high drawling tones, as he glanced around the office, looking like a dressed up dog in a circus. Deliberately he lifted up his nose and sniffed again. "Ahem, very suspicious, I must say——"

Mr. Hollis coughed explosively. "Get on with your work, Edgar! What the devil are you grinning at?"

Edgar furtively was holding up, for Phillip to see, a cut-out photograph of the feathered Parisienne with her leg extended from split skirt to golden shoe, doing the naughty naughty Gaby Glide.

"You be careful, my son," said Downham to Edgar. "Remember what the Bard says about groping for trout in strange waters."

"That's enough of that sort of thing, I think," remarked Mr. Hollis abruptly, as he scrawled his signature furiously. "Maddison, pay in, if you please."

"I say, what—what is all this?" asked Little Freddy. He stared at Edgar's corner. "Haven't I seen that bird in here before? What is it, a stork? And what is that thing like a little dog?"

"Mr. Maddison's clobster, sir," replied Edgar briskly.

"Good gracious me," ejaculated Little Freddy.

"Here you are, my lad," said Mr. Hollis, handing over the paying-in book. "Edgar, I want you to take a note at once down to the Minories, and await a reply. You will tell them, of course, that you are waiting for a reply."

"Yessir," cried Edgar, springing up, and smoothing down his diminutive silver-button'd jacket. He wore this with a peaked cap out of doors, the silver disc of the moon as badge in front.

Phillip returned briskly from the Westminster Bank across the way, as Little Freddy was leaving.

"Fop," remarked Mr. Hollis, as the door closed. "Still, apparently he gets business for the Life Office."

Mr. Howlett was treading downstairs with his usual care.

"Oh, Maddison, I'd clean forgotten about the territorial camp," he remarked pleasantly. "Of course, both you and Downham will be going this year. When is it, in August? My word, that stoat's scent is pretty strong. Has anyone else noticed it?"

"Have we not?" remarked Mr. Hollis.

"With your permission, sir, I suggest I take the first fortnight," said Downham, "and Maddison goes when I come back. I don't want to miss the Office Tennis Tournament, sir."

"It's all the same to me," said Mr. Howlett. "Will that suit you, Maddison? You'll have your fortnight at the end of July in Devon, then another in Sussex after an interval of two weeks here with Mr. Hollis. There's never much business in August."

"That's all you know about it," remarked Mr. Hollis, decisively. "With young Maddison here learning to type, it won't exactly be a picnic for me. However, Horatius will hold the bridge, as always."

This semi-serious grumble was interrupted by the tobacco man with his bag slipping in; and the sight of twenty-four one-ounce packets of Hignett's Cavalier laid out on the counter, eight each for the seniors, six for Downham, and two for Phillip, at fourpence farthing an ounce, brought general contentment to the office.

As he went home, carrying bittern and clobster, Phillip thought of an answer about the tablet of soap. Why did he take it? "A year ago I used Pears Soap, since then I have used no other."

Chapter 7

EXCURSION

THEODORA MADDISON, a chronic hunger-striker, was released from Holloway Prison for the sixth time in the middle of June. Two of her teeth had been broken by steel goads forced into her mouth while wardresses held her down on the floor of her cell. After that, a doctor had squirted liquid from a rubber tube thrust up one nostril and down the throat into the stomach. It was like stuffing a turkey, he remarked for the hundredth time: a remark which made the wardresses, lips pressed in narrow lines, exchange bleak glances, for they were as sick of the remark as they were of the doctor; and as secretly sympathetic to the political prisoners.

In addition to the broken teeth, Theodora's left eye was injured. Just before her last arrest, for being likely to cause a breach of the peace in Hyde Park, she had been knocked down by a man, her face had been stamped on by another; helped to her feet, umbrellas were poked into her face by indignant bystanders.

Now, free for awhile, she went with her great friend Sylvia to convalesce at Lynmouth. The cottage stood near the quay, above the river and facing the Severn Sea. There she hoped to gain strength for further effort in London.

"For," she wrote to Hetty, "our victory cannot be delayed much longer. Unemployment is rising, every where are signs of unrest due to the malformation of the body politic—in the docks, in the factories, at the pitheads, in Ireland. The head of the body politic—the gross extravagance and immorality of the rich, with a few noble exceptions —is conjoined to a withered body: the extreme penury of the working classes, the hopeless destitution of the out-of-work. Our struggle will go on, even as the one in olden times, among the catacombs of Rome——"

Within the envelope was a note for Phillip, in her minute writing, with its Grecian letters α, δ and ε mixed with English letters.

"Do come, dear Boy, and stay for as long as you want to. Bring your rod; there are plenty of trout in the Lyn."

Wearing his new pair of five-shilling grey flannel trousers with his twelve-and-sixpenny Donegal tweed jacket, and carrying an old black gladstone bag with a small second-hand greenheart fly-rod bought at Sprunt's the pawnbroker's for fifteen pence, Phillip set out for his holiday. The excursion train was due to leave Waterloo shortly after 8 a.m.

While people were still abed he walked down Hillside Road as the sun was casting long shadows of houses in the fresh cold air of morning. The seeds of the chestnut trees were balls of bright gold above the dusty surface of Charlotte Road. Randiswell was a-shine, empty and silent, except for two labouring men cycling to work, and the Borough water cart laying with pink permanganate spray the dust at the side of the road. Everything looked new, and clear, and calm.

A whole fortnight of freedom lay before him, in a place which Father said was one of the loveliest in the West Country. Father had given him the bag, which being cracked in places, Phillip had had botched. Also some old flies in the leather case stored with other things in Grandfather's uniform case in the loft over the bathroom. The gut was brittle and yellow, but the flies, said Father, might do for a pattern.

"Blue Upright, Olive Nymph, and the dropper is a Pheasant Tail," he had said, moving them with his pink filbert-shaped finger-nail. "I used them once, long ago, on the Lyn, and the trout took them readily. You might find it worth while to have them copied by a local fly-tyer."

"Thank you, Father."

"And you are welcome to take my fly-rod, if you care to."

"Thanks all the same, Father, but I think my own will be enough."

There was sixpence change out of half-a-sovereign for the return excursion ticket from Waterloo to Barnstaple. This train would take much longer than the express, having to stop at so many stations; but that would make the journey all the more interesting. He had a packet of mutton sandwiches, half a pound of Garibaldi biscuits, twelve oranges. And of course his Civic pipe, with its satisfying crust in the bowl, and not one speck of loathèd putty outside; for after a dozen boxing lessons, he was smoking again. The chaps on the Hill had agreed with him, comparing pipes, that it was a real beauty. It was also a personal triumph that David Wallace, on his recommendation, had changed to Hignett's Cavalier from Murray's Mellow Mixture. The two had more in common, too, since he had agreed that David's Pioneer pipe, which had a silver band like the Civic, but an amber mouth-piece, was one of the best straight-grained bowls to be seen anywhere. Peter Wallace did not smoke; Peter was still aloof, rather curt; it may have been because he was in hard training for the bayonet-fighting championship.

Besides the two Wallace brothers in the London Highlanders, there was Mr. Bolton's son, quite old of course, being twenty-four; and cousin Hubert, another aspirant for the bayonet-fighting cup given by Lord Cheylesmore. The tournament was to take place in the coming autumn. Perhaps when Willie came up from Rookhurst to work in the Moon he would join too; then there would be six London Highlanders living within a hundred yards of their corner of the Hill, surely a record!

Sitting back in the third-class carriage, feet up on the seat opposite, bag and rod safe above, *Nights with an Old Gunner* open on lap, Civic well-packed and little skeins of smoke straying past the nostrils, Phillip felt joy within himself trilling, trilling, trilling.

The train drew out of the dark station, and ran among hundreds of polished junction rails. Smoky London with its tall chimneys and rows and rows of grimy stacks was soon left behind. He was keen to see Brooklands, which Father said would be on the left side of the train after about half an hour. If his luck were in, he might see some racing cars rushing down from the banking to the Railway Straight, which lay beside the line. He knew Brooklands only from reading about it; and from imagining himself winning some fantastic race at enormous speed, gripping the wheel to control a skid, while in reality scorching on his bicycle.

Nobody was racing on Brooklands track, which came suddenly into view beyond pine and silver birch trees. Still, it was a wonderful place. His eyes glanced about to get every detail as he stood at the open window, before the grey oval track rushed away backwards with the train gathering speed. Hurray! He was on holiday. He did a jig in the carriage, and then hung from the rack, turning himself inside out until a jingle of coins made a search of the floor necessary. Counting up his money, he found it all there. This decided him to enter his expenses in his pocket book; everything must be entered there, just for the fun of seeing how much he had spent by the time he got back.

Every moment of the eight hours in the train was enjoyable: rushing past cornfields and over bridges, the approach to Salisbury and the thin blue pointed tower of the Cathedral; the long afternoon in the blazing sunshine, both windows open, and the many stops where people, all most interesting, got in, everything about them fresh—feathers on hats, leather gaiters, collars, ties, colour of bone buttons on jackets, breeches laced or buttoned—whether their boots and shoes were more worn at the heel or the side—how they were shaved or the kind of moustache or beard they wore, and why none of them seemed to be pimply, like so many faces seen in the streets of London (barber's rash, Father called it)—rings on their fingers, the different kinds of watches and chains they wore. Every face and characteristic was fresh, so were the station names, barns, shapes of fields and hills and churches, the slow speech of porters, butterflies drifting in the open windows as the train stopped to unload, or shunt into trucks laden with brightly painted farm machinery; and most wonderful of all, a box of ferrets, in the guard's van, pink noses and white whiskers, scratching claws.

After Exeter the fields of red-gold wheat seemed to have been saturated with the everlasting blaze of the sun; the earth red in fallow to have been burned in some great furnace. How far away seemed Wine Vaults Lane, and the rush-hour over London Bridge, how remote his old life upon which vaguely hovering thoughts lay unresolved behind objects ever new and strange upon his sight and feeling. He had been standing at one or other open window more than six of the eight hours in the train, without one moment that was not of full interest. They stopped at Exeter, a city as remote as the sun, which made the top of the carriage hot to touch, and the wind coming in the open window as from the earth-red furnace.

Thereafter the train ran in a valley with woods on the distant slopes of hills, sometimes approaching a river in a stony bed which turned away again in a deep-cut curving course and came back suddenly as the train thundered over a bridge, and he saw below green and white rushing water. The sun was now ahead of the train, when it had been behind all the way from Waterloo to Salisbury, thereafter swinging out in a great burning arc but never ceasing in brilliant blaze of harvest light, pouring down its beams of the hue of red-gold wheat, the red-gold sample of Squarehead that Uncle Jim Pickering at Beau Brickhill had let him trickle through his hand, and hold in his palm; tawny, warm-looking seed, burned that colour by the harvest sun.

He took out a letter from his pocket and re-read it yet again. It was from Cousin Willie at Rookhurst, saying that his application for a post in the Moon had been accepted on the recommendation of one of the directors his father knew. He would be coming to London at the beginning of August. It would be tremendous fun when Willie came. Even Father was looking forward to it. Willie's mother, he said, had been one of the loveliest women he had ever seen.

The river widened into sudden sullenness. It moved slowly, with scum on it, under oakwoods which came down to its steep sides, as muddy as the reaches of the Thames when the tide was out. Could they be near the sea? He leaned out of the window, and saw, faintly under the spiky western sun, a pale length of sand with heat-hazed hills beyond. This must be Barnstaple! He put bag and rod on the seat before him, alert with excitement.

Aunt Theodora had written that he must stay in the train until the second stop, at the town station; and then change to the small-gauge Lynton train he would see awaiting the London train on the opposite platform. It would take almost two hours to Lynton, but the country was very beautiful, she said. Sylvia would meet him at the Lynton station, if she was not able to come herself, and bring him down to the cottage.

He got into the miniature Lynton train. The engine looked like a green oblong tank, with a red cow-catcher in front. It had a big polished brass dome like an immense fireman's helmet rising out of the middle of the tank. There were only three carriages, one of them almost all made of glass, the first-class one. He got into a third, and stared about him, at the swans in the river, wooden ships moored at the quay on one side, and the number of traps and carts drawn by horses on the road seen through the opposite window. There was only one other person in his carriage, an old farmer with mutton-chop whiskers and a square sort of bowler hat on his head.

At last the tiny engine gave a discordant shriek of its twin brass whistles, and with much chuffing, and rattling of the carriage, started off. By the rapid chuffing it seemed to be racing, until by comparison with the people and houses outside it was seen to be creeping. The longer it took the better. To ride in such a train was an adventure which he would like to go on for ever.

The engine puffed and huffed out of the town, and up a green valley with oakwoods on either side, and meadows thick with rushes, where sheep and red cattle grazed. It passed over very small bridges, and left whiffs of steam through cuttings like a story-book train. Once it stopped, for a bullock on the line. He saw large birds soaring in wide spirals far above a hill, and counted seven, one above the other, sailing serenely in the blue.

"Good lord!" he said to the bewhiskered farmer opposite, "they must be buzzards!"

The farmer grinned, revealing brown stumps of teeth. "Aiy," he said, "they'm 'awks."

"Aren't they rather rare?"

"Noomye!" shouted the farmer. "Serradwads fessans us calls 'n."

He wondered what this meant. It must be dialect. It seemed appropriate with the name of the little station, SNAPPER, where the farmer, who was almost as round as a barrel, and seemed to have some of the contents of one inside him, got out. Head out of window, Phillip asked the guard what was the local name for buzzards.

Turning to the same farmer, the guard shouted, "What be they birds up auver, Jem?"

"Aw, they'm 'awks, I reckon! Us calls'n serradwads fessans yurrabouts, midear, it ban't thik praper name, noomye, 'tes only what us calls'n yurrabouts like."

"Oh, thank you," said Phillip, as puzzled as before, for he had not understood a word of it.

The safety valve of the engine was screeching with the head of steam got up for the long haul to the moor. The engine driver had blown his whistle, and the train had started off again, when Phillip heard shouting, and poking his head out of the window he saw the figure of a parson running and waving his black shovel hat. The train stopped with a jerk.

"Afternoon, Joe!" shouted the parson to the driver. "Billy Chugg's bees have been playing again." As he passed Phillip's window, he stopped and said, "Hullo! I haven't seen you before, have I?" When Phillip replied that it was his first ride on the railway, the parson said, "Get your things—no, leave them where they are, they'll be quite safe—and come with me into the end coach. You'll get a much better perspective of the curves from the tail. There's a grand view of the Chill'em viaduct, in the declining sunlight. The infra rays reflect beautifully from the white Marland brick. Let me give you a hand with your bag."

While the driver waited, Phillip transferred bag and rod to the end coach.

"Very few visitors know what to look for on this line," the parson continued, seating himself opposite. The engine screeched once more; and making an enormous show of power and speed, rattled on slowly.

"Once over Collar Bridge the gradient rises one in fifty for the next eight miles," went on the parson, as he thrust a hand into a jacket pocket, pulled out what looked like a pinch of dust, and threw it out of the window. Phillip wondered why he did not stand up and turn his pocket-lining inside out by the window, if he wanted to clean it out. Instead, the parson removed the dust pinch by pinch, throwing each little bit out of the window.

"You'll notice we ricochet from side to side from here onwards. It's a bore, but not due to any intemperance on the part of the engine, but to the eccentricity of the landowner in not allowing the engineer to follow the best levels when the line was first surveyed."

Having said this in his dry voice, the parson sprang from his seat to fling another pinch of dust out into the air. As the train rounded a long curve, he continued to throw out pinches.

"We go under the road in a minute, rocks in shadow. I must hold my fire."

The noise of wheels echoed back from rocky walls green with ferns.

"Now look out, dear boy, and observe the effect of the declining sun on the brick of the Chill'em viaduct! 'A rose-red city, half as old as Time', you know the allusion, no doubt. We have to put on all power here, to get up to Chill'em station."

While speaking, the parson was collecting more dust meticulously from his pocket. Phillip wondered if he were throwing out seeds—as he had once done himself.

The train was climbing through the woods; and suddenly was upon a bridge of several arches, but much taller than those seen from the train to London Bridge. It was built of white brick apricot-yellow in the light of the westering sun.

"Some visitors object to the white bricks, they look too much like a London underground lavatory, they complain, but I tell 'em it's the clay of the country, from Dolton and Marland beyond Bideford. The materials of the country can't be wrong. We're seventy feet above the road, now. That's the view I wanted you to see."

The hillside station was enwound along its margins with rambler roses, hollyhocks, and sunflowers. Phillip saw the name was Chelfham. No one got out, no one got in. They seemed to be the only passengers in the train.

As they went on, the parson explained that he hoped to see

in a year or two, upon the sides of the cutting, various flowers in bloom, including stocks, wallflowers, pansies, night primroses, and balsam. "Good for bees," he said, "as well as adding to the gaiety of nations. Don't you agree?"

"Yes, sir," said Phillip. "I threw out some bluebell seeds last year on the Bermondsey embankment, near London, but none have come up yet."

"Good man," replied the parson. "Good fellow. They will! You're on holiday from Town? Got your rod, I see. Nice length for the glen, for sideway casting under the bushes. Fish wet or dry? Hawthorn gets 'em this time of the year, dapped, when the water's gin clear. You fished the Lyn before?"

"No, sir, but my father has. Oh, by the way, I wonder if you can tell me the local name for a buzzard?"

"I don't know of any, unless it is 'hawk'."

"I heard someone just now calling them something like 'serrards fessans', and have been wondering what that means."

"Oh, I can answer that! Sir Edward's pheasants!" cried the parson. "The woods are so poached by fellows coming out from Derby, this end of Barnstaple, that Sir Edward hasn't a bird left. So the hawks are, in effect, his only pheasants, I suppose. Well, I wish you a pleasant holiday. I get out here at Bratton. Good day to you!"

The parson got out among more roses and hollyhocks. "Don't forget to try a hawthorn!" he called out, as he prepared to get up into the trap waiting for him.

"Good day to you, sir!" cried Phillip, waving his straw hat out of the window.

He was now alone in the train: rather a sad thought. His eyes became melancholy: the moment, the friendship, was gone for ever. To console himself, he sucked another orange, thinking that the parson was rather like Mr. Mundy, hail-fellow-well-met with everyone, high or low, riding his bike on the Hill, against the regulations, and on the pavements. Mr. Mundy even rode his bike into the Free Library, balancing while he got the swing doors open.

His new friend had told him to look out for the four farms on the hillside—Knightacott, Narracott, Sprecott, and Hunnacott— and for the streams sometimes passing over the top of engine and coaches by wooden aqueducts. Phillip looked for these, until the train had climbed away from the deep valley. From now

on it ran through rocky cuttings and high embankments on which
yellow furse bloomed, filling the carriage with its sweet smell.
Bees wandered through the open window, like the butterflies
of hours ago; long ago in the morning of the day whose eternity
was now ending.

It was a dream country, floating on sunshine, the world lying
far below. Were some of the shaggy men with dogs, drovers of
cattle, descendants of the Doones? The train had stopped at
Black Moor Gate; in a drowse of dream he listened to strange
words and voices of rough shaggy men with sticks in hand
shouting at bullocks among barking shaggy dogs. All seemed to
share one language. At last the stamping was finished, and with
the cattle truck coupled, the train went on, crawling to Parracombe Halt. Thereafter views of the moor, purple above the
far smooth azure Severn Sea; then a louder chuffing of Yuffing
Yeo, or whatever the old engine was called, echoed from the trees
of Wooda Bay—another name mentioned by Father, Little
Wood Bay. They were now surely at the highest part of the moor.
It was shimmering, with the shimmer of a bee's wing! Leaning
out of the window, he gazed upon the calm, grey-blue sea
stretching to a layer of white bubbled clouds above a far land.
Good lord, it must be Wales!

He had travelled a great distance to be within sight of Wales!
He waved his arms, and jigged upon the carriage floor.

The last orange was eaten, the last glaze of the sun upon the
sea was glimpsed, and then Yuffing Yeo was running down above
the oakwoods of the Lyn valley, to the terminus on the side of
of the hill above the town. Alas, the journey was over. He said
goodbye to his carriage, and to the valiant little engine that had
pulled him to his destination; and got out, to the melancholy
belving of cattle behind—and saw he was the only passenger.

A woman with projecting teeth stood on the platform.

"Are you Phillip?"

"Yes."

He raised his straw hat, and stared at the strange face which
smiled and said a name of which he heard only the first part,
Sylvia.

"Dora is rather tired, she is so sorry she was unable to come.
She thought you might like to walk up to the town, and go down
the cliff railway. It's rather an experience, if you haven't done

it before. You must have had a trying journey, nearly twelve hours! Can you manage the bag, if I carry the rod?"

"Yes, thank you."

He did not like her face. She seemed dowdy. Her smile seemed rather forced. He had no idea that she had suffered in prison. He walked in silence uphill beside her, awkwardly. After the long sunny day, it was dull in the shadow. It was different, too, from what he had imagined.

"I expect you are tired after your long journey, Phillip. May I call you Phillip? Do call me Sylvia. Everyone does."

"I'm not tired, really, thanks all the same." He did not like to call her Sylvia. She had a nice smile.

He felt that she would think him rude. Father had often told him he was rude, without manners. Uncle Hilary, said Father, had noticed it too. He walked on, feeling like a ghost of himself, rather forlorn that this was the first time he had come to the seaside without Mother and the girls. He felt very sorry, now, for having spoiled their holidays, so often in the past, by his bad behaviour. It was too late now. What was Mother doing at that very moment? Perhaps playing chess with Father; or next door playing picquet with Gran'pa. She was at everyone's beck and call, including his own. Why was he always so impatient with her? He never really meant to be. Poor little Mother, her cheeks often grew flushed, and her eyes had the shine of unshed tears in them, when Father was more beastly than usual; and now he, her son, who did at least know better, as often as not, criticised her too.

He did not know that his thoughts came from nervous exhaustion. He had imagined so much that his power was gone.

At the top of the climb were shops and hotels. He felt more cheerful to be in sunshine again. Several boys and girls in riding coats and breeches and little bowler hats were passing down the street on ponies, followed by a groom. He heard two speaking so politely to one another that they seemed almost unreal.

His guide led him along a narrow road beside a curving stone wall, obviously a garden wall, to a sudden view of blue sunlit sea and red cliffs far below. It was almost breath-taking. He stopped and stared with delight.

"Isn't it beautiful?" said Sylvia.

"Yes," he said fervently.

They came to a big painted iron water tank and a glass office, with a turnstile before it. Sylvia bought two tickets. This was the cliff railway, she said. He saw steel lines with grease on them going down fearfully steep to a tiny roadway below. He saw the tiny white fringe of sea breaking on grey boulders. The sea was nearly black, like a stain, beyond a dwarf quay. He felt giddy, and put down his bag; smiling at Sylvia to conceal his feeling. She noticed that his hands were clenched.

"It is rather awful the first time one sees it, like the view of London Bridge and Billingsgate from the Monument," she said. "It certainly terrified me."

"I'm not very good at heights," he smiled.

"The odd thing is that one doesn't notice it at all when going down. It's rather clever, the way it's worked. They let water into a tank underneath the top lift, then down it goes, slowly, pulling up the one below, on a stout cable. At the bottom the water is released into the sea, and our cab is ready to be hauled up in its turn. Newnes, the *Tit-Bits* man, had it built."

"Oh, really." He was amazed to think of *Tit-Bits* being heard of in Devon.

"Sir George's house, on the hill up there, was burned out last year. They've blamed it on the party, of course. We had nothing to do with it, actually, but it was a good advertisement to us, all the same."

He was not afraid of going down, once he was in the cab: on the contrary, he felt satisfaction that he was quite calm. On firm ground once again, Lynmouth with its jetty and light-tower, fishing nets drying, boats at anchor, and blue water and tiny cottages was better even than he had expected from the picture postcards stuck in Mother's book.

"Can it really be you, Boy? How you have grown! What a pleasure to see you again!"

How old Aunt Dora looked! Some of her teeth were gone. She looked yellow and wrinkled. Of course, she had been ill.

She took his hand between her two slender hands, hesitated whether to kiss him, decided he was too grown-up, and asked forthwith if all at home were well. He gave her his parents' messages of good will, and followed the ladies into the cottage, thinking that if he had seen Aunt Dora anywhere else, he would not have recognised her, so thin was she. The fair hair he remembered was ashen grey; and worst of all, the gaps in her

front teeth made her voice sound funny. It looked as though he
were not going to have a very nice holiday.

During tea of boiled eggs and brown bread and salty butter,
followed by raspberry jam and cream, in the cottage with the
sound of the Lyn rushing around the boulders in its bed below,
the light came back into Phillip's face, and met the light in the
face of Theodora, and in the face of her friend Sylvia. They were
both really very nice and kind, he thought, and ever so jolly:
how very strange that they were also suffragettes.

Chapter 8

SUMMER'S LEASE

THE EARLY days were a delight of sun and sea and heather; of
steamers nearly dissolved, under faint smoke-trails, in the misty
blue of the Severn Sea; of fishing boats sailing offshore in waters
sometimes reflecting the red precipices of unscaleable cliffs; of
green and white tumbling water in the tree-shadowed glen, Lyn
noisy with spray of fall and cascade; of gravelly pools lit by
sun-shafts piercing the green glooms of the forest rising to the
sky where gulls sailing over were like tiny specks of winged
sea-shell. Hawthorn flies, heavy with black lace and trailing
wings, coupled on ash and oak and alder leaves, sometimes fell
into the pools between the smooth boulders—*splash!*—the lovers
died together. He must get some quickly!

Aunt Dora told him of a cobbler who tied flies. He bought a
dozen hawthorns for sixpence, and was shown how to tie a turle
knot through the eyed shank, with gut wetted to prevent it
snapping. There were other flies, too, said the cobbler—the
true water-flies which hatched out of the stream, not from the
earth and trees like the heavier hawthorn flies, and beetles and
moths which fell in from above by accident. The true flies were
Blue Upright, Pheasant Tail, and Olive Dun.

He watched the true flies over the morning waters of the glen.
This was what he had read about. They were little slow whorls
of light, rising from the clearest water, to seek rest on the leaves
of ash and alder. There they shed their skins, wings and all:
and prepared to mate. They were spinning over the runs and
pools in the afternoon and early evening, rising and falling to

drop their eggs, while the swift spotted trout watched from under water: to leap, sometimes to feel the prick of the "hypocrit", as he thought of his fly being dapped gently in imitation of a spinner.

Proudly, casually, he took home his first red-speckled trout, for Aunt Dora's and Sylvia's breakfast.

What fun it was in the cottage; they were old, yet they seemed so light-hearted. Strange, too, that there were no disagreements, no arguments. What was wrong with them? And what masses of post they had: almost as much as came in every morning into the office, renewal premiums not counted.

In wonder at his marvellous new life he had to send off post-cards; many postcards, each with a variation of that statement. Poor people, left at home! So coloured postcards went to Mother, Mrs. Neville, Gil Fitcheyson, Aunt Dorrie, Cranmer, Willie at Rookhurst, David Wallace, Hubert Cakebread, Aunt Liz Pickering, Mr. Graham, Hern the grocer, Desmond at school in Essex, Mavis at Thildonck (give my love to Petal), Tommy at Brighton—and who else? Ah, he had forgotten the Branch! Mr. Howlett. Downham? He hesitated some time: he could not bring himself to write to Downham. To Mr. Hollis? Yes. But— might not Downham feel left out, if he wrote only to Mr. Howlett and Mr. Hollis? Edgar? Well, that might offend Mr. Hollis. So three more, these three please. They were written. Who else? Polly. The idea set up a discord in him. To Helena Rolls? No, no! Why not? NO!! Might he, perhaps, send one to Mrs. Rolls? Yes, that might be all right: she always spoke to him in a very friendly tone.

So, greatly daring, he sent a coloured view of Hollerday Hill to Mrs. Rolls, with *This is a delightful watering place, the country of the Doones and Lorna, with every good wish from Yours sincerely Phillip*; and then the date, 22 *July* 1914.

Composing that, and especially the address, left him feeling slightly shaky; so buying sixteen green ha'penny stamps, he stuck fifteen of them on at all angles, a gesture of his new freedom; but the sixteenth was set with every care, exactly upon the rectangle provided for the purpose.

Coming out of the little post office, which sold everything from cast-iron cooking pots and cough linctus to voluminous bathing costumes and tomatoes, he saw the blue sea and his mind at once was transfixed with the eyes of Helena Rolls.

When they were posted the morning seemed vacant. He perked up on hearing the notes of a horn, and looking up the street, saw some blue-coated men in white breeches and grey bowler hats by the arched bridge over the Lyn. He ran up the street, and soon was among wet hounds, which bayed dolefully and dripped water from the hair under their bodies and slung drops from their waving tails. He learned that an otter had been hunted down through the glen, and lost under the bridge.

Then a hound bayed among the boulders in the bed of the stream below, and the small red-faced man in dark-blue uniform blew the copper horn again, and cried out a sort of nasal chant. He took off his grey bowler and scooped it towards the river bed. The hounds plunged down into the water, and baying loudly, ran and swam towards the sea. Someone said the otter had gone that way.

This was exciting. He ran down to get a better view. He saw his aunt and her friend looking out of their door.

"Shameful," said Sylvia. "So many against one small animal."

"It will get away," said Aunt Dora. "They won't turn an otter in this water. It will get down to the sea, if I know anything about the beastie."

He hastened away down the street, to get a view from the sea-wall beyond the cottages. The green and white water poured and rushed among the grey boulders, on which gulls sat, making their yakkering cries. The tide was coming in, past the black posts of the salmon weir or trap at the edge of the boulders on the other side. Weeds made the water dark blue. Somewhere among them the otter was swimming, underwater. What would it look like? If only he could have one glimpse of it.

He got down. Oh, what luck, it was crawling out of the water, brown as seaweed, dragging a long thick tapered tail on a boulder! Shaking itself, spiky-haired, looking back! He saw its whiskers and its flat button-eyed face as it stared. It stood up, seeming to sniff the air. A gull dived at it, hung with yellow webbed feet yakkering; the otter gave it the least look, then sinking down slipped head-first into the water. It was gone! Although he searched from the shore, he did not see it again. Then, looking up to the wall of the quay above, he saw many brown crabs laid there, having been lifted from a steaming cauldron. They looked like a row of broken brown houses.

The otter-hunters went into a hotel, while the hounds sat in a yard, licking one another, yawning, and rolling on their backs in the dust, while the huntsman in navy-blue uniform and black nailed boots talked to them out of the corner of his mouth. His horn was placed between two buttons of his jacket. Phillip hung about, wishing he had remembered to bring his Brownie camera. He wanted to go into the hotel, to listen to what they said; but felt not good enough.

Later, he followed them up the steep hill to the town above and the railway station, where he watched the hounds put in a closed waggon. Many of the otter-hunters got into the carriages. They had come from Barnstaple, he learned, where the kennels were.

Well, that was an adventure! When the engine had puffed away, he went for a walk along the cliffs, high above the sea with its ships looking so tiny upon the wide silvered spaces to Wales. The cliffs below were wooded. All the trees had gnarled limbs. The path rose and fell among them. He thought how wonderful it would be if he could build a hut, secretly when no one was about, on the slope of the cliff, and live there on the simplest food, cooking on a wood fire. He could shoot rabbits and pigeons with his saloon gun, catch trout in the Lyn, grow his own potatoes, and drink only water.

The dreaming boy walked many miles every day. He followed the cliff path to Wooda Bay, and continuing along the twisting shaly track to the beacon of Highveer Point, turned inland above the valley of the Heddon stream. Here sheer leaden screes gleamed dully on the opposite side of the valley—hundreds of thousands of tons of flaky rock slidden down the side of the hill. He scrambled down to the river below, and followed a flowery path to an inn where he had bread and cheese and beer, sitting outside with the sweat drying on his shirt, face to sky, to get all the burn he could from the loving sun.

By following the stream up to near its source, he came to Parracombe. His shoes were shiny at the cap with heather and bramble. After tea, he caught the same train back to Lynton that had brought him that afternoon which seemed to be so long ago— far back in the hourless summer.

Every morning he set out to climb the long hill up to Countisbury, and onwards across the moor, wine-dark with heather, yellow with furze, to County Gate. He was in Somerset! That

wonderful, romantic name! He went down to Badgeworthy
Water, excited that he was in the country of Jan Ridd and Lorna,
and Carver Doone, and actually having tea at the farmhouse
where the great Jan had lived. His long legs, seeming tireless,
carried him up the valley and through the Doone stronghold,
past thorns holding ever so many old magpie nests, and up to
the wild moor, walking hour after hour with the burn of the sun
upon his face. He wanted it to be black by the time he returned
home. Onwards, onwards! Up coombe sides steep with the
sounds of his own breathing, feet swishing through heather, while
pipits flew up from among the rocks with faint cries at his passing.
No one but himself, in league upon league of empty moor. He
felt clear and happy as running water.

He came to a stony track, strewed with dried droppings of
moorland ponies, and plunged through knee-high bell-heather
down to water and drank from cupped hands. After a rest, up
again, with pounding heart, to find once more the cool breezes
of the highest ground. This must be somewhere near Exe head;
for southward lay mile upon mile of lower moorland, and beyond
a shimmering prospect of woods and patchwork fields dissolved
in sky.

Westward lay a molten line brimming upon the moor. With
a shock of delight he knew it for the open Atlantic. He held out
his arms to it, closing his eyes for joy of the discovery. Then off
with clothes, to dry them. Sunshine seemed to buoy his naked
body, so that he had no self left, only something looking out of
his eyes, part of the sky.

Spreading his clothes on wiry bushes of heather, he lay back,
eyes closed once more, while a pipit flitted with chipping cries.
He wondered if he should look for the nest, though it was bound
to have young so late in the year. He would not distress the little
mother by searching for it. But supposing he was near the nest,
even lying on it? He got up, moved his clothes to a compara-
tively bare place on the edge of a bog, marked by white tufts of
the cotton plant in flower, and settled down again, to enjoy his
sun-bath.

Faint white wisps of cloud floated still in the height of the sky;
he felt his eyes absorbing the blue space, until he was part of it,
part of the remote blue thought of the sky, and in that most pure
thought was his vision of the soul of Helena, for ever unattainable,
like all beauty, all thoughts of the soul. Why was beauty always

sad—because however much one loved beauty, it was forever unattainable? Yes, that was the answer.

One late afternoon in his second week he was jumping from thick tussock to thick tussock of purple moor-grass growing in a dry bog with shaking white tufts of cotton grass, making for Hoar Oak Water which, according to the map lent by Aunt Dora, lay at the bottom of the unseen coombe somewhere in front of him. He was on his way back after a twenty-mile circuit. By this time the toe-caps of his brogues, and the heels, were worn rough and thin by nearly two hundred miles through hard heather-stems of the moor. He was lean and brown as the heather. Day after day had been hot—bright in a dream of summer, of all summers that had ever been, and would ever be, for the world was now timeless as it was remote. He was one with the sky, he had found completion. A holiday into eternity, he thought to himself, again and again.

Coming down from the high ground of the moor, making for Hoar Oak Water, he thought that all the north-running streams ran to the sea at Lynmouth; so if he missed Hoar Water, he could find his way home by any other stream. His friend the fly-fishing cobbler said that he would know it by the old grey oak which grew at the bottom of the coombe, near the head-waters. The tree was a boundary mark between Somerset and Devon, and was probably four centuries old.

As he strode down a cleft in the moor, beside a runnel of water, walking on a path in the heather trodden by ponies, he heard thunder behind him, and stopping to look back, saw a flash coming out of a rock-like cloud that was drifting, and even as he stared, tumbling through the sky, solid-seeming yet breaking into fragments in silent weight. He had never seen one move with such speed. Its presence seemed to chill the whole moor with livid light.

He began to run as the thunder came in heavier blows. The cloud might be a colossal iceberg, so cold was the air rushing from it. Several birds, which he thought must be blackcock, glided over the line of the hill, uttering cries when they came nearly over him; then shifting direction they beat away across the coombe.

Before him lay a grey stump, with splintered top; the dead Hoar Oak. A track led away from the brook. He hesitated

whether or not to follow it. A hissing purple flash of lightning
upon the brow of the hill behind decided him. He began to
count, while hastening along the track, and had reached ten
when the thunder broke; and glancing back, saw only obliter-
ating grey.

He ran full speed down the track. He had been caught in
thunderstorms on the Hill, and much enjoyed them from the
shelters there, or the Refreshment House by the elms; but this
was different. It was frightening. Behind him played several
kinds of lightning: long jagged electric blue threads forking into
the ground; rose-coloured fan-like effusions which made everything a momentary glowing pink; green slashes that *hissed* a
moment before the sky broke.

The ground was jumping with water. He gasped with icy
shock. Shirt, shoes and trousers were heavy with water, dragging shapeless. He could see nothing beyond the smaller stones
of the track dancing knee-high. He knew not where he was
walking, but walk he must, or perish in cold.

Thunder rolled continuously; reddish burnings arose upon
the watery earth, or hovered as balls of fire, or shot sideways
like expanding flares illuminating the massive sheets and torrents
of the rain. White streams of water, suddenly suffused with pink,
were everywhere gushing down through the heather; while
through all was a roar that was frightening until he realized that
it was the little Hoar Oak Water rolling its bed of boulders to the
sea.

By the time the lightning had moved further away, and rain
settled to a heavy fall without turbulence, he could see to walk
again. His shoes squelched, so he lay down and held them over
his head to run out brown liquid and small stones. It made
walking a bit better, but there were blisters on both heels.

The track turned into a lane between banks of lichened stone
walls, on top of which beech trees writhed in many old cuttings
and layings. While he walked up the enclosed track the rain
suddenly ceased; and looking back, he saw blue sky in patches,
with high white clouds moving above. Their shadows raced over
the sunlit moor. It was so surprising a transformation that he
stopped to watch it; and while he watched, instantly he was
surrounded by warmth and light. Tiny, jewel-like glints of
purple, blue, green, and red trembled in the grasses and on the

beech leaves beside him. Already his clothes, like the earth, were steaming.

He took off his shirt, and wrung it out; and whirling it round his head, walked down the beechen grove, singing. Then in the pleasant grove he got out of his trousers, wrung them out, and continued to sing to an audience of bullocks watching through a gap in the beech hedge. They backed away, heads low, while the trousers went round like the sails of a windmill.

Saying goodbye to the bullocks, waving shirt and trousers, he went on up the grove, which ended at a sunken red lane arched over by trees. The lane was extremely steep on a surface of bare ribbed rock, so that he had to walk gingerly, to prevent himself from slithering.

Seeing a green valley below, and a road beside a river, he put on his trousers, and continued downhill until he came to a group of white-washed cottages, and a high arched stone bridge under which thick brown water was rushing. There was a monkey tree growing in the garden of a cottage. He put on his shirt reluctantly.

A farmer told him he was at Barbrook, and the lane he had come down was Beggar's Roost. Lynmouth was down the road. He went happily on his way, sun hot on back until he entered the shade of trees upon the road cut through rock; and all the rest of the walk was in shadow through the forest until the bottom of the long steep hill into Lynmouth, through which he hobbled with blisters, but rejoicing in his adventure.

Where had he been? Was he quite sure he had not caught cold? Good heavens, no! Then, going upstairs to change, he noticed two gladstone bags packed and standing under the dresser, side by side.

He looked at the labels. *Passenger to Dublin, via Holyhead.* Perhaps Sylvia was going away. For some days she had been talking about Dublin, a name known to him chiefly through Father reading bits out of *The Daily Trident.* He had neither listened to nor cared what it was about. Something about Carson, F. E. Smith, Orangemen, and Home Rule.

When, during tea, Aunt Dora said that she felt she must go with Sylvia to Dublin, in case civil war broke out, he began to take interest.

"Do you think you could look after yourself, Boy, for the remaining three days of your holiday?"

"Rather! I can cook, you know. Trout, eggs and bacon, toast, anything! Anyway, bananas and bread and butter are enough for me."

"You see, Boy, the news today is very grave. Our national living has been wrong in England for some years, and if those of us who know this don't act now, we may all be plunged into something which might very well be the final catastrophe of Armageddon, foretold in the Old Testament."

What rot, he thought: like the Salvation Army. He cared only that he would be having the house to himself. If only Desmond were with him!

"You may be wondering why we are going to Dublin, Boy. You see, Sylvia heard when you were out this morning that our soldiers, to their shame, have been firing on an unarmed crowd in Dublin, most of them children. One little boy was shot in the back, there was a little girl with her ankle shattered, whlle several parents were killed, and many more wounded."

"*Our* soldiers did it? But why, Auntie?"

"Well, you have heard of the Home Rule Bill, have you not?"

"No, Auntie."

Dora looked momentarily helpless.

"Well, Phillip, the Orangemen, or Irish Unionists of Northern Ireland, have armed to oppose the Home Rule Bill. And, you see, while arms for them are virtually permitted by our Government, they are forbidden to the National Volunteers, the Southern Irish that is. So they landed some secretly. The Viceroy sent soldiers to seize those arms, at Louth, where they were landed. On their way back to barracks the soldiers opened fire on an unarmed, jeering crowd, and some of the bullets killed the children."

Phillip was only half listening. A fisherman on the quay had told him that salmon would be running in the "fresh", and they would take a lobworm among the boiling water of the boulders. The thing to do was to water a lawn with mustard and water, then up would come the lobs. Could he ask Aunt Dora where there was a lawn?

" . . . you will be mobilised, won't you, Boy?"

"War, Aunt Dora? You mean civil war in Ireland? Father said something about it, I remember now. The Terriers are home defence, you know. We're really more a sort of club than anything else."

She looked at him with a gentle smile. He was so young, so unaware of the world. Pray God that he, and thousands of boys like him, would not be drawn into the threatening cataclysm.

"Do you ever read the newspapers, Phillip?"

"No, not much."

"You have heard about the assassination of the Austrian Archduke Ferdinand at Sarajevo, surely?"

"Only sort of, Aunt Dora. I say, do excuse me, I want to ask the cobbler something, before he leaves his shop. I won't be long."

When he had gone, the two women sat there in silence for awhile. Then Sylvia said, "That poor boy is typical of the European millions, Dora. What does he know of the dark forces?"

"It is the backwardness of time that conceals the truth of the present, Sylvia."

"We are all part of it, Dora. Even the warnings of that noble man, our great friend Keir Hardie, seemed to me to be exaggerated, when he told me, a year or two ago, that Haldane's Army Bill, then before the Commons, meant, finally, war and conscription. I listened to him with sympathy, of course, but being involved in moment to moment problems of our own struggle, I thought that his attitude was too remote. I suppose Keir Hardie found me wanting."

In the morning the two women left by the early train, and Phillip, to his satisfaction, was left in charge. He had instructions to leave the key with a neighbour, who would come in and clean up the cottage when he had gone.

On the following Sunday night at nine o'clock he caught the return excursion train from Barnstaple, and arrived, after sitting upright in a carriage all night with nine other people, at Waterloo station shortly before six in the morning. On the way home he had a carriage to himself, and turned inside out between the luggage racks in sheer exuberance of being alive. August Bank Holiday lay only a week ahead; Desmond would be coming home from school, and cousin Willie be living with him by then. What fun they would have together! He would take Willie to his secret Lake Woods, with Desmond, and they would fish for roach.

Chapter 9

SOMETHING IN THE AIR

IT WAS very hot in London, though cool in Wine Vaults Lane. No artificial light in the downstairs office now; but upstairs, in his narrow frosted glass partition, Phillip worked under an electric bulb as he sat before the tall Remington machine, making out Fire and Combined Household policies from proposal forms, and at moments pausing to imagine the sun upon the heather of Hoar Oak Hill, and the clear gravelly runs of the Lyn.

When he got home he found the front door ajar. He stood on the hall mat, listening to Father's voice in the sitting-room.

"You mark my words, Hetty, Lord Roberts knew what was to come as far back as 1908 when he said at Quebec—I cut it out of the *Trident* at the time—here it is—'They refuse to believe me, and we sleep under a false security, for I do not hesitate to affirm that we shall have a frightful war in Europe, and that England and France will have the hardest experience of their existence. They will, in fact, see defeat very near, but the war will finally be won by the genius of a French general named Ferdinand Foch, professor of the Military School in Paris'."

Phillip crept silently away. It was awful to be home again. He went next door, and had tea with Grandfather and Great-aunt Marian.

Later that evening, when he had told him of the Dublin journey, and Father said, "Preposterous idea! Dora's a muckraker," Phillip got up and left the room. They heard the front door close behind him.

"Curious chap," remarked Richard. "You can't tell him anything nowadays."

"In 1908 Lord Roberts, in Quebec, said we would have a frightful war in Europe, and come near to defeat, Mr. Hollis. Hark, what's that paper boy crying? Perhaps it's started already!"

"I hope not," said Mr. Hollis. "I sincerely hope you and Lord Roberts are not right, Maddison. Here, Edgar, stir your stumps, forget your pictorial harem, and go out and buy me an evening paper!"

"Yessir, certainly, sir!"

The messenger went smartly out into the narrow sunlight of the ͺLane, disappearing in the direction of the distant voice.

"Though I must agree with you," went on Mr. Hollis, "that things look pretty bad. Even so, we ought to keep out of it. We've got a Navy, haven't we? And we're an island! As Napoleon once said, we're a nation of shopkeepers and tradesmen. While we rule the seas, we rule the world, my boy! We've also got most of the world's gold. Nations, like families, can't exist without money. A modern war would soon exhaust the European nations' gold reserves. In three months any country at war would be bankrupt. Contractors have to be paid for their armaments and supplies, you know! Take my word for it, there won't be any war. So get on with your work, young feller-me-lad. No martial glory for you, you sunburnt trout tickler."

Downham was at luncheon, so was Mr. Howlett. Mr. Hollis was dressed in his tail-coat and striped trousers. He was going to meet young Roy Cohen at the Piccadilly Hotel, and, he said, get the new clothing factory insurance of Moses Cohen, Ltd.

"Someone in this Branch has got to get new business, you know, Maddison."

"Quite right, Mr. Hollis."

It was Friday, the last day of July. Desmond was home from school, with Eugene his Brazilian friend who was a nice fellow; Cousin Willie was arriving that afternoon at Waterloo; Monday was August Bank Holiday. Then, very soon, camp at Eastbourne! Life *was tremendous fun, really.*

And yet—and yet—somehow, under everything, a feeling of coldness, of longing, of dread, was growing; and the feeling became centred on the talk of war, which, stealthily, and in secret, was a thing to be desired. War—everyone spoke about it: the fellows at Head Office; Father; Mrs. Neville; Gran'pa; Mr. Bolton—everybody. The tobacconist spoke of it when he had gone to buy a sixpenny ounce of mixed cigarettes—yellow Russian, fat oval Turkish, strong black French, red-silk-topped Ladies, Italian with streaky thin rice-paper, African with paper ends screwed up, violet-tipped for passion. Secretly, awefully, fearfully, one part of him desired the excitement that was war to become more and more; while another part of him quailed before a vast, fathomless darkness. As these feelings grew side by side in his mind there persisted a vision of hatless French soldiers slouching along a road, treeless, houseless, bare, a road leading nowhere, from nowhere. There was no fighting in this picture: nothing like the pictures of *Valour and Victory*, stories of the Boer War: only an endless straggle of ragged soldiers, some without arms, others with rifles slung on shoulders, all walking very slowly, listlessly, from nowhere to nowhere.

Edgar returned, breathless.

"All papers sold out, sir! I tried four pitches, sir!"

Edgar's hair was smarmed smooth with oil. He would be sixteen on the morrow. Phillip determined to buy another sixpenny ounce of mixed cigarettes for Edgar's birthday.

"I thought this might do instead, Mr. 'Ollis."

Proudly Edgar put a copy of *John Bull* on the counter, and, under it, Mr. Hollis' penny.

"Good God! That rag!"

"I thought you might like a read of it, I bought it wi' me own money, sir. There's your penny back, under it, sir."

"Oh," said Mr. Hollis, his voice becoming winsome. "How very civil of you, Edgar! Thank you indeed! So you follow Horatio Bottomley, do you, eh?"

Edgar smirked in his sudden importance.

"H'm," said Mr. Hollis. He opened the middle pages. "'To Hell with Servia'. Well, that's frank, anyway." He glanced a few moments, then folded it again and put it on the counter. "Thank you, Edgar!" He gave a nod to the messenger, who stood by the counter. "I think," he went on, as Edgar did not move, "that perhaps your periodical would be better in your drawer, Edgar."

"Thank you, sir," said Edgar, returning to his corner.

"This is a respectable office," said Mr. Hollis, *sotte voce* to Phillip. "Between ourselves, Horatio Bottomley is one of the biggest rogues out of gaol, and that's putting it mildly. He's escaped the penalty of dubious finance again and again, solely owing to his knowledge of the intricacy of company law. He's a witty devil, too, in his way. This story is vouched for by my father-in-law, Carlton Turnham, the civil engineer, you know. Bottomley called one day on someone called Chumley, spelt, of course, C-h-o-l-m-o-n-d-e-l-e-y. To the butler he said, 'Is Mr. Chol-mon-deley in?', 'No, sir, but Mr. Chumley is. Have you an appointment, sir?' 'I have,' replied Bottomley. 'Who shall I

say has called, sir?' 'Oh, Mr. Bumley.' Ha-ha-ha, you see the
joke, of course.''

Phillip laughed as he closed a shiny black reference book, and
said, "Very good, very good," while wondering what exactly the
joke was.

A newspaper boy's shouting came down the Lane.

"No, not now, Edgar, I have to go out." To Phillip, "Where
is Howlett, does he ever do any work? If he's not back inside five
minutes, I shall leave you in charge of the office, young feller. So
for God's sake don't start playing jokes on anyone who may come
in!''

"Certainly not, Mr. Hollis."

To Phillip's disappointment, Mr. Howlett arrived back a few
moments later.

The senior clerk, with a glance at his gold watch, said to Edgar,
"Fetch me a taxi, quick as you can, my lad! I have a business
appointment and must not be late."

"Yessir!" said Edgar, dashing out once more into Fenchurch
Street.

"I thought you were going out to lunch with young Roy
Cohen," said Mr. Howlett, mildly, taking his pipe out of his
mouth.

"I am; but I could hardly leave young Maddison in charge
here. Where the devil is Downham? Is office routine at this
Branch to be taken seriously, or is it not?"

"I should say that the office routine is liable to considerable
upset, judging by the latest news," replied Mr. Howlett, quietly.

"Oh?" said Mr. Hollis, pausing as he brushed his jacket with
the office brush.

Phillip saw that Mr. Howlett's face looked quite different from
what it had ever looked before. It seemed longer; the eyes
larger. Mr. Howlett's manner was so serious that it seemed to
add to his height. The creases were not noticeable in his trousers.
He looked strangely unlike himself in this new quiet seriousness.
Mr. Hollis responded to this new Mr. Howlett. Mr. Hollis'
appearance of always being in a hurry, which had always seemed
to amuse Mr. Howlett, left him. Mr. Hollis awaited what he had
to say, brush in hand. Movement was suspended for perhaps
two or three seconds; but to Phillip it seemed, while it lasted, to
be for ever.

Mr. Howlett said, in a low voice, "The Czar has ordered

general mobilization. I've just come from Lloyds, where they rang the Lutine bell."

"Good God!" exclaimed Mr. Hollis, putting down the clothes brush. "In that event the fat is in the fire with a vengeance!"

Phillip felt a cold shiver pass through him, and then the fearful longing for war, like a dark spectre.

He remained in the office after Mr. Hollis had left in the taxi. When Downham returned he was supposed to go upstairs, to continue the typing of policies; but when Downham did come back, he followed his impulse and without a word walked out into the sunshine of Fenchurch Street. He must be free of the shaded Lane, and his dark thoughts, for a moment or two.

The usual traffic of heavy horse drays was passing up and down the street, but now it seemed as though all movement was half-dissolved, insubstantial in the brilliant summer light, which was somehow part of the news. He walked towards Aldgate, drawn by the brilliant feeling of light, away from his usual self, to be separated from that life. He felt on the verge of finding that something which had always been shut off from ordinary living. He remembered how he had first felt this something when singing to himself as a small child, left alone for a few moments in a tepid bath in the kitchen, by Minny his German nurse—the gas jet very low and blue—and singing to himself in a minor key. It was a strange sort of happiness. He had felt it later in the Backfield; and in the loft under the roof of his home; and later still in moments of Whitefoot Lane, and in his "preserves". It had been strong during the holiday in Devon, high upon the moor in the burning sun. It was another life. He, the Phillip that lived at home, the Phillip seen by others, by himself in the mirror, was for the moment left behind, like the skin of a mayfly after it had flown.

It was much more than sad feeling, the lonely tepid-bath gas-jet singing feeling of childhood; it was more than an alone-feeling; it was a state in which he could know things without thinking— not the kind of thinking the Magister urged the boys at school to do—he could almost *feel things themselves*, rather than theorems.

He surprised himself by this sudden thought; and found he had come to Aldgate Tube station.

Newsboys were shouting. Men in top-hats, straw-hats, bowlers, cloth-caps—everyone except orthodox Jews with tallow faces and black whiskers and hair under rather high black felt hats—clustered to buy papers.

While he was looking at *The Globe* on the corner of Mark Lane, he saw Peter Wallace. He had seen Peter once or twice in the Lane, and at London Bridge; but they had never spoken, only nodded, until now. Peter, hatless too, also had a paper.

"Do you think that war will come, Peter?"

"My gov'nor says it's inevitable between Germany and the Slav States. For one thing, there are no more Central European wheats or barleys being offered on Exchange now. Our agents say that the Germans have bought the lot. No British government can permit that interference with normal trade."

"How do you mean, Peter?"

"Well, it's obvious, surely. The City exists on trade, and trade exists on free markets. Free markets exist on the freedom of the seas. Grain is a fundamental commodity. The Germans have virtually closed the Baltic. So we're bound to be at war within a week. Q.E.D."

Phillip was greatly impressed. He remembered that Peter had got First-Class Honours in the Oxford Senior—"Oh, I see! Well, I must go now. When are you going to camp, with the first or second lot?"

"I'm with the first contingent."

"I'm with the second."

Peter Wallace turned on his heel. Phillip felt that Peter had never liked him since the day he had called him a coward. If only he had learned to box! He hurried back to Wine Vaults Lane; and went through the door quietly, a little apprehensive.

"What's the latest?" asked Downham.

"The German Government has sent a twelve-hour ultimatum to Russia, to stop mobilization. And a friend on the Corn Exchange told me what is not yet in the papers—the Germans have closed the Baltic. So we'll be at war within a week."

"Closed the Baltic? What, here in the City?" scoffed Downham. "How did they close it? Padlock the door?"

"That's right," said Mr. Howlett's voice from upstairs. "The Germans are stopping all grain leaving Danzig and other Hanseatic ports."

"Well, sir," Downham called up the stairs, in his flattering voice, "Wallis, of the Accident Department, our company Colour-sergeant, telephoned to Regimental Headquarters just before I left Head Office, and they said that the camp is still on, so it looks as though only the Navy will be involved. For the present, at any rate, sir."

"Ah," said the voice of Howlett, from the roost above the stairs.

It was half-past three by the clock on the wall. Phillip thought of Willie's train arriving at Waterloo in about twenty minutes' time. He had been trying, all day, to bring himself to ask Mr. Howlett for permission to leave early, in order to meet the train; but ever since his late return after Whitsun, he had, as Mr. Hollis had advised him, been watching his step.

"Well," said Mr. Howlett, who *did* look like an owl as he spoke, peering round the frosted glass door where, amidst much muttered indiarubbering, Phillip had spent the Saturday morning before the tall Remington typewriter. "Well, Maddison, I suppose when we meet next, on Tuesday morning, our fates will have been decided. I'm closing the office now. You'll appear here on Tuesday, I suppose? Are you staying at home for the Bank Holiday?"

"Yes, sir." As he got up, he said, "Mr. Howlett, do you think war will come to England?"

Mr. Howlett removed his pipe. He was the serious Mr. Howlett of the previous afternoon.

"Between ourselves, I think it will be a miracle if it does not. The *Telegraph* here"—he tapped his folded newspaper—"says that we cannot stand aside if Germany marches to attack France through Belgium. The present Government attitude, you know, is only to guarantee the Channel Ports. But if we stood by while France was beaten, it would only be a question of time before our turn came. That, at any rate, is the argument, and I must say I agree with it. Only a miracle, in my opinion, can now avert war. If the worst comes to the worst I suppose Hollis and I will have to carry on as best we can, without the help of Downham and yourself."

Mr. Howlett said this so sincerely that Phillip wished he had worked harder. He lowered his eyes before the kind, owly gaze. The dark fear came over him. Why had he wished for war to come? Now it might be too late to un-wish it.

"Well, we must not meet trouble half-way, Maddison. If you and Downham are mobilised, I shall have to apply for someone from Head Office. It's a good thing for you you took your holiday when you did, for it looks as though none of us will be able to have ours. I cannot possibly leave for Cromer to join my wife and family this afternoon, as I had arranged." Mr. Howlett put on his panama hat. "I shall remain at home until I know what is going to happen. By Tuesday, as I said, things will probably be decided one way or the other. By the way, did your cousin arrive yesterday without mishap?"

"Yes, thank you, sir."

"I suppose he will be starting next Tuesday?"

"Yes, Mr. Howlett."

"How old is he?"

"Willie's seventeen, sir, a year younger than me—I mean I."

"It would be rather curious, wouldn't it, if you were mobilised, and he came here to take your place? Don't look so alarmed! I am not suggesting for one moment that anything like that might happen! But if there is General Mobilisation, quite half Head Office staff, and the branches too, will have to go, you know. By the way, have you any news about your uncle, George Lemon? I was so sorry to hear of his trouble."

"He arrived in Australia, sir, to help on my other uncle's sheep and fruit farm."

Phillip did not add that one of the first things Uncle George did upon his arrival was to set fire to the farmhouse, after which act—to secure attention to a grievance that his plans to irrigate the entire continent of Australia by pumps operating on perpetual motion from power to be supplied by the water which they were to pump had been ignored—he was removed to an asylum.

"Ah, there's nothing like an open-air life to bring a man back to health," said Mr. Howlett, genially, puffing his pipe. "Well, we'll meet again on Tuesday."

Palely in the narrow sky over Wine Vaults Lane floated the half moon, its grey human effigy in part obscured by the shadow of the earth.

Phillip could hardly believe that "Uncle Dick" was the same person as "Father". He talked quite differently, like he did when in the old days he had come to visit them on Hayling Island during the summer holidays, and had played tennis with Captain Spalding at Dr. Robartes' house. He had been proud of Father, then. Mavis and Doris looked different, too, while Mother seemed ever so happy.

In fact, Willie was a general favourite, and had almost taken the place of Zippy the cat, whose funny face during the years had been almost the only common denominator by which tenderness was released in the Maddison household.

"Well," said Richard, after he poured a glass of sherry for his guest, a second for his son, a third for himself, "well, success to you, Willie!"

The two girls and Hetty, hurrying in from the kitchen, drank lemonade. After the toast, Richard faced the shoulder of lamb on the dish before him. Phillip watched him use the unfamiliar stag's-horn-handled carving knife and fork, which had come out of the silver-plate box that afternoon. He felt rather proud that they were having dinner at night, instead of supper.

"You know," Richard was saying, "*The Trident* reported mysterious engine noises over the Essex marshes and the Thames estuary at night, a year or so ago; obviously Zeppelins come to spy out the land, and to test their instruments. I say this—and mark my words!—if England does not honour her guarantee to Belgium, it will be her turn next! Those Prussians are at the back of it all. They destroyed the old German states and principalities. They glorify war as the highest human activity. Peace, they say, rots the nation. Yet, Willie my boy," as he handed round the plate, "you owe your very existence to Bismarck, for if he had not killed your great-grandfather and his sons, your grandmother would not have fled to England, and married your grandfather! And where would we all have been today, if it had not been for that fact?"

"Lying fallow, sir."

"What? Oh, I see!" Richard was surprised at his nephew's remark; then, "Quite right, my boy! You have your mother's wit, I perceive."

So genial was the voice that Zippy leapt lightly on Richard's chair, and opened its mouth to mew plaintively for a tit-bit.

"Ah, Zippy knows, don't you, naughty ickkle Zippy——!"

Phillip did not want Willie to hear Father talking his soppy cat-talk, so he said quickly, "Oh, Father, we are planning a sort of tennis tournament on the Hill on Monday, and will you join us?"

"Tennis, Phillip? It is so long since I played, old man. I'd be awfully stiff, and out of practice."

"You played jolly well on Hayling Island, when you beat Captain Spalding. Didn't he, Mum?"

"Yes, you played splendidly, Dickie."

"Oh, come now——"

Richard looked pleased to be invited. However, he would not answer directly. He was out of the habit of being invited.

"Let's wait and see, shall we? Why, anything might happen between now and Monday."

"We'd love you to come, sir," said Willie.

"Yes, rather, do come, sir," added Phillip, half-consciously imitating his cousin's manner.

"Oh very well, since you so kindly invite me——"

Hetty felt she was going to cry. She went outside, ostensibly to see that she had turned out the gas in the oven. It was all so strange; it was almost sad; Dickie looked *happy*. She knew it was because Willie took after his mother. Poor, poor Dickie!

Unaware of her emotion, Richard went on with the carving. The mahogany table, lengthened by an added leaf brought up from under the floor, bore upon it some of the family silver, including the stag's-horn-handled carving knife and fork. The rest of the plate stood upon the sideboard. Tea-pot, coffee-pot, jugs, and tray were massive affairs of nodulous silver, part of a set left to Richard, while still in his teens, by the will of a great-uncle. Only once before, in nearly twenty years of married life, had Hetty seen the stuff, which had been locked in the iron-bound square oak box in Richard's workroom until he had brought down some of the pieces to show her, for the second time, the previous afternoon. She and the girls—Mavis had come home early from Belgium—had cleaned them, brush and rags and saucer of Goddard's plate powder on newspapers spread upon the kitchen table. They were heavy and ornate, more clotted and penduled than any house-martin's nest ever was with mud and feathers: ugly and depressing as the earth's surface around a coal-mine, with which this silver had a direct connexion, since it had been a gift to Augustus Maddison from his early Victorian partners and associates of a mining company upon the Durham family property; but in Phillip's eyes, at least, the sight of it was pleasing. "My boy," she had heard Richard say to him, "this will be yours after I am gone—provided the Germans don't get it first."

He had unlocked the oak box the afternoon before, on coming home from the City, impelled by thoughts of what he should do with the plate if the Germans invaded the East Coast, and got so far as London. Had not Blücher remarked once, *What a city to sack!* (Blücher's words after the Napoleonic War were, *Was für Plunder!* as he regarded the unplanned muddle of the place— a literal translation being *What bloody rubbish!*). Richard had a vague idea, if the worst came to the worst, of burying the box under the house. The trouble was, the trap-door in the lavatory floor was not anything like big enough for the box.

Anyway, in Willie's honour, the silver was in use for the week-end; then it would be locked up again. "After all," Richard had said to Hetty, "the Royal Navy will have something to say to any attempted invasion!"

The next morning something happened which the master of the house declared to be "without precedent". Through the letter-box came a special Sunday edition of *The Daily Trident*. Phillip took it down to the breakfast room. No one had ever dared to look at the paper before Father had seen it.

"Do you know, Willie, I have taken this paper since number one came out, and never missed a single copy! Let me see, it must have been a few months before you were born, old chap. It was in the spring of 'ninety-six; you were born in the following winter, I remember."

Richard looked at the face of his nephew, seeing upon it the lineaments of his adored Jenny, who had died when the little chap was born. He saw upon his nephew's face the same glow, the same inner shining, as once upon the face of Jenny.

"Well, it looks as though our fates have been decided, Willie boy, since the *Trident* has come out on a Sunday! Let's see what it says, shall we?"

"Yes please, Uncle Dick!"

Fear of war, yet longing for war to come, moved again in Phillip.

"On second thoughts, I think that perhaps we should wait for your aunt, don't you?"

"Yes, Uncle Dick."

Phillip got up from the table, and with long silent strides, one of them taking him up the three steps in the passage, entered the kitchen.

"Come on, Mum, hurry! You know what Father is—if you don't come, he'll prolong it for ever. I *must* know!!"

"I won't be a minute, dear. I'll be as quick as I can."

"Hurry!"

She was waiting for the kettle to boil, in order to fill the hot-water jug, and the tea-pot.

"Why can't he tell us at once?"

"Father is only being considerate, dear, he wants me to hear, too. Just coming, Dickie," she sang out. Then to Phillip, so that his father might hear (she was taking no chances), "Don't forget both taps, Phillip."

"All right, I know the form!"

All were now seated at table; and then (it may not have been entirely due to the influence of the silver plate) Richard decided to say grace—an event that had not occurred in the house for many years. After that he waited while Hetty poured out the tea —while Phillip fumed and sighed. The cups having been passed round, Richard concerned himself with his guest—salt and pepper for his plate of haddock, and butter for his bread. Only when everyone had been served did he open the special edition of *The Daily Trident*.

Phillip's third or fourth sigh was overlaid by a low whistle from his father.

"Listen to this, I say! GERMANY BEGINS WAR!—Precautionary Measures—Russia's Partial Mobilisation—British Fleet Puts to Sea—('Thank goodness we shall not be caught napping!')—Mr. Asquith on the Crisis—('"Wait and See," I expect, is that Old Woman's contribution, Hetty')—Extreme Gravity—('Well, I'm glad anyway he realises our danger, Phillip')—Financial Strain ('They say in the City that a Moratorium will probably be declared, to stop a run on the Banks, Willie')—Foreign Bourses Demoralised——"

At this point Zippy ran in through the open french windows, tail up, mewing at the smell of haddock. Seeing the cat, Richard began to speak to it in what Phillip called (out of his father's presence) his soppy feline lingo.

"Zippy, my little Pippy, where have you been, you naughty, porty catty? I called you for your milky-pilky-wilky, but you did not come, did you, Zippy Pippy Wippy?"

"And so you missed the newsy pewsy, Zippy Pippy Wippy, about the Foreign Bourses being Demoralised," said Phillip.

Hetty tried not to laugh. Richard was not pleased with what he considered to be his son's unexpected lampoon of himself; but he maintained his new equilibrium.

"Where were we?" he said. "Oh yes—'Foreign Bourses Demoralised'. INVASION OF LUXEMBURG—FRANCE'S CLAIM ON BRITAIN—Germany the Aggressor—'To be able to Claim British Support'—('They are frightened, you see, the French, and no wonder, after eighteen seventy! I was only a bit of a boy at the time, Willie, but I well remember my father saying that the French, who forced that war upon the newly federated German States, were decadent, living on illusions of Napoleonic glory, instead of keeping their powder dry—well, that seems to be about all, except——') TODAY'S CABINET, Last Efforts to Limit War, Great Britain's Position—(ah, here's something)—The Kaiser's Order, 'Mobilise Our Entire Force,' he says, 'and Safeguard the Empire'."

Richard passed the paper to Willie.

"Well, I am going for a cycle ride," he announced, getting up from his chair. "It may be the last chance for some considerable time. But before I go, I propose to write a letter to Winston Churchill, at the Admiralty, to warn him of a danger that he may not have foreseen."

These words had a quietening effect on his listeners. Doris was frightened; but she did not show it in her face when in the presence of her father. Then her face was invariably expressionless; her spirit remote, withdrawn. She had never recovered from the shock of being beaten by him, when, a small child, she had suddenly announced that she had a big knife to kill him with, if he made her Mummy cry.

Phillip wondered whatever Father was going to write to the Admiralty. He might be able to find out later from Ching, if he saw him, for Ching was in the Admiralty. Anyway, what could Father possibly know? Then he remembered reading a story in *Pearson's Magazine*, some time back, about a German battleship called the *Von der Tann* getting into the Atlantic through the Channel with masked lights, to sink scores of British ships until brought to book by British Dreadnoughts, and sunk, after a terrific fight. Father had been very impressed by that story, in fact he had given it to him to read, saying, "If ever there is war, this is what might happen to our merchant ships, Phillip."

"Father, what are you going to write to the Admiralty? Tell us!"

"Ah, wouldn't you like to know!"

Richard wrote his letter, carefully with stylograph wire-point pen, sealed the envelope, stuck a penny stamp on it, and posted it at Fordesmill, as he passed on the Sunbeam. He had warned the First Lord of the Admiralty that the German Fleet might try a surprise dash down the Channel, with masked lights, under cover of darkness, in order to raid Atlantic shipping; and as a loyal citizen he felt that it was his humble duty to point this out, in case it had not occurred to the responsible authorities. He had the honour to be, their Lordship's most obedient servant, Richard Maddison.

No reply or acknowledgment ever came; but Richard, who as a boy, a would-be cadet, had failed to get into the Navy, had done his duty.

Bank Holiday tennis on the Hill. A day of sun and wind, white cumulus clouds passing swiftly across the blue, dry elm leaves rustling above a sun-baked gravelly soil, kites flying, distant Crystal Palace glinting along its grey scales. The thud of tennis balls on strung catgut (one or two strings broken), how proud he was of Father's swift service, coming down from the racquet held at the top of his extended right arm, whipping just over the net, flicking in low swift bounce upon him. Willie as Father's partner was jolly good, too, and beat him and Desmond. Then Eugene played with Desmond, and they beat Father and Willie. Eugene had a crafty, slicing, underhand service, which made the ball break in all directions. Phillip thought that it wasn't quite sporting, just like a foreigner. Still, Eugene wasn't half bad.

Father looked almost distinguished. He was glad he had asked him to play. He had been nervous about it at first, in case Father became cross. His relief therefore was the greater. Father wore old-fashioned brown-striped white flannel trousers, but they looked quite nice. Then Mavis and Doris and Petal came up to play, with cousin Hubert and Maudie his sister, at the next court. It really was a wonderful Bank Holiday. It felt somehow to be the last of the old kind of Bank Holidays. A pity Mother had to miss it all, having to do the housework. The wind blew, warm and sunny, the atmosphere was very clear. When the play was over, the question came uppermost again, Would Great Britain stand by France?

Thomas Turney sat on his usual seat, Panama hat on head, his hands clasping his thick yellow lemon stick, his ginger cat as usual squatting underneath the seat, watching feet passing on the gravel path. Mr. Bolton walked up the gully, in covert coat, gloves, and bowler hat, to stop, as usual, and speak with his acquaintances, while Bogey the pug-dog rested in the shade underneath the seat, snuffling beside the cat. On the seat with Thomas Turney sat Mr. Krebs, the pink-bald German. Phillip went to speak to them, while the others were playing. Mr. Krebs did not talk much. Mr. Bolton said that his son had gone off to the London Highlanders camp near Eastbourne, with Peter and David Wallace, and his cousin Hubert Cakebread. "Quite a local contingent."

Phillip said he was going later. Thoughts of sea-bathing and fishing for the rest of the summer enlivened him. Perhaps he could take Timmy Rat!

"Well, whether England comes in or not, the war can't possibly last long, as I was saying," said Thomas Turney. "I give it three months at the outside. No country's economy could stand the strain of a modern war longer. What do you say, Krebs?"

Mr. Krebs sorrowfully shook his big bald pink head. "It is beyond me, Mr. Turney, it is beyond me quite. I am South German, I do not like vaw."

Mr. and Mrs. Bigge passed, the little woman bowing and smiling, the tall gentleman beaming. She said to Phillip, "Now you have your cousin, I expect you're happy, aren't you?"

"Yes, rather, Mrs. Bigge."

Oh hell, the Pyes were approaching. It was too late to get away. He waited, inwardly squirming.

"Ah, Mr. Turney, I hope I find you well! Momentous news, is it not? A challenge which I trust we shall not refuse! I do not think I could properly hold up my head again if we stood by while——" Mr. Krebs looked at his watch, got up, raised his hat, bowed, and walked away.

"Well, goodbye, Gran'pa. I'll see you at Phillipi!" and raising his hat to Mrs. Pye, he hurried back to the grass court, unsquirming as he cursed the image of Old Pye, sanctimonious old humbug, fondling Helena Rolls like that years ago, at his Magic Lantern Party! He felt lithe and vital in his new white flannels, white socks and shoes, Donegal tweed jacket, and Old Boys' silk scarf round neck. If only Helena Rolls could see him! If only

E

Willie could see what a wonderful girl she was. Alas, Helena was
away with her people at Shanklin, in the Isle of Wight.

All day the sun burned bright in the blue spaces of the
wind.

Richard lay back in his deck-chair, his eyes shut. He was
alone in the garden, alone with the hot brilliance upon his face,
alone with his newspaper on the lawn beside him. The nesting
boxes in the elm above were forsaken, the young titmice hatched
and flown. Flowers wilted in the dry beds. The peach espalier
he had trained, years before, against the garden fence, was dead.
It had never borne any fruit, in London yellow clay and acid
smoke.

Beyond the hot gaze of the sun upon closed eyelids, brow, and
face, he felt the glow, the inner shining that still moved him in
the face of the rare, the incomparable Jenny, who had died in her
beauty, so young. She had entered his soul with the first glance
of her tender brown eyes, a glance so loving, yet so self-possessed,
as she took his hand and held it while he congratulated her and
brother John at their wedding. All his young years floated before
him in a golden dream—his mother's death—his empty life until
he met Hetty, so like Jenny, and yet—— There was only one
Jenny. *Ach Isolde, Isolde, wie schön bist du——*

Richard had never told Hetty; but she had divined his feelings
the moment she had seen them together, during that beautiful,
beautiful Lynmouth summer holiday. Poor Dickie, poor lonely
bearded wheat, dreaming of the rose in the hedge!

When Richard awoke, a strange sight met his gaze: a young
cuckoo, brown-barred, was perched on the fence dividing the
gardens. It uttered a thin reeling cry, and a robin flew to feed it.
It cried again, and a hedge-sparrow brought it food. Then it
flew away, and sat in the oak tree at the bottom of the Rolls'
garden.

How could it find its way, alone, to Africa, he thought, and
then, what a wonderful thing was instinct. He would tell the
boys about it at supper. What a jolly little fellow Willie was—
and what a difference he had made already to Phillip. Richard
felt a sudden sense of freedom, the first he had ever felt in his
own home.

Chapter 10

PENUMBRA

RICHARD was not the only one who felt that life was becoming clear at that time. Men who had been familiar strangers for years on the same suburban platform now exchanged the same newspaper opinions. Almost every one of a hundred thousand faces under straw-hats undulating on the pavements of London Bridge bore a look of new resolution, on the Tuesday following the August Bank Holiday.

Phillip and Willie, sharing a newspaper in the train, read that Germany had demanded free passage for her armies through Belgium, against France. "Necessity knows no law", Bethmann-Hollweg, the German Chancellor, had declared in the Reichstag. Belgium had appealed to England for help. And yet Sir Edward Grey had spoken of taking action only if the Germans bombarded the Channel ports!

"I hope to God we declare war, Willie."

"So do I!"

Feeling themselves to be marching, they crossed London Bridge. Phillip pointed out the Tower Bridge, the Monument, and then, his knowledge of guiding being exhausted, they stared at the spars and rigging of ships at wharf, the dingy barges moored in the Pool, the down-river funnels and high white superstructures of steamers.

"You go that way, Willie. Ask a policeman for the Mansion House. Then you can't miss it."

At No. 42 Wine Vaults Lane he dared to ring up Head Office, ask for the Country Department, and enquire of Willie how he was getting on. They agreed to meet for first luncheon.

The room at the top of the Moon Fire Office building in Haybundle Street was cool and airy. Waitresses in grey-and-white striped uniforms, starched white coifs on heads, with discreet smiles put before them ninepenny plates of tongue and green salad, followed by bread and cheese. There were large portions of Gruyère, Gorgonzola, Cheddar, Wensleydale, or Cheshire, of which they might cut as much as they liked.

Phillip ate Gruyère with mustard, having observed, when he had first used the luncheon room, that Costello, who had left

Heath School some years before himself, always had mustard with
that holey cheese. Costello was a first-luncheon man; but they
had seldom spoken. Costello flipped large pieces of Gruyère
spread with mustard into his mouth from the point of his knife,
as a gesture of superiority, or independence, thought Phillip, who
considered it to be rather bad manners. He himself put his cheese,
on broken bread, always unobtrusively into his mouth. Costello
was in the London Highlanders. Today Costello was sitting
beside Furrow, a hefty member of the London Rowing Club, who
actually knew that he, Phillip, was in the same Company, as
himself. Phillip was flattered when Furrow spoke to him.

"Well," he said, on rising, "I expect you've heard that the
Camp has been cancelled? This time next week we'll be somewhere on the East Coast, with any luck."

"Yes, rather!" agreed Phillip.

The cousins arranged to meet again at Head Office after the
day's work. The afternoon in Wine Vaults Lane passed strangely.
Everybody seemed to be out of their offices, talking, looking at
newspapers. The Government had sent an ultimatum to Berlin,
requesting the German Army to evacuate Belgium by midnight.
And the German Army was pouring on through Belgium! It
meant war. Nobody could do any work. Even Mr. Hollis was
absent. There was no paying-in at four o'clock, as all banks were
closed, because of the Moratorium. Phillip went out and got a
newspaper, returning with face tensed as he cried to Mr. Howlett,
"Sir! The King has signed the order for General Mobilisation!"
He felt a chill strike his spine.

"You'd better go, I think, Maddison. There's nothing more
to be done here. Goodness knows where Downham is——"

Phillip said goodbye to Mr. Howlett and to Edgar, and left.

Everywhere in the City streets, as he hurried to Head Office,
were groups of men standing about, talking. He hurried through
the shaded, nearly empty Leadenhall Market, with its high glass
roof and pet-shop at one corner, where Father had bought
Timmy Rat; through Leadenhall Street, down Cornhill, and so
to the Royal Exchange. There a strange sight met his eyes. People
were waving hats and cheering. Soldiers with fixed bayonets were
marching to the Bank of England. People were cheering. It
was terribly exciting. Tramp, tramp, tramp, moving as one man.
The Guards! They were no longer in the familiar red jackets and
black bearskins, but wore flat service caps and khaki trousers

with puttees. Good lord, there was Cranmer! Looking straight ahead, Cranmer with the others wheeled up the narrow street under the high black stone walls of what Gran'pa called the "Old Lady of Threadneedle Street"

"Crikey, my old pal Cranmer, whom I told you about, my corporal of the Bloodhound Patrol, must have joined the army! I haven't seen him since he played footer for the Old Boys' team, so that's where he got to! Fancy Horace a soldier! I vote we don't go home. Let's stay up and see the sights!"

"Rather!"

They climbed on top of a bus going past St. Paul's to the Strand. The Strand was a place he knew to be rather wicked, ever since Father had forbidden Doris to sing the popular song, *Let's all go down the Strand (and have a banana)*. Marie Lloyd had sung it at the Hippo, and added as a leering aside *Have a banana?*, while the trombones went pom-pom-pom-pom-pom, and her blue eyes had glittered with a slow wink, her top teeth sticking out. She was, in Mother's phrase, vulgar without being funny. It wasn't very nice, really. But Doris had been quite innocent of the double meaning; and when she had repeated the words at home, afterwards, and Father had chided her, her face had gone blank, as usual. In the kitchen Doris had said, "I didn't mean any harm, Mum! I don't think it's fair! But Father has always hated me, I know."

They got off at the end of the penny ticket and went to have tea in an A.B.C. shop. "Boiled egg, portion of cottage loaf, with butter and jam, twice please, pot of tea for two." This *twice* business was the correct way to order for two. And when Willie offered to pay, "No, no! It's my treat! I wonder what your friend Jack Temperley is doing now?"

"Helping with the corn harvest, Phil. I say, do you think your regiment will want volunteers? I'd like to join, if I can."

"We're not up to strength in 'B' Company, anyway."

"Do you think they would have Jack?"

"Well, you're supposed to have some Scottish blood, you know. They are fairly hot about not calling it Scotch, by the way. Scotch is used only for whiskey, you know. I say, where are all the people going to? Let's go and see."

They found themselves below Nelson's column in Trafalgar Square. The agitation seemed to be around an old man with a white beard and cloth cap who was speaking with a Scottish

accent that the world could yet be saved from the cataclysm if
only the wor-r-rkers in all countries maintained their solidarity
against the capitalists' greed for expansion! If the wor-r-rkers of
all countries held out against the capitalists' greed to seize the
markets of their rivals! If the wor-r-rkers united themselves against
the capitalists' lust for greater profits! Against their urge to get
greater power to suppress the living standards of the wor-r-rking
classes!

"He's got a red tie on!" said Phillip. "He's like one of the
Socialists on the Hill on Sunday afternoons in winter."

"That's Keir Hardie," a man said, overhearing the remark.

Good lord! Aunt Dora and Sylvia knew him, then! Phillip
looked at the old man with new interest. He was stirred by his
way of speaking. He was startled when some men near him began
to shout against him, "Little Englander!"

There was a scuffle. Men were trying to pull the old man off
the plinth by the lions. His cloth cap, amid jeers and boos, was
thrown into the air.

"Are they going to hurt him?" Phillip asked a policeman near
him. The policeman did not reply.

"Boo! Boo! Boo! Filthy blackguard!"

A man with angry snarling face said savagely to Phillip, "That
creature, to our country's everlasting disgrace, is a Member of
Parliament! Why, he's illegitimate!"

"Move along there! Get a move on!" shouted the policeman.
A terrific agitation of jeers and boos were drowning what Keir
Hardie was saying.

"Lock him up! Why don't you go to Germany? Yah! Boo!"
Fists were held up, the crowd pressed, Phillip was shifted off his
feet. Willie looked very startled, he thought.

Another part of the crowd was now singing *God Save the King*.
The singing spread, the ugly look on faces was gone. Phillip did
not feel like joining in. Now that war was to start at midnight,
he felt only slight chill and fear. Oh God, what would happen?
Then he saw that a cordon of police was pushing itself around
Keir Hardie and the people with him, who had such anxious,
serious faces, with the look of Aunt Dora's in them. The pressure
of the crowd bore them away. Looking back, he saw mounted
police, with them an inspector in blue pill-box hat and tight
tunic with silver buttons, walking their horses into the crowd. It
was awfully exciting, and it was also terrible. Where were the

people all going? He followed, with Willie. The crowd went under a heavy-looking grey arch, and along a straight wide road, with trees lining it, tall cream-painted mansions on one side rising above it. And on the other a park, with trees and grass. It was fun to follow the crowd—suddenly, far away in front was a familiar newspaper-view—good lord, it was Buckingham Palace!

The two boys returned home at twilight, the half-moon hanging in a sky flushed with calm hues of sunset, eager to tell how they had seen the King and Queen come out on the balcony of the Palace, with the Prince of Wales, to the tremendous cheers of hundreds of thousands of people, waving hats and yelling themselves hoarse long after the Royal party had gone in again. But when Doris opened the front door, she put her finger to her lips, and whispered, "Father is playing the gramophone. *Please* don't make a sound, or he'll stop it!"

They went quietly into the sitting-room, where, in the warm twilight of the french windows wide open to the garden, Father's and Mother's faces could just be seen. Most beautiful music, that he had not heard before, filled the room. It made him think of the sun, which was dying, and saying goodbye to the earth, a golden god slain in the darkness. He crept slowly, and very quietly, to be alone on the steps leading into the garden. After the music Father lit a candle by the gramophone in the corner of the room, to see the labels of the records.

"What was that one, Father? Could we have it again, please?"

Strangely, Father actually consented to play it again. He said it was the *Liebestod* from *Tristan and Isolde*. Once again the dying sun was saying goodbye to the earth it loved, since it had made all things on the earth. The strings rose in crescendo, waves of the dying sun-god sinking into the sea; and when it was ended he tip-toed through the room to the front of the house, and from the open window watched the moon of broken silver lying low in the dusk of the calm evening. Voices came from the dark grass, laughter and far-off yodelling cries of happy boys, a star shone very small. He thought of Uncle Hugh, and what he had told him about the South African War.

A low double whistle came from the bottom of the road. He knew that whistle. He jumped over the sill and went down to

meet Gerry, who was walking up, just visible in the darkening
night that was so warm, so alive.

"Hullo, Gerry! Heard the news?"

"Have I not! I'm going to join your little lot tomorrow, with
Bertie."

"Oh, topping!"

He saw the big hanging cloth-shaded light in Mrs. Neville's
flat. Desmond's new friend Eugene was staying for a month at
the flat. He felt a little unwanted. Were not he and Des all in all
to one another? Had Gene, with his queer brownish-yellow face
and little brown eyes, taken his place as Desmond's great friend?
How quickly life was changing. Even with Willie come to live
with them, it was rather sad, when you thought of the old days.
It was rather like the new music Father had played.

When he returned with Gerry, the gas was lit in the sitting-
room and the music over. That was rather sad, too. The solitary
candle-light was gone. It would never be the same moment ever
again. Did a candle-flame sometimes dream of the sun?

He dared to ask Father if he would play the record again; but
Father said, as the keys on his bunch jingled at the gramophone
lock, "No more now, old chap. Doris, it is past your bedtime,
please!"

Doris got up abruptly, said "Good night all," and left the room.

"Well, Gerry, how are you? I suppose you will find yourself in
the Navy before very long, things being what they are?" He
took out his watch. "In two and a half hours, this country will
be at war. The ultimatum expires at midnight."

Phillip felt the cold chill strike him again, as though the sun
was really dying. Darkness! He reassured himself by thinking of
guarding the East Coast. Gerry was saying, "We shall be at war
in one and a half hours, Uncle Dick, surely? Berlin time is an
hour before ours."

Father looked serious, Phillip thought.

"Our ship left Hamburg yesterday morning, got away in time,
I guess, too. The Deutchers are an hour earlier over there. They
wanted to know if we had had special orders to leave, but we
weren't telling!"

"And you had better not tell us, Gerry, old chap! Official
secrets, you know." Father waggled his finger in warning.

When Father had gone out of the room, Phillip said, "Come
on, tell us! Did you have special orders, Gerry?"

"You bet your life we did!"

"Tell us, come on, be a sport!"

"No flies on Winston Churchill, my boy. Well, the square-heads mean business, all right. You should have heard them cheering in Hamburg. Bands playing, and everything."

"What were the special orders?"

"To vamoos like hell, all lights doused except navigation!"

That night, when the others were in bed, Richard went quietly to the front gate, and with a screw-driver removed the ten brass letters of *Lindenheim* from the top bar. Returning into the house, he took out his rifle and inspected it; then his special constable's arm-band, which he had kept in his desk for a quarter of a century. If the Germans made a sudden raid on London in the night, like the Japanese at Port Arthur eight years before, he would be ready to do his duty, if called upon.

"General Mobilisation has been proclaimed by mounted heralds in the City," said Mr. Howlett, returning from luncheon, the next day. "Head Office will lose over eighty men, in all departments. Thank heavens it isn't anywhere near quarter day! By the way, I've got your salary cheque, but I'm afraid the banks are still closed, owing to the moratorium. When they open, there will be no more gold sovereigns, I'm told. Instead, the banks are to issue new one-pound and ten-shilling notes. In the meantime, can I be of any assistance, Maddison?"

"Thank you sir, it is quite all right."

"Well," said Mr. Howlett, "I suppose you ought to report to your headquarters? By the way, at a special meeting today at Head Office, the Directors agreed to pay full salaries of men away in the Army, with all annual rises due to them, for the duration of hostilities. That is, of course, in so far as individual men are required to serve, of course, by the Government."

"Lucky devils!" exclaimed Mr. Hollis, seeing delight in his junior's face. "You'll have three months holiday at the Government's expense—if it lasts so long, that is. You'll be sitting on your bottoms in some Martello tower, waiting for an invasion that never comes, thanking God for the Royal Navy, while Howlett and I sit here in this dark little hole and do the work you and Downham will be paid for, you blighters! Seriously, Maddison," he added, with a smile, "I wish I were twenty years younger. I'd be off like a shot, I can tell you! Then you"—

turning to Mr. Howlett—"would have to do all the work of the Branch!"

"Well," said Mr. Howlett, easily, "it takes all sorts to make a world, and when you get your own Branch, Hollis, you'll be able to have things your own way." And putting a pink cheque on Mr. Hollis' desk, Mr. Howlett went slowly upstairs.

Outside a newsboy was yelling in Fenchurch Street. Without waiting to be told, Edgar nipped out to get *The Pall Mall Gazette*.

Mr. Hollis spread the paper on the counter. Phillip looked over his shoulder.

FIRE AND SWORD IN BELGIUM

GREAT GERMAN ADVANCE

Battle Near Liège

Town Ablaze

Populations Cut Up

Phillip set out, with a curious feeling of being hollow, to Headquarters. In Fenchurch Street a newspaper boy was yelling. He bought a *Globe*, and returned to show Mr. Hollis.

IS LORD HALDANE
DELAYING WAR
PREPARATION?

What Is He Doing
At The War Office?

The Nation Calls for
Lord Kitchener.

"Good God, you back again?" exclaimed Mr. Hollis.

"I thought you'd like to see this, Mr. Hollis."

"That's very civil of you, Maddison. Let's see what it says, shall we, what?"

"H'm, Haldane's pro-German, of course. I remember when he said that Germany was his spiritual home. Time he was kicked out. Time you got to your regimental Headquarters, too, or you'll find you're kicked out."

"Goodbye, Mr. Hollis, once more."

Mr. Hollis gazed at him.

"Goodbye once more, you natural history specimen!"

Just then Downham came in, sporran swinging, neat fawn-spats, glengarry ribands dangling. He pointed at Phillip. "Orders to report at Headquarters forthwith. Hullo, Hollis. I came round to collect my cheque, and to say goodbye. The news is that the German Fleet has come out, and there's been a hell of a scrap in the North Sea! Some of our ships have gone down, and hundreds of transports are steaming for the East Coast and the Thames Estuary!"

"My God!" cried Hollis. "Port Arthur over again! It's that idiot Churchill!"

Upstairs the door opened. "What's that, what's that? Hullo Downham! What did I hear you say?"

Phillip felt as he had felt when, having set the Backfield alight, he realised it was spreading too fast for him to beat it out.

"You'd better go, I think, Maddison," said Mr. Howlett very quietly. "I think I'll get confirmation from Head Office, all the same."

They all stared while he was on the line. "Yes sir. Very well, sir. We shall just have to, that is all. Good day to you, sir."

He hung up.

"Well, I spoke just now to Reed, the General Manager. There's no official confirmation of a naval action, except that a heavy cannonade has been heard all the afternoon off Southend. One of our agents rang up, apparently. Territorials should not wait for mobilisation papers, Reed thinks: the postal arrangements are bound to be a bit late, with the extra work suddenly put upon them. Anyway, as war has been proclaimed, there seems to be no point in delaying. So I suppose this really is goodbye, Maddison!"

Mr. Howlett shook hands first with Downham, then with Phillip.

"Goodbye, gentlemen, for the fourth time," said Phillip, clapping on his straw hat, and quickly leaving the office, not wanting to leave with Downham. He hurried, not to Headquarters, but home.

He was obsessed with an idea that he must get his pair of brogue walking shoes repaired. Those French soldiers, straggling along an open road, from nowhere, in broken boots! If he had extra thick soles, he would be all right.

Immediately after Mrs. Feeney had opened the door to him, he got his brogues and took them to Freeman, Hardy and Willis in the High Street, asking for the thickest possible clump to be put on each sole, and a heavy studding with nails.

This done, he hastened home to try on his uniform. So far he had done no more than take it out of the kit-bag since bringing it home the previous winter. He had been shy of the kilt. He must hurry, to try it on before Father came home. Then he must report at Headquarters.

"Mum, will you give me a hand?"

"Yes, dear, of course." She was curious to know if anything in the way of knickers was worn under a kilt; but forebore to ask, as he took it out of his bottom drawer and laid it on the bed.

"I think I'll have my cold tub first."

Bath over, towel wrapped round middle, he hopped back into his bedroom. He tried on the kilt. It was pleated, pale pinkish grey, rather like the colour of the bells of the ling on Exmoor as they were fading. Wound round the waist, and fastened by two straps, it hung free, though he had a sort of naked feeling until he found the brooch pin which secured the skirt end. He put on the thick woollen hose, held up by garters with forked ends, that showed below the turned-down tops. Then his second-best pair of black calf shoes, and spats to be strapped under the soles and buttoned to just below the calf.

To view the effect he ran up to Mother's bedroom, to look at himself in the long mirror of the wardrobe. Oh, he looked awful! Pigeon chest! Sparrow knees! Owl eyes! He would never dare to go outside like that!

"Well, dear, why not put on shirt and jacket first?" Hetty laughed; but seeing his face, became helpful. Had he not forgotten his pouch? Or did he call it a sporran? He said he did not know. It was used for a purse, anyway. It lay in the corner of the drawer, underneath his old yellow-faded school cricketing trousers. Seeing these, Hetty went out of the room, not wanting him to see her tears.

He fastened on the empty purse; then buttoned up his khaki jacket. He tried the glengarry bonnet with the white-metal badge pinned to its side—the lion of Scotland, the Cross of St. Andrew, and the rather frightening motto.

"May I come in, dear?"

"Yes, Mum. Do I look awful?"

"You look very nice, dear. The kilt suits you. Do come downstairs, and let Mrs. Feeney see before she goes."

Mrs. Feeney, bonnet on head, empty porter bottle and last of the mutton bone wrapped in *The Daily Trident* within her black American-cloth bag, was about to depart out of the kitchen.

"My, you look quite handsome, Master Phillip! Fancy you a sojer! Good luck, Master Phillip! Ah, well! Good-day, m'am! See you next Wednesday, all being well," the old woman cried cheerfully, as she let herself out by the front door.

He went next door to show his new finery to Gran'pa. He found him reading *The Evening News*, which contained a report of gun-fire heard off the coast of Kent, but "further reports of a naval action were unconfirmed." He decided to report the following morning.

Three times that evening he started to leave for a walk on the Hill with his cousin and each time he changed his mind, nervous of what people might think of him. He hung about in the front room, in a mortifying fix, occasionally irritable with his mother; and ashamed of his behaviour before Willie. Finally, he changed back into ordinary clothes when a carriage pulled up Hillside Road, in which were Mrs. Rolls, her two daughters and small son, and their luggage. Mother said they had been recalled from the danger zone, the Isle of Wight being so near Portsmouth, by Mr. Rolls, who for the past hour or so had been clipping the privet hedge in front of his house. Mr. Pye, also, was clipping his hedge immediately below.

It was the presence of the two men that had over-awed Phillip; he had to pass them before reaching the Hill.

He told Willie about Helena; Willie told him about his girl, in Rookhurst, an artist's daughter named Elsie Norman. Mutual confession drew them closer; made the friendship real; and with renewed confidence Phillip leapt upstairs, three at a time, to put on his uniform once again. They went down to Aunt Dorrie's in Charlotte Road, to see if Hubert had any news. There they found not only Bertie, but Mr. Bolton's son.

In the company of Corporal Cakebread and Sergeant Bolton, all three in uniform, Phillip's pride rose up. Bertie, ever friendly, re-adjusted the glengarry bonnet from over his left eye to his right.

"You'll be a credit to the regiment yet, young Phil!"

Over the road, in the garden of the house by the red pillar-box, Peter Wallace and his brother David were also in uniform. They came out, and talked on the pavement. With them was their youngest brother, the tall, lean, buck-toothed Nimmo. Nimmo said he was going up very early on the morrow to try and join. As his father had been a sergeant in the regiment in the old Volunteer Corps days, he probably stood a good chance. He was sixteen, but would pass for nineteen. He was going up on the early workman's tram, to be in plenty of time.

"Yes, the earlier the better," said Sergeant Bolton, "many recruits have applied to join at Headquarters, and quite a number have been turned away."

Willie looked at Phillip.

"Mobilisation notices should arrive tomorrow morning."

Although this had been expected, and accepted, Phillip was stilled by the news. It was so final. General Mobilisation! Tramp-tramp-tramp, of marching men! Somehow——

He went with Willie to see Desmond and Eugene in the flat. Mrs. Neville was alone. She said, "My word, Phillip, you *do* look nice, dear!" Then she said that Desmond was out with Gene, on their bicycles.

"They went fishing, dear, I think to the Lake Woods, anyway, it was to that place you all went to together on Saturday afternoon last. Oh, those roach! How anyone can eat them, I don't know! Even Mazeppa turns up his nose at them, don't you Mazeppa? Well, goodbye, boys, if I don't see you again later on. Desmond and Eugene will be back anytime now."

"I see, Mrs. Neville. I must get my shoes now, I think."

So Desmond had taken Eugene to *his* Lake Woods, to *his* preserves? It was like everything else, the old world he had known, fast falling into pieces.

PART TWO

'THE GREAT ADVENTURE'

" It was then that the country in her need
turned to the despised Territorials."

1914, by F-M Viscount French
of Ypres, K.P., O.M., etc.

Chapter 11

MILITARY ARDOUR

"Mother, promise you won't forget to post on my shoes, will you? It's terribly important! I'll send you an address, as soon as I know where we are going." He hesitated. "May I have a word alone with you?"

Hetty followed her kilted son into the front room, the place of many a secret conference. She must, whatever happened, keep her attitude of cheerfulness. Perhaps the war would end, as Dickie said, after a great naval battle. Such a pity it all was; poor, poor Belgium. She had prayed that Mère Ambroisine and the others at the Convent would be safe.

"Mum, please advise me. Ought I—I mean, dare I—you know, say goodbye to the Rolls? But we hardly know them, do we? And you know what they must think of me."

Hetty looked at her son's face, so anxious under its holiday tan. He was still her little boy, a child at heart, despite his pretended grown-up ways! But she must not show her feelings.

"I think it would be all right, dear. After all, you are going to serve your Country."

"I daren't! You know, don't you, Mother, how I feel? Oh, I must leave now. I shall be late for my train!" He stood there, divided. "Perhaps I might ask Willie to go and ask them first? No, that would look awful! Look, if anything happens to me, will you tell Helena that—no, it doesn't matter. Goodbye!"

He kissed her hurriedly, and turned away, and went out of the house, Willie matching his steps beside him, up to the gully leading to the Hill. She watched them from beside the aspidistra fern on its stand, clasping her hands before her as she tried to restrain her tears. Try as she might, she could not stop thinking of the goodbye of Sidney Cakebread and Hughie, off to the South African War. Now all these boys——

Hetty was smiling when she went back to the others.

Soldiers in uniform, Richard had told Phillip at breakfast, were free to travel in trains and buses, according to *The Daily Trident*. So Phillip, getting into the nearest carriage with Willie (carrying kit-bag)—people smilingly making way for them—rode up to London free in a blue-upholstered first-class carriage, a fact which raised his spirits.

Headquarters was all faces, movement, equipment, rifles, grey kit-bags. The drill hall was portioned off into eight sections, one for each company. Letters on the wall denoted the company areas, "A" on the left to "H" at the far end. He went to "B" Company and was told to draw rifle and bayonet from the Armoury downstairs.

Hundreds of men in all sorts of suits, morning coats, tweed coats, blue serge, carters' jackets, were waiting to join up. Willie stood among them.

Later in the morning, his bayonet was collected, without its sheath, and taken away with many others in a wheel-barrow. They were, said Lance-Corporal Mortimore, to be sharpened on the grindstone. "Useful for opening sardine tins," he said, in his clear, rich voice. He was a dark, jolly fellow, very friendly, often laughing.

After some drill by sections, they paraded outside in the street for a route march. They were in drill order, wearing webbing belts with bayonets only. Rolled greatcoats, water-bottles, entrenching tools, ammunition in side-pouches were left in line on the floor of the company area.

As they marched off, rifles at the slope, angles varying considerably, some people on the pavement cheered. Phillip felt proud to be taken for a real soldier defending England. Led by Captain Forbes, sturdy and red of hair, brows, and moustache—the Fiery Forbes who had led the famous, record-breaking London–Brighton march—they entered a park behind tall railings, through an arch guarded by a policeman. He felt he was seeing the world already, the fabulous West End. They passed carriages driven by coachmen, footmen beside and behind, with folded arms, equipages of the very rich. Most of the carriages were empty; only one here and there contained an old lady, alone, or with a companion. Lance-corporal Mortimore said that the horses were being exercised, as the families were away. He wondered what this meant. The man next to him, with whom he had exchanged names, Baldwin, told him that they were in Hyde Park. The big houses opposite were most of them occupied by millionaires, Park Lane.

"Good lord! Of course!" He stared at them with wonder and amazement, for here came the heroes of magazine stories, poor but aristocratic, handsome and debonair, raising faultless Lincoln Bennetts and often misunderstood by vulgarian millionaire fathers of heroines.

At the other end of Hyde Park some of the beautifully polished carriages were stopped by soldiers. "They're commandeering horses for regimental transport!" said Lance-corporal Morti-more. The word *commandeering* had a familiar, a martial ring about it, from stories of the Boer War in the book *Valour and Victory*, a childhood Christmas present from Willie's father, Uncle John. Phillip thought that Lance-corporal Mortimore must be a very important man in civil life to know so much. He had a crisp clear voice, and urbane bearing.

When "B" Company got back, they piled arms in the drill hall, and before being dismissed, were told to find their own lunches, and to be back at 2 o'clock. They would be paid 2s. a day in lieu of rations for the time being; and £5 10s. for equipment money—shirts, socks, towel, razor and case, table-knife, spoon, fork, comb, clasp knife with tin-opener, tooth brush, shaving brush, and housewife fitted with needles, threads, buttons, etc. Five pounds ten shillings! Plus salary, plus overtime! If the war ended soon, he would buy that wild-fowling gun!

He looked for Willie, but could not see him, so he went off with Baldwin to a Lyons teashop. After poached eggs on toast and an apple dumpling each, they walked around the streets before returning. They saw more drivers of carriages, carts, and even a milk float, being interrogated by soldiers wearing spurs and bandoliers. Baldwin bought *The Pall Mall Gazette* and read out something about a man called Jaurès who had been assassinated in Paris. He had been a traitor, in contact with certain elements in Germany, while the Germans were invading his country.

"They say we have some like that in our country, too," said Baldwin. "I heard that the police raided the crypt of a church in Sydenham, where many Germans went, and found it full of rifles and machine-guns."

"Good lord! That's quite near where I live!" It was just like some of the magazine stories he had read in the past.

"The parson has been thrown into the Tower, so I heard."

They agreed to be friends. Willie was still waiting in the queue when Lance-corporal Mortimore said he had heard the battalion was up to strength. Soon afterwards Willie came over to their part of the hall, and said this was so. They were talking together when the bayonets, each stamped with the number of the rifle, came back in the wheelbarrow. The new edges did not seem very sharp. At four o'clock "B" Company was told that they might go to their homes for the night, and report again at ten o'clock the next morning.

Suddenly Phillip said, "I say, Willie, how about the Moon?"

"Which moon?"

"Our Moon, of course."

"What d'you mean?"

"Did you get permission to join up? I mean to say, well, about your salary?"

"Oh, I asked first. I think I'll try the London Rifles in Sconhill Row. Some of the chaps in my department are in that lot. See you later, at Aunty Hetty's."

Phillip decided to see London by omnibus, since travelling was free. But soon he felt lonely, and seeing a 36 got on it and rode to the bottom of Randiswell Road. He hoped that Desmond and Eugene would see him from the flat window. Would they call out to him? He walked slowly round the corner of Hillside Road, rifle slung over shoulder, feeling depressed. The old place looked very much the same. Thank God he had not gone to say farewell to the Rolls!

Then, hesitating half-way up, he turned back to tell Mrs. Neville his news. He stayed to tea, learning that Gene and Desmond had again gone fishing in the Lake Woods. But they were his woods! While he sat there, unspeaking, he saw Mother coming down the road, with Aunt Dorrie. To surprise them, he gave the family whistle through the open window, and hid. Mrs. Neville said they were looking to find who had whistled.

"Don't keep your mother in suspense, dear. Stand up, there's a good boy. I don't want her to think——"

He showed himself at the window. Mother waved. When he went out to see her, her face was pink, her eyes shining. Aunt

Dorrie, too, seemed glad to hear the news that Bertie and Gerry would be returning that night.

"Well goodbye, Mrs. Neville, if I don't see you again!" he called up to the open window.

"Any message for Desmond, dear?"

"Oh no, it doesn't matter, thank you all the same."

He went to Aunt Dorrie's house, hoping that Petal would be there, to play and sing to him some of her lovely songs by Grieg. Bertie and Gerry had just arrived home. He felt cheered up to see them. The good news was that Gerry had got into the battalion. Young Tommy Turney, the bird's-egg thief, who was big for his age, on holiday from Brighton College, said he wanted to join up too.

"You're too damned young, Tommy, you're only fifteen."

"But Nimmo Wallace is only a year older'n'me!"

Nimmo, being tall, had declared his age as nineteen, and got into the Highlanders.

"I don't think it's fair," said Tommy, "the war will be over soon, and why should I miss the fun?"

The Russians were already advancing into East Prussia, "irresistible as a steamroller", said *The Daily Trident*.

Every morning for a week it was a joke in the family to say, "Goodbye boys, see you tonight!" as Phillip and Willie left for their headquarters in London. Willie, having advanced his age by a year and a half, had been duly sworn into the London Rifles.

All over the London hoardings were large posters of stern Lord Kitchener, menacing eyes and heavy black moustache, pointing at you. He looked like an angry giant. Underneath were accusing words in large black letters.

YOUR COUNTRY NEEDS YOU

The talismanic heavy-soled brogue shoes, for security along some remote and lonely road in retreat, were not yet back. They had been sent away to the Leicester factory, said the branch manager of Freeman, Hardy and Willis. He wore his lighter shoes; they had given him blisters on the daily route marches through the parks of Hyde, Regent, and St. James'. If only his campaign clump soles would come! He must break them in, ready for that dim future ordeal.

One morning they were told that the battalion was to hold itself in readiness to move at an hour's notice; so no-one could sleep at home any more. According to Lance-corporal Mortimore, the battalion transport had its requisite waggons, limbers, and water-cart. This last was the subject of some jokes; large and square, it was of the familiar type used for spraying pink permanganated water to lay road-dust in summer. It bore on its riveted iron sides, in letters of white paint, the words

SHOREDITCH BOROUGH COUNCIL

New and terrible Krupp guns, firing 17-inch shells, had shattered the forts of Liège. They had been kept a secret until the moment of attack. The shells came down direct out of the sky, and broke the steel cupolas under which the guns of the forts were protected. At Dinant, on the Meuse, German officers had raped women in the public square, said *The People*, while private soldiers held the women spread-eagled on the cobbles. Elsewhere German drunkards had cut off the hands of little children, for sport. They had burned down Louvain, and all the art treasures there, like the Goths and Huns of old. That was German *Kultur*! They shot old men and old women, too. "Necessity knows no law." Had not the German chancellor himself said it? Supposing the Germans landed in England!

The battalion moved to an empty school in a City square. Companies slept on classroom floors. He chose a spot next to the fireplace, with Baldwin, to be apart as far as possible from the others. Thank God Baldwin did not snore. The hearth-stone under him was hard and cold. He kept waking up.

During the daytime, another problem. The tops of the lavatory doors were cut off short, the lower ends too, showing feet. When his turn came, he went in, feeling shame, then anguish; he *must* be alone, unseen; his feet would be seen from outside. A face looked over the top, went away, as he stood there. He waited in painful indecision and heard Church, whose face had looked over, say loudly outside, "Choosy sort of cove, isn't he? Waiting for the seat to cool!"

Phillip stood with his toes pointing to the playground for a minute, and then went out. He would wait for the darkness.

Drill, drill, drill on the hot asphalt; squad, left turn, right turn, slope arms by numbers, order arms, present arms by numbers, porte arms; squad, stand at ease, squad, stand easy! Squad, 'shun! Fix!—Bayonets!—the right hand man, Church, runner-up for the company boxing championships, taking three smart paces forward, looking to his front: seizing rifle from the order and placing it between his knees, crouching—right arm held out, looking to his left, while every eye in the squad watched him as a model—the right arm in a semi-circular sweep seizing the bayonet haft—pause—bayonets flashing in the sun— clicking on the locking device of rifle-muzzles—the right-hand man springing to attention again—three paces smartly backwards into line again. Hours of tedious drill upon heat-radiating soft asphalt.

In the yellow coolness of the long summer evenings there were concerts in the playground. They sat around, in little groups, listening in stillness to the singing of Corporal Geddes, of "D" Company—everyone knew his name, because of his exceptionally sweet and tender voice: a silver tenor, said Lance-corporal Mortimore.

I'll sing thee songs of Araby
And tales of far Kashmir

and then, when the quiet clapping and moderated cries of *Encore!* (rather strange after the wild applause at the Hippo) were over, Corporal Geddes sang again.

Little white bride, in the midst of the heather!
Small white window, warm and bright!
Through the cold and the stormy weather
Donald is coming to you tonight!

The first stars were points in the sky above the walled playground.
It seemed strange that the sky, right in the middle of London,
could be a deep indigo blue. Lights gleamed in the streets beyond
the guard at the porter's lodge. Moved and isolated by the tender
floating voice, when it was over he got up and walked to the gate,
as he had several times each evening, in the hope of seeing
Mother's face. He had written her a postcard telling her he was
confined to barracks until further orders, and hinting of being
kept there in case of invasion. Would she ever come up to see him?

The sentry stopped men going out into the street. Would
there be enemy spies, watching what the battalion did? Some
spies had already been shot at dawn in the Tower.

Then there were those hundreds of *en tout cas* tennis courts,
laid at strategic points in private gardens on high ground over-
looking London—Barnet, St. Albans, Hampstead, Sydenham,
Highgate—by Germans before the war as bases for the 17-inch
German howitzers to bombard the capital.

Warehouses on Thames-side had been raided, found to be
filled with German machine-guns, ready for *Der Tag*.

A wireless transmitting set had been discovered in the steeple
of a City church, giving movements of troops.

One of the King's uncles, in the Royal Navy, was a German;
he ought to be kicked out of it.

Bread shops in the East End had been wrecked, after children
had been poisoned with arsenic put in the flour by the German
owners of the shops. These and many other rumours had passed
over the hot asphalt.

Germans were being killed in thousands, in tens of thousands,
as they advanced, sometimes drunk on ether, arm in arm to
meet the death-dealing fire of *mitrailleuse* and *Creusot* rifle of the
gallant allies fighting for Civilisation, while cowardly German
officers, ready to shoot anyone wavering, followed on behind,
wearing jackboots and monocles, fighting for Barbarism.

He saw Bertie near the gate. Did he know why they were
being kept in London? Was it in case of a desperate last throw
of the Germans, invading across the North Sea?

"Well, the fact is, old man," said Corporal Bertie Cakebread,
"the water-cart of the Shoreditch Borough Council has sprung
a leak, and Billy Bolton the sergeant is trying to swop it for one
belonging to the Marylebone Borough Council. No, joking
apart—we haven't got our horses yet."

Bertie had transferred to the transport section, under his friend Sergeant Bolton, who was going to be made a second-lieutenant, he said. Fancy Mr. Bolton's son an officer!

He returned, cheered by meeting Bertie. Another man was now singing *Glorious Devon*, followed by *Drake Goes West*. He cried *Encore* with the others, and clapped, as befitted one having a particular interest in both subjects.

Yellow light over the Square changed to a penumbral green, then imperceptibly to a dusk of blue above black outlines of spire and roof and chimney pot. Baldwin and he went to their room as the thrilling *Last Post* of buglers echoed around the shadows. Time to get down on the floor again, to try and sleep, after thinking of home, Mother. Newspapers laid over the stone made it a little less cold, in the wakeful early hours of the morning.

Perhaps Mother would come on Sunday. After breakfast, there was a battalion parade in full marching order. First the cyclist section, then pipers and drummers followed by buglers with burnished copper bugles on green tasselled cords, then the Commanding Officer, the Earl of Findhorn on his charger, Adjutant beside him. The second-in-command, nicknamed the Iron Colonel, stern-looking martinet with heavy brown hongroised moustache, hero of the Boer War, waited on a high grey horse at the gate, to take up the rear. He was an honorary Colonel. Phillip regarded him with a mixture of awe and pride. He looked made of iron.

As they marched through Regent's Park, behind the pipers playing *The Road to the Isles*, to the lifted hats of men on the pavements, he felt the pride of being a London Highlander. Thrillingly he looked back and saw the long column of tramping men, swinging kilts and sloped rifles, company after company, all in step. His blisters were still raw under the 'New Skin' plaster he had put on them; but when his feet were hardened, things would be all right. Why did not Mother send his campaign clumps? He tried not to step otherwise than full on the ball of each foot, but it was agony. The day was extremely hot, his pack heavy, tunic under webbing belt clammy with perspiration. The pouches, with their fifty rounds of ammunition on each side, in clips of five brass cartridges with round-nosed nickel bullets, made his shoulder bones ache. O, for a pint of shandy-gaff, he could drink it all straight down. A hot breeze rustled the dry leaves of the trees, a harsh sound. Left-right, left-right, the man in front bobbing up and down, kilt swinging, would this spittle-frothy route march never end? O, to be in the Lake Woods, fishing under the rhododendron bushes, free to go anywhere, like Desmond and his new friend Eugene.

After dismissal by companies there was a rush for the chained, heavy iron cups in the playground; O, so slowly did the push-taps pour, would it never be his turn, O the scorching asphalt playground under his flaming blisters.

Phillip and Baldwin were now good friends: the friendship of young men without egotism, confiding in one another, yet retaining each his soul in privacy. Truly they were private soldiers. Baldwin was fair-haired, round-headed, slow in speech, sturdy and strong. He played rugger for the Harlequins, and was in shipping insurance at Lloyds.

Rumours came fast in the afternoon. The General was coming; the Bishop of London was coming; there had been a great victory in France; the Russians were deep into East Prussia; Prince Louis of Battenberg, after sending Naval Defence Plans to Berlin, had been put in the Tower.

The second rumour came true. The Bishop, surplice over khaki service jacket with its black badges of a chaplain-colonel, addressed the battalion. Officers with gold-leaf cap-peaks and red tabs stood behind him. The Bishop spoke from a trestle table on the justice and righteousness of the war to stop aggression, to uphold the Christian ideal against the false doctrine that Might was Right. He who draws the sword shall perish by the sword, was his text.

Never before, he declared, in the known history of mankind had a nation's conscience been clearer upon the issues involved— between supercession of God before national militaristic idolatry on the one side, and intercession on behalf of civilisation based on Christianity on the other; between the forces of Satan, and the commandments of God.

"This leads to the question which every man listening here, now, must put to himself: Is it not better for the defence of Britain, for the preservation of your cities and homes, to slip over the 'silver streak' and meet the enemy on the continent, rather than wait for the enemy to come across and treat our cities, our homes, our mothers, wives, sisters and sweethearts, as the French and Belgian women had been treated? Let every man hearkening to these words of mine ponder in his own heart and decide in his own conscience whether or not he should volunteer for service abroad. The General Officer Commanding the London District has asked me if I will do this; and having examined my own heart, and after prayer to God for guidance, I have replied, that I am myself ready and willing to serve the troops of the London Division in the field, if so I should be ordered.

"The Territorials, or such of you as may volunteer, will in all probability be employed on lines of communication, in order to release regular soldiers for the firing line, in the great and difficult fighting that is to come, when the main Armies are joined in battle."

The Bishop then uttered a prayer. The sun shone on his white hair as he bowed his head. When he got down from the trestle table, Phillip could see that he was receiving the thanks of the General, the Earl of Findhorn, and the Iron Colonel.

Both these awesome figures, their left breasts adorned with South African War ribbons, the sleeve-cuffs of their cutaway jackets braided with four speckled khaki bands, each with its embroidered cloth crown and stars, their tartan breeches and highly polished riding boots and spurs, had made a deep impression on Phillip. He regarded them as almighty beings from another world. The company officers also were from that other world, high above him. Their faces were different from those of ordinary people. They looked cleaner, somehow, although not all were good-looking. Many of them, he imagined, lived in Park Lane, and, until the war, their hats were faultless Lincoln Bennetts. No doubt they drank champagne with their evening dinners in expensive hotels of the West End.

While they stood easy, Phillip asked Baldwin what Captain Forbes did in private life. "Or has he a large private income, perhaps?"

"He's a partner in one of the oldest firms 'in the House'—the Stock Exchange. Morty's father is 'in the House', too; but Morty's on the stage."

Phillip was surprised to learn that all the officers had served in the ranks, it being a rule of the regiment.

"What, the Earl of Findhorn, a ranker!"

"No, the C.O. is always a regular, usually a Coldstreamer."

"How about the Iron Colonel?"

"I don't know, Phillip."

"Oscar Hatton?" said Mortimore, overhearing. "He joined as a private, after Charterhouse and Heidelberg, in eighteen seventy-nine. That makes you think, doesn't it?"

"Eighteen seventy-nine! Thirty-five years ago! But he has still got brown hair!"

At this point "Colours" said quietly, "Pay attention, men. Stand at ease, Captain Forbes wishes to say something."

Beside Captain Forbes stood Lieutenant Ogilby, both wearing swords in polished brown leather scabbards.

"Now, men, about volunteering for foreign service—it is realized, of course, that some of you have domestic and other responsibilities which must weigh in any decision you may make. On the other hand those of you who feel themselves free, and are nineteen years of age or over, can give in their names to me now."

Fiery Forbes had got so far when the battalion sergeant-major, a massive figure wearing a Sam Brown belt, sporran, and glengarry like those of the officers, approached to give Captain Forbes one of those salutes which, it was said, almost made the asphalt playground open in cracks. He was from the Coldstream, and had a line of campaign ribbons across his left breast, the first one being, according to Mortimore, for the landing at the Battle of Hastings. He had a very big head, and a moustache on his huge upper lip like a hedgehog. Each of his cheeks was ruddy-brown as a crab-shell, so was his thick neck, which seemed longer behind than in front, since he carried his head very upright with chin held down. When he gave an order, it was always out of the side of his mouth, his upper lip screwed sideways and his teeth showing—a fearsome figure, speaking in bolts or jerks of roaring, harsh Glasgow accent.

Cane under left arm, standing rigid, the battalion sergeant-major barked, "With the compliments of the Adjutant, sir! The Commanding Officer to address the battalion, sir! The Adjutant will take the parade, sir!"

In tense silence "B" Company waited, listening.

Phillip felt that something had happened. Perhaps the Germans had landed on the East Coast.

Captain Forbes ordered "B" Company to stand at ease. His eyes were bright, he looked alert.

The Adjutant called the battalion to attention. All down the square the company commanders reported, in turn, that their companies were present and correct. Then the Adjutant turned to the Colonel and saluted him. "The London Highlanders are present and correct, sir!"

"Thank you, Captain Menzies."

"London Highlanders!" cried the Colonel. "I need hardly add to what the Lord Bishop of London has already told you. It is a great honour for this battalion to be selected for foreign service, and in keeping with the high standards the regiment has always maintained since its foundation by the Highland Society, in association with the Caledonian Society, over half a century ago. This is a moment to recall to you the fact that Scotland and France have been traditionally friends for centuries, ever since Douglas and Sinclair rode with Jeanne d'Arc and Dunois at Orleans and Beaugé. Our friendship has endured up to, and beyond, the Union with England. We Scots, as well as those of you who are of Scottish origin, know very well that Scotland largely owes its existence today to that friendship. We have a chance now to show our gratitude in a practical way, when France, with Belgium, is fighting for her life against a ruthless invader determined to destroy her national existence, and ours with it."

The Colonel held up a piece of paper. In the silence Phillip could hear the chirping of sparrows among the chimney pots of the school buildings, with the thudding of his heart. In a louder voice the Colonel cried,

"London Highlanders! News has just been received that the British Expeditionary Force has since this morning been in action against the enemy!"

There was a depth of silence after this announcement: then wave upon wave of cheering broke out among the lines. Arms arose, holding aloft glengarries. Baldwin cheered and waved beside Phillip, who felt himself like a speck of chilly dread among the gleeful excitement. He saw a flight of pigeons, passing overhead, suddenly flutter to the break-up, and turning, fly rapidly away. Then the massed excitement took him and he shouted with the rest.

Five minutes later, stepping up to where Fiery Forbes stood, "Colours" beside him with note-book, he said he would volunteer

for foreign service. Then stepping back a pace, he saluted: and
it was Baldwin's turn. They had agreed to go together.

It was rather strange to learn who had not volunteered. Lance-
corporal Mortimore said he was expecting his commission to be
gazetted: and several others, who looked big and strong, had
decided for Home Service. Among them was Downham. He
was a single man, and like Lance-corporal Furrow of Head
Office, a member of the London Rowing Club. It was all a bit
of a surprise, for many of the smaller chaps, not looking half so
strong, like Kirk and Blunden, had put down their names. Even
so, what had he done? What would Mother say? He had
thought that everyone else would volunteer, and had not liked
to appear different. But when he heard that the three Wallace
brothers had volunteered, as well as Bertie and Gerry and
Sergeant Bolton, Phillip felt reassured.

Soon afterwards Gerry sought him out to say that Aunt Hetty
and Aunt Dora were waiting by the gate. Hurrying thither, he
told them what he had done. Then seeing Mother's rather sad-
smiling face, he felt slight panic. Bayonets! His panic was controlled: but it showed itself in the sharpened features, and
clenched hands, as observed by both women. To Dora, he was
still the unhappiest little boy she had ever seen.

"Perhaps I can take it back, Mum. I can ask 'Colours'."

"You must do what you think right, Phillip, of course,
naturally," said Hetty.

Newsboys in the street beyond the sentry were shouting. They
listened.

BRITISH EXPEDITIONARY FORCE IN ACTION!

"My heavy shoes, where are they? Why have you not brought
them up for me, as I asked repeatedly? I must have them, I
must!"

"They will come soon, I expect, dear. The man in the shop
said the factory had a lot of orders for the Army."

"I knew that would happen!" he said, with strained look.
"That's why I took them at once! Oh well, I must say goodbye
now," he said, unable to bear the further thought of being seen
talking to his mother at the gate.

When they had gone, he wandered about the playground with
Baldwin. He did not speak to the Colour-sergeant. "Colours"

would suspect him of being what he was, and always had been, cowardly.

As far as that went, Phillip deceived himself: for the Colour-sergeant, a married man with three children, had not volunteered.

Chapter 12

AS IN TWO GLASSES

THEODORA MADDISON left her sister-in-law at Charing Cross, out of consideration for Hetty's feelings having refrained from saying what she believed: and suffering because of the self-imposed restriction. Poor Hetty, she thought, poor Hetty; all that little mother could do now was to hope and pray. It would be a crime to enlighten her about the dreadful reality of the war, which was sweeping away more and more people in its evil deluge of hysteria, and darkening the very sun of truth.

She had listened to the Bishop's address, keeping silent afterwards. She tried to reassure Hetty by a calm and unruffled presence. She must dissemble her real thoughts. What did the Bishop know of living truth? Had he not visited Holloway Prison seven months before, and declared after his "investigation" that the "alleged ill-treatment" of Suffragettes had no basis in reality? The rich and the comfortable lived in an entirely different world. It was easier for a camel to go through the eye of a needle, than for a rich human being to know the truth of Christ. Theodora, making her way back on foot to Old Ford, heard again the sudden cheering, saw the wild delight, the excitement, as part of the maniac flashing of bayonets throughout the world.

In the grey city of Dublin, before the outbreak of the war, she had watched a grim prelude of what was to come. The voice of a half-starved child still haunted her, as it cried out from among the crowd to the English soldiers marching to the docks. *You killed my father!* The tattered mite had shaken her small fist at the hard faces below the undulating, sloping frise of bayonets fixed on rifles at the slope. She and Sylvia had been at the inquest of the Dubliners killed when the troops had fired into a crowd. The jury had been magnanimous, blaming not the soldiers, but the Government, declaring that the military were illegally on the streets.

The scenes at the boat station had been of the same spiritual devastation. Dense, dark crowds swayed before the big locked door, an almost senseless packed mass of reservists in civilian clothes, younger soldiers in khaki; children screaming in the pressure of bodies, drunken men cursing and quarrelling; white-faced babies carried on the shoulders of women blasphemous, piteous, or praying aloud to the Saints and the Mother of God. Periodically the great door opened as though to Gehenna, revealing a double line of burly uniforms of the Royal Irish Constabulary. For hours the struggle seemed to go on, thousands of people fighting to get past the door through which, she thought, not one of them truly wanted to go.

When at last she and Sylvia got through to the other side, the scene on the platform and around the booking counters was of a deeper sadness. Hundreds of drunken soldiers lurching about arm in arm, caps on backs of heads; staggering, glass-eyed, as they sang, or spewed. Many were lying down in pools of their own urine upon the platform. Oaths, curses, swinging blows upon heads and bodies; wailing of little frightened children, weeping red-eyed mothers. They behave like that because they do not think, Sylvia's voice said beside her. But they *dare* not think, she replied; and that was why not one man, or woman or child among them all was doing what he or she wanted to do.

To Dora the scene at the boat-side was the climax of the Aeschylean drama. Here women in the poorest clothes, wives of men, surplus of the labour market, who had taken the King's shilling as an alternative to starvation—here the women had broken through the thin, undernourished restraint which had buoyed them white-faced and staring until then. They clung with loud sobs and moans to their men. Some of the younger ones, who had not been able to get up the gangway to the ship, in despair of being able to pick out a loved face in the immense mass of figures crowding the rails high above, were sobbing, faces in hands, doubled up, against the walls of a warehouse. O, the sad gestures of love!

And then, in the strange manner of humanity, as the ship was under way, slowly edging from the quay, a transformation had come about in the spirit of place and scene; and into her mind had come the Latin tag, *Dolor decrescit*, for at some point, starting either on the ship or from the quay, people began to wave and cheer; and the emotion spread until every ship in harbour and in dock was blowing its sirens, answered by short jubilant blasts from the departing transport. Minute after minute the excitement was kept up; and when at last Kingstown had receded and the wake was spreading wider and smoother to the Irish shore, then within the ship could be heard shouted tuneless choruses, aimless yelling, discordant cheering.

So the evening came on. As she stood upon the small enclosed cabin-class deck, she noticed, with a sense of premonition, that the planets Mars and Venus were in conjunction, low in the north-west. Did the planets affect human life, indeed all life, upon the inhabited earth, as the Ancients had thought? The moon visibly did so: Diana ruled the tides, some said the seasons of seeding and fertility; and the menstrual life of women, linked to the periods of the moon, was a fact that needed no proof. Mars and Venus together, sinking down to the ocean, their lights a reflection from the sun certainly; but so was the light of the moon.

Ah, there was the moon, near to the full disc, rising up over unseen England—England, land of her fathers, country of great wealth side by side with abysmal poverty, at war with the country of her mother's family, cousin nation against cousin nation! She thought of her friends in Austria and France, in Hungary and Greece, in Italy and Germany; of those members of the League of Youth in Vienna, so ardent for beauty to come into the lives of the people, for universal peace in which to build a life based on the age-old dreams of the artists and poets, from the dawn of Hellas and onwards down the centuries of nearly three millennia of great visions of ineffable beauty. Was Europe to suffer the fate of the Greek City States, warring one with another until even the radiance of Hellas was extinguished?

In the East End of London, Sylvia and Dora found on their return a dilemma which at first very nearly daunted even those dedicated women. Hundreds of reservists had been called to the colours, and their families were left entirely without support. Women were starving, for many of the factories where they had worked were closed, in panic of the unknown. A man earning fourteen to eighteen shillings a week before the war, sole support of wife and half a dozen or more children, had not been able to save. Prices had risen sharply in the shops on the day after war was declared; and they went on rising daily.

As soon as it was known that Sylvia was back—for she was

the leading spirit in the women's political movement—her premises were thronged with white-faced mothers, some with babies in arms, others in rickety prams and so weak that they had ceased to grizzle. O, the pity of the little discoloured bundles of skin and bone, regarding her with the sad eyes of age, lying helplessly in muted weakness!

As the hot August days went on, some families were threatened with eviction unless the weekly rent, which had taken up to a third of the former weekly wage, was paid. There was a small unemployment benefit available to a few trades, under the National Insurance; but this affected only about one family in six. Again, Poor Law relief applied only to the crippled, not to the "able-bodied"; so this could not help the wives whose men had gone.

Breasts of nursing mothers shrunk bag-like from lack of food. Dora sold some of her few remaining securities, inherited from her father. They were sold far below their peace-time value; still, bread and milk must be bought. Sylvia opened a depot; the news spread swiftly; long queues of mothers, with prams and soap-boxes on wheels—the trollies which had taken piece-work garments to clothing factories and shops—formed outside the old house.

A letter was sent to *The Times*. Money came by post, enough to revive hope. A milk centre was established. *Sylvia will save us* ran the wild, hopeful cry through the streets.

Old people, as they waited for bread, told of the corn-fields they had known as children, when the old ford was across the stream which was now the canal. Behind the house was a decaying small hall, turned into a meeting room before the war. Its rough interior brick walls were colour-washed. At one end was a platform; at the other a wooden archway with niches wherein stood plaster casts of Greek figures—the Venus de Milo, Homer, the Delphic Apollo among them. Into this hall shuffled the head of the queue, through the house from the open front door: young mothers, lily-pale of face, bearing themselves with such fortitude, she thought. She was inspired by their patience, by their beauty as of twilight before the halls of Aides; their eyes dark-ringed, brow and cheek of Persephone lost to the sun. What pride they had! Tidy clothes, however poor and worn, clean aprons over threadbare shirts, hair closely braided, or twisted tight in curling pins! They were neat, they were presentable even on the brink of collapse, out of respect for themselves and for their adored leader. *Sylvia will save us.*

Some of the infants, their legs no thicker than a man's thumbs, were too ill to digest cow's milk. What was wanted was albumen water. In Sylvia's weekly broadsheet appeals were made for eggs. A clinic was formed, a woman doctor gave her services. How could they be found *work*? "Everything pawned, and nothing coming in." It was a common statement.

One woman, expecting a baby, another in her arms, three mites hanging to her skirts, fainted in the queue. Another with six young children, two of them twin babies, said that for nearly three weeks they had been fed only on boiled white bread. Prematurely aged, the young mother lived in dread of eviction from her one tenement room wherein always by day and night arose the whimper of hunger. A third, also with six children, had had no food for four days.

And yet—and yet——

"But look what the Germans are doin' in Belgium, miss!"

"Alf Burgess dahn our street bin'n lost 'is job, why don't 'e go for a sojer? A big strong man like 'im, eating food what's needed for the children, 't'aint right, miss!"

Alfred Burgess came to see Sylvia. Before the war he had aided the suffragette movement—and lost several jobs on account of his loyalty. He was white to the lips with starvation. "What do I do, miss? Even the missus says as 'ow I ought to go, miss." Later that morning Alfred Burgess, his wife's nerve-thin nagging yet audible in his mind, had gone for a soldier, feeling he had betrayed Sylvia. O for the pen of Euripides!

"Their minds cannot hold out against hysteria, and the lies of the yellow press, Dora. You see, they will not even save themselves! Their loyalties are divided between our movement, and what they think of as their country. Their country—look at it——" Sylvia pointed at the shabby street, the decaying houses, the melancholy and patient mothers waiting in the queues. What would be the end of it all? What would happen to Sylvia? Dora saw her as one pre-destined to be crushed by the dark forces. Her mother and sister, both militant sufferers in the cause before the war, had already publicly disclaimed her.

But the little body known as Grannie Nobbs was of undefeatable stuff. She came to whisper, bonnet nodding, that coppers' narks had been planted among the mothers. "I'll mother'm, I will! But look out, Miss Sylvia, don't say nuffink to strangers abaht th' war bein' all wrong, see? If 'ey do arst yer, tell'm vose

what arst no questions'll be to'd no lies, see?'' Black tags of her
bonnet shaking grimly, Grannie Nobbs, black shawl over black
bodice, shuffled away.

An old man with weary eyes in a face of great beauty and
suffering, his white and silky hair giving him the look of an old
North Country sheep-dog who had lost his sheep, appeared one
day. His eyes brightened when some of the mothers exclaimed,
"Gawd bless yer, Mr. Keir Hardie, sir!"

To Sylvia he said, in private, "I have heard that a lot of our
lads have fallen down out there."

The old man sat still on a wooden chair for some time; then
with a long sigh, as he rose to go he said, "As Jaurès remarked
before the hand of the assassin struck him down, 'Away and seek
pardon of God and man'."

"You know," said Dora, "I have a feeling that the corner has
been turned, dear Sylvia. The first confused rushing of the un-
prepared to meet the unimagined is over. Have you read Queen
Mary's Message to the Women of Great Britain? How simply
it is worded; I am sure she wrote it herself."

In the firm belief that prevention of distress is better than charity,
I have inaugurated the "Queen's Work of Women Fund". Its object
is to provide employment for as many as possible of the women of
this country who have been thrown out of work by the war.

I appeal to the women of Great Britain to help their less fortunate
sisters through this Fund.

"That is all very well in so far as it goes," remarked Sylvia,
"but what is it but charity? It is only a sop to us, because we
have shown that we refuse to accept the Gadarene Rush to
destruction."

"A sop to us? It is giving a lead to the entire country, surely?
After all, dear Sylvia, it is what you have done here in the East
End. Now through the Queen, who has a sense of high duty, the
nation will be awakened to its responsibilities."

"I have no quarrel with the Queen. She is both gracious and
her life is ruled, as you say, by a sense of high duty. But the
Crown is, after all, only a figurehead. It is the System that must
be changed. I shall continue to oppose the war and the ideas
of the entire nation while the continuance of the war is being

urged. In this I am with Keir Hardie. Dora, in his eyes when he came here yesterday I saw death. He is stricken in his soul. Now if you will excuse me, I have some work to do.''

Dora knew that Sylvia was near the point of exhaustion herself. She seldom slept for more than an hour or two at a time. Often her lamp was burning until the small hours, into the dawn and the day, while she sat at her table, papers everywhere, envelopes, pamphlets, articles for her weekly broadsheet, begging letters, letters written to men, called up, on behalf of wives who could not write themselves, or lacked paper and penny stamp. If she was curt at times, was it not the momentary rigidity of one steeling herself for the "mental fight" of William Blake, "till we have built Jerusalem, In England's green and pleasant land"?

Later, when a committee was proposed to look after the district east of Aldgate, and Sylvia was asked to sit on it, Dora received a slight shock to see that the letter came from a Lady Tofield. She must be, she thought, the wife of the son of the man who had bought all the farms but one of her father's property in Rookhurst. The Tofields were brewers, and wealthy people. Now that war had come, at least farmers would have a good market for their produce, after the long years of Free Trade, which had brought riches to the new industrial classes, but impoverishment to the countryside where there was no wealthy man to act the squire.

What a pity it was that the family property had had to be sold! Phillip and William should now be at the university, afterwards to set-to and farm the land in partnership; instead, both had become two very young urbanised pawns in what was basically a European Industrialists' War, for markets, Germany being the latest competitor.

And having restored the balance of her mind according to her ideas, Dora went to look after her babies in the clinic.

The War Office announced that separation allowances were to be paid to the wives of men called up or enlisted: one shilling and one penny a day for the wives and an additional two pence a day for boys under fourteen and girls under sixteen. The soldiers might allot to their families, further, up to half their pay, which was a shilling a day. There were inevitably long delays in these payments; while rent of up to six shillings and sixpence a week must be met.

Lady Tofield's Committee had not yet been formed, let alone done anything. So Dora sold more of her depressed Consols, and went out among her few remaining friends, begging.

On Sunday afternoon she visited Hetty, who gave her five pounds.

"It is out of the little nest-egg Mamma left me, so it is quite all right to give it to you. But you won't mention it to Dickie, will you, Dora? You see, he thinks I have no idea of the value of money. Perhaps that is so; but I am sure Mamma would be glad to know that the poor little children will be fed because of it." Hetty was thinking of Phillip, when he had been born, wasting away because she could not find the right food for him.

She went next door to see Mr. Turney, who wrote her out a cheque for ten pounds, asking her not to make it known.

"I don't want to be besieged by beggars, he-he-he!" Then seeing Dora's face at this unguarded remark, "Things will come right, Dora, don't you worry over-much. The Government has an immense amount of work on its hands, and it takes time to organise under entirely unforeseen conditions, y'know. This war will make a lot of changes—it has already put my three grand-sons into kilts, Scotsmen all, he-he-he! War, like roguery, makes strange bedfellows. Stay to supper, won't ye? Marian has got some macaroni-cheese baking in the oven, with sliced tomatoes on top: 'twill do you good, I say. Bolton is coming, have ye met him? His boy's another Scotsman for the duration! Bolton saw them all marching through the Green Park the other afternoon, and a fine sight they were, too, he tells me, pipes skirling and kilts swinging. I've just been reading again that passage in Henry the Fifth, before Agincourt. Wonderful stuff, wonderful! The Prince of Wales, now, I wonder what part he will play in the war? M'friend on the Hill, who is reporter to *The Morning Post*, tells me the Army is in France, but the Prince wasn't allowed to go with his regiment, the Grenadier Guards."

The old man fell into a reverie. When he looked up he said, "Why, bless my soul, surely you were here, Dora, when I read the prologue before Agincourt, the night that Sidney Cakebread and m'boy Hughie were leaving for South Africa? Of course you were, I recollect now. Newman was here, wasn't he, yes; and Sarah——"

He took out his red silk handkerchief and wiped his eyes.

Dora thanked him again for his gift, saying it would bring such happiness to so many; and leaving the room, went into the kitchen to say goodbye to "my dear, dearer, dearest adopted Aunt Marian," whom she hugged, being hugged in return.

Mr. Turney called her into the front room as she was about to leave.

"This bread question will ease up, you know, when the United States grain shipments reach our ports. The *Telegraph* said some days ago that it was a record wheat crop this year. Competition will bring down prices, and I shouldn't be surprised if the Government puts on some sort of control, as it has already for bacon, margarine, and sugar."

"And a jolly good thing, too, Mr. Turney! The Canadian exporters declared their solidarity with the Mother Country almost as soon as war was declared, but that did not prevent them from substantially putting up their prices, well knowing that they had nothing to fear in competition with the Central European grain harvest!"

"Ah ha, I know what you are thinking, Dora! But reflect a moment that it was Free Trade that kept the prices down, in the normal course of buying in the cheapest market, before hostilities upset the balance!"

"The Shop Assistants' Union has complained, Mr. Turney, that many of their members have been put on half-pay 'on account of the war', yet it is noticeable that the shops have also raised their prices."

"Supply and demand, Dora, supply and demand! As I said just now, everything is abnormal. No one knows from one minute to the next what is going to happen. Things will settle down. The cry is already, 'Business as usual.' I see Kitchener has appealed for another hundred thousand men; their going will further add to the dislocation. People think it is going to be a short war, but I am beginning to doubt it. Both the Germans and ourselves are very strong. As for Russia, I don't have all the faith in Russia that the papers seem to have. Her industrial strength is not very much, and it will be industrial strength that will tell in the end, you mark my words. Steel!"

Theodora smiled wanly as she thought of bayonets. "Let us hope that all people will come to their senses, Mr. Turney, very soon."

"I wish I could think so, too, Dora, but facts rule this world, you know, my girl, not theories. Are you sure you won't stay and take some macaroni pie? The Germans will be buying up all they can, I expect, from Italy. Won't you change your mind?"

She thanked him once more for his kindness and generosity, and went next door. Unfortunately she allowed herself to be drawn into an argument with Dickie, a foolish thing on her part, as it upset Hetty. Together they went to London to see Phillip.

The next evening Richard remarked to his wife,

"Dora had better look out for herself, now that this second Defence of the Realm Bill has become law. It declares here that anyone found to be spreading 'reports likely to cause disaffection or alarm among any of His Majesty's forces, or among the civil population'—as the act declares—can be arrested and tried in the ordinary course of the law."

"Oh, I am sure Dora would never do anything like that, Dickie."

"Well, I am not so sure."

A few minutes later he found more in *The Daily Trident* with which to justify himself. "Listen to this, Hetty! It is from an article by Lady Frances Balfour. I think it disposes of Dora's exaggerated claims for her 'deserving poor'.

"Let there be no complaining in our streets. Women can save the situation by accepting it. We have heard of women giving tongue over the counter because the full tale of their goods could not be delivered at the usual price. Such people are as deserving of being treated as deserters as ever any soldier is who runs from the rifle fire of the entrenched position he has to take."

Hetty was saved from reply by double *rat-tat* on the front door. She hurried up the stairs; but Doris from the front room got there first.

"A postcard from Phillip, Dickie! Would you like to read it?"

"You read it out, old girl. After all, he's your best boy."

"'Everything all right. *Send my campaign clumped brogue shoes as soon as you get them.* Great concentration of troops to the coast any moment now. Also post my Civic pipe with brogues. Tell Father to get a pull-through for his rifle. Please don't join a Ladies' Rifle Club, the kick would dislocate your shoulder. Hope all are well, including the Girls, Timmy Rat, and Gran'pa. Love to all, Phil'."

Richard laughed. "He's developed a pawky sense of humour, since wearing the kilt, hasn't he?" He picked up his paper once more. "Funny that he should mention the Women's Rifle Club —one has been formed, you know, by the Amazons. Pity Dora doesn't join, too. I wonder why he suggests a pull-through for my rifle—I am not likely to lose it, now Master Phillip is no longer here."

"I expect Phillip meant it kindly, dear."

"Of course I know that! Do you think I am a fool? There is no need for you to defend him to me, anyway."

"Of course not, dear, naturally. Well, I think I'll go and see Papa for awhile, Dickie, he does so look forward to his game of bezique. I'll be back in time for a game of chess."

She took the postcard with her out of the room. He had wanted to read it himself, to look at the post-mark, at his son's handwriting; but it was addressed to the boy's mother, and not to him; and she had a perfect right to keep it to herself.

Hetty came back into the room. "How silly of me," she said. "I was taking Phillip's card with me. Perhaps you would like to see it, dear." She put it beside him on the tablecloth, while he continued to read his paper.

"Thanks," he said, as she was going out of the door. "Oh, before I forget it, what about those campaign clumps of his? He seems most anxious about them."

"I got them this morning, and posted them off, Dickie, straight away."

"What were they like?"

"The soles seemed to be nearly two inches thick, Dickie."

"Good heavens, I thought he was now a Scotsman, not a Dutchman!"

He waited until she was gone before he took up the postcard, an expectant light in his eyes.

Chapter 13

ELASTIC-SIDED HIGHLANDER

PHILLIP's faith in heavy-nailed campaign clumps was gone by the time the battalion reached the granite-setts of London Bridge at half-past six on the summer morning. The sun was already hot in the eastern sky above the Tower Bridge. There were a few people about to cheer the skirl of pipes and tramp of feet; but enough to make him proud of being a London Highlander, to forget his disappointment in the shoes. But by the time the battalion had marched over similar jarring setts along tram-lined Kennington, crossed Clapham Common, and reached through Wandsworth the brigade rendezvous by the windmill on Wimbledon Common, the skin of his feet was broken and raw in a dozen places. Fortunately they piled arms, and could lie on the grass.

Reveille had been at 5 a.m., with coffee and biscuits. They remained on the Common for three hours, then Captain Forbes led them away to an empty school for the night. It was now 6 p.m., and they had had no food since the early-morning biscuits. After dismissal, a wash, and patching of heels with the black plaster called "New Skin", Phillip and Baldwin went with others to look for a restaurant. Sam Isaacs' was thronged; but they managed, after waiting an hour, to get two seats, for coffee with fish-and-chips.

If the first day had been trying, the march next morning absorbed all memory of its fatigue. It began with great spirit in the bright air of morning, as the outer suburbs of London were left behind. The Highlanders were the rear-guard battalion; they swung along to the beat of drums with thin high tuneless fifes, followed by massed bugles, and, proudest of all, the skirl of the pipes playing *The Road to the Isles*. Songs arose; cheering; laughter, as the sun climbed up.

Then, as the dust arose with the heat, fife, bugle, drum, and pipe were silent; songs were no more; the landscape passed in jagged monotony with the trudging tramp of shoes sweat-dull in the dust of the white lanes, stirred and restirred by the rhythmic tramp of feet: grit, sweat, aches, blisters, glare, and thirst. As the sun brazed the zenith, the permanently undernourished of the other battalions of the brigade recruited from poorer districts upon the old marshes of the Thames, in twos and threes, in half-dozens, wet-haired, thin and white of face, open-mouthed with exhaustion, began to stagger into gaspless shade beside the road. Phillip, desperately shifting equipment weights—rifle slung, rifle sloped, rifle slung again—hands clutching shoulder webbing to lift weight of pack forward—to take the ache from collar bones, body running with wet, feet burning, throat parched—Phillip yet noticed their thinness, whiteness of faces, and why were so many covered with pimples, and often greenish boils? Were the eruptions on their faces due to sun-stroke? Had the great heat driven the poison from their bodies, with the perspiration which poured from them? Hundreds were lying in the shade on the grass, absolutely done in.

Phillip, together with every marching man in the brigade, carried fifty-six pounds; rifle, ammunition, water-bottle, haversack, entrenching tool, bayonet, rolled greatcoat strapped on back with mess-tin in khaki cover on top. Every step forward in the torrid heat of the glaring day he felt must be the last. He saw himself flinging himself upon the grass in the shade, there to lie for ever and ever. He thought of snow, of ice—never again would he complain of being cold. He blinked to loosen the grit upon his eyeballs, he clenched his teeth to keep on, tunic yellow-thick with dusted sweat, feet burning, flames of pain and the next ten minutes' halt at the end of every hour was a thought beyond a thousand thoughts of broken glass, with which his shoes were filled.

Under dust and glass and flame were the songs of the morning, when more and more men and a dog had gone to mow a meadow, or in a tavern in the town with true love sat him down; now the ribald chant, composed by Collins and Kerry, the beery comics of "B" Company, which periodically had been roared along the length of the battalion before the August sun had climbed to splash down its molten brass, was a horrible scissoring inside the head, words mixed up with an unbearable multiplication of hose and spats scissoring and swooshing short-shadowed in the dust, dust, dust.

> We don't give a damn
> For Will-i-am
> We know the Crown Prince is barmy!
> We don't give a (HUSH!) for old von Kluck
> And all his bloody old army!

> Hoch der Kaiser!
> Donner and Blitzer!
> Salmon and Gluckstein!
> BAA-A-AH!

Aa-aa-ah! Was ever pint of shandy-gaff so welcome? Another; then a third; and from the billiard room of the Red Lion he hobbled out beside Baldwin, each to buy a ha'penny picture postcard and ha'penny stamp; and having dashed off pencil messages to parents, they walked, curiously insubstantial, down the village street. A cobbler's shop was open; and going inside, Phillip asked the old man if he had any second-hand shoes—"I want a pair well broken-in. No nails. I don't mind how light they are."

The cobbler had only a pair of elastic-sided boots, of his size. These fitted; and when spat straps were fastened, only a small section of black elastic was visible. The dust would soon hide that.

"They belonged to his rivirince, but he won't need they again, I reckon."

"How is that?"

"He be dead. I be asking two shillin' for 'em."

Having packed up his campaign clumps, he took them to the post-office, and labelling them O.H.M.S., addressed them to his father. "He's a special constable. They may come in handy, especially as taxes are going up all round," he told Baldwin.

Feeling much relieved in his new boots, which, he hoped, together with "New Skin" would end the pains of marching, he went with his friend and, coming to a river, decided to bathe. No one was about; so getting out of uniform, they slipped into the water from under a decayed wooden platform beside an empty mill, and swam in the mill-pond. Gone were the desperate thoughts on the march; this silent swim starko was worth every step of it.

Lance-corporal Mortimore had fixed up a supper of ham and tomatoes with the landlord of the Red Lion which rounded off the day. As for sleep under the billiard table, what more could one want, after the hearthstone in the classroom of the school? For with wood under him, and with the pneumatic rubber-cloth pillow which Aunt Dora had sent him under his head, sleep, beautiful sleep was only ended by the morning sun pouring into the room.

For the next day's march the Highlanders were to be the leading battalion in the brigade. Lance-corporal Mortimore, who had shared with two of his especial friends a bottle of champagne at supper the previous night, advised them to rub soap inside their socks, to prevent blisters. Phillip did this in the lavatory, not wanting his boots to be seen. His heels were black with "New

Skin", and with the extra soap on his toes, he hoped to last out the march. Looking in the mirror, he thought that he would have to shave soon; it was nearly a week since he had done so, and small black hairs here and there on his chin were distinctly visible. He intended to let his moustache grow, but it was very slow. The sunshine might hasten it.

At the end of a torrid march, again wringing-wet with sweat, the battalion reached East Horsley, and passed under a tall brick arch and through grassy fields to the long hovel or cart-shed where "B" Company was to sleep the night. Beyond was a grey mansion with towers. For the first time since mobilisation the battalion cook-house was set up, manned by volunteers who were excused marching, and rode on the waggons, to conserve their energy. Phillip and Baldwin were detailed to draw the half-section's dinner. They bore back two big black iron trays in which several porterhouse steaks had been fried over a roaring fire of beech boughs, which had made the cooks' faces extremely red.

"My God!" said Lance-corporal Mortimore, gazing at the contents of the trays. "Burnt offerings, if ever there were any." He stabbed a steak with his bayonet. It was dry and frizzled, lying in gravy like flaked tar. "I prefer a bloody sacrifice, where a steak is concerned. Well, thank God we've got our health and strength! 'I owe it all to Phospherine'." Opening his clasp knife, he hacked off dried strips. "Help yourselves, boys. I'll be in the 'Duke of Wellington', if anyone asks for me."

After chewing and swallowing, Phillip and Baldwin went to look for a shop, to round off the meal with biscuits and chocolate. There was a foot inspection at four o'clock; until then they were free. Having bought some licorice bootlaces, bull's-eyes, and nut-chocolate, they went exploring, and found under some trees a pond where fellows were bathing, the Wallace brothers among them. The pond was shallow, black mud on the bottom, but it was cool and refreshing.

"Good heavens," said Mr. Ogilby, at the foot inspection. "What is that stuff on your heels?"

"'New Skin', sir."

"H'm. Do your shoes fit?"

"Yes, sir."

"Let me see them, will you?"

Phillip uncovered the elastic-sided boots.

Mr. Ogilby prodded one with his walking stick.

"My shoes were a bad fit, sir, I bought these yesterday, all I could get, sir."

"I see," said Mr. Ogilby, quietly. "Let this man see the medical orderly, sergeant, and get those heels looked at. Aren't you the man who had those enormous soles on his shoes on the first day's march?"

"Yes, sir."

"Did you march yesterday, or ride on one of the G.S. waggons?"

"I marched, sir."

Mr. Ogilby nodded, as once more he turned over the late vicar's elastic-sided boots.

"Not exactly regulation, are they. Still, until your feet are healed, you had better continue wearing them. But the medical orderly should see your feet."

Phillip did not dare to ask where the battalion was going, so that his second-best pair of shoes, which he posted home on receiving the heavy pair, could be returned to him.

He chose for his bed that night an old faded blue cart, under the hovel or cart-shed. He laid hay in it, and awaited the last of the sunset. On the side of the blue cart was painted in white *Lionel, Earl of Lovelace*. He was the owner of Horsley Towers, where the officers had been invited to dinner that night, lucky dogs.

The chaps began to come back from the Wellington, among them Collins and Kerry, the half-section comics, leaning on one another, and singing. Kerry was small and perky, with pince-nez glasses and a furze-bush moustache; Collins was big and heavy, with a rather bloated, clean-shaven face. His lips were thick, and the lower one hung down.

Phillip forgot himself in romantic musings as the sun disappeared, then he took off his tunic, and put his feet through the sleeves for warmth. Having wrapped himself in his greatcoat, he settled down back to back with Baldwin. The last of the sunset diminished in the west; tawny owls were calling among the trees —and night had come to end the second day's adventure. Despite his hot and aching feet, where the iodine had bitten, he fell asleep at once.

Onwards again through another radiant morning; but whither? He had written to Mother to "stand by" to post his old shoes to an address he would send her. Did Lance-corporal Mortimore know where they were going?

"They never tell you a damned thing in the Army," said Morty. "They've got us body and soul now." He laughed, with his usual good humour.

Again they marched to the massed copper gleam of bugles, the colourless high wind of the fifes, to the skirl of *The Road to the Isles*. This march took them, after the third ten-minute halt, when collar-bones once more were aching and shirts and tunics dewy with sweat, past a row of cottages before which stood women with smiling faces and little girls wearing ribbons in their hair, holding out baskets of apples and pears. There were feminine cheers and cries, waving of hands. Thereafter endurance in great heat, as the sun passed the top of its harvest arc; the ten-minute halts flat on back, eyes closed, neck on hard pillow of rolled greatcoat.

They arrived that afternoon, lips rough with fine dust, at Reigate, to be billeted in an empty hall; and after a meal of skilly, they were marched to open-air baths in fatigue dress. Water again glorified all. Tea tasted of skilly grease, and it was not hard to guess that it had been brewed in the remains of the skilly, since washing-up of dixies was on a par with cooking. Afterwards Phillip took Baldwin looking for old bird-nests in the hedges, while telling him of past days in Knollysley Park and the Squire's woods along Shooting Common. In return, Baldwin told him of rugger matches at Twickenham, the Rectory Field at Blackheath, and other famous places, with the Harlequins.

During the next day's march, as they approached a bend in the road, unexpectedly they were called to attention. A whisper went down the column, *The King!*

"'B' Company! Eyes right!" Fiery Forbes cried fiercely.

Phillip saw a group of four blue-uniform'd figures, their tunics buttoned to the neck, red-gold tabs on each side of the stiff collars, red-banded blue hats with thick gold braid on the peaks. They wore riding boots with spurs, and stood on a raised grassy bank above the road. The central front figure, dark-bearded, wearing gold spurs, held an arm at the salute. Phillip held the muscles of neck, eyes, and shoulders rigid before the majestic figure.

"'B' Company! Eyes front!"

Undulating rifles, glengarries, khaki-covered mess-tins above rolled greatcoats jumped into view again, with swinging kilts and dusty spatted shoes moving in unison in a haze of grit.

"'B' Company! March at ease!"

They passed three black Daimler cars, one with the Royal Standard on its bonnet, drawn up on the other side of the road.

"March easy."

Once again blisters were burning on heels, where the "New Skin" had rucked up, and all his woollen clothes felt soggy.

Chapter 14

WAR CORRESPONDENCE

RICHARD was amused, and pleased, when he received his parcel, labelled O.H.M.S., containing a present of the campaign clumps, together with a long letter roughly scrawled in pencil, from his son. The contents of the letter surprised him; then he began to doubt; and one passage, about the photograph Hetty had sent to Phillip, made him wonder if he ought to let her see it. It was a little unkind, he thought. After all, she was his mother.

"The boy still draws the long bow in places, I fancy."

"He is still very young, Dickie."

"He has a graphic style, but I fancy he has exaggerated at times. It is odd, too, how he contradicts what he has written almost in the same breath. Almost he seems to be in two minds at times. Well, read it for yourself. Only I ought to warn you, first—he does not apparently take to a certain hat."

Hetty hesitated before taking the letter from the envelope, into which he had neatly returned it.

"Are you sure Phillip would like me to see it, dear?"

She meant her words to convey that Phillip naturally wanted to confide in his father, and not in his mother.

"Why, don't you want to read the latest from your best boy?"

"Yes, dear, of course, naturally."

Camp Hill Camp,
Ashdown Forest,
Crowborough,
Sussex.
30 August 1914

Dear Father,

Will you please send me two one-ounce packets of Hignett's Cavalier once a week as I can't get any in this hole. The hardships of this life are awful. It takes a lot to exhaust me, as it does you, but after a 20-mile march without food and full kit and rifle in the brazen sun, one flops down and gasps for water and breath. On the first day out of London we passed literally hundreds of chaps, grown men and youths, lying still on the roadside, overcome with sunstroke and exhaustion. I am afraid that poor old Desmond who at present has not very good enduring powers, would have gone red in the face, then stumbled and collapsed. Many of the boys in the L.H. went sick with blistered feet (blisters often the length of their soles, and often broken blisters) but not one fell out!

I have posted you the brogues, as they might come in useful for your special constabulary work, as your shoes fit me, therefore mine will fit you.

Here we sleep like pigs, twelve wedged in one bell tent, and with unwashed hands, face, and body. No water is yet laid on. Thank God the food is now good and plentiful, though coarse and badly cooked generally. At first when we arrived here on the highest part of Sussex, we slept under the stars. Breakfast—undrinkable "tea" (no milk or sugar) and 3 Huntley and Palmers biscuits. For dinner uncooked boiled mutton only. (The cooks have given up trying to roast.) $\frac{1}{2}$ the chaps couldn't eat it, but I wolfed 2 lbs. of it.

For tea, as breakfast, except that it was greasy with the old boiled mutton; and 3 Huntley and Palmers Lunch Biscuits. Rain lashed down all the first night, before the tents arrived (they were lost on the railway with our commissariat). Result—several men high temperatures, two with pneumonia. No drinkable tea the next morning, and only 3 loaves per 12 men for all day. Starvation, slow and terrible! Luckily I can stand it, and damp and hunger and hardship do not affect me. Even with tents it is pretty awful. And the life is hell itself. Now it is dry again, black dust lies on everything. We have nowhere to wash—hands, face, body, all grimy. Work all day, digging with entrenching tools, marching, attacking by rushes in extended order, and nothing to do at night except to sit in dusty dark tents. A pipe is the only consolation, but baccy is low—nowhere to get more. There are just tents, and miles of heather. There are 12,000 men here in all, twelve battalions of the London Regiment; three brigades; one division. I have enquired about Willie, but he is not down here with the London Rifles.

I believe if ever I come back I shall be changed evermore. All the chaps are already hard-bitten and slowly soured. Enough of this—I can stand these conditions.

Don't let Mother waste any food by sending it to me just yet as we may shift any minute night or day. Navvies at Newhaven are digging trenches and blowing up houses and trees to clear the way for mountain guns, we hear. An invasion may come if our Expeditionary Force is destroyed. The Terriers are for relieving regulars, but the L.H. and a few crack regiments will fight in France. We expect to get new kit, and 2 days' leave soon, so when I send a telegram get the house full of food and tell Desmond to stand by.

When I come home after the war (how long will it last? I hope Germany will go broke soon, it is costing her £3,000,000 a day) we will have a good time, tennis, etc., and we will spend a holiday at Lynmouth. Will you, on a Sunday, if you have time, put my Swift in preserve?

Next quarter day you ought to receive £6 5s. and about £1 11s. 6d. overtime. Don't write a letter of acknowledgement, I know you are very busy with your special constable work, etc. Just pay into your own account. If you have a holiday next year with Aunt Dora, take my little rod, but don't lose it. I want something to remind me of my holiday in Glorious Devon with Aunt Dora.

By the way, are taxes up? If you are hard up, don't forget you can use my salary in the common pool of the family. Spend it if necessity arises, I shan't expect it back at all, and am not really earning it. So if you are pressed at home, spend my £50 a year on Mother and yourself and the girls as a present. Please keep this letter, as it is also my will. I am afraid this war will mean the ruin (financially and otherwise) and break-up of many English families. Be sure that if I go abroad, I will fight like a devil and a Maddison against the barbarians who are doing the Fiend's own hellish work in wrecking the peace of Europe, and causing grief and anguish in millions of homes. If ever there is a bayonet charge I will be one of the first to stab and thrust at them.

Don't forget to put up the new bird boxes in the elm tree by February, for my tomtits. I took the old ones down, as they were rotten.

My face is dark mahogany. I am what is known as a hard-bitten, silent, cursing tommy! (French Foreign Legion kind.) We must send every available man to France. We shall want millions there. Perhaps more.

When we barter for terms in Berlin, we shall be backed up by an enormous army to *enforce* our terms.

We *shall win* in the end.

But the cost!!

It will nearly mean death for England.

Please write your opinion of the war's course, in length. I will keep it.

Mine is this (keep this letter).

The Germans will crush the Allied Forces abroad. We shall send all our available men across the silver streak. They will go in an unceasing stream, but each time Germany will, by force of numbers and particularly machine-guns, decimate us. This will go on for years.

We shall lose the flower of our youth. But there will come a time when the Germans will have to subside.

But meanwhile our original Expeditionary Force will be no more. More will go abroad—they will likewise fall, until we shall be able to take the offensive.

Russia will be no good in the offensive. She will not reach Berlin, and be not much good to us. Germany will send a force over if she reaches the Channel ports.

It will be swamped almost immediately. Now it will come to this. *Every available man*, except those needed for home defence, will be on the continent, *millions and millions*! We shall lose an appalling amount.

France will never recover. She will be crippled for hundreds of years. Russia will not be much violated. Her forces will be scattered, and repulsed. Germany will gasp for breath for centuries. England will be exhausted for years, but will otherwise be intact. Our fleet will preserve our shipping but our trade will disappear for fifty years or so. That is my opinion. Please send me yours, with the baccy. Keep this letter as a "curio".

P.S. Ask Desmond to come and see me on his bike one day here. Tell Mother not to send me news like this, "Namur has fallen", "English eating heartily of dead Germans", etc. etc. I see newspapers here. However, I welcome local news such as the convent at Thildonck, etc., and what is happening at home. Does the Hill seem destitute of fellows? Has slacker Ching joined up yet? Tell Mother I *don't* like the photo she sent me: it is one of the worst she has ever had taken. The huge hat on her head is like a beehive with a flower garden. Tell her to send me a nice one, as for instance the one taken at Beau Brickhill. I don't like to think that Mother only sent me a badly taken photo, even if Woods did take it in his studio. I would like one of the family group I took in the sitting-room with the old Brownie—a time exposure. It is with others in my top bedroom drawer.

Do ask her to arrange a shoal of letters here. I should like a half-dozen every post. But tell her not to come down here, we are out training all the time and have no time to see anyone.

Give my love to Mother and Mavie and Doris and to yourself and all.

Love from your affectionate son,
Phillip.

P.S. Don't forget to repair and to nail up the nesting boxes before Jan. or Feb.

"Well, we've had our orders," said Richard, with a laugh. "You must get another hat, that resembles neither bee-hive nor

garden, and I must see about his nesting boxes with the car-
pentry tools of mine he ruined long ago. I wonder he did not
tell me to give Timmy Rat his daily airing on the Hill! But
perhaps that is to come, when he finds the field-marshal's baton
in his haversack!" He was really pleased with the new directness
apparent in the letter. "He is like his grandfather in that, I
fancy; my father wrote a forceful style."

Other letters in the same strain arrived; then a week later,
Hetty had one, meticulously written in ink, on Y.M.C.A.
writing paper. She was relieved that it had come after Dickie
had left for his train, for she felt that he ought not to see it: the
tone was so different, and might disappoint his new regard for
Phillip.

> 9689 Pte. P. Maddison,
> "B" Company,
> London Highlanders,
> Crowborough, Sussex,
> 6 September 1914.

Dear Mother,
Today is Sunday. I have just wandered to the Beacon Hotel where
the L.H. men are entertaining their visitors to luncheon. Nearly
everybody has someone to see him on Sunday. I have nobody:
I am as an orphan, an outcast.
Still, the journey is long, the days are hot, the travelling irksome,
so perhaps I am too unreasonable to expect a visitor.
Even the poor boys in this camp—those who in times of peace
are carters and the like—are visited by parents and relations, those
who, perhaps, can ill afford the railway fare from London.
However, it is no use my speaking, because we may go away
at any minute. We may go anywhere.
Perhaps I shall not see you again in this life—one never knows,
and any opportunity there was is now gone for ever.
> Love to all,
> P. S. T. Maddison.

P.S. Do you think it advisable to get rid of my suits and saleable
things at home? In all probability I shall never have need of them
again. So if Father wants the room, get rid of the contents.

Hetty waved to Mrs. Neville as she went down the road, to
do some shopping. Then as she turned the corner she saw the
postman on his bicycle. Yes, there was one for "Lindenheim".
Her heart beat faster as she saw it was addressed, in scrawled
pencil, to her. Then up went Mrs. Neville's window.

"Any news of Phillip, dear?"

"Yes, Mrs. Neville. He is a little homesick, I think. He always asks after you, and Desmond."

"Yes, I asked Desmond to write to him, but you know what boys on holiday are; and these two, Eugene and Desmond, are mad on fishing, going out first thing in the morning as far as Westerham and Tonbridge, and coming back late in the evening. Do give my love to Phillip, won't you, dear?"

Hetty went on to see her sister Dorrie, and there read her letter. It certainly did seem that he had two distinct sides to his mind, as Dickie had said.

Same old address.

Dear Mother,

I know that I asked you *not* to come down so don't take any notice of my previous letter complaining. If I can't get leave next Sunday, I will write. I shall know Sat. morning, so will wire if I get it. You can only come to the camp here by pass which I have to procure, and they are very difficult to obtain.

Love to all,

Yrs affected son,
Phil.

P.S. Send my dear old Civic pipe. I have the bulldog shape; I want the one I bought after I burnt that huge Artist's Incinerator. How is Desmond? Tell him there are two brothers Church, here, who left soon after he went to Rodings College. Can't he cycle down with Eugene to see me? It won't be too far, if they start early.

Phillip's tent, one of twelve in "B" Company lines, was third from the bottom. The next tent down was occupied by what he thought of as the Leytonstone Louts, owing to the slight cockney voices of some of the occupants, who were always wrestling for fun, and bumping the sides of their tent. Several of them came from Leytonstone, a district he knew only from the many renewal notices he had made out, and from Downham's remark about it being a ghastly place to live in. Among them were Martin, with serious face and long clean-shaven upper lip, and Kerry and Collins, the beery comics.

Not all were from Leytonstone, that village once of Essex, but now enclosed within rows of industrial London's brick houses dulled by fogs of the low-lying clay-lands: two of the tent were the brothers Church, sons of the City tailor who made Mr. Howlett's suits, and also the uniform of young Edgar. The

Church brothers had been, Phillip discovered, to Desmond's school near Chelmsford.

In the new canteen marquee one morning after parade, Phillip asked the younger Church if he had known Desmond, saying he was his great friend.

"What, that kid in Lower School, who blubbed and blubbed when his mater left him, and tried to run away? At least the 'Leytonstone Louts', as I overheard you describing us the other evening, don't behave like that!"

Shocked by the unexpected remark, Phillip stammered, "I d-didn't mean y-you were one of them, Church, I meant the others."

He saw Lance-corporal Furrow standing near, listening.

"What others?"

"Oh, you know. Martin, Collins, and Kerry—they come from Leytonstone in the East End, don't they?"

"So that makes them louts, does it?"

"Well, I didn't exactly mean it that way. It was a passing remark."

"Well, here's another passing remark. Your name ought to be von Madigsohn."

"I don't understand what you mean."

"You ought to, being a German. It means 'son of a maggot'."

"Will you fight?" cried Phillip, hotly.

Lance-corporal Furrow put his arm between them, and swung Phillip back. "Get out of the canteen, if you can't hold your drink!" he threatened. "Get back to your tent!"

Nothing more was said about the fight—for the time being.

Chapter 15

BLEAK HILL

To Phillip in his loneliness Ashdown Forest was a wilderness; but to Norman Baldwin, who was twenty-four years old and engaged to be married, the views were what he called glorious. From the high ground of six hundred and fifty feet covered with bell heather and ling, fringed by dark clumps of pine, he saw with his lady-love the Martello towers built behind Pevensey Bay against Napoleon, and the far shining sea. The smooth grey-green South Downs lay below them, from Eastbourne in the distance to the dark beech hanger of Chanctonbury in the west beyond Shoreham Gap.

Norman's girl came down every Sunday. They walked for hours, holding hands, integrated by love, a feeling of eternity upon them as they looked southward towards the high beacons of Firle and Ditchling, the castle of Lewes, the skiey rampart of the Devil's Dyke. Northwards lay the escarpment of the North Downs, the wooded Weald between; and when Norman had seen his girl off by train from the station, thither he returned with Phillip in the twilight, to stare towards the faint glow of London, whither she was returning, taking his heart with her.

One such Sunday Phillip returned to camp before Norman. Within the tent Lance-corporal Mortimore was sitting, singing softly in his light and tender baritone voice *A Broken Doll*. There was a bottle of whiskey and a siphon of soda-water before him, and a large hamper. He had been on the musical comedy stage before the war, and that afternoon a party of friends had come by motor car to see him.

"Hullo, you look depressed, dear boy. Have a peg? Help yourself. Haven't you got a girl to visit you? You ought to have, with those eyes of yours."

"Oh yes," replied Phillip. "Only at the moment her people are not very favourable."

"You don't know when you are well off, dear boy."

"Hark, the cavalry trumpets!" said Phillip, to change the subject.

"The Roughriders are on the next hill, dear boy. My brother's with them. Won't you change your mind and have a drink?"

"No, thanks all the same."

He went out of the tent and stared at the ridge beyond the pines to the west. The cavalry! Thunderous charges, sabres flashing, cheering, Uhlans scattered! He thrilled at the thought of the glory of the cavalry.

Many times Phillip had knelt by the piano in the front room, while Doris accompanied his song, *The Trumpeter*.

"God-forsaken spot, isn't it?" said Mortimore, cheerfully. "No wonder they call it Bleak Hill!"

Sanitation was no longer an excruciating worry for the shy youth. He had been a little chary of standing at the edge of

the great round pit dug in the heather below the lines of grey
conical tents, the vast urinal filled to the brim with yellow
liquid; but the series of little oblong holes, called dogs' graves,
for squatting in the open, had been too much for his reserved
nature. After one glance on the first day he had left, despairing
of ever being able to be like the others there, talking as though
it was nothing unusual. He waited until night and found a
place in the heather, digging a small hole, and relaxing in
privacy and peace. But one night the orderly corporal, Lance-
corporal Furrow, going his rounds smartly, black cane with
regimental crest on silver nob tucked under arm, surprised him.
"You filthy little tyke!" His name and company were taken
and reported to the orderly room.

After breakfast the following morning the Colour-sergeant
led him to Captain Forbes' tent in the officers' lines. While he
waited outside he saw within the tent a green canvas bed and
camel-hair sleeping sack, a rug, a folding table on which was
a lantern and a silver-framed photograph of a lovely woman; and
Fiery Forbes' sword, belt, and revolver-holster hanging on the
back of a canvas chair—symbols of another world, awesome
and slightly feared, of the rich.

While fox-haired aloof face was speaking, his own face assumed
the helpless bewildered expression he had always used to conceal
his mind when faced with the condemning power of authority:
his only defence when apprehended for leading his own life.
Captain Forbes said tersely,

"I consider that it is a damned disgraceful thing for any
member of the company to have done. There can be no excuse
for it. If such a thing occurs again, I shall take a most serious
view of it. Do you understand?"

"Yes, sir."

Fiery Forbes turned away. He saluted. The Colour-sergeant
told him, quietly, to go back to the lines.

The next morning he went to the dogs' graveyard, which now
had a loose hessian screen around it. Overcoming his nervous-
ness that the other men there would look at him, he squatted;
and left with secret exultation that it had not been such an
ordeal as he had dreaded. No one had spoken to him. Thereafter the morning visit was, in a slight way, something to look
forward to.

They went for route marches along the gritty lanes through the heather. In hot September sunshine they extended over the wiry, toecap-scratching stalks for attacks on distant ridges. Sometimes Colonel Findhorn and the Adjutant rode up to watch them, followed by their grooms. One morning "B" Company advanced up a slope to storm an imaginary trench with fixed bayonets. Early in the advance Phillip and Baldwin were told off by Mr. Ogilby as casualties. They had to lie down in the heather, pretending to be dead.

"A bit of luck for us," remarked Phillip. Both were sweating. The sun blazed on their faces, on their red-lidded eyes. The bells of the heath and ling were colourless and shrivelled in summer's decline, but bees still burred past to the yellow nuggets of the gorse.

"This used to be part of a great forest," said Baldwin. "In Saxon times it was called Anderida. I suppose, when William the Conqueror defeated the Saxons after the Battle of Hastings, many of them hid here, and lived on the wild deer. The Normans must have killed thousands of leading Saxons, in the years following Hastings. The Germans, if they won, would probably do the same to the English aristocracy."

"They have missed their chance of winning the war, now. They're retreating on the Marne."

"Do you think the war will be over by Christmas, Phil?"

"No, I don't, Norman. I think Castleton is right, when he says in *The Trident* that it will be a long war."

"I hope we see some of it before it ends, anyway. It would be bad luck to miss the fun." Distant cheers floated through the air. "That means we've stormed the trench. Don't you think we ought to join them now?"

"I votes we stop here, Norman. After all, we were ordered to sham dead. With any luck we can spend the morning lying down. No one can see us here."

"But we're supposed to exercise some judgment, you know."

"I'm going to lie here. They can't blame us if we obey orders."

Baldwin lay down again, his better judgment overcome, the sun soaking into him.

"Did you see that wounded soldier the other evening, in the village, Phil?"

"From the front? Good lord! What did he say?"

"He said it was simply terrible out there."

He was startled; yet, somehow, he had known it was like that. He had known it when he had had the heavy clump-soles put on his shoes.

"I had an uncle in the Boer War. He said it was hell."

"That's what this chap said. He said nobody could have any idea of what it was like, unless they had been there. His regiment was cut to pieces with all the others, at Le Cateau. We lost most of our guns there. He said the retreat was as good as a rout. They went back ninety miles in twelve days, marching all night, and fighting all day, with little food and no sleep all that time."

"What else did he say?"

"Kitchener was no good. He tried to take over from Sir John French, after some French general had been shot for cowardice."

He felt the shadow of life, that he had always felt, very near him. He had *known* it would be like that; he had never wanted to cheer, as most of the others had, after the Bishop had asked them to volunteer, and the Earl of Findhorn had spoken of the British Expeditionary Force meeting the Germans.

He heard thudding hoofs in the ground. Then he was looking up into the almost sallow face of the Iron Colonel, crossed by its great sweep of brown moustaches.

"What are you men doing there?" asked the deep bass voice.

"We're dead men, sir."

"Stand to attention when you speak to an officer!"

Colonel Hatton wore the Queen's ribbon of the South African War. Lance-corporal Mortimore joked about the Iron Colonel, calling him Tin Ribs. He said the only action he had seen was in the Modder River rout, when he was wounded in the bottom by a Boer bullet as he ran away. He carried a fly-whisk of white horse-hairs on a rhinoceros hide handle. His face was as brown as tea, deeply lined. From Morty had come the further information that he was the senior partner in a famous City firm of bullion buyers. He looked gold, somehow: dark leather, saturated with gold. The deep bass voice exclaimed,

"Report to your company immediately!"

They turned away.

"You there! Salute an officer after he has spoken to you! Who is the older soldier of you two?"

"I am, sir," said Baldwin.

"Then take charge! Order your squad to slope arms! Salute as you move off!"

"Yes, sir. Squad, 'shun!" said Baldwin, red in the face. Phillip prayed he would not laugh. "Sloo-oo-oope—hipe! By the left, quick march! Squad, eyes left!" Baldwin struck his rifle butt with his right hand, as he trudged beside Phillip, who was now drawing his breath inwards with small clucking noises, a silent inverted laugh he had invented in the class-room for use with a blank face. It sounded like a donkey braying far away in a tunnel without echoes.

"I knew I was right, you know, Phil. What's the joke?"

"I thought you were going to say sloo-oope—off! And the Iron Colonel telling the dead to salute him!"

"Come on you slackers!" shouted the Colour-sergeant in the distance. "At the double!"

"Double, double, boil and bubble!" laughed Phillip.

Bleak Hill was now less bleak. A large Y.M.C.A. writing marquee, and another for the canteen, stood beyond the lines.

The two friends usually went there to write letters in the evenings, at one of the small tables provided. Then there was the daily pint of shandy after morning parade. Sometimes Phillip saw Gerry or Hubert there, and the Wallace brothers, always together; but having their own friends all they said to one another was "Hullo", or "How goes it?". Being in different companies made them almost like strangers.

"Good lor', look at this, Norman! *The Trident* suggests that women be armed, and formed into commando bands, in case of invasion. Tommy rot!"

"I bet it's the suffragettes."

"Oh no, they aren't like that, Norman."

"Here's an interesting article in the *National Review*, Phil. It shows what a near thing it was, our declaring war. No, keep it, I've read it."

While he was reading, there was shouting outside. They ran out with the others. In the sky, with churring engines, was an airship. Someone said it was a Zeppelin. He was excited. Would it be fired on? If only he had his rifle! Then the Iron Colonel galloped up, saying it was the "Beta", from Aldershot.

"Lucky for it there isn't an aeroplane gun on Bleak Hill," said Baldwin. "Or some fool must have shot it."

Phillip went back into the marquee to send the news, a little exaggerated, to his mother.

Two days later, Hetty took the letter next door to read to Papa and Aunt Marian. She left out the passage that he had asked her not to tell Gran'pa, substituting one of her own, which in effect reversed what Phillip had written, about the socks.

> Crowborough Camp.
> 14 September 1914

Dear Mother,

Please don't join a Commando Band. You are not fitted for such work. (Though that bee-hive hat with flowers on it might do to give protective coloration!) We have not fired our rifles yet. How is Father liking the Rifle Drill and special police work?

You mention again the Russians which many people say they have seen. It is all rot about them landing in Scotland. It has been officially denied, besides they may as well go via the North Pole. Thanks for the sweater. It keeps me warm at night. We have only one blanket each. I now have four pairs of socks (not sox, as you write) so don't trouble to send me a lot, except one *thick* pair made by yourself, which I shall treasure highly.

I can bear the hard work now without any trouble. We had manœuvres today, and each man had to dig a mound for himself as cover when lying on the ground under fire. It is a greyish black soil, tough with heather roots, and round pebbles.

I am in the Y.M.C.A. marquee here, with writing paper, tables, chairs, etc., where one can sit for nothing and write letters.

An airship sailed over camp just now and was lit up by a search-light. Great excitement, we nearly shelled it, but the Iron Colonel galloped up in time and pointed out that it was an English type, in fact the Beta. A narrow escape for the ship, as we had already charged our magazines, and loaded the aeroplane gun!

We are all to be inoculated soon, a nasty and unhealthy business.

You must not mind my going abroad. It is not probable that we shall relieve regulars at Malta, as you suggest, because the Colonel has said that we should if needed (when trained) go to Belgium to guard lines of communication, etc. It is probable that if the L.H. does go (and in my opinion we shall be needed against those never-ending masses) only about one-fifth will return alive: the others will join their comrades in the deep, deep, sleep.

Still, I must not alarm you: I have had a very happy life, and I have volunteered because I know you and Father want me to help the Allies in my best manner.

Why does not Desmond write? Is he coming down on his Rudge? Don't forget to ask everyone to write occasionally, as it is nice to receive a letter when the others do. Your letters are always rather scrappy.

Desmond is quite happy with Eugene, I suppose. If he does not cycle down soon, it may be too late; his holidays will be over, anyway. I hope Grandpa is well and all right. Don't tell him, but the socks he sent are unwearable, a thick ridge all down the middle of the feet under the sole. Who made them, Aunt Marian? Say nothing, I don't want to seem ungrateful; but they are unwearable. However they can be used for bedsocks (*not* sox).

Give my love to Father and dear Doris and Mavis.

It is very hard to leave home and friends and have only the memory of them left.

I wonder if I shall ever see Reynard's Common again, and play tennis on the Hill?

My tame jackdaws and my jay, the kestrel with a broken wing, where are they? I would like to think that the kestrel can now fly, that he hangs aloft the scenes of my boyhood, guarding the spirit of those days under the sun. But all I can do is to wonder; for 'tis in Higher Hands than mine.

I must close now with great love to yourself and all the others,

Your loving son, Phillip.

P.S. Tell Father to read the September "National Review". He will be surprised at the warning of the writer against the Cabinet.

It is well worth reading. It says that in the Black Week, Haldane didn't want any interference on the part of England: Asquith didn't want any Expeditionary Force: and Churchill saved the situation by ordering Naval Mobilisation "on his own" before declaration of war.

Also: the Territorials at the event of war are untrained: we have no army really: all are practically raw recruits now in England. A glance at the other battalions here proves this. They are a frightful lot, weedy and undisciplined.

P.P.S. If we start for an unknown destination, I don't think I shall ask you to see me off, at say, Southampton or Dover, because it would perhaps unsettle things for you all.

Thank you for the tobacco (Father). And also for the cakes and chocolate (Mother). We share all parcels in our tent. We are now used to hardships and enjoying ourselves.

The Bishop of London came down for a bit. He called in at every tent. The tents were grey-black, thick with dust; but we beat them before the Bishop arrived in the lines. His sermons were excellent.

I will send you a little book he gave each of us.

P.P.P.S. Jack Hart, who was expelled from school (remember?) is now I hear with the Royal Flying Corps in France. He joined at outbreak of war.

Don't forget my list of things. And please buy me a little oil lamp from Benetfinks in Cheapside. We have only candles in the tent. And send my old water-bottle in "the servants bedroom". I am reading a very funny book Lance-corporal Mortimore lent me, the "Diary of a Nobody". It is awfully funny. Try and get it. I think I must be rather like Lupin, Mr. Pooter's boy—a trial to poor Mr. Pooter with the beard (??!!)

So please get Lupin's old water bottle from "the servants bedroom", with the straps. Most of the bottles here are busted and we can't get any more. Now I must close, with anxious expectation of clothes, lamp, bottle, etc.

Your affec. son "Lupin." (nicknamed Maggot).

P.P.P.P.S. I apply every week for leave—no luck, so far.

Dinner was the usual skilly which had steamed away until the fresh vegetables added were nearly dissolved, and the meat threaded or fibrous. There were sometimes dumplings which had white unkneaded flour at their cores. Skilly was followed by treacle tart, the *spécialité de la cookmaison*, said Mortimore, who had a weekly hamper from Fortnum and Mason in Piccadilly. The thin pastry was invariably burnt, the treacle dried brittle and brown. Skilly was preferable to the hunks of leathery mutton or frizzled and blackened beef. They ate outside their tents, on or beside the neatly piled blankets. Morty dished out the skilly for the members of his tent, while making his usual sort of joke about the food, such as,

"Even Doctor Watson would not need to be told that the chef had not received his training at the Ritz. Maggot, dear boy, take away that horrible crock and return it, *clean*, to the so-called cookhouse, will you?"

Each man in the tent took his turn at what was called orderly dog, fetching the grub from the cookhouse, returning dixie and baking pan after cleaning in the heather.

"It's not my turn, Morty, today. It's Kirk's."

"Kirk is on headquarters guard at six o'clock tonight, and has to get his equipment smartened up, dear boy, as well as go on parade this afternoon, so don't argue, but take those beastly things away. Whatever names they bear, they smell the same, as

the Bard certainly would have said, had he been here. Go on,
be a sport, dear boy."

Phillip sat still.

Morty raised his handsome eyebrows.

"Skedaddle laddy, skedaddle. It won't take you a couple of
minutes."

"But I want to take my spare shoes to the snobs shop, to be
re-soled, ready for all eventualities."

"You can take them tonight. And don't let the Quartermaster-
sergeant charge you for them, the old robber. He tried it on me.
The Army pays now. Come, show your elasticity, dear boy!"

When Phillip did not move, he said, "Come on, Phil, don't
muck about with discipline. You could have done it and been
back by now. Don't try and fight the army."

Still Phillip did not move.

"Very well, since you ask for it."

After early parade next morning for Swedish drill, an orderly
came with a message that Captain Forbes wanted to see Maddison.

"But I haven't shaved," he cried, in panic. His face was
lathered, his cut-throat razor was open in his hand. His looking-
glass was fixed on the outside of the tent below.

"That baby fluff can wait," said Church, appearing in the
tent-opening. "Why ever they let you into the battalion, I can't
imagine."

"You Leytonstone lout! Will you fight?" shouted Phillip, in
sudden rage at the sight of Church's rabbit teeth.

"Any time you like!"

"After parade tonight, then!"

Ironical cheers came from the lower tent. Collins' face looked
out, with Kerry's "Yah boo, von Maggot!"

"Leytonstone louts!" cried Phillip.

"Choice of weapons rests with the challenged," laughed Morty.
"Entrenching tool handles, or do you prefer the razor? No
offence, dear boys!"

Phillip wiped his face hurriedly, put on tunic and glengarry,
and ran to the Officers' Lines.

An angry Fiery Forbes cried, "If this sort of thing occurs again,
I won't take you overseas! I don't want, and won't have, any
petty trouble-makers in my company! The discipline of my
company is based, in every particular, on loyalty between all

ranks! Now if you waste more of my time, or Corporal Mortimore's time, you'll go back to the second battalion. Have I
finally made that clear?"

"Yes, sir."

"Then go and apologise to Corporal Mortimore."

Phillip remotely hoped that he would not be taken overseas;
yet it would be awful if he were sent away as a washout.

When he got back to the tent, he found Morty in a state of
glee. An orderly had come with a chit from the Adjutant to say
that his commission had come through. He was a second-
lieutenant in the Roughriders. Already he was gazing at the
new pair of fawn cavalry twill breeches he kept in his kitbag.

"I'm sorry about the dixie, Morty."

"That's all forgotten, dear boy."

More excitement was to come a few minutes later. The
Colour-sergeant came down the lines, and, looking into the open
flap of each tent, spoke while holding a paper in hand. From each
tent as he left it there arose cheering.

"Morning parade is cancelled. The order has just come that
the London Highlanders will proceed overseas at forty-eight
hours notice."

The effect on the members of the tent who were inside at the
time was varied. Elliott threw himself on his back and waggled
his legs in the air, cheering happily. Douglas, a dark, handsome
rugger-playing Old Blue, looked thoughtful, then happy. Slade,
a big, quietly genial fellow, always the same, red of face and
country-looking although he had worked all his life in a bank,
smiled contentedly. Little Blunden, who looked so sturdy and
tough, said, "Well, anyone who wants to help himself to my food
box is at liberty to do so." Tommy Atkins, apple-cheeked
gospeller, who read his Bible morning and evening, and prayed
kneeling down, with hands clasped, said: "Well, that is what
we all have trained for, boys, and it is God's will." Kirk, a
delicate youth with pince-nez spectacles, sat with thin nostrils
open wider than usual. Baldwin flushed as he smiled quietly. A
chill struck into Phillip, which remained, although now he had
a good excuse to get out of fighting Church.

Morty dug into his kitbag and produced a bottle of champagne.
The whole camp was lively, cheering arose everywhere.

"A loving cup, dear boys! You'll have to drink out of your
tooth-mugs, I'm afraid."

When the human effervescence had subsided, with that of the liquid in the tooth-mugs, the subject of leave became linked with speculation about the battalion's destination. Gibraltar? Malta? Egypt? Perhaps India? Lines of communication in France? Possibly even South Africa, since some of the Boers were known to be openly on the side of the Germans.

Excitement settled when it became known that there would be no embarkation leave. Thinking of his mother, Phillip felt darkness filling him. Why had he asked her specially not to come and visit him? The other chaps had had their mothers and fathers down. But he could not very well have asked her without Father: and he did not want the others to see him. It was nothing to do with being half-German, that was all rot. It was—well, Father might say awkward things, or be cross with Mother. He had envied the others of the tent, Douglas, Kirk, Morty, Norman, who had been so friendly with their fathers.

Morty had already packed. "Help yourselves to the hamper, dear boys." He said he intended to give himself a week's leave in London, to be fitted for his uniform before reporting to the Roughriders depôt.

"Think of me with a bit of fluff dancing at the Grafton Galleries tonight, dear boys, after a dinner at the Trocadero and a revue. Seriously, I'm damned sorry I'm not coming with you."

Before Morty left, Phillip asked him if he would send off a telegram for him at the station. "Oh course, my one and only Elastic Maggot! No offence, dear boy: you ought to know what a silly old ass I am, by now!"

Phillip wrote the telegram and gave Morty sixpence.

"My dear old top," said Morty. "I won't hear of it! I'll send it off as soon as I get to Crowborough, count on that. Any more telegrams?" Putting them in his pocket-book, "So long, dear boys! We'll all meet again in Berlin, and drink hock, and eat that sauerkraut! Come now, all together, the 'Hymn in Praise of Camp Cooking'!"

Lance-corporal Mortimore led off with the words of his famous song.

> *We have fat ham for breakfast, turnip jam for tea!*
> *Skilly for dinner, or cold Maconochie!*
> *Oh, take away those dixies, and wash them well out!*
> *For soon we'll be eating sauerkraut*
> *NO DOUBT!*

G

Phillip shouted the last two words with the others. He joined in the cheering as handsome, gay Morty walked up the lines. They watched him so far as the top, where he blew them a kiss, and was gone.

Chapter 16

A LUNCHEON PARTY

"Your parents have come, and are looking for you," said Douglas; and Phillip, trying to fit his greatcoat into the new khaki valise which had been issued that morning, promptly went to find them. He greeted them with a salute, having observed an officer greeting his wife like that. The next thing was to get leave to go with them to Crowborough, to the Beacon Hotel, for lunch.

"Just a moment, Mother, I'll see if I can find the Colour-sergeant. Things are a bit mucked up this morning. I won't be long."

Unable to find Colours, he ventured up to the Officers' lines. Captain Forbes' tent was empty. What should he do? Seeing the grey head and moustaches of the Earl of Findhorn for a moment in the opening of his tent, he went with some trepidation towards that distinctly awesome presence. Outside the tent he stood to attention, and saluted. The lean face with an irritable expression looked at him with distaste.

"Who are you?"

"If you please, Sir, my Father and Mother have come to see me, and may I have permission to——" He stopped, as sharp little teeth appeared under the moustache, with a snarl of anger.

"What the devil——! Get out! Get out!"

Phillip turned and ran away, jumping over guide ropes and dodging round tents until he found himself in "F" lines. Bending down, he hastened through "G" and "H"; and walking briskly downhill, came to where his parents were waiting at the bottom of "B" lines.

"Don't look back! Follow me! It's all a bit of a muck up today, anyway the Colonel said I could get out, so I take it he meant the camp. This way, please don't look back, just follow me along the track. It's about two miles to the hotel."

The room adjoining the main dining-room of the Beacon
Hotel was small, and crowded with tables. They entered, among
officers and other ranks sitting quietly with their relations. Seated
before his father and mother, and speaking scarcely above a
whisper, he asked how things were at home.

"Oh, much the same, old chap," said Richard. "Timmy
Rat misses you, I think, but we are looking after him for
you."

"S-sh! Not so loud."

After awhile Hetty said, "Zippy is very good with him, Phillip,
he hardly ever gets on the copper. We see that he has plenty of
water, too."

"Oh good."

He stared at the table. The meeting he had imagined so many,
many times had been entirely different.

It was a slight relief when Baldwin appeared at the door, with
his red-haired girl. Phillip had been introduced to her; but he
did not greet them. He kept his eyes on the table. All the tables
were filled. He did not think of asking them to share his table.
In his father's presence, mild as it had been for a year and more,
he could never think. He sat there impotently uneasy. Baldwin
and his girl went out again, silently as they had come in, as
though also over-awed by the presence of officers there.

"Your sister Mavis is coming as a stop-gap, to work in the
office after Christmas, you may be interested to hear, Phillip."

"Oh, I see."

"Yes, dear, she is learning to type now, at Clark's College in
Fordesmill."

"Oh." Then, "How is Timmy Rat? And Gran'pa?"

"Oh very well, dear, Gran'pa and Aunt Marian asked me to
send their love."

"Oh, thank you."

"I think you may be interested to hear that Mr. Rolls has
joined the Rifle Club, Phillip," said Richard.

"Oh." Phillip's eyes were on his plate.

"When I saw Mrs. Rolls the other day, dear," said Hetty, "she
said that she is organising a Knitting Party connected with St.
Simon's Church, to knit socks for soldiers."

His agony lest others overhear the name of Rolls was equalled
by a momentary wild hope that Mrs. Rolls might have told
Mother this as a hint that Helena was going to knit some socks

for him; but the hope died when she said, "How are your socks, dear? Both Mrs. Bigge and Mrs. Neville have asked for your measurements, so I expect you will have plenty before long."

To this he could not reply.

"By the way, before I forget, Phillip. It was most kind of you, old chap, to offer us all the use of your salary while you are away; but at the moment it might be the best thing to have it paid half-quarterly into a deposit account at the bank, until such time as you may need it. The first payment, as you know, is due at the end of the month, at Michaelmas."

"Thanks," said Phillip hastily, hoping that Father would not mention the amount. Some of the fellows in the battalion were quite rich, and he did not want them to know that he had been earning only fifty pounds a year. Hastily he sought another subject.

"Mother, I did tell you we saw the King, on our march down here, didn't I, in my letter?"

"Yes dear. I wish I could have seen him. What did he look like?"

"Oh, just like the photographs, only sort of browner, his beard you know. His eyes sort of looked heavy underneath them. There were three other officers with him, all in blues."

"How very interesting, dear."

Sipping soup scarcely tasted, or realized, Phillip saw Douglas' face at the door. When Douglas had gone, Mother said, "What a very nice man, dear! He was so helpful when he saw us looking for you. He brought us to your company lines, and apologised for not being able to take us into the Officers' Mess, explaining that he was not an officer."

"He's just got a stripe. He was at the Bluecoat School."

"I could see there was something fine about him. Oh well, I did my best to get you a presentation for Christ's Hospital, when you were small."

"Douglas comes from Fordesmill, you know."

"Ah! I thought I had seen his face before, dear."

"Have you fired your Lee-Enfield rifle yet, Phillip?"

"Not yet, Father," he said, in a low voice. Why did Father speak so loudly?

"I suppose you will, before you go?"

"I don't know, Father." How could he stop Father?

"But surely, my boy, before you go overseas you will fire at least once on the range?"

Fried slices of plaice were hurriedly swallowed.

"Perhaps Phillip will, dear, there's no knowing. Anyway, you may be going to Egypt, may you not?"

"They haven't issued us with sun-helmets," he whispered. Thank God the officers were going out. "We've got our new valises. There's a rumour we are going to have the short rifles, the ones with the wooden stock extended up to the muzzle, but I really don't know. All I know is that our names, numbers, regiment, and religions are now being stamped on identity discs."

Hetty tried not to think about it. Richard, too, was feeling worried. There had been an article in *The Daily Trident* about the need for the powers-that-be to think in terms of modern warfare, particularly in the part that the machine gun was going to play in the battles to come when the main armies confronted one another. The Germans had a great many machine guns. While Phillip and his fellow territorials had not even learned to fire their rifles!

Hetty could see that Phillip was in agony about further questions. Richard took the hint, and chose what he thought was a subject of general interest.

"Well, tell us if you have seen anything of the Russians that came down from Scotland, old chap."

"I don't think it's true. Also, it has been officially denied, as I wrote and told you."

"Well, a lot of people appear to have seen them on their journey south, as they travelled down from Leith. Some porters were seen brushing snow out of the carriages afterwards—that at any rate was the tale, Phillip. If they did come from Archangel, and have crossed over to France, they may just turn the scale, you know. And it is hardly likely that any arrival of reinforcement troops would be mentioned in the papers, is it?"

Richard's words did nothing to lessen his son's taut fears of his father appearing dogmatic before the other fellows in the room. Phillip swallowed tasteless food; and after coffee, said he ought to be getting back to camp. Trying to make light of the gloomy situation, he said, "I hope the Colonel doesn't recognise my beastly physogg!"

It was now Hetty's turn to try and make light of what, after all, was only an aggravation of the usual awkwardness between father and son, a condition that almost her entire spiritual life at home had been devoted to removing.

"Perhaps he won't remember it, dear, with so much on his mind at present."

"You don't know him like I do," muttered Phillip. "He's a martinet."

"Anyway, he must be used to your ways by now, dear!" she said, with a smile; which remark produced in him a scowling sigh, as he stared at the tablecloth. The waiter was sweeping up the crumbs, preparatory to laying fresh knives and forks.

"Well," said Richard, "we had better be moving."

Outside in the sunny air of a calm September afternoon fresh fears assailed Phillip. "I say, please don't be offended, but do you mind if I don't see you off at Jarvis Brook Station? I think I ought to be getting back now—I haven't a pass, and the military police may report me. Well, give my love to everyone, including Mrs. Neville and Desmond, Gran'pa, Aunt Marian, and everyone you can think of. Don't let Tommy go anywhere near my bedroom, will you? Or he'll pinch the rest of my birds' eggs."

"No, dear, of course not." She opened her purse. "Now, dear, I have brought this for you." She took out a small silver and ebony crucifix. "It was mine as a girl at the convent at Thildonck, and and if you wear it round your neck, I am sure it will keep you from harm, wherever you are. And you won't forget your prayers, will you?"

He took it hurriedly, and put it in his breast pocket. "I'll put it on the leather bootlace which Baldwin said is best for our identification disks. Well, I think I ought to go back now. Goodbye Father, goodbye Mother."

He saluted, and was about to turn away when Hetty said, "Give me a kiss, dear." He flinched at this; but removing his glengarry, kissed her lightly on her cheek. He shook his father's hand.

"Well, do your best, old chap! Good luck!"

"Yes, Father. Goodbye."

He saluted, and turned away and without looking back strode along the road leading to Ashdown Forest. Hetty turned, and waved her handkerchief to the striding figure. Richard took her arm, to comfort her.

Chapter 17

CIGAR FOR A SOLDIER

WHEN he arrived back in camp a company parade in fatigue dress was just assembling. Douglas, new stripes on his jacket, said that they were to be inoculated against enteric fever. This fact had given rise to the rumour that their destination was Egypt, or even South Africa. But it turned out to be an anti-typhoid injection, which pointed to France, where the water was notoriously bad to drink.

A dab of iodine on bared upper arm, then the needle, which Captain MacTaggart, with pursed lips, pushed hard into nipped flesh. Why did some chaps faint, he wondered. To his surprise Furrow, the powerful rowing man, was among them. He stood up all right; but an hour later he began to shudder violently, perhaps because he had gone to the washing benches, stripped, lathered all over, and emptied a pail of cold water over himself.

There was a big fire of wood flaring up in a space near the canteen marquee. He managed to lug four blankets there, and lying down to cover himself up, teeth clenched, head throbbing, shaking in every limb. After an hour under blankets the paroxysms passed. Feeling sick, with aching arm, he returned to lie down in the tent. Shivering, he pulled his blanket over his head, and slept beside his rifle.

Others were lying there, pale and quiet. By tea-time he felt better. He felt considerable cheered when Colours came to tell them that the Commanding Officer had succeeded in his request to the Commander-in-Chief, Home Forces, that each man be given twenty-four hours' embarkation leave. Half companies were to start the next day after morning parade.

Leave was in two batches. Phillip was in the second. After Saturday morning parade he and others of the half company were given railway warrants. Off he and Baldwin hurried to catch the fast train from Jarvis Brook to London, free until Retreat on Sunday night.

With keen anticipation he showed his pass at Wakenham station to the porter. The porter looked at it, then waved him through with his clippers, as though unaware that he had returned. Outside the station the houses looked small, drab, forlorn. He saw for the first time that they had slate roofs. Banana skins lay in the gutter, with pieces of paper. He went into the newspaper shop, to buy some Cavalier tobacco; the wooden-legged man who gave him his penny-ha'penny change from sixpence did not seem to recognise him, but returned to study of the League prospects. Football, was there still *football*? He hurried away up Foxhill Road, anticipating the wonder of his arrival home—and Desmond.

At the top, opposite St. Simon's Church, they were playing tennis in the club. His heart accelerated. Peering through the shrubs he saw Helena Rolls, all in white, playing a set.

He hesitated, feeling twisted inside; then not daring to reveal himself, he hurried onwards. Home, Mother's face was now prominent in his mind.

The Hill was just the same, though somehow looking more bare. There was the slow form of Mr. Krebs walking towards him, arm in arm with his grey-haired wife. Would Mr. Krebs recognise him? He remembered he was a German. Mr. Krebs looked straight ahead, Mrs. Krebs smiled. Phillip saluted. Mr. Krebs seemed startled—ah, he had recognised him after all! He raised his hat, showing bald pink head as he bowed. Phillip strode on, feeling a little happier.

He passed the West Kent Grammar School, much enlarged since the L.C.C. had taken it over as the Wakenham Secondary School. The old grammar school was still there, its wasp-dug and flaking old red brick enclosed by new clean high walls. It did not seem alive, it had been suffocated by the L.C.C. He went down by the sheep-fold, glad to see the Crystal Palace glittering on the ridge some miles away; but it seemed to be much nearer.

Vaulting the hurdles, he crept down the steep clay bank above the gully, seeing the same old blackish-red hips on the trees, and same curled dry notched brown leaves fallen under them. Yes, summer was ending. Soon the rest of the leaves would fall, and old sparrow nests be shown in bare branches. He stopped, closed his eyes: why, why did life change so?

The front door of the Rolls' house was open. He passed, looking straight ahead, hoping he would not see, and have to speak to Mr. Pye, should his sallow face be visible in the next house. He got to the safety of Gran'pa's house, looked in at the window, saw no one. He shut away a piercing thought of Grannie, of Uncle Hugh, of the old faces, the old days——Ah, Mrs. Bigge peering round her gate! He was glad to see her.

"They're all waiting for you, Phillip. How well you look! We are all proud of you in Hillside Road. Go in, dear, don't waste time with Aunty Bigge, as you used to call me. Mother is waiting to see you! What days we're living in, to be sure!"

"Yes, Mrs. Bigge. I hope you are quite well?"

"Yes thank you, dear."

"And Mr. Bigge? And Norah?"

"They had a spree all by themselves at the sea-side, you know, without Mother. Now in you go, bless you!"

How terribly quickly the time had rushed away. It was Sunday afternoon.

"You ask him, Mum, please. I daren't."

"I am sure Father would do so at once, dear, if you asked him yourself. Besides, it would please him if it came from you. He is very proud of you, you know."

Mother and son stood in the kitchen. He had left the sitting-room ostensibly to carry in the tea-tray, but really to ask her to ask Father to play the gramophone.

Down in the sitting-room sat Richard, Mavis, Doris, Petal, Mrs. Neville, and Desmond. It was four o'clock. At a quarter past five he would be leaving to catch the half-past five train from Wakenham to London Bridge. They were all going to walk over the Hill together, to see him off.

He glanced at the Ingersoll alarm clock on the dresser shelf, ticking away alert as Mrs. Feeney. Only another seventy-five minutes! How small the kitchen looked, how dark. How small Mother was, really. He had never thought of her as small before.

"The kettle will soon boil, dear."

Why did Mother pretend to be so cheerful? Yet somehow, it was all part of the kitchen, with its varnished wallpaper, faded and yellow; the clock on the wall that used to ring the morning alarm but had stopped owing to fumes of the gas-stove, which had made its brass wheels green; the table, the chairs, the scullery where Timmy Rat lived in his box on the copper-lid; the pail under the sink with the swab and hearthstone in it used by Mrs. Feeney; the plate-rack over the sink; the small window above, the door with its several bolts and chain; the empty water-butt

outside where he had once put some roach and so been found out
taking Father's things.

"I think I'll just run up and take a last look at my bedroom."

He opened the corner cupboard, with its faded gummed label
stuck on the door, *Private*. How dark it was inside, all the light
shut out by the house next door, and the roof. There lay his
"treasures"—the most valued custard-box of birds' eggs on saw-
dust: half-cured skins of birds, and the stoat, and various claws,
wings and skulls from gamekeepers' gibbets: his model stationary
steam-engine, with steam-hammer attachment and circular saw:
his model yacht *Dipper*, which Mother had given him for winning
his scholarship: the set of conjuring tricks, and box of chemicals
with which he had not experimented for years, since Father had
discovered that one of the little red pill-boxes had been labelled
potassium ferrocyanide, declaring it to be a deadly poison. The
box had cost 1/-, from Murrage's, an old Christmas present. A
score of memories smote him, of his lost childhood. There was
his pocket accumulator in its curved transparent celluloid case,
which leaked sulphuric acid, and was charged for 2*d*. at Wether-
ley's in the High Street. It bubbled considerably, and had lit
several bath-nights, standing on the soap-dish, until Father had
forbidden its use, vitriol being dangerous, he said. Its place had
been taken by the big flask-like bottle holding dark-yellow
potassium chromate, a single-cell battery so heavy and clumsy
that it had fallen into the bath, out of which he had hopped so
quickly that the *Boy's Own Paper* he had been reading had got
soaked and dyed yellow. How he had scrubbed the bath, to get
rid of the yellow stain: then the *B.O.P.* had stuck in the lavatory
pan, and had to be torn into little shreds with pincers to get rid
of it, in panic lest he had stopped up the drains for ever.

On the wall was fixed his cigar-box telephone, with carbon
rods balanced to make a diaphragm: he had laid wires across the
ceiling, above the door, along the passage and so to Mother's
bedroom, where a similar cigar-box was fixed behind her bed.
The telephone had worked, too. The trouble was you had to yell
to be heard in the cigar-box at the other end, to make sufficient
vibrations to move the carbon rods which regulated the current:
and so you could never be sure if it was your shout that was
heard in Mother's bedroom, or your telephone voice. He had
put it up without permission, but Father had never spoken about
it, although he had driven screws into the wallpaper and made

some false-move holes in the plaster. After the accident with the single-cell potassium chromate battery, there had been no more telephoning.

And there, standing guard over his boyhood "treasures", stood the bittern on its small wooden stand, covered all over with pepper to discourage moths. It was time to go down. He felt a thin wire-like feeling of almost desperate pain to be leaving his bedroom now. Voices came up through the floor, as they had when he had lain awake at night, listening to Father's mumble at Mother: and where he had, long ago, lain in terror waiting for Father to come upstairs to punish him with the cane. He sat on the bed, mourning, until he heard Mother's footfalls coming up the stairs. He went to meet her.

"You ask him for the gramophone, Mum. I *can't*!"

"All right, dear. Come on down now. I put the pepper on your bittern, as you asked me."

"You can have it for Christmas dinner if you like, with some salt added!"

"It may well come to that, if prices rise any more!" she said, gaily.

When they re-entered the sitting-room, which used to be called the parlour, he suddenly remembered, Father said, "Now old chap, would you like me to play the gramophone?"

"No thanks, Father."

Richard looked at Hetty. Then he got up from his chair, and selecting the key on his ring, unlocked the top.

"There you are, old chap. You play anything you like."

Mrs. Neville looked across the table at Phillip. She wore a hat rather like a large pale green pork pie with ribbons round it.

"I hear your gramophone has a beautiful tone, Mr. Maddison."

"What would you like to hear first, Mrs. Neville?"

"Oh, I am sure your choice would be better than mine, Mr. Maddison!"

"May we have the one by Wagner, Dickie? I am sure Phillip would like it."

As the *Liebestod* filled the room Mrs. Neville surreptitiously wiped the corner of her eye. "Ah, how it brings back Covent Garden!" she exclaimed in her creamy voice. She had once gone there to hear *Traviata*.

Petal smiled at Phillip. Everyone was sitting very still, as always when Father played the records. When the *Liebestod* was finished, Father looked at his watch. Mother said—why *did* she have to say the obvious?—"We must not be late at the station, Dickie," rather anxiously.

"Oh, there's plenty of time yet," he said, airily. "Petal, what would you like next?"

"May we have Paderewski, Uncle Dick, please?"

"Yes, the *Waterfall* one!" exclaimed Phillip. It was one of the Études, tumultuous and sad. As the record was playing, he saw Mrs. Bigge's hat move along the level of the fence beyond the half-open window. She was listening.

"May we have the *Humoresque*, Father?"

This was a song set to the music of Dvorak. Mrs. Neville watched Hetty's face as the lamenting words came with the sad plaint of violins.

> *When the ice was on the fountain*
> *And the snow was on the mountain*
> *Donald came no more to greet me.*
> *Come back, my laddie, come back and love me,*
> *Why did you die and leave me . . .*

Mrs. Neville said boisterously, to cover her emotion, "Phillip, you would choose that, wouldn't you, you bad boy! Don't heed him, Mrs. Maddison. I know Phillip of old! Why, when we hear from him next, he will probably be adopting some of the monkeys on the Rock of Gibraltar, and putting Timmy Rat's nose out of joint when he hears of it. I am sure animals understand what we humans are saying, half the time, and how they must laugh at us!"

Mrs. Neville's jollity eased the feeling in the room. She went on,

"Haven't you got one of Harry Lauder, Mr. Maddison? My idea of a send-off for Phillip is *Stop your tickling, Jock*. Though," she added, in her creamy, best-manner voice, "I must say that your selection of records is a very fine one indeed."

"I have not got the record you speak of, Mrs. Neville, but here is the next best thing, perhaps," and Richard put on *Over the Sea to Skye*.

As the plaintive tune and words for the defeated Prince Charles

Stuart filled the room, Mrs. Neville could not restrain a drip of tears. Fortunately Thomas and Marian Turney appeared at the open french windows before, as Mrs. Neville remarked later to Desmond, Mr. Maddison could put on *The Dead March in Saul.*

Richard was glad of the intervention. He greeted his father-in-law and Miss Turney with an affability that was, for the occasion, genuine.

"Well, Phillip m'boy, how are ye?" said Thomas Turney. After awhile he chuckled and said, "Now then, Phillip, you're in the thick of things, so tell us the secret about the Russians from Archangel."

"Oh, those Russians!" exclaimed Mrs. Neville. "The number of people who have friends who have seen the snow on their boots!"

Before Phillip could have his say, that it had been officially denied, his grandfather, chuckling, went on, "Two hundred thousand Russians! They certainly were white but not with snow, he-he-he! As ye know, Hetty, I talk sometimes on the Hill with a fellow on the staff of *The Morning Post,* and he tells me that one of the large wholesalers in Leadenhall Market— he-he-he!—received a telegram 'Two hundred thousand Russians arrived from Archangel', and they were—he-he-he!—eggs!"

Mrs. Neville laughed as heartily as Thomas Turney: Hetty hovered between amusement and concern for Richard, for whom the explanation was a disappointment. He had believed in the arrival of two army corps of Russians. He went to the gramophone, took off the record, put it in its cardboard case, and closed the lid softly. As he did so Phillip got up and left the room. Richard said, with an air of conspiratorial intimacy,

"I think if you will all excuse me, I will go and see if the boy wants to ask me anything before he leaves."

He found Phillip sitting by the pot-board in the kitchen, changing his shoes. It was some effort for Richard to say,

"Well, old chap, look after yourself out there, won't you. And don't forget to write to your mother sometimes. If there is anything I can do for you at any time, do not hesitate to ask me."

"No, Father. Thank you very much."

"I'll keep an eye on Timmy Rat for you, of course."

"Oh, thanks."

With light, almost bantering voice, Richard went on, "Do you remember the large black spider, with the pale yellow spots on its back, which used to live in the corner up there, all one summer?"

"Yes, Father. I found one like it once, in a crack of the garden fence."

"I don't suppose you remember the spider we saved from a watery grave in the bathroom, when we paid our first visit to this house, do you? Let me see, it must have been"—he made a pretence of calculation—"March, eighteen ninety-seven—you were nearly two years of age."

"I remember, Father. You put the spider on the window sill."

"So I did. Fancy you remembering that!"

"I thought it was very kind of you."

Richard felt the words like a blow. He said, when Phillip stood up, "By jove, are you going to wear the 'campaign clumpers' after all? Won't they be too heavy?"

"Yes, on second thoughts I think they will be, Father."

Almost feverishly he plucked at the laces.

"No great hurry, my boy. You have ten minutes: then you ought to be toddling along. By the way, it might be as well not to mention the fact that you had a German grandmother. Some of your cousins, I expect, are now fighting on the other side."

"I noticed that you had painted over the letter-spaces of the name on the gate."

"Well, it is just as well to take no risks in these times, Phillip. I hear, between you and me, that many German shops in the East End have been smashed by the mobs. In one case, an attempt at arson was made. So you see, old chap, the less we say about it, the better for all concerned. Here's Mother—I expect she will want to have a word in private with you, so I will leave you with her."

Mother and son went into the front room. He closed the door, to whisper words which revealed to her the doubt and longing that obsessed her little boy—O, he was still that, she could see.

"Mum, do you think I ought to go in and say goodbye to the Rolls? Would Mr. Rolls be cross, do you think? Oh no, I daren't! What would they think if I did? Anyway, they may be going to church. But, Mum, when you write, you will tell me any news about them, won't you?"

"Yes, dear. I am sure that both Mr. and Mrs. Rolls regard you as a brave boy."

There were footfalls outside. Now it was time to leave.

Richard decided that, as he would probably not be asked to accompany his son to the station, he would first find an excuse for remaining behind. "Well, I'll say goodbye now, old chap."

"Here y'are, Phillip m'boy," said Gran'pa. "I've had to give up smokin' 'em. I gave one each to Bertie and Gerry, who came home yesterday. It's a good cigar—a Corona. Would ye care for one, Dick?"

"No thanks, Mr. Turney, I've chucked smoking."

Phillip went into the scullery, where his white rat was awaiting him, whiskers twitching, pink eyes bright. Timmy sneezed: he had a chill. Phillip scratched his ears, the rat closed his eyes, warm in his owner's hands. Then, "Goodbye, Timmy," whispered Phillip, and putting him back in his box, closed the door.

As in a dream, it seemed, he was walking up the gully, Desmond beside him, with Mother and the girls. It seemed only a moment since he had come down there, the day before.

Under the elms, by the Refreshment Shelter, he said, "Please, Mother, I think I would rather go on, with Desmond only. Please don't mind. Only if you all come to London Bridge, there will be a lot of chaps, and besides, I—oh, I can't explain. You go back now, with Petal and Mavis and Doris."

"Yes, dear, of course, naturally. Just as you like. We'll go back to Father, he is all alone. Don't forget to write, will you?"

"Of course not."

He kissed her, said goodbye to Petal and his sisters, and went on with Desmond, feeling less cumbered.

"I want to join up in the London Electrical Engineers, Phil, but Mother says I'm too young."

"You look much more than sixteen, Des. But surely you'll have to stay at school?"

"My guardian may give permission. He's my uncle."

"Oh, yes."

"My father's separated from Mother, you see."

Phillip wondered why Desmond spoke in so low a voice, as though there were some secret in his life.

"The London Electrical Engineers operate searchlights, and I am keen on physics. Our science master is now an officer with them. The Zeppelins used to fly over our school at night, you know, spying out the land, before the war. We used to hear the engines up among the stars."

"I would much rather work a searchlight than footslogging!"

Desmond went with him to London Bridge Station. As they waited on the platform, Phillip said, "How is Eugene?"

"He's very well. He's with his father. We did start once, to come and see you at Crowborough, but his bike kept getting punctures, so we turned back. It's quite a journey, you know, eighty miles both ways. And to be frank, I didn't want to run the risk of seeing the Churches again."

"No, they're not much cop. I nearly had a fight with the younger one. Well, Des, I can't tell you how glad I am you are my great friend."

"Phil," said Desmond, looking at him steadily, "I shall miss you very much." He had gone pale. There were many faces under the dark and dirty glass roof—all soot, sulphur, and grime. The faces were part of it all—and the sorrow of living. The last Phillip saw of his old life was his great friend's oval face and waving hand among a fluttering of many waving hands and set faces along the gloomy platform.

He settled into his corner, and lit the cigar as the train rattled over the points on its way to Croydon; but before the train stopped at that junction, the Corona was lying on the permanent way, more or less in line with instalments of his tea. It was the inoculation, he decided, as he wiped his mouth and faced the future with shut eyes.

Chapter 18

LINES OF COMMUNICATION

It was a fine day in the third week of September when the London Highlanders, made up to strength by a draft from the Second Battalion, marched away from Ashdown Forest behind the pipers playing the *Marseillaise*. This tune, or its approximation limited to the minor scale of the bagpipes with their fixed buzzing bass note, immediately confirmed the rumour that they were off to France.

As a fact, the Colonel did not know the destination of his battalion, beyond Southampton. Sealed orders were to be given him after the transport had steamed beyond land: but to be on the safe side, the grey-haired, regular soldier, seconded from the Coldstream, had ordered the Pipe-Major to teach his pipers the

French national anthem. As time had been short, the pipers were practising the difficult tune on the way to the station.

As they approached the town, after an interval of silence, the pipes played *The Road to the Isles*, the regimental march, and at once an air of braced alertness moved down the swinging length of a thousand-odd men.

From the scouts wheeling bicycles, then the Pipe-Major and his pipers, then the Commanding Officer and his Adjutant on grey chargers, the Regimental Sergeant-Major just behind on foot—first-class warrant officer, also of the Coldstream, dressed like a commissioned officer except that his tunic was buttoned to the neck instead of being open for khaki collar and tie—all the way down the column to the second-in-command at the rear, the Iron Colonel with his gigantic brown moustaches and brooding military impressiveness, the battalion was braced in more senses than one. Indeed, before they moved off from the old bare-trodden lines of Bleak Hill—the leading fours of "B" Company overheard the Adjutant saying with a laugh to Captain Forbes, "I don't know how you feel, Fiery my boy, but I feel like a Christmas tree!"

The Company Commanders, breeched and spurred, rode horses; the subalterns marched at the head of their sections. But astride or on foot, all officers were encumbered for war with various articles of equipment suspended or attached about their leather belts and braces. There was the rucksack humped on the Iron Colonel's back, his long sword in leather scabbard hanging from the frog attached to his belt on his left side, under the stuffed haversack; water-bottle, revolver in holster and cartridge wallet, on his right. Thus sword in one hand, pistol in other, map-case and field-glasses dangling, he saw himself going into action, to rehabilitate himself in his own eyes for the funk, sheer blue funk, at Modder River! This time it would be a case of do or die! The Iron Colonel had a sovereign sewn under each crown and stars of each cuff, in case he were taken prisoner, as in South Africa.

As for rank and file, they were even more loaded by webbing belt and straps. They carried at the slope the newly issued Mark I rifle; one hundred rounds of ammunition, in clips of five within the pouches pressing on their ribs. Entrenching tools hung over the base of each spine, upon the left thigh lay haversack, bayonet, and entrenching-tool handle, a water-bottle on the right. The new valise held greatcoat and mess-tin, with spare shoes, socks, and shirt—said to be fifty-six pounds weight in all.

On the station platform Phillip noticed a new kind of officer, near several staff-officers in red-banded hats and tabs. He had a brassard on his right arm, a white band with the letters R T O in black. Eight men to a third-class carriage, was the order.

On the platform Colonel Findhorn stood chatting to the Brigade Commander. Beside them was the graceful figure of the General who had inspected them the day before they had struck camp. Everyone knew his name, Sir Ian Hamilton, hero of the Boer War; and immensely great to Phillip since the General had stopped by him as he passed down the ranks; he said only a few words, but in those moments Phillip had felt his whole self to be alive. The General, who had a smiling face of unusual amiability, said, "This man has a look of Robbie Burns about him, Colonel." Then to Phillip, "Do you know who I mean?"

"Yes sir, and James Hogg, the Ettrick shepherd lad, too."

"The poets will be wanted after this war," said the General to the Colonel; and the kind eyes passed on down the ranks.

Standing with others, at the open window, Phillip watched the General who did not look heavy-bodied like other old officers, and had a manner like that of Mr. Rolls. Eagerly he regarded the handshakes, the slight bows with heels together, the salutes, the smiles among the great ones. Then the Earl of Findhorn stepped back, gave the General a full salute, and got into his carriage, followed by the Iron Colonel and the Adjutant. The anxious-faced Railway Transport Officer blew his whistle; the civilian guard waved his green flag; the engine screeched; Sir Ian Hamilton and his staff stood to attention while Sir Ian saluted. A roar of cheering, in which Phillip joined, broke out along the length of the train as it moved away from the platform.

Equipment off and stuffed on racks, they examined their new rifles. Baldwin told him that they had a flat trajectory for six hundred yards, superior to the old long rifle's four hundred. The order was that no man was to charge his magazine until ordered to do so. They had rattled and clicked away with bolt and trigger while in extended order in the heather of Ashdown Forest, but always with imaginary ammunition. There was no firing range.

Two of the Leytonstone tent were in the carriage, Collins and Martin. Collins suggested a game of nap. Phillip had learned this game, and the more interesting solo whist, in the tent. Before learning, he had considered the men seen in trains, newspaper over knees, flipping out cards, to be rather low sort of people. Now, with a paper over his knees and those of Martin, Collins, and thin little Kirk, who wore pince-nez spectacles, he gambled happily with ha'pennies and pennies. The others read, talked, or looked out of the window.

One of them, Tommy Atkins, was writing a very long letter. Tommy Atkins was his real name, not one nicked on to him. Tommy Atkins was exactly what the mythical British soldier was supposed to be, always cheery. Like Phillip, though in a different way, he had never quite mixed in with the others. Tommy was apple-cheeked and alert, with a small black moustache. He was ever ready to help others in any way he could with good advice, as well as practice. He had a tendency to preach the good life, and neither drank alcohol, smoked tobacco, nor used swearwords.

Tommy Atkins was something of a joke in the company; a nice joke, owing to his cheerful unselfishness, a sincere rather than an amiable nature. He had unusual habits; he washed all over every evening before putting on a white night-shirt to sleep in; then lying down in his place, feet to pole, he read the Bible; and knelt up, eyes shut and hands folded before him, to say his prayers. When at first he had been ragged good-naturedly, he replied, always with energetic cheerfulness, that he was a member of a Christian civilisation. Phillip had greatly enjoyed the cross-talk between Tommy Atkins and Lance-corporal Mortimore.

"So you think this is a Christian civilisation, do you, Thomas my son?" Morty would enquire, with his disarming smile.

"Certainly it is, Corporal! It is built on rock, not on sand."

"London, the centre of it, is built on clay. How do you account for that, Tommy?"

"Part of it is built on chalk, Corporal; but I speak metaphorically."

"Have a drop of this wine, Tommy. It came from limestone, which is allied to chalk, and sunshine—Beaujolais, very special, Tommy. It will liven you up."

"I am already quickened by the Spirit, Corporal."

"You sly dog, been at the whiskey, have you? Well, never mix malt and grape, they say."

Imperturbably Tommy Atkins opened his Bible. No one ragged him then.

Cards flipped on the newspaper; coppers clinked.

"Do you believe in gambling, Tommy?" asked Collins, looking up.

"I do not, Collins, but carry on with your game, if it seems right to you. But look out of the window, man, the Downs are in sight!"

A grey-green extended hump lay above the heat mist.

"I'll go the bundle," said Collins, closing his cards.

"We must be going along the coast to Southampton, behind Brighton and Worthing and Chichester! Hurray!" cried Elliott, hanging between the racks by his hands. Phillip did the same; Collins took the opportunity to give him a hard slap on his backside.

"That's for bloody well sucking up to the General."

"But he asked me a question, and I answered it!"

"Arse crawler!" said Collins, contemptuously. "Come on, it's your deal."

"That remark injures yourself," said Tommy Atkins.

"I don't think I want to play any more, thanks all the same," said Phillip.

The train ran on steadily, passing over many points behind towns which Tommy Atkins obligingly named from time to time, after scrutiny of the map in the glass case above his seat. So they came to Southampton, as he had prophesied, in the late afternoon, entering above marsh grazing where red and black cattle stood tail-swishing at trodden places in the dykes, and ragged ranks of thistles yielded shining floss to the heated airs above.

The railway lines were shining, too; and floating thistle-seeds were sucked into the carriage past the gazing eyes of one who was feeling that the world he had hitherto known, which had been leaving him in some unrealisable way since the far-off excitements of August Bank Holiday, was now at last come to its end.

Remotely, as with the moon's pale shade in the September sky, his mother's face looked upon his mind. He fingered the crucifix under his shirt, and felt the reassurance that, unknown to him, he had lost since childhood; when his father had taken from his cot and forbidden further use of the silken scrap of his mother's old petticoat which had served, with his sucked thumb, as sub-stitute for lost warmth and safety. Tears, sobbings of aloneness in dark fear had followed; but the father had been firm in this duty. The sooner the donkey boy learned manly ways, the sooner he would cease to whine, to cry at the least reprimand; the donkey boy was then two years old.

The troop train drew into the port. He stared at a row of brick back-to-back houses, where in tattered-looking gardens small tattered-looking children waved from porch and cinder path. Each garden, he noticed, had its faded wooden rabbit hutches and wired-in hens. Leaning sunflowers hung their brown heads askew in little shabby garden after garden. Each head hung as though weary of its weight of seed, its green and twisted neck tired of following the sun so many times around the sky, only to die when its race was run.

When its race was run—it was a sad and yet beautiful thought, first heard from Uncle Hugh, and recurring to him in secret since his earliest memory of faces and moments passing—Minnie his German nurse; Mona Monk the little maid who had wheeled him in the mail-cart on the Hill until her father had gone to prison; the early days at Beau Brickhill when Great-uncle Toby Thacker was still alive; the woods in Whitefoot Lane; cycling with Desmond to the Fish Ponds on Reynard's Common; the catkins and red-speck flowers among the tracery of the hazel coverts of Shooting Common about the time the chiff-chaff flew across the sea from Africa; and the nightingales filling the new green wood with their dark purple notes above the acres and acres of bluebells, to announce the fullness of sap and egg. Well, he had had a lovely life, and now perhaps his race was run. He stifled the anguish of his thoughts by staring fixedly through the window; relieved that now it was time to put on his equipment, within the carriage slowing in sudden dimness, as it moved under a long covered shed.

They piled arms in the centre of the platform. They were told to sit down, but not to fall out except to go to the lavatory on the dock at the end of the shed. At once he used this excuse to look around.

He pretended not to see the upright iron shelter, painted green, on the dock, for an excuse to walk beyond. It certainly was an unfamiliar lavatory, like a long green barrel which showed a

man's feet below and the top of his head above. He walked past
it, looking at some silent Lascar sailors, various objects on the
quay, including big wooden crates marked with the government
broad-arrows. There was an enormous rectangular pile of rolls of
galvanised barbed-wire. Beyond the grey stack stood something
that he had seen before only in photographs; a howitzer with its
short thick barrel pointing into the air; and the sight was
startling.

Its shield was gashed and holed. Part of the barrel was pitted
deeply, little ragged craters amidst gougings and jagged cuts.
If steel could be so torn by shell-fire, as though spattered upon it,
how much more so would the flesh and the body of a man!
Hitherto his vision of death upon the battlefield had been of men
falling, shot through the heart, the cheer ceasing on their lips;
somehow the body was borne off, covered with Tricolour or
Union Jack, to be buried with reverence, while bugles sounded
in the sunset of the hush of battle; the noble soul at rest, understood at last by all in death.

The sun was going down over funnels, masts, and cranes.
Chains were rattling, dirty men with greasy faces walking up
planks with small wooden boxes on their shoulders. He hurried
back to Baldwin, and tried to feel that this was the Great
Adventure.

They waited on the platform, whiling away time writing
letters, smoking, wondering. The haversack ration of cheese and
bread had been eaten in the train. They had only their iron
rations—a blue tin of bully beef each, and six hard thick biscuits,
in a little linen bag. The iron ration must not be eaten until the
order was given.

Phillip had some apples and chocolate, and Baldwin had a
nut cake, so they shared.

Dusk descended. At last a stir, an order, rattle of piling-rings
and knock of butts, shuffle of leather on wood; and up a gangway.

The transport was a rusty iron steamer, with a Lascar crew.
Gleaming dark eyes under black ringlets passed noiselessly above
bare feet. One murmured in a thin voice, "The la-dies from
hell", with a grin of very white teeth. Baldwin said, "That's
what the Germans call the Jocks." Ladies from hell! He saw
himself running in huge elastic-sided boots, bayonet outheld as
in practice through the heather of Bleak Hill, his face contorted
as in the pictures of soldiers in the Boer War, yet grinning like

Grannie in *Little Red Riding Hood*. He felt cold and hollow. If ever in a charge, he would keep a bullet in his rifle, to save himself when a German came to bayonet him, at the last minute. The water below slopped oily between ship and dock. Then in the darkness the quiet pulse on the iron deck became a trembling. Water swirled below, glittering in the lilac light of the arc-lamps spluttering on the quay. They were leaving England!

A long thick row of glengarries above shoulders hunched over the rails hardly moved as the lessening garish lights began to slide round behind the wake of the transport. The order was given, *No Smoking*. There were submarines about, it was murmured. Suddenly he saw that the officers were above them, leaning easily upon their rail. A breeze found their kilts, and he turned to go below, to see what the sleeping quarters were like.

There were none. There was a rusty iron deck, partly covered in. They dumped their accoutrements with others against the canvas-shrouded rails, then set out to look around the ship, to find out if there was any beer to be bought. He met Gerry, and was greatly relieved to see him. "How about a beer together?"

"No luck, young Phil. There's cocoa in the galley aft, thr'pence a cup, a damned swizz. How're y' feeling?"

"All right. How's Bertie?"

"He's on another boat, with the transport. See you later."

From the dark little galley lit by an oil-lamp hot cups of thick cocoa were being passed out, to the chink of coins. Threepence, sheer robbery! However, it was warm and sweet, which was something.

They returned to the rails. As they were looking into the dark, without warning their eyes were hit almost painfully by blinding light, the searchlight beam lifted away, washing the waves before swinging back to light the funnels. And all the way down Southampton water to Spithead ship after ship at anchor in the roads saluted with long blasts on their steam-whistles, while searchlight after searchlight picked up the transport. It was exhilarating; it gave a feeling of England's regard to the men standing in penumbral darkness, while over the short waves moved in succession trails of tinny light to whiten the rows of faces.

A last greeting came from the signal station on the hill above the East Foreland of the Isle of Wight. W-H-A-T S-H-I-P I-S

T-H-A-T spots and dashes of light spelt out in Morse. The answer from the bridge was met with another signal from the Isle, which Journend, one of the battalion signallers standing near spelled out G-O-O-D L-U-C-K. The entire battalion broke into cheering; cheer after cheer passed away into the night until the impulse was gone, and upon the darkened ship there fell a silence above the throb of engines, in the night spectral with waves breaking upon the receding shore of England.

Phillip had forgotten the nausea of the night when the transport hove to for the pilot outside Le Havre. As they moved nearer he saw upon the quays French sentries in red trousers and long blue coats with the ends turned up, carrying rifles with bayonets like the one he had bought at Murrage's long ago. Word soon went round from the pilot that they were the first transport to arrive in the port after the evacuation caused by the Germans crossing the Marne. People and sentries on the quays were waving.

"I hear the Colonel's orders are to report to the Director-General of Communications in Paris," said Baldwin.

"Who told you, Norman?"

"Journend, in the Signallers. Only keep it to yourself."

The news raised Phillip's spirits, already calmed by what the newspaper which Baldwin had brought with him, said. The leading article stated that victory might be nearer than was supposed. The Germans in the East had been stopped by the Pripet Marshes; the Austrians had suffered a great defeat from the Russians, who had captured the fortress of Lemberg; and on the Marne and Aisne the enemy had lost many guns, and thousands of prisoners. He stood happily by the rail, in warm eastern sunshine bringing out the blues and pinks and greys of the houses of the town on the hillside.

They marched through narrow streets, led by pipers playing the *Marseillaise*, to the shrill cheers of the populace. They marched on cobbles, in which lines of steam trams were laid. There were many halts, due to traffic. The street was hot, the air smelt of the grey drain-water trickling in the gutters. The women all looked fat and blowsy. Some wore wooden sabots. They had a grim look when their faces were not animated by obvious jokes as to what *les écossaises* had under their skirts.

Flies were a nuisance. "They like the taste of British sweat, for a change," said Collins.

They marched on, roaring out *It's a long way to Tipperary*. After three hours without a fall-out, and many checks, the battalion arrived at the top of the long hill leading to a field above the town, surrounded by a barbed-wire fence. It was littered with paper and bottles. Here they were to spend the night. There were not enough tents, they were told they would have to sleep out. It was a dispiriting place, for no one was allowed to go into the town. But by trusting children beyond the wire with English silver, bottles of wine and long loaves of bread were to be obtained. Phillip gave a florin to a boy, but did not see him again.

In the morning the camp, which previously had been used by French troops, was cleaned by fatigue parties. Then the battalion marched down the hill again, to the Gare des Marchandises. Another long delay; more children sent off for wine and bread and chocolate. He tried again, and was lucky. A long loaf of bread, a bottle of red wine! And just in time, for grey-covered trucks on which *Hommes 40 Chevaux 8 (en longue)* was stencilled in white paint, came clonking and jerking past them, into the siding. A rumour faster than the train said they were for Paris. This was the life!

"I only hope we get a chance of a smack at the Germans before it is all over," said Baldwin.

"Same here, old son!" replied Elliott.

Only half the battalion, under the Iron Colonel, boarded the train. This fact confirmed that they were for lines of communication.

Everything seen through the open spaces on either side of the moving truck was of keen interest. He kept telling himself, with secret thrills, that he was in France. He must send a postcard to Mr. Howlett. At 42 Wine Vaults Lane they would be preparing the Michaelmas renewal notices very soon now. Was Mr. Thistlethwaite, in top-hat and frock-coat, still coming into the office to talk to Mr. Hollis about the way he had been ill-treated by his old company? Had Downham got his commission yet, for home service? Did Mr. L. Dicks still smell of fish-and-chips, and Mr. J. Konigswinter look as though he ate only salt and pastry? What was Downham doing at that moment? He would be in clover, with twenty pounds every half-quarter paid by the Moon, in addition to his officer's pay. He himself wasn't doing so badly, a shilling and twopence a day, and office salary adding up all the time. Perhaps the war would last six months—he hoped it would, anyway—and if he spent only his army pay he would have at the end of it enough to buy a second-hand motorbike, and be able to turn up at the Old Heathians Fourth Footer matches on a N.U.T., or a B.A.T.!

The picture faded; the train, carrying the right-half battalion dragged its slow journey towards the night. After much stopping, and restarting, to melancholy little toots of the driver's horn, it drew up at Villeneuve, a junction south of Paris. They were marched to billets in an empty school. Things didn't look too good when a sentry was put on the door, and no one was allowed out.

In the morning, washing and shaving in an open yard before the usual burnt bacon and bread and tea for breakfast; and then they were marched to the junction of a hundred shining converging rails, above a revolting litter of tins, paper, faeces, where swarms of fat blue and green flies besieged their faces and necks for the salty sweat as they were told off into squads, each under a French *Sous-officier*, to make orderly piles of rusty shells which had been tipped out of trucks all anyhow. It was hard work, for each shell weighed about a hundred and fifty pounds. They were painted with pale blue or yellow bands.

"Old stock, if you ask me," said Baldwin. "Drop one, and the whole shute might go up."

"You volunteered for this, old son," remarked Elliott, two of whose left-hand fingers had been crushed already. Elliott, a fairly quiet chap at Bleak Hill, seemed to have taken on the sardonic rôle of Mortimore, without Morty's gaiety.

"Honest work never harmed anyone," said Tommy Atkins, cheerfully. "And it's helping to win the war."

"In what way, old son?"

"That is not for us to say. The sooner we've done the job, the sooner we shall be free to stop."

"You've got some hopes, old son."

"I have hope, Elliott, and I have faith, two things that cannot be taken away," replied Tommy Atkins, his apple-face glistening.

"And I have two purple fingernails, old son, so let's call it quits."

At the end of a week, just as they were getting into the way of handling the shells, they were sent to another siding, to unload French wounded who had come down from the Aisne, and carry them on stretchers to horse ambulances. They lay on straw in the

familiar grey trucks, some groaning, others deathly still. The
stench was sickening; the straw was wet with urine and faeces;
flies crawled on open wounds which ran with pus, or were slippery
with twisting maggots. Eyes stared wild and fixed above the
straw, hair and beards dishevelled; they muttered, groaned,
sometimes screamed when being shifted on to stretchers. One
man's feet were splintered bone through broken boots; another's
arm was a bloody stump into which a brown bandage cut,
twisted by a stick, the end of which he held dog-like in his teeth.
The flesh of the shoulder was a blackish blue. A retching smell
came from it. When accidentally he touched the soldier's cheek,
it felt sickly hot. The man's head did not move.

"Dear man," said Tommy Atkins. "He's got gangrene. Or
lockjaw. Don't take it to heart, Maddison, help me get him on
to the stretcher. Only God should be taken to heart."

When the trucks had been cleared he had washed his hands;
but still the smell remained. He tried to force himself not to
sniff his fingers; but again and again the hand came up, and
he had to swallow to stop himself from being sick.

"The French never were exactly famous for their sanitation,"
said Baldwin. "Every well in Villeneuve, despite its name, is
probably crawling with typhoid, and no wonder, when you see
that there are no drains, or if there are any, they just empty
out beside the wells."

They had been forbidden to drink any water except that
drawn from the water-cart, saturated with chloride of lime.

The medical officer, Captain McTaggart, organised a temporary hospital in a factory building closed since the war.
Volunteers were called for orderlies. Tommy Atkins was the
first to volunteer. Phillip and Baldwin preferred to work on the
loading of trucks, the shells having all been stacked.

There was an odd bearded old soldier living in the yards, who
called himself Mad Jack, with a row of dirty ribbons which he
said were got in thirty years' service. He appeared to have no
unit, and tried to attach himself to the Highlanders, and get put
on their nominal roll. Baldwin said he was probably a deserter
and was playing mad, to avoid being shot when caught. Mad
Jack did no work, he slept in a hay store, and played pitch-and-
toss with anyone, including what he called the "'eathen French
frogs", for sous, to get red wine. Another practice of his was to
pinch bully beef, and "flog" it in the *buvettes*. Then one day

military policemen appeared in the yards; and Mad Jack was last seen crossing the tracks at a fast pace, a sack of stolen rations over his shoulder.

Upon an evening soon afterwards they all entrained for Orleans, where a railhead camp was being made for troops of the Lahore and Meerut Divisions, on their way from India.

After a week at Orleans he thought of himself and Baldwin as old sweats, a term learned from some regular soldiers who, having recovered from slight wounds, were there on light duty before being sent back to the front. The light duty was putting up tents in rows; digging latrines, and trenches for water pipes to fill canvas drinking troughs for horses; and erecting a barbed-wire fence around the camp.

After 5 p.m. each day they went into the town, having to report back at the guard tent at 9 p.m. They went to the Poisson d'Or for steaks and sliced potatoes, excellent with the local mustard, and red wine, twice a week; they were paid five francs every Friday, when their brown pay-books were initialled by Mr. Ogilby. Phillip had written half a dozen letters home, saying that no post had come to him so far, but he was well and enjoying himself, and the war would be over by Christmas.

The swallows had gone from the reeds by the river; mists lay over the water at night; leaves broke from the trees. Fishermen stood on the bridge over the Loire unspeaking, their long poles before them. Sometimes one caught a very small fish, slightly bigger than a sardine. Was it a gudgeon, or a bleak? He did not really want to know. It was not an English river.

In the second week of October they read that the Germans had captured Antwerp. Many prisoners of the Naval Division, sent by Winston Churchill, had been captured. The Germans were losing thousands of men in their mass attacks, but in spite of enormous losses, they were advancing. The old sweats in the camp were darkly pessimistic.

"The Ally-mands will be feeling the benefit of all we're doing here," said one. Some of them were court-martial cases, serving sentences of ten and twelve years' hard labour for insubordination, the sentences to begin *after* the war. They were supervised by military policemen armed with revolvers—they did all the worst jobs, like emptying latrine buckets into wheeled carts. When they were fit for duty, they would be sent back up the line.

He was shocked to think that some of the heroes of Mons could be treated like that. Ten years' hard labour for answering back a sergeant! But all regular soldiers appeared to be treated harshly, quite differently from Territorials.

One night in the Poisson d'Or an old French soldier of 'Soixante-dix—the war of 1870—told them that Lille had fallen. Les sales boches were advancing, to the ports of le Manche. Coupez les gorges! he cried, drawing his finger across his throat, and pointing to the north.

"Vous!" he shouted, spitting between his sabots. "Vous! Soldats anglais! Allez! Allez!" He flipped a hand angrily towards the north. Growled agreement supported his words.

"I suppose they think we're letting the French do all the fighting," said Baldwin, quietly.

Suddenly, in the fourth week of October, the order came for the detachment to entrain the next morning. Mr. Ogilby told them that all the other detachments were being recalled at the same time, to reassemble as a battalion. The Germans were making a supreme effort to capture the Channel ports, he said; news which they had already gathered from the smudgy-printed local paper in the Goldfish estaminet.

The London Highlanders were about to be flung into the battle.

PART THREE

"THE RED LITTLE, DEAD LITTLE ARMY"

"It seems to me that we have never realised what
we asked these men to do. They were quite
different to professional soldiers . . . I wonder,
sometimes, if the eyes of the country will ever be
opened to what these Territorial soldiers of ours
have done."

1914 by F-M. Viscount French
of Ypres, K.P., O.M., etc.

"The British Expeditionary Force was the finest
of its kind that ever took the field in Europe.'

General Oberst von Kluck,
Commanding 1st German
Army in 1914.

Chapter 19

ALARUMS

ALL NIGHT the train moved north, halting and shunting in sidings under spluttering purple arc-lamps. At each stop there were shouts, the stamp of horses, and often a jabber of argument outside the truck wherein they were trying to sleep on one another's legs, thighs, even boots. Some were sitting up, others a row of bent backs and head on arms along the one bench. The door rolled open to excited French talk. Wearily he thought that French troops were joining the train. At last the feeble toot of the engine-driver's horn announced the *en avant*, to the accompaniment of more ringing jolts of buffers striking, clank of chains, and the wheels underneath the floor began to grind again.

An increase of lights, jolts, stops, and shakings across points was vaguely noticeable in the small dispiriting hours. With the first pallor of dawn came relief from vain attempts to sleep. Rising into the mist above grey roofs and walls was the Eiffel Tower.

"I wish I hadn't drunk that red wine."

"So do I."

Collins gave a loud belch, without putting his hand up. He *was* a lout, thought Phillip.

Once clear of the capital, the train seemed to be making up for lost time. It puffed steadily through the misty countryside, which passed by slowly.

"We're in no hurry, so we may as well ride."

Their iron rations, six hard thick biscuits in small cloth bag, and blue tin of bully beef, were still uneaten. The sergeant's face looked in at the window space, and told them to open a tin between two men, for breakfast.

"Hurray!" cried Phillip, thinking of Mortimore. "English cooking! Vive la France!"

"Sergeant, what about the lats? Where are they?" asked Tommy Atkins.

"When in Rome, do as the Romans do, my bonny lads! Only don't go dropping yourselves off by mistake," and the sergeant walked to the next truck along the running-board.

The sun was rising up and they felt more cheerful. Looking out of the open window space, he saw several French soldiers crouched down on the running-board, holding to the rail, red trousers down. It was rather fun that way. He rejoiced that he had kept a newspaper. All along beside the track was a litter of paper and empty ragged ration tins, extending as far as he could see. Thousands of troops must have passed that way.

The journey became tedious. They passed slowly through another large station, marked *Beauvais*. At midday they were at *Amiens*, where the train stopped. No one was allowed to leave the truck. The bully beef had made him feel rather sick. Then someone said tea was coming; and soon afterwards two men were told off to go to where smoke arose near a signal-box. They returned carrying the familiar black dixie between them. Who cared that the tea tasted of skilly? It was hot, that was all that mattered.

Soon the old familiar song was rising from the truck,

> *We don't give a damn for Will-i-am,*
> *We know the Crown Prince is barmy!*

but now von Kluck was properly rhymed, as in the original composition.

Walk over the contemptible little British Army! had been the Kaiser's Order of the Day to his troops at Aix-la-Chapelle, according to *The Daily Trident*, while they had been in London. Let all the Allemands come, the London Highlanders would show them! That was the mood of the moment.

In the darkness of that night, after twenty-two hours in the truck, the train stopped at a station lit by arc-lamps subdued by the mist. On the top of the iron posts—*St. Omer*.

Shadowy cavalrymen on the platform told them it was the headquarters of Sir John French. Among them was a familiar hodden grey kilt. The scout saluted Mr. Ogilby.

"All London Highlanders form up on the platform!"

Following the scout and Mr. Ogilby, the detachment was

marched to French cavalry barracks where the rest of the
battalion was said to be. They marched under an arch, seeing
flames against a wall. "Fall out for a meal!" Two black-faced
cooks stood by steaming dixies, cursing French coal. "Here
you are, laddy, a hot meal!" It was bully beef stew with lumps
of biscuit, but it brought a glow to life. Carrying half-filled
steaming mess-tins to the strawed loft over the stables, they sat
and ate with their spoons. The straw was damp, but who
cared?

Elliott sat next to Phillip. Phillip rather liked him. He
envied him, in a way, for having a girl of his own. She had
come to see him with her parents every Sunday at Bleak Hill.
All he had noticed about Elliott's girl was that she had a very
white skin, and Cambridge-blue eyes the same colour as her
dress; and she had smiled at him. He had wondered how
Elliott had seen anything in her; but still, she was his girl.

"Letters! Letters!!"

The wonderful, life-giving moment when the post-corporal
appeared with letters and parcels, hundreds of letters and parcels
carried in sacks up the wooden steps. In the candle-lit loft men
were soon living in the past. He saw that Elliott had a thick
wad of letters from his girl.

He himself had two parcels from home, each containing a cake,
a tin of *café au lait*, chocolate, some soap, a pair of socks, and a
packet of Hignett's Cavalier. An almost formal note in one of
the parcels informed him that the enclosed tobacco had been
paid for, in accordance with his declared wish, out of the money
Your Affectionate Father had in trust for him.

There were four letters from Mother. He read them in a happy
feeling of aloneness shared by the haze of his wavering little
candle-flame beside him on his mess-tin lid. The letters were
more or less identical, feeling as though Mother was always
in a hurry, each beginning *My dearest Boy*, and ending, *Ever
your loving, Mother*. There had been a moment in the loft, before
the hot meal, when he had felt that he must tell his officer he could
not face the unthinkable gap between present and future: that he
was lost in darkness for ever and ever; but now, as the pages
shone in the candle-light, he re-entered the world which lived
in Mother's handwriting.

The sentences said little in themselves; but in them was all
happiness, all life, all safety.

They were all well at home, and hoped he was, too. Father was working long hours, as more younger men from the Moon had left to join up. Mavis had begun work at Head Office, in the Country Department. Willie had stayed with them for his first leave, after inoculation, and sent his love. He was such a kind boy, so sympathetic and helpful, Father thought very highly of him. Of course Father was very proud, too, of his own son. Gran'pa sent love, and asked him especially to keep his feet dry, and not to run unnecessary risks. He was going to send him a red chest-protector, for his lungs. Mrs. Neville sent her love. She had promised to write to him, so had Mrs. Bigge. Mrs. Rolls had enquired after him, and sent her very good wishes. Ah! she was knitting a pair of socks for him! He must not forget his prayers, God would always answer his prayers. He had answered her prayers when her little son was such a long time in coming into the world. There was one sentence underlined. *Do write when you have a moment to spare, dear, and don't forget to mention Father, will you, lest he feel that you do not care about him.* Mavis and Doris both sent their love, and would write to him. Aunt Marian also sent fondest love. Timmy Rat was well. Father had hung a mutton bone on the tree in the garden for the titmice. He asked her to say that he would not forget to repair the nesting boxes.

Phillip cut a slice of cake and ate it, after closing the tin and hiding it under his valise. It was Mother's own cake, the well-known flavour of raisins, currants, and beef-dripping, with the usual burnt paper on the bottom. He hesitated several times before putting the segment of burnt paper, from which he had gnawn every hard fragment of cake, into the sack provided for waste-paper. Many times he had seen Mother put paper in the baking tin after smearing it with margarine, then the cake into the oven. And perhaps, as she was playing chess opposite Father, "Oh dear, I had almost forgotten my cake!" and then hurrying footfalls along the passage and up the steps to the kitchen. He could see her now, her head bent down to look inside the oven.

After a pause he rose and put the burnt paper in the sack, to reassure himself when he sat down again by a touch of the letters in his breast pocket.

Then down the ladder into the yard to brush teeth and wash,

up again to arrange bed, blow out candle, lie down, immediately
to induce before closed eyes pictures of his home, scenes and
faces in the silence of the corridors of the mind.

One by one the candles died out, until only Elliott's shone in
the dark dusty loft, as he sat up writing. At ten o'clock he blew
out his flame, and settled down with the muttered remark,
"God bless the man who first invented sleep."

In the morning they marched out of St. Omer along a road
lined with poplars, turning off into a lane which led to rolling
hedgeless fields of stubble whereon grass and clover was growing,
and plowland extended to the skyline where teams of large
grey dappled horses were at work. There were copses in the
hollows and lanchetts, and against the sky a clump of beech
trees. It was rather like the Kent country on the way to the
Salt Box.

Across this land the battalion carried out an exercise, advancing
in companies in line to a distant objective: first in artillery
formation of half-sections at each point of a diamond; then at a
signal from the Company Commander to his subaltern officers,
into extended order. It began to rain as the advance took place
up the gradual slope to the ridge, on which a group of staff-
officers was standing. After the charge, with cheers, and the
position captured, a line of trenches had to be dug in the brown
loamy soil, which became stickier as rain fell steadily. It was
slow work with the short-handled entrenching tools. About four
o'clock, when they were wet to the skin, water squelching in
muddy shoes, the exercise was stopped; and the trenches ordered
to be filled again. There was no grumbling, although they had
had no food since breakfast at seven o'clock that morning.

As "B" Company marched at ease over the stubbles, and
Captain Forbes was walking beside his section, Phillip saw a mouse
running and jumping away through the big wet clover leaves.
Captain Forbes saw it at the same time; and Phillip saw his eyes
bulge as, raising his walking stick, he ran after it, striking at it
again and again as it darted sideways, until a final heavy thwack
like the stroke of a cane, stopped it. Captain Forbes hit it several
times, making sure the mouse was dead before returning to
walk beside the company once more, a satisfied look upon his
face. Phillip recalled the poem of Burns he had read, about
the mouse's nest turned up by the plow, and wondered

vaguely why Captain Forbes had been so determined to kill a stray mouse.

The march back lay along a track under a sort of plateau. They were passing below a raised bank near a windmill, when he saw some men in forage caps standing above.

"Royal Flying Corps!" exclaimed Baldwin.

Looking up at the faces above him, he saw, with a start, the be-spectacled grinning face of Jack Hart among them. He had a sergeant's stripes on his sleeves. At the same time Jack saw him, and waved; then they had gone past. He told Baldwin about Jack's legendary wickedness. And now he was a sergeant!

At the end of the march the company entered in twilight through the iron gates of a large building set among trees. It turned out to be a new and unfinished convent. A high wall surrounded the grounds. The rooms within were wide and lofty, without doors; the building had no lavatories, no kitchen range, no fires where their clothes might be dried; but what matter, they were under a roof.

"Wonderful how cheerful the men always are, isn't it?" he heard Mr. Ogilvy say to an officer of another company.

"Yes, a wonderful feeling to be with them, Bruce."

These untried men accepted all that came, buoyed by a feeling that was not yet of the present. Tommy Atkins perhaps expressed that feeling—though not by his words—by the attitude that all was in the hands of God—an attitude which had not yet become discredited at its face value; for all were yet amateurs of war and its machinery, mental and physical.

They were indeed happy to be under shelter. Candles winked on the parquet floors, as stew was eaten hungrily, followed by tea, drunk out of unwashed mess-tins. It was hot, it had rum in it. Firmly Tommy Atkins refused his portion. Animation filled the room flickering with shadows on the walls; each candle-light was a personal beacon of security and shelter; and when the post came, with three letters for him, from Mother, Desmond, and Father, Phillip wanted nothing more.

After a game of solo with some of the fellows, he and Baldwin went outside to explore the grounds. Against one wall the cooks' fires smouldered, beside a heap of branches for the morrow. Tommy Atkins stood there, cheerfully sipping from a mess-tin his own brew of rumless tea.

The clouds had lifted. A star shone in the clear sky. There was a slight hillock among the trees, and seeing several men standing there, they wandered that way. As they drew near, Phillip sensed something strange in the attitude of the men on the hillock. No one was talking as they stared towards an open space through the trees. As the two friends joined them a cock pheasant flew crowing through the darkness, a thing unheeded by the watching group, so intent were they upon something else. What could it be?

Under distant clouds ran a faint flicker of light. A moment later he saw it appear again, but as a suffusion, a glow which spread up and died, only to flicker again and play like remote summer lightning higher in the sky. A dull blow came on the light breeze, then another. The horizon was faintly reverberating, glowing fitfully, trembling with light.

So still did they all stand there that he could hear the sycamore leaves breaking from the trees above, falling from branch to branch, coming to rest in the darkness around them. The guns of Ypres!

Rain fell in the night, and during the next morning and early afternoon; and when the London Highlanders left the convent it was still raining. They marched through the square of St. Omer and out of the town to a long line of omnibuses standing on the right of the road. Wet to the skin again, with sodden spats and shoes, they clambered upon the familiar solid-tyred Tillings-Stevens buses, greeting them like old friends, despite their boarded windows and grey paint, for when last seen they had been of the streets of London.

"I votes we ride on top, Norman."

The bus was a 47. Surely it was lucky? He explained that it might be one that he had often raced with his friend Desmond up Brumley Hill in the old days, on its way to the George and Dragon, Farnborough. "I hated the coming of the buses, with their hordes of people invading the countryside, and stripping the woods of bluebells. Most of them, from Shoreditch, went only for the ride, and to booze at the George and Dragon, so they did not do much harm to the countryside. We'll see more on top, Norman."

It was a hopeful remark, for the day was already sinking into twilight. The bus swayed along the pavé road, following another of a long column in front, often skidding, and once striking a tree with its off-side rear hub. Cheers could be heard from down below when this happened. The road was narrow, lined by trees on either side. On the slippery sett-stones the pace was a crawl. Trees beside the route were darkly lit by the glare on the eastern horizon to which they travelled, intently staring. During the many stops the rolling cannonade came directly upon the wet wind. The scene was romantic to Phillip, despite the growing immediacy of fear under the incredulity of the whole thing. Was he dreaming, after all? How *could* they put Territorials into battle? Perhaps they were to be used to help the wounded, as they had at Villeneuve. Why was it all happening? *Could* he be killed? He felt himself going pale, and with an effort evaded frightful thought. He could not be killed; for what would Mother do if——

Baldwin was silent, too. Neither spoke more than a word or two. They had already agreed to stand by each other, whatever happened.

The sky was now lit up by almost continuous flashes far ahead of the black avenue of trees.

"It's rather like the early bioscopes in a way, isn't it, I mean the flickering, Norman. I remember when I went to my first flicks at the Electric Palace—I saw it all through three times, and when I got home, my father sent me to bed and forbade me to go again."

"I saw my first films through several times, too, and went home late, but my dad didn't mind particularly."

They were sitting in a front seat, their laps covered by the tarpaulin apron which still remained. Looking down, he saw that the engine was boiling, steam hissing up from its radiator cap. The convoy of thirty-four buses had stopped for a battery of French guns to pass. Could they be the famous seventy-fives? The newspapers had praised these wonderful guns, firing their *rafales*, or continuous fire. How wonderful if they were!

On went the convoy again, the bus grinding in low gear, the solid tyres damping down the shocks of the sett-stones. They passed through a town, entering another straight avenue of trees. This road was congested. Wagons and lorries were moving both ways. The rain had stopped, and the moon shone clear. They removed the tarpaulin from their knees, hoping it might dry.

All hopes of a billet for the night went as the convoy moved through another town, the tall trees seeming to lead direct to the great arc of thundering light which was the battle raging for Ypres.

"My God, Norman, look at the play of light on the clouds!"

"It's rather wonderful, when you think of it."

"Do you feel frightened?"

"Not particularly."

"Same here."

There was another wait, prolonged and cold, between the over-arching trees. Ambulances drawn by horses moved slowly below, each with a red cross on a white square on its canvas hood looking black in the moonlight. The noise of gunfire was now so great that the grinding of the iron wheels of the ambulances on the *pavé* was unheard.

He touched the wet twigs of the tree near his head, and by the feel judged that it was an elm. The thought that soon he would be leaving for ever the tree, so quiet and fixed in its life, became a vast blanching fear; he threw himself down and his head cracked with stars as the whole earth split white. Was he wounded? The bus seemed upright. Baldwin was holding his head as he saw when, his ears still ringing, every part of the trees around them seemed petrified. There was a third smiting report, followed by a fourth.

They learned from the bus-driver that it was a battery of naval guns firing from a railway siding. Even so, it was alarming. Like ghosts of their former selves, among other pallid faces the length of the convoy, they sat and waited, shaken by the tumultuous night.

At last, cold and tired, unspeaking, they arrived at their destination, climbing stiffly down the stairs of the bus and passing in single file into what seemed to be a cathedral, with a tall belfry and smaller fretted towers and pinnacles along its roof, glintering in the nearly rounded moon.

"Lead on, lead on!" said Mr. Ogilby's voice. Then Sergeant "Grannie" Henshaw's voice was saying, "This way, follow me! No smoking, anyone!" He was known as Grannie Henshaw because he was a kindly, slightly fussy, elderly man, a bachelor who had been in the battalion for over twenty years.

To Phillip's relief, most of the shells seemed to be bursting beyond the town. The bursts outlined roof-tops and chimney-stacks. Away from the scintillant night he followed others through a door, to find himself inside what looked like an immense timbered hall, with a carved oak seat extending around and under walls which were painted with large pictures, seen dimly in the light of hurricane lamps on the ground. An agitated civilian, wearing a funny hat, sash over one shoulder and tied round his waist, was gesticulating to Captain Forbes.

With relief he heard that they were to sleep there for the rest of the night. Two blankets each were issued, but no tea or food.

"Get what sleep you can, you fellows," said Mr. Ogilby, walking round to where they had dumped their equipment on the seat. "And no smoking. The mayor is anxious about fire, as this is a historic building, apparently. Is that clear? No smoking. Breakfast will be at six o'clock. It is now nearly three, so get down to it."

"Well, we don't get much money, but we do see life," said Elliott, when Mr. Ogilby had gone away. Phillip went to find cousin Gerry, at the other end of the hall.

"Hullo, young Phil. How goes it?"

"Oh, not so bad. I say, I've got a spare cake. Would you like it?"

"Can you spare it?"

"Of course I can. How's Bertie?"

"Haven't seen him. The transport remained behind. I bet he's cursing that he'll miss the fun."

Gerry had not seen the French wounded at Villeneuve. Did he really think it was fun? He wished he were with the transport. He went away, returning with the cake. On the way back he saw Peter Wallace, and stopped to speak to him before he realised that he, with David and Nimmo, was cutting into three pieces a pork pie. Would be think he was cadging?

"Hullo, Peter. How goes it?"

Peter grunted, and looked at him sourly.

"Remember old Purley-Prout, Peter? I wonder where he is today?"

"What do I care for your dam-silly questions?"

"Oh, I only just wondered. No particular reason, really."

"At least he wasn't half German."

"Nor am I; I'm only quarter."

"What do you want?"

"Nothing, really."

"Then take it and go."

Nimmo smiled at him, and winked. Phillip strolled away, trying to look as though he had merely been having a friendly chat with Nimmo. Was that why Father had removed "Lindenheim" from the front gate? Thank God for Baldwin.

The floor of the Salle Pauwels was cold, despite two blankets, while the noise of the guns never ceased throughout the four hours of fitful sleep. In the wan light of hurricane lamps they had half a tin of bully beef and biscuits for breakfast. Hardly were the lumps swallowed when an increased cannonade seemed to shake the whole lofty building. Then buckling on equipment, they fell in for rifle inspection. When new ammunition of pointed bullets was exchanged for the old blunt-nosed clips, with two extra linen bandoliers, his heart gave a sickening bump. Surely they would not be sent into action, when they were lines of communication troops? Still, there was hope when they were told to tie two blankets over the shoulder, like a plaid. Perhaps these were to wrap the wounded in? This small hope died when Captain Forbes addressed the company.

"Well, men, this is what we have trained for. The battle now raging may be the last big battle, and the decisive one, of the entire war. The enemy is doing his damndest to get the Channel ports. To do this he must first capture Ypres, where we are now. If he does capture Ypres, the whole of the British Expeditionary Force, and the Belgian Army, will be cut off. The Kaiser, we know on good authority, is not very far away, waiting to move forward with his troops. The regular soldiers are tired. They have been in action continuously since Mons, and so the London Highlanders have been given the honour of supporting them. I have here a message from the Colonel. "It is my proud belief that every London Highlander will remember the high traditions of the regiment."

He paused. "Now, men, break ranks quietly and fall in on your markers in the square outside."

Cold as cocaine Phillip followed other silent men through the arched door, and so into the Grande Place. Under a grey sky and upon the regular grey cobbles he saw a row of long-snouted guns, painted in colours of decaying cabbages, standing in the square. A man in wooden sabots went by, peaked capped and muffler'd, beside a loaded little cart drawn by a dog. Military

police with red-caps and revolvers in holsters, and the company
markers standing to attention in front of the Halles aux Drapiers,
were the only other people visible in the square, except a soldier
with a beard, and only one button on his tunic, on guard near
the guns. He said something to Elliott, who gave him a cigarette.

"What did he say, Elliott?"

"He's Royal Garrison Artillery, and says the guns have been
taken out, as they've got no shells for them."

As they marched in the direction of the firing, he saw some of
the refugees read about in the newspapers. They were in a side
street, loading their household goods into carts and hand-
barrows. They looked dull-faced, unsmiling, in best black clothes
and black cloth caps. Down another street were rows of grey
motor cars, stretching to the end. An enamelled plate on the
corner house read *Rue des Chiens*.

"Road of the Dogs! Look at all those motor cars!" he exclaimed, for a joke. "Each one is owned by a rich dog—but
all their shovvers have been called up!"

"Perhaps they volunteered for home defence only."

"Seriously, Norman, I wonder what those motor cars are for."

The sight of a French sentry, in blue coat, kepi, and red
trousers, gave the clue.

"Good lord, they must be the Paris taxicabs painted grey,
the ones we read of in the newspapers, Norman, that took reserves
up to the Marne!"

"This place is mediaeval," said Baldwin, a few minutes
later, as they marched through a gap in the massive red-brick
walls, between two stone figures of lions. "These are the ram-
parts, and the moat."

Decaying water-lilies lay on the surface. Phillip wondered if
roach and carp lived in the water. He felt, now that he was
no longer frightened, glad that he had not missed the adventure.
And his salary was piling up all the time, for when he got home
again!

In the new mood of optimism, he felt pride as he saw the kilts
swinging and the rhythmic movements of the leading company
turning to the right up a long tree-lined road. There were grassy
meadows extending on either side. Beside the road hundreds
of cavalry horses were picketed. Coming down the road was
a procession of refugees leading piled-up carts, some with old

people perched on what looked like feather-bedding—stick-like people with grey, expressionless faces. The cobbled road led on straight, the feather-like poplar trees on either side drawing closer together and dipping once before rising up to the horizon.

They marched on into a misty landscape of plow and stubble, ending at woods against the sky. Each man marched unspeaking now, for slate-coloured smudges of smoke hung over the woods, beginning as little black balls that spotted the sky and drifted into the general grey, other spots and smudges taking their place. Among them appeared yellow writhing caterpillars, much larger than the black spots, which Phillip thought of as the dung droppings of yellow hairy caterpillars.

The blows of the gunfire seemed to arise through the bones of his heels upon the hard cobbles.

Then his mouth filled with water as a coarse downward buzzing grew louder and louder and in the field three hundred yards away on the right four massive black eruptions arose and instantly seemed to break the very day with four stupendous rending crashes.

"Halt!"

The rear companies waited, white-faced, while the leading company marched on, to allow an interval between them.

"Them's Jack Johnsons," said a cavalry soldier, one of a score guarding horses tied to a picket-line on the grass near the road. Leaning against branches were clusters of lances with bright points, and pennons below the blades.

The trooper explained that the rest of the squadron was in the line.

"What's it like up there?" asked Elliott.

"Bloody terrible, mate."

"How far away are the Germans?" asked Phillip.

"Just over that ridge. Why, you blokes in a 'urry to git at the Allymands?"

"It's not a bad idea," replied Elliott. "It's what we came for. When do we attack?"

At this, other troopers gathered round. They were unshaven; one had almost a ginger beard; their cap badges were missing, and their shoulder numerals. Some of them had marked the numerals with indelible pencil.

They stared at the rolled blankets. "Blime, goin' on a picnic? Where you blokes from? You don't talk like Jocks."

"We're the London Highlanders," said Elliott.

"London Islanders? Then we're the pushin' Horse Marines."

"We're territorials," explained Phillip. "For lines of communication."

"Ah, Saturday ar'ternoon sojers!"

"Blime, you blokes come to the right place fer lines o' communication!"

They were reservists from East London. They asked about the prices of food. Was there a shortage? Had it gone up? Was there enough to go round? Phillip wanted to hear about the front. He wanted to ask about any special tips, what to do in order to avoid any undue risk. He dared not ask. O, it was too late now——

" 'B' Company, lead on."

"Good luck, mates!"

"Thanks, same to you."

As he slung his rifle, he heard one of the lancers say to another, "Blime, Burlington Berties wiv'out umbrellas!"

Soon his kit was weighing on his collar bones. He marched with thumbs under the webbing straps, to ease the weight. They passed wounded soldiers moving down the road, some with bloody bandages, walking slowly, uniforms crumpled, torn, shapeless; without interest in anything. Others were sitting down by the wayside. They looked like ragged clay-men. One was trying to light a cigarette, holding a matchbox in fingers coagulated with blood dripping from an arm bandage. His face was clay-coloured, like all his trousers and tunic. His puttees had dropped round his ankles. More refugees were coming down the road. By contrast, a kestrel was hanging in the air over the field less than fifty yards away, fluttering its wings as it watched the stubble below, apparently indifferent to the noise.

"Halt! Fall out on the right side of the road. No man to leave the ranks without permission!"

On the other side of the road was a château, white in pale sunlight. Dismounted troopers with polished bandoliers and boots and spurs, looking strangely smart, were on guard outside the open iron gate. He lifted his head to watch them present arms as the Earl of Findhorn, the Adjutant beside him, walked through the gate. Motor-cycle dispatch riders, white-and-blue bands on arms, were arriving and departing all the time. There

were red-cap military policemen on duty, with revolvers in their
holsters, and hard faces.

The heavy black shells, the Jack Johnsons, were falling in the
fields. A soldier told them they were after the naval guns.
"We've got a battery 'id away, see. The Alleyman's searchin'
for it."

"Why don't the naval guns fire back?"

"They only fire when the Alleyman attacks, mate."

"When do you think they will attack next?"

"They're coming over all'v'e time, mate."

"Then why don't our guns fire?"

"They ain't got no shells left. They only gets a ration'v two
shells a day, each gun, see."

After about ten minutes Colonel Findhorn was seen to be
returning with several other officers, among them a General
with a big grey moustache, hatless. Phillip noticed his highly
polished riding boots, as he walked to the tall iron gates with
the Colonel. There he stopped, smiling. After shaking hands, the
General turned back, and the Colonel, between a redbanded
staff-officer and the Adjutant, walked to the head of the battalion.

Baldwin, who had been talking to a despatch rider, said the
General was the corps commander, named Haig, of the whiskey
family.

"Fall in, 'B' Company."

They crossed over a railway line embedded diagonally in the
pavé. Wounded men were limping down the road, bearded,
hatless, ragged, their faces set beyond desperation. One was
lying in the ditch, beside a spread of dark blood. Field guns
were now firing on both sides of the road. Their reports smote
hard on the ear-drums. The 18-pounder shells tore narrow,
screaming furrows in the air as they sped away to the horizon.
More and more German shells were arriving in front, very close
to the road, darkening the mind with their prolonged and
terrifying bass droning, growing deeper and louder until the
whole sky was being opened for rending metallic crashes in black
smoke. Fragments hummed and buzzed through the air, spun
and whistled to fall to earth with little plops that seemed almost
as slight as the clay-bullets of rival-band days in the Backfield
long ago.

A wild half-thought faded in his mind of a policeman in uniform to stop it all.

Phillip was not the only one unsteadied by fear. Drivers of limbers and waggons on the road, and other mounted troops, ducked their heads as each shell droned down. Dead horses lay about. He thought with some sort of slight relief that, as he was second in his file of four, Collins on his left, and Elliott and Baldwin on his right, would save him, if any splinters came their way. Then the morning was filled with a rising crackle as of thorns in a fire, an increasing crackle of musketry that grew more and more with hundreds of black spots of shrapnel over the woods in front.

Nearer and nearer the dreaded noises of rifle and maxim-gun fire they marched, up the rising straight road, coming to a dark spruce plantation on the crest of the rise. Here, he saw with relief, the companies ahead were turning. Shells were falling away in the wood, up in the unseen front. Bullets cracked, seeming a foot or two above their heads, causing them to duck every time the alarming crack was heard. A bearded soldier standing by a fire, over which a large black iron kettle was hanging on a tripod of sticks, said in a calm voice, as they passed by, "Keep yer 'air on, mates." He seemed entirely unconcerned, so Phillip thought that perhaps after all things were not too bad.

Some of the shell-holes in the yellow, sandy soil had a little water in them, at the bottom. The sides were of broken lumps of yellow clay, blackened as by a coal fire. Going deeper into the wood, they passed other unshaven soldiers, who were smoking, and laughing at some joke.

"Whatyer, Jocks!" cried one.

His friendly tone encouraged Phillip to ask where the Germans were. Cocking his thumb over his shoulder, the soldier said, " 'Arf a mile, up by the Gellyvelt cross-roads."

"Do you think they will get here?"

"Naoh! If any pushin' Alleyman do, 'e won't pushin' well git back!"

"He pushin' well won't," agreed Elliott. Then seeing the face of Tommy Atkins, he said, "The main explodent of every human oath, old son, is directly related to what has been described as an overrated pastime. And when you consider it, moreover, all life is, in its various origins, more or less of an explosion."

"Long words won't excuse foul language, Elliott. And in my opinion you as an educated man should set a good example."

"That's what the monkey said to the looking-glass, old son."

At the next halt, Phillip looked at an oak that had been severed by a shell splinter, and thrown across the path. The trunk was broken, or smashed, in every ring or layer, which had split into scores of frayed ends, like huge wooden pen-holders gnawed by the children in Wakenham Road School. He thought of Cranmer, and how he used to squirm and cry on the floor when Mr. Twine gave him the cane, which swooshed down again and again with all Mr. Twine's strength, as shown in his fierce eyes and distended nostrils. Why had Mr. Twine always chosen Cranmer for the cane, day after day? Was it because Cranmer was so ragged and dirty, without stockings or boots, and cried so easily, not having had any food to eat before coming to school, and therefore he could not pay attention? Cranmer never did anything wrong in the classroom, except to smile at others. These desperate pictures rose up and died away in his mind, as he followed Baldwin in front, the company now in single file.

At last there was a halt. Mr. Ogilby told them that they might take off blankets and packs, and lie down. No sooner had they done so, when a series of high descending screams swooped upon the wood, and four black blotches burst simultaneously in the grey sky above the trees in front.

"Keep your heads down when you hear them coming," shouted Mr. Ogilby; but they needed no telling.

Bullets were now cracking incessantly overhead, clipping off twigs. In one of the treetops was a sort of brushwood shelter, reached by a rough ladder made of pieces of sawn-off branch nailed to the trunk. Phillip asked Baldwin if he knew what it was. Baldwin suggested a look-out post, perhaps a sniper's platform. Mr. Ogilby glanced round and said to Phillip, "That's for pigeon shooting. The ladder doesn't look particularly safe, does it?"

"No, sir," agreed Phillip, pleased that his officer had noticed him.

Captain Forbes came and knelt on one knee by Mr. Ogilby. Listening, Phillip heard him say that the battalion was to take over the first-line transport of the Coldstream, which had been cut to pieces.

"Have your men got their iron rations intact, Bruce?"

"Yes, Fiery, I inspected them this morning in the Cloth Hall."

Captain Forbes took out a gold cigarette case, and offered it to Mr. Ogilby. He lit both cigarettes, which were gold-tipped, and casually spun the matchstick away.

The sun now shone weakly upon the resting company. Phillip felt pleased that he no longer minded the bullets cracking overhead. He lay back and closed his eyes, wondering what Desmond would think when he learned he was at the front. Pigeons flew over, wheeled, and returned the way they had come. Lifting his head, he stared at them, then caught his officer's eye again. Mr. Ogilby smiled; glanced up at the shelter above; Phillip felt warmly grateful to him. Mr. Ogilby was popular, quiet-spoken, and always courteous to them. A brother of his had come to visit them in a Minerva motor car at Bleak Hill, bringing some dark-plumaged birds with feathery feet which he had recognised from prints, as grouse. The officers must have wonderful food in their mess. Skeuse, Mr. Ogilby's batman, said they had drunk a toast with one foot on the mess trestle-table at dinner, on the last evening at Bleak Hill.

He closed his eyes, trying to sleep. Ricochets occasionally fell down from the height of the sky, making sounds strangely like bird cries. Some were like the plaintive whistle of the buzzard on Exmoor; others had the descending cry of a curlew prolonged to a dying fall. *That note again; it had a dying fall*—he saw the English master at school, repeating the phrase, the only one he had remembered from *Twelfth Night*. How strange that Mr. Ogilby's voice should be saying,

"It's Hallo'e'en tomorrow, Fiery. I'd very nearly forgotten."

The firing east of the wood seemed to have died down. A battalion runner came to tell Captain Forbes that the company was to return to Hooge Château, the divisional quarters they had passed on their way up. They formed up and marched back, past batteries of 13- and 18-pounders beside the road now silent, the gunners drinking tea, and smoking. Obviously the German attack had failed.

"I wonder if they stop fighting to have their dinners, on both sides."

"It looks rather like it, Phil. I don't know about you, but I'm peckish. This is rather fun, isn't it?"

"Have a biscuit? I'm beginning to enjoy it."

The pipers led the battalion into a field just outside the village they had passed on the way up. There they halted, while company markers were spaced out by the Regimental Sergeant-Major. Then, in front of the red-brick château, the Divisional General, who had commanded the London Territorial Division in peace, went round the lines with the Earl of Findhorn and other officers, inspecting them. The officers spoke affably, and all looked cheerful. Perhaps they would not be wanted after all, he thought with wild joy.

After the inspection, they fell out near the road, and ate what food they had in their haversacks. They remained there all the afternoon, resting, indifferent now to shells bursting at regular intervals some distance away. The news had been confirmed that the German attacks had been beaten off that morning.

At five o'clock the order came for the battalion to march back to Ypres.

Now exhilarated, uncaring of shells dropping as though aimlessly in the fields, Phillip marched with happy confidence beside his comrades down the long straight incline, seeing in the distance, exactly in the middle of the road between the poplars, the tall blue belfry of one of the great churches of Ypres silhouetted in the last light of the sun now leaving the plain of Flanders. His mind was fixed on the arched door leading into the painted Hall, on the ultimate moment before lying down on the floor, wrapping blankets round himself, and sleeping. This hope became joy as, coming to the centre of the city, he saw, drawn up upon the wide cobbled Grande Place, two lines of motor buses. The fellows were saying that they were going back to St. Omer, and so to the lines of communication. This was the life!

Chapter 20

ACTION

WHEN the battalion was halted in the shadow of the Halles aux Drapiers, all officers were called to the Colonel. On their return, the company sergeants were called to Captain Forbes.

"This is the situation, as far as is known. A new attack has developed, and the Germans have penetrated between the high

ground of the Gheluvelt ridge where we lay in reserve this morning, and the Wytschaete-Messines spur to the south. If I had a
map I would show you the position, but we haven't any. Briefly,
the enemy holds the ridges, which command the roads into
Ypres. This very square where we are now is the centre of all
roads to the front. If he gets here, our Army won't be able to
move as an Army in the cramped space behind us and the sea.
There won't be enough railway to bring up the necessary
supplies."

Captain Forbes continued. "All the troops are in the firing
line, where they have been continuously since the Retreat. The
London Highlanders are the only reserve at present, though a
French corps is on the way."

Phillip watched the sergeants, as they all stood very still.

"Well," went on Captain Forbes, "it looks as though it is up
to us. Sir John French himself has sent the order that we are
to be placed in immediate support of the cavalry holding the
Messines ridge. The men are tired, and hungry, I know; but
there will be a meal of sorts waiting for them where we are going.
There are enemy agents in this town, so do not mention what I
have just told you. The Commanding Officer is most particular
about this. However, there is no harm in passing on to your half-
sections the news that an open wireless message was intercepted
this morning, from Brussells, to the German general in charge of
operations on this front, that the Kaiser is arriving at Courtrai
tomorrow, which incidentally is Hallo'e'en! That fact speaks for
itself. The Germans are bringing up two new corps, possibly a
hundred thousand fresh troops. The London Highlanders are
the only reserve, at present, of the British Expeditionary Forces."

Phillip saw that the officers, and the sergeants, had serious faces.
He felt something fluttering in his throat, as he stared into the air.

With a sort of dream-incredulity he was sitting in the bus,
seeing before him the old panelled advertisements on roof and
wall—Steedman's Teething Powder for Babies, Bluebell Metal
Polish, Lipton's Tea, Dr. Toogood's Trusses and Surgical
Appliances, Bird's Custard Powder—when he took notice again,
he was aware, behind the driver's seat, of a theatrical poster
advertising *The Glad Eye*.

"Good lord!" he heard Baldwin saying. "I went to a Saturday-
afternoon matinée with Mary, to see that!"

It showed a Barribal girl with dimpled rouged cheeks, hobble skirt, and little black hat with a feather in it entering one open door of a taxicab, while a handsome, sprightly man raised his hat by the open opposite door.

He. "My cab, I believe."
She. "Mine, I think."
He. "Ours, I hope."

Phillip always thought of Uncle George Lemon whenever he saw the poster.

He stared at this unreal relic of the past, seen many times on the hoardings outside London Bridge Station. The bus was drumming on his ears. Did Baldwin feel it, too? Yes; it was the guns. He felt he was going to be sick; and grabbing the rifle between his knees, he made for the door, and climbed up the stairs, and found an empty place beside someone. The air was fresh; he felt better; it would be too awful to be sick before the others.

As the daylight lessened, the great trembling flickers and vibrating cones of light filled half the entirety of the sky over the German lines. Shells could be seen bursting in fans of fire a mile or two away. Small red stars were pricking the sky-line all along the east, to the left side of the bus. Away in front a ruddy glow played upon the clouds. He listened to the voices of unknown men near him saying it must be a village on fire. He stared around, losing himself in the romantic scene. All along the eastern horizon, far up to the north over his shoulder, was a sight that thrilled him. This was War! He imagined some mighty giant forging a giant horse-shoe upon some colossal anvil, hammer-blows resounding, sparks flying from the iron in a myriad curves, each to die in sullen splashes of fire upon the darkness. It was terrible. It was wonderful.

The night breeze blew upon his cheeks as he sat there; the convoy stopped to let long files of cavalry pass. Hundreds of horses. They clattered past below, taking the best part of half an hour to go by.

The man beside him was Collins, like a flat tyre without his fellow-comic Kerry. The two had nightly returned from the canteen, arm in arm, singing songs in deliberate discord, pretending that it was necessary to support one another—Collins big and bulky, unsmiling, clean-shaven with sloppy lips: Kerry small and perky, pince-nez spectacles on fox-sharp face and a brown moustache that he had cut and brushed up at the ends in imitation of the Kaiser Bill. Collins and Kerry had been inseparables—they even belched and broke wind together—until orders had come for overseas. Both had been home service before, but Collins had changed his mind. He and Kerry had parted coolly.

Perching on the end of the seat (for Collins' bulk took up most of the room) Phillip said to him, "It's a rather wonderful sight, isn't it?" Collins made no reply, but sat as before, chin on tunic. He must still be angry for being called one of the Leytonstone louts, thought Phillip.

The convoy was moving in front. After a series of grating crashes in the gear-box, the bus moved on with a jerk, followed by a slither. They passed over what looked like a canal, water gleaming with the fiery hues of the sky. The journey was slower than that of the previous night, which seemed now to be such a long time back in the past. More halts. Refugees, mounted troops, horse-drawn waggons passed. He was shivering with cold when at last they entered a village, and were ordered to get out, and fall-in.

They stood in the flickering darkness, under a church; they waited with hope of billets, following with their eyes the forms of Captain Forbes and the new Colour-sergeant passing down a row of cottages, the officer banging on each door with his stick, then the flash-light of an electric torch, and some of their numbers ordered in by Mr. Ogilby. The platoon officer had already told them that a cooked meal would be arriving soon, after which they must get what sleep they could. They must not take off their shoes.

"We may move at a moment's notice."

Phillip and Baldwin were among the last to go into a barn behind the cottages. It was a wooden affair, with a ladder up to a loft, cracks in the floorboards, and in the upright plank walls which gave glimpses of the dilating sky; but it was dry, with hay soon spread.

Unwrapping his blankets, he made some sort of a bed. The loft was shaking with the distant explosions, which seemed to travel through the ground. Then Lance-corporal Douglas' voice shouted from below that grub had arrived; and Phillip followed the others down the ladder. The field-cooker had not turned up; only a ration of cheese, with hard biscuits. Phillip was surprised how hungry he was. There was tea, sweet with sugar and rum. He soon felt cheerful, and went out into the street, where G-S waggons and horses were drawn up. With relief he saw cousin Bertie.

"Hullo. I thought you were back at the convent."

"We came up to take over the Coalie's transport."

"Coal?" Phillip thought of leather helmets, grimy faces.

"The Coldstream. The transport is about all they've got left."

Someone had got hold of a bottle of wine. Phillip and Baldwin went down the street, looking for the estaminet. It was on the corner, open, a dim light on the counter. Baldwin opened a tin of Maconochie and put it on the stove, watched by an old woman in sabots with a wrinkled face, in black bodice and skirts. She stood and watched with monkey-like eyes from the doorway leading to the back kitchen beyond.

"Allemands no bon. Obus *poom*! No bon!" she muttered, as the oil-flame jumped with the reports of 60-pounder guns firing in a field some distance away, the shells screaming low over the cottage.

"Anglais!" said Baldwin. "Bon, n'est ce pas, madame?"

"Avez vous du bif-tek, madame?" enquired Phillip.

"Si si," she replied, and turned away to light a candlestick. Phillip followed her into the back-kitchen. With the light in her hand she went through a door and down three steps. Looking down, he saw that the entire floor of the little cellar was piled with bully-beef tins.

"Un franc!" she said, holding up a finger, while retaining a tin in the other.

"Bully bif no bon! Mon ami et moi, nous desirons bif-tek frit avec pommes-de-terre, madame!"

"Ne hichny niet! Allez, allez!" she cried, shooing him away. Phillip laughed with Baldwin at the idea of buying bully pinched from the troops.

There was a pot of coffee on the stove. They each drank a tall thick cup, with rhum, and shared the tin of stew; and feeling more cheerful, went out into the street, in time to listen to an altercation between the Quartermaster and the Army Service Corps officer in charge of the buses.

"I'm sorry, but my orders are to return with my convoy to Ypres immediately after your troops have de-trained."

"Look, old boy, my chaps are going into action, and as I told you before, all our transport is back at St. Omer. We've been allotted the first-line Coldstream transport, to take up rations and ammunition to the line. If I have to use them as second-line transport, to go all the way back to rail-head to draw supplies, where's my first-line transport?"

"I'm sorry, but that's nothing to do with me. You should indent with D.A.D.O.S. for more transport."

"By that time the Germans may be in Ypres! We are under orders to go into the line at a moment's notice. Where will our boys be without supplies? I need three of these buses, and as your superior officer I am ordering you to leave them here, with their drivers!"

"Then the responsibility must rest entirely with you, sir," said the young A.S.C. officer, who was a second-lieutenant, while the Quartermaster was an honorary Captain. "This is my first convoy, sir. I only arrived from the base this morning."

"That's all right, I'll give you a chit."

The Quartermaster wrote in his Field Service book, signed it, tore it out, gave it to him.

"That will cover you, my lad."

Phillip had already realised that the Army Service Corps had a much better time than the infantry. Herbie Low, who lived down Hillside Road, and had enlisted at the beginning of the war, got six shillings a day pay. The A.S.C. were always in the rear areas, far behind the front. An idea struck him, and he went to find his cousin. "I suppose there isn't a vacancy in the transport, is there, Bertie?"

"Not now, at any rate, young Phil. But there may be. By the way, you should address me as sergeant. I came up because the Coldstream sergeant was killed when a salvo of Black Marias fell on their picket line. Fed up with foot-slogging?"

"Well, sort of—Sergeant."

To Phillip it seemed that he had hardly lain down in the moon-chinked loft before Sergeant Henshaw's voice was saying, "Come on, wake up, there! Corporal Douglas, get your men fallen-in by the church!"

"Come on everyone, out of it!"

In silence they folded their blankets, then down the ladder to where rifles and equipment were piled by the wooden wall below. "It's four minutes to midnight," said Baldwin, peering at his wristlet watch.

While the company was forming-up by the church there was the sound of a multitude of trotting hooves. In the moonlight a mounted column came down the *pavé* street, tall helmets gleaming above the horses. They were French cuirassiers. Behind them came flat British caps, and Phillip saw they were all mounted on grey horses.

"How's it going?" called out Elliott.

"Fine, laddie! There's bluidy thousands won't goose-step afore the Cayser no more. Who are you?"

"London Highlanders. Territorials."

The news spread down the squadrons. There were friendly cries, some cheers.

"Gude luck, London Highlanders!"

"Same to you, Scots Greys!" More cheers, this time from the London Highlanders.

The trotting of horses died away to the north. They waited in the street of St. Eloi, until the order was given to return to billets, but to be ready to move again before dawn.

Heedless now of gunfire and remote crackle of musketry Phillip curled up in his corner of the loft; then, warm again, stretched his legs and worked his feet to and fro, as the tensions of day left his mind. Touching his crucifix, he prayed voicelessly for safety, and had sighed himself to sleep when, "Good lord!" said the voice of Elliott, across the loft. "It's Hallo'e'en, old son!"

They awakened to crashing gunfire. Out of the hay they crawled, unspeaking. Down below hot tea was ready, with bread and bacon. Afterwards an inspection of iron rations, ammunition in pouches, field-dressings. Water-bottles to be filled from the chlorinated water-cart. Cloth bandoliers of the new Mark VII ammunition were handed out. In clips of five, they looked like pointed nickel teeth.

As the *pavé* with its steam-tram rails began to gleam with the grey sky, brutal torpid downward dronings filled the air above the dark church, seeming to Phillip to be growing heavier and more massive while he waited in a cold sweat of utter defence-lessness, until one tremendous metallic rending upon another

rose with wafts of blackish smoke in which darker objects were
thrown up into the dawn beyond the tiled roofs of houses. Were
these Black Marias? Then the first British aeroplane seen in
France drew his gaze upwards, as the biplane passed over the
village, the painted Union Jack under each lower wing clearly
visible, and the helmet'd heads of pilot and observer looking
over the side of the fuselage. They waved: a cheering sight.

The London Highlanders marched away from St. Eloi,
passing fields where an occasional small stack of hay or corn
stood. They came to a road beside which peasants in peaked
caps, double-breasted jackets, and *sabots* were slowly pulling
up lines of roots and throwing them into a long waggon shaped
like a boat. They stopped work and stared as the kilted troops
marched past. Hardly had they gone by, when Phillip saw, with
others, a strange-looking aeroplane circling in the sky above
them. Its wings were curved back at the ends—it must be a
Taube! Had the peasants been signalling to it, he asked Baldwin,
when a few moments later Black Marias began to drone down,
buzzing fatly, hugely, to burst with black rending, in pairs, two
short of the road, two beyond it. The nearest was a hundred
yards away; even so, splinters buzzed and hissed past alarmingly.
One fell with a tinkle on the *pavé*, and Phillip stepped out to pick
it up for a curio; he dropped it, blister-hot.

After two more 8-inch salvos the shelling stopped. So far it
was not bad, he agreed with Baldwin. He was relieved that he
could stand it. If that was all that was going to happen when
they were in reserve, he was glad he had come.

As they marched into a village of red brick and tiled roofs,
shelling started again. What made his heart drum hollow in his
white-bone-seeming ribs was wondering where the next one was
going to fall. He began nervously to work his teeth, while
trying hard—how silly it was—but anyway try to think whether
or no the insurance policies of such buildings in Belgium had a
clause, like the London Tariff policies, stating that in the event of
war, riot, or civil commotion—how did the clause end? If he did
not finish the thought, a shell would fall beside him with its
colossal rending iron crash. Think of Mr. Hollis' face, quick! But
in the way was Mr. Howlett's benign face puffing Hignett's
Cavalier from his pipe until—down! down—tiles, bricks, stones
went up in one black shattering explosion which hung a haze of

brown dust in the air, falling slowly down rather like pictures of a water-spout at sea; then the smoke was drifting away. He was surprised to realise that he was still marching on. Could it be himself who was walking on, upright? He tried to swallow, found his throat was dry and prickly. Far away he heard a cry of *Stretcher bearers!* The order was given to halt.

Why were they halted in the Square, when the shells were falling right into it? In white-faced panic he was aware of others only as khaki flat movements, except the pink side of Baldwin's face. Why did they not lie down? More terrible swooping, groaning noises came corkscrewing in massive black steel upon them. He felt split in two as he saw one actually bursting upon the *pavé*, with a hot, screaming noise, more rending than when the shells had plunged into the clay of the fields. Why did they not move away at the double? Only fools would remain where they were! *Obviously* that Taube had signalled back to the batteries, just as the English Farmans did! Fools, fools, fools, fools! his mind screamed, seeing in his mind the irritable grey-moustached face of the Earl of Findhorn when he had gone to his grey Boer-War-rotten bell tent to get leave to go with Father and Mother to Crowborough. The Earl was not really a London Highlander; he was a regular officer of the Guards, where the men, according to Baldwin, were treated with the harshest discipline. When they were drilled on the square, with rifles at the Present, the blood showed round the nails of their right-hand fingers, so hard and continuously were they ordered to slap their rifles at the first of the three movements. They were automatons. *Theirs not to reason why, theirs but to do and die.* O God, was this going to be like the Modder River battle, which Uncle Hugh had told him about? Why did they not double off and get on to the flanks like old Purley-Prout always did, unlike those Berehill and Fordesmill fools whose men came right up to the camp in frontal attack upon the Dowager Countess' paddock and banged away on the barb-wire fence with their poles!

Memories of Boy Scout "manoeuvres" with present fears and dreads raced in panic through the head of the hare with the thoughts of a fox. Instinct suffered; it was utterly stupid to stay there. At last he managed to say to Sergeant "Grannie" Henshaw,

"Why, oh why, are we standing still here?"

"Because that is the order," said "Grannie" Henshaw, as he twirled and retwirled his moustache.

When the scouts returned, with their reports, the order was given to about-turn; and the battalion marched back the way it had come for three hundred yards and turned off the road, near a large red-brick building beside a wood. The brick building reminded Phillip of the Randisbourne Home of Rest, for many old people were being brought out of it. But these were dressed in black, whereas the Infirmary people wore red.

"Poor devils," said Baldwin. "I suppose that's a sort of Workhouse. I suppose the Germans are over the skyline? They're rather awful, those big shells, don't you think?"

"Norman, I don't think I can stand much more," said Phillip, his tongue clucking in the dry roof of his mouth. He thought whitely that he never was any good at things like fighting, football, or boxing. His throat had always dried up at the school sports, so that he could never run properly.

"You'll be all right, Phil. The only thing to do is to keep on. It's the only thing one can do, really. Anyway, we'll stick together."

"It's the noise I find so awful."

"Same here. Did you notice Collins shaking and muttering while we waited just now? I thought he was going to throw a fit."

"Did you see Martin when he was hit by a bit of whizzing brick on the ribs?" asked Elliott. "He looked white as a sheet as he cried out 'Send for the stretcher bearers'."

"You've made a pun, d'you know it?" said Baldwin.

"How d'you mean?" asked Phillip in a shaky voice.

"The Scots Greys called this place Whitesheet."

"I don't damn well wonder at it, old son," said Elliott, with attempted jocularity.

While waiting by the Hôspice he heard the Colour-sergeant telling "Grannie" Henshaw that the battalion had been ordered to debouch from the village by the road along which the steam-tram lines led up to the sky-line a quarter of a mile beyond; but the scouts had reported it was "very undesirable". He said also that the battalion was now in support of the cavalry brigade holding the crest—reassuring information to Phillip, who thereby had hopes of returning to Ypres that night, and perhaps steak and fried potatoes in an estaminet, before a proper night's rest in the Cloth Hall.

"Fall in, 'B' Company!"

At first it seemed that his hopes were to be realised; for after passing through the village once more, they turned into another road leading down a long gentle slope towards distant woods and villages. While marching, they had a fine sight below them of a battery of Royal Horse Artillery galloping up, swinging round with the guns in line, and soon the 15-pounders were recoiling with their short stabbing scarce-visible puffs followed instantly by sharp cracks and the *paa-a-angs* of swishing shells. As they passed the battery, not more than fifty yards off the road, some of the company waved, Phillip with them. Those gunners had been out since Mons, and now he was with them, he, Phillip Maddison! He longed to fire his rifle at the Germans. Enemy shells were still womping down as though aimed anywhere. He felt he had had his baptism of fire. I shall be all right now, he told himself.

Leaving the battery behind, the battalion swung off the road and moved down a cart track beside a small brook, and followed its course towards a wood about six hundred yards in front. He wondered if there were any fish in the brook. Perhaps he could make a fire in the wood, to dry his clothes before riding back to Ypres. This seemed to be a distant possibility, as they were ordered to halt and fall out at the edge of the wood, near a farmhouse where peasants were still walking about. Perhaps they might get some hot *café*.

"All officers to the Colonel, sir," said a scout, saluting Captain Forbes.

Phillip watched the officers going to the Earl of Findhorn. Each one came to attention, and saluted him where he stood with honorary-Colonel Mordaunt Hatton, the gaunt brown-moustached warrior with his Queen's, Coronation, and Territorial Decoration ribands, thin long legs, and riding whisk with its white horse-hair fringe for flicking off flies. First came Major MacAlister, who was on the Metal Exchange; Captain Mac-Laglan, the son of a bishop, of "A" Company; Fiery Forbes and his friend Captain McQuaker, a small, pale-faced officer known as "Oats", of "G" Company. "Oats" was remarkable to Phillip in that he was the only officer he had ever heard to swear, or seem to lose his wool. "Oats" McQuaker once, at Bleak Hill, had run down "G" lines crying out in his high voice, "Come on, you blighters!" just before battalion parade. Beside him stood Captain Millar of "C" Company, a man with a rather dour appearance; Captain Duncan of "H" Company; Captain Orr of "D", Captain Mackae of "E"; and portly "Jumbo" Meiklejohn of "F". Phillip and Baldwin watched as the officers stood and listened to what the C.O. was telling them.

When the C.O. turned and pointed up the steep slope towards the rattle of firing, Phillip felt a stab of fear. He forced himself to breathe slowly, to keep himself steady.

Martin, one of the Leytonstone tent, monkey-anxious beside him, said, "Christ!" He looked thin and white as a sheet.

Shortly afterwards Captain Forbes returned with Mr. Ogilby and Mr. Tennant. All their faces were very serious. They had a conference with Colours, and the company sergeants. Captain Forbes pointed with his stick in the same direction. Phillip swallowed the moisture which flowed into his mouth suddenly, and turned aside under necessity to urinate. Several other men were doing the same thing, but he hardly noticed them, so harsh seemed his breathing to himself. Lily-livered, lily-livered, he thought wildly, struggling against the scenery becoming lop-sided.

An agonising thing occurred, after they had fallen in. When the order to charge magazines was given, and Phillip tried to push home the bolt, he found that his rifle was jammed. The bullet would not enter the barrel chamber. He tried again and again. In desperation he struck at the knob of the bolt. It jarred forward. But the tip of the bullet broke off. So did the next one. With sudden hope that he would not be expected to go into the trenches with a faulty rifle, he went on legs that seemed filled with water to report the defect to Lance-Corporal Douglas. His mouth opened, but no words came. His jaws worked only, his breath seemed solid.

"Get back into line!" ordered Lance-Corporal Douglas.

Phillip went back to find Baldwin.

Captain Forbes blew his whistle.

"Mr. Ogilby, lead on your half company!"

Captain Forbes' teeth were unusually visible, as he gave the order in a voice higher than usual.

The orders from the Colonel were that the battalion was to advance in columns of half-companies up through the wood.

"D" Company, in the centre, was to give direction. The objective
was a windmill on the crest beside a farmhouse with a red-tiled
roof. Both landmarks stood beside the road from Wytschaete to
Messines. The road ran along the top of the slope, from north
to south, sixty metres above sea-level. The Germans occupied the
reverse slope beyond the road in further dead ground to the east.
On the right of the ridge, the C.O. told his officers, the enemy
had obtained a footing in Messines, beside the road. That would
mean a certain amount of enfilade fire. The companies, in
rushes by half-sections, while the other sections lay down to give
covering fire, would cross the road and reinforce the trenches
held by the Carabineers.

An Indian regiment, Wilde's Rifles, had helped to hold the
ground with the Carabineers since the previous day. All their
European officers having been killed or wounded, Wilde's Rifles
had been ordered back, but some remained. The London Highlanders would now deploy, for the advance in columns of half-
companies.

Phillip followed the man in front. The centre company was
already taking up its position in the dead ground through the
trees. "B" Company passed behind them.

The advance was to be made in three lines, with the men
extended to five paces. It took about ten nervous minutes to
deploy.

"B" Company's position was on the right flank, in the second
line. While Phillip waited behind an oak tree at the verge of the
wood, he tried again to load his rifle. This time, the leading
cartridge jammed. He wrenched back the bolt, the brass cartridge flipped out; he rammed back the bolt. The next cartridge
stuck again. He struck it with his fist, uttering a wild cry: the
tip of the nickel bullet broke off.

"I can't load my rifle!" he complained, as though to the tree.
No one else took any notice of him; no one heard him. He tried
once more, without success. Then looking at the next man,
Elliott, he saw that he too was fumbling with his bolt. Sergeant
Henshaw came running up. Phillip waited for him to pass, while
trying to think of what to say. Shells were plunging down into
the wood, with the noise of electric trams stopping in the High
Street, only a thousand times darker, coarser. He heard distant
shouts, the blowing of whistles. As "Grannie" Henshaw

approached, he saw that his nostrils were distended. Beads of sweat glistened on his forehead.

"Sergeant——"

"Grannie" Henshaw took no notice. Phillip caught hold of his tunic. A face, no longer that of "Grannie" Henshaw, turned to him and cried, "I can't listen to anything now!" Then, with hand to ear, he stopped, looking towards Mr. Ogilby.

"Fix bayonets! Fix bayonets, everyone! Fix bayonets!" shouted "Grannie" Henshaw. Phillip saw officers drawing their swords.

Nearer whistles were blowing. Captain Forbes and Mr. Ogilby were swinging their arms for the advance. Phillip stood by the tree, as he fixed bayonet, "Grannie" Henshaw muttering to himself as he fixed his.

"Please, Sergeant, really, my rifle is no good! I can't load it!"

"It's the same with everybody else! You must load singly. Don't you ever listen to orders? Now go forward, like a good boy, and do what you're told!"

With a lingering glance at the tree, as to a friend he must leave for ever, Phillip made himself walk forward with the others, like a man walking through ice giving way before him. With shaking fingers he took a clip of five cartridges from a pouch and wrenched off one. Where to put the other four? For a few moments it was an imponderable problem. Then he thought of his right-hand lower tunic pocket. But it was already full— Civic, matches, pouch, bundle of letters from Mother. With a sob he tore at the contents of the pocket, trying to wrench away a fistful. He threw all away as though his life depended upon it— red rubber Crocodile pouch of Hignett's Cavalier, box of Bryant and May's matches, pipe, talismanic letters. He shrieked at himself in his head as he freed other cartridges of their clips and dropped them in his pocket. Mother, mother!

His life depended on a pocket full of cartridges. But supposing a cartridge still would not feed-in? *Father was right. They should have been given a chance to fire their rifles.* He pulled back the bolt, and at once saw that the spring of the magazine was not strong enough to push the cartridge, already in position, into the chamber. The front stop clips were the wrong shape for pointed ammunition. The pointed end of the bullet would not feed-in level; it tipped up, and when rammed in by the bolt, was sort-of crushed. It was liable to explode like that, quite apart from the jamming.

Removing the magazine, he shook out the remaining cartridges, and put them in his pocket. Then slipping a round into the barrel, he closed the bolt, and fired it into the air. The butt in recoil struck his cheekbone, for he had been holding the rifle loosely: but the blow was not felt in the wild and trembling frenzy now that he had found out how to load. He looked from left to right, saw the long lines of men as far as the trees, and then with a secondary ice-shock realised that nothing could now save him from what was to happen when he reached the crackle of the skyline.

Mr. Ogilby was moving his sword from his head towards the right. They were too far to the left. *Right incline!* shouted Baldwin's voice only just audible in the noise. *Right incline!* How thin his own voice felt. He could now hear machine-guns firing. Each bullet passed with a sharp hissing. He broke into a sweat. Why was Baldwin kneeling down? He seemed to be sick. Then he saw that he was vomiting blood from his mouth. He fell sideways, hands clutching face, fingers streaming bright red jerking blood.

Movement thereafter for Phillip became automatic. He was stumbling over brown furrows of a plowed field, near a tall hedge red with hawthorn haws. There were stacks at the far end of the field, and a windmill. Near the windmill was a farmhouse, with a red roof. He was a walking mass of perspiration. A jumble of memories rose before him, his head was filled with a high singing note, a steel wire seemed to make him go on after each automatic bending down, arms shielding face, from great black metallic-rending crumps in the field. He thought wildly of himself as a bony skeleton rushing down Westerham Hill on his unsteerable rigid Swift, white dust rushing up behind, the pace too fast on the hill too steep to put on brakes after he had turned the corner and seen with awful suddenness what lay below him, the straight steepness of the white dusty road, on which he would skid and crash if he put on the brakes. It was the same sort of feeling now, a thin steel wire from below his stomach to above his eyes.

With a broken-glass-like glance to the left, he saw the brown mass of Wytschaete as a flat and painful upright surface. In front he could see the straggling first line of attack beginning to bunch like iron-filings under the hidden magnet of the field. Black blots of shrapnel were thick in the sky, floating above the huge up-spouting steel-fragments of Jack Johnsons. *Like repels like*, he thought again and again, with working teeth. He passed several new holes smoking as though fires had been burned in them. The ragged clay was cracked in great lumps, some black-brown. Then to his distant surprise he saw a hare crouching between two craters, angular and terrified, its ears magnetised back over staring eyeballs. He could have touched it when it seemed to burst as it leapt away, racing. Who had left part-filled sacks in the furrows in front? When he came up to them, his white-faced eyes as though floating nearer, he saw they were dead Indian soldiers, with pale green faces. An Englishman lay near them. His face was all deeply red-brown, like the neck, swollen. His neck had a congealed wound in it, but no blood outside. The blood must have spread up, just inside his skin. Another had no legs. Only the broken-off trunk was below the tunic, with a thick vest in pink wool unravelled around the trunk. The pale face lay sideways, on an arm, pale, asleep without legs. Rifles lay by other dead men sprawled all ways, unmoving. It would be no good trying to speak to them. It seemed an eternity, as he moved past them.

He was aware of loud cracks in the air, just by his ears. He saw earth spirting: and as he lay down upon the furrows, follow-ing others, a spark glowed in the earth near his eye for quite a second after a bullet had struck. The spark died quite slowly. They were getting up again. He heard screaming. Looking to the right, to the windmill now abruptly large, he saw that several men of the line in front were gesticulating on the ground. One man was beating his arms in the air. A face was lying stare-eyed, kilt over chest, two little blue punctures in the white stomach. Farther on, a man sat on the ground, his eyes glassy, blood coming out of a hole in his throat with little rippling pulses. He had a surprised look on his face. Phillip gazed as though from a sort of isinglass-brittle unrealness at all that was happening with-out meaning beyond terror.

Some of the men were lying down. Others were running forward, doubled up. He saw Captain Forbes standing still, looking towards him, sweeping the line forward with his arm. Some were running half-right, with rifles at the trail. He found himself running with them, surprised that he was doing it. It was like running for a train in a dream. All the steam-screeching engines in London Bridge Station under the sooty glass roof were now out of control. Earth was flung up darkly on the rocking buffets of black explosions. There was a ditch in front, and men crouching down in it, beside a stack. He ran to be among them, but terribly slowly, feeling awfully puffed, the wire pulling him back from reaching the safety of the drain in the ditch. With infinite slowness he pushed against the drag and lay down, and the grass and nettles and bits of straw came large and the earth beat through his body until he recovered, among men tearing at the lip of the ditch with entrenching tools.

Beside the stack, a few yards away, he saw the Iron Colonel sitting chin on chest, his brown riding boots and spurs stuck out in front, his fly-whisk and sword beside him. When he crawled nearer the shelter of the stack, he saw that something had happened. The Iron Colonel was asleep and snoring harshly. Bubbles of blood were being half-blown from his nostrils upon his big moustache. His batman, who had been his valet in civil life, sat beside him. As Phillip watched, he put a folded towel on top of the Iron Colonel's head.

"What's happened?" he asked, vaguely wondering why his own voice sounded so far away.

"Colonel Hatton was struck by a splinter. I heard it go through his glengarry with a sort of crack. Just as we got to this stack, it was. He would insist on coming. I advised him not to, but 'It's death or glory this time', he said to me."

The batman held out the cap. Phillip saw that it was torn, and sploshed with a mess of grey mixed up with brown crossed tufts of hair and little broken bits of reddish bone. Colonel Hatton's cheek was very lined; he had never been close to it before. His unshaven stubble was white. His dark-brown hair at the roots was white, too.

Phillip wondered why this was. Had his hair become white with shock, from the roots up, so soon?

"Pass it down to advance in short rushes," shouted a man up the ditch.

Peeping round the edge of the stack, Phillip saw men were scrambling across the road. Most of the shells were bursting away to the right, near the village. The faces of men about him were not those of "B" Company. An officer appeared. His revolver was in his hand. He was Captain McQuaker, who had shouted at Bleak Hill, *Come on, you blighters!* He was always pale, his face sharp: it looked just the same now, but he spoke with composure.

"We must reinforce the Dragoon Guards, in trenches over the road! So no covering fire, you fellows. Go one or two at a time, keep your heads low. The Germans hold the edge of the village, and have the road in enfilade, so don't bunch."

Captain McQuaker saw the figure sitting under the stack with his valet. "Who is that? Not Colonel Hatton?"

"I regret to say that it is, sir," replied the valet.

Captain McQuaker kneeled; examined the wound. "I'll send someone to fetch stretcher-bearers," he said. He looked at Phillip. "Who are you?"

"'B' Company, sir."

"You're in support?"

"Yes, sir."

"Better stay here and prepare to give covering fire during the section advance, until I return."

"Very good, sir."

Phillip tried not to show his thoughts on his face. He sank on one knee, and peered as though earnestly towards the unseen enemy, hoping that the officer would then forget him, and detail someone else for stretcher-bearers.

Led by a sergeant, men were getting up out of the ditch, and dashing across the road. One dropped his rifle. It clattered on the *pavé* in the middle of the road. Phillip saw him turn round, holding his arm. The man made as if to come back, but knelt down instead, as though to fasten his spats. But very slowly he toppled over, face down on the road.

Captain McQuaker pushed through the thorns, and bending down, tried to lift him up. His glengarry fell off as he did so. He seemed unable to lift up the man, as he bent over him. He seemed to sit down, then turn over on his back, then his legs began kicking. A machine-gun was now very loud, from the dark-brown houses of the village. Bullets flipped bits of stone and sparks from the cobbles.

Cowering within himself, Phillip felt that it would be no good trying to rescue Captain McQuaker. Besides, Sergeant Henshaw had said he must do what he was told; and Captain McQuaker had ordered him to prepare to give covering fire. And, anyhow, he was too afraid to leave the shelter of the stack. Peering cautiously, he saw that Captain McQuaker's kilt was awry, showing his testicles squeezed back behind his bottom. There was a great dripping gash behind one thigh. The hair on his head stuck out at the back. It seemed very strange that an officer could be killed.

Other men crawled to the side of the stack. Their faces looked sweat-swelled, their eyes bloodshot. They said they were "C" Company. They told of losses from shells and machine-gun bullets from Messines on the way up. Their company commander, Major MacAlister, had been blown to rags by one of the Johnsons.

"God, what a bloody muck-up it all is!" said one of the men. The voice was familiar, but he did not recognise the face, which was grimy.

The huge black bursts were spouting up regularly. One roared down just behind the stack; but everyone had already thrown themselves flat. After the burst, and the stink of it, his ears cracked and went deaf, for some time. When he could hear again, the same voice was saying, "What's our own artillery doing?" He saw that the speaker was Costello, of Head Office. With great relief Phillip cried,

"Hullo, Costello! Remember me, from Wine Vaults Lane? About your question just now. A gunner in the Grande Place told me that a lot of those batteries we saw there, the harlequin-painted ones, had been withdrawn because they had no ammunition. Those other batteries, up the Menin Road, were rationed to six rounds a day."

"You're a bloody cheerful bloke, I must say!" replied Costello. Then he said to Lance-corporal Furrow, who had crept to the stack, "I wish the bloody Germans would show themselves! Anything is better than this blasted shelling."

A wounded man kept asking for water. Phillip gave him his, the man drank most of it, then began to groan. Phillip realised he himself was thirsty, but could not drink, owing to the man's blood all over his bottle.

"Where do we get water from, when our bottles are empty?" he asked.

"There's bound to be a pump in that farmhouse. Only we'll have to wait until dark."

They lay, speaking less as the morning wore on, in the shelter of the corn stack. Costello killed a rat, as it peeped out of the

stack beside him, with a blow of his fist. He slung it on the road.
It fell near the two kilted figures. All day the three lay there,
never moving, while high-explosive shells plunged down from
the sky.

The red sun, distended among black and grey layers of cloud,
cast a purple pallor over the plowed work behind the stack.
Through thick and heavy tiredness Phillip heard the wheezy calls
of a partridge among the furrows, and wondered vaguely if the
bird was of a covey broken up by shelling. All day he had lain
with others on sheaves pulled from the stack, close against the
northern side, while bullets had cracked past from Messines four
hundred yards to the south, sometimes thudding into the straw.

The Iron Colonel had died in the afternoon, moaning "Mother
—Mother", his batman holding his hand. The batman cried as
he covered his master's face with the towel.

"I don't know what the world's coming to," he had said, at
intervals during the afternoon, as he rearranged the towel respect-
fully with soft hands.

"What will happen to you now?" asked Costello.

"Oh, I shall go home. You see, I am not an enlisted man. On
the contrary, I retained my civilian status, being Colonel Hatton's
valet for the last twelve years. I wear the kilt as a courtesy, if
you follow my meaning. Oh no, I am by no means a military
man."

He rearranged the towel deftly.

No one had eaten. There was no hunger. Phillip's fingers felt
hot and thick, like his feet and his wrists. All fear was gone,
except for shells, and that was momentary. To bullets hissing
over the stack, or whizzing and scolding in richochet off the *pavé*
road he was indifferent. He was only afraid when he thought of
his mother, and how she would be if he were killed. That thought
always unnerved him. What would she *do*?

At times he had felt a sort of satisfaction that he was actually
under fire. This feeling stayed with him as he watched the sun
go down in the dark clouds of the west, leaving upon the furrowed
field a sort of purple penumbra, a faint ruddy light, shifting as
he stared. Was something wrong with his eyes? He asked a man
of "G" Company, sitting next to him. He noticed it, too. Looking
round the stack, they saw that the play of light over the field
came from burning buildings in Messines. They stood up.

Lance-corporal Furrow told Phillip to act as sentry, eyes across the road.

In the dusk Phillip heard voices. Leaving the shelter of the stack, he walked into the field, feeling strangely free in the fading light, by which he could just discern figures approaching across the furrows.

"Halt, who goes there?"

There was sufficient light to recognise the Earl of Findhorn, with the Adjutant and the Staff-sergeant. Staff, as he was called, was next in seniority to the Battalion Sergeant-Major, and like him, a Coldstreamer. Behind were two scouts.

"What company are you men?" asked the Adjutant, in his conversational voice.

"Two of 'G', three of 'D', two of 'B', sir," said Furrow.

"With your permission to speak, sir," said Costello, in a polite voice, "Colonel Hatton is here, under some straw. He died this afternoon. A shell splinter, in the head, sir."

The Colonel said nothing. The Adjutant turned away to look at the body.

The Colonel wore his British warm, with no visible equipment, not even a revolver. His right fist clasped a tall thumb-stick, like one Phillip had seen the otter-hunters carry in Devon. Not the ones in uniform, who carried poles, but the others.

He heard the Colonel tell Staff in his high, rather thin voice, to arrange for stretcher bearers at once. Staff turned away and spoke to a scout. "Get a move on, my lad." The scout hurried away over the field.

"Hatton had no business to leave battalion headquarters," the Colonel said to the Adjutant.

"No, Colonel."

The Adjutant turned to the group by the stack. "Have any of you men seen Captain Forbes?"

"No, sir," said Furrow.

"Or any other officer?"

"Only Captain McQuaker, sir, lying on the road," said Phillip, putting himself forward. "He went to the rescue of a wounded man, and was hit immediately."

"Didn't any of you men attempt to bring Captain McQuaker in?" asked the Colonel, an edge on his voice.

"Please, sir, it was a machine-gun, sir," said Costello, standing to attention. "I was not actually here then, but I understand that the others considered that by showing themselves it would draw more fire, and perhaps kill them both, sir, if they were wounded. And if I may say so, sir——"

The Colonel turned away, and said something to the Adjutant. The Adjutant pushed through the hedge. He came back a minute later.

"Oats is dead, I'm sorry to say, Colonel. Hit through the head," he said in the same level voice.

While they had been talking, an odd figure had shambled up, with a face that looked strange; it made queer little glottal noises; and when it came nearer, was seen to be an Indian with his lower jaw entirely shot away, and his tongue hanging loose. He looked deeply dejected; but when Staff spoke to him in Hindustani, he brightened.

"Get the bodies of the two officers away on stretchers," said the Colonel to Staff.

"Sir!"

"And see that this man goes at once to the First Aid Post."

"Sir!"

As they were moving away, Staff said, "Corporal Furrow, have your men at the stand to, with fixed bayonets. And remain 'ere until an officer comes. Look out for Allemans coming up from yon." He pointed to the east. "There's bloody thousands over there. And don't get down-'earted!"

"Right you are, Staff!"

When Staff had gone, Costello said in Phillip's ear, "You get no thanks from that bloody guardee Findhorn! There's esprit de bloody corps for you!"

Costello seemed to be almost another person, thought Phillip.

In deepening dusk he watched files of men moving away from the road towards the wood. What was happening? At length he asked Lance-corporal Furrow if they ought to be going, too.

"You'll stay here," said Furrow, "until I give the order."

"What are we supposed to be doing, corporal? I mean, we could have remained in the wood just as well, and waited for the dark."

"You do what you are damned well ordered to do!"

Phillip felt more sure of things when Mr. Ogilby came along, with Sergeant Henshaw. They had been down the hedge, near the windmill, all the time.

"Ah, Lance-corporal Furrow!" said Mr. Ogilby. "'B' Company is to reinforce the Dragoons in the trenches over the road, with 'A' and 'H' Companies. You fellows of 'D' and 'G' are going to be withdrawn to the edge of the wood, to join 'F' and 'E' and half of 'C' in battalion reserve. In the meantime, wait here under Lance-corporal Furrow until you get orders from one of your own officers. Is that clear?"

"Certainly, sir," said Furrow, looming huge.

"Keep a good lookout, old chap," whispered Sergeant Henshaw, as he and Mr. Ogilby went away behind the hedge.

Phillip remained apprehensive, while others of the stack party were obviously cheered by the idea of going into reserve. Apprehension became fear with the dark. Those "bloody thousands" of Germans!

When Sergeant Henshaw returned, with other men of the section, Phillip began to think how he missed Baldwin.

They filed through a gap in the hedge, and crossed the road on tip-toe into a field where some stumbled, as upon hundreds of human heads. But it was only winter swede-turnips.

"Pick your feet up, boys," whispered Sergeant Henshaw. "No talking, mind, no talking!"

They filed away in the dimness lit by flames from Messines on the right. Shells were starting to come over again, bursting with red-black gashes low in the darkness of the night. Bullets cracked past. They moved with heads held low, fearful always, picking their way over the level darkening field.

In front before their feet were thuds, tiny spirts of red. Unexpectedly they had come to the trenches. Phillip saw men standing below, firing away over the field. He scrambled down, and following the man in front, pushed past other soldiers, who greeted him with cheerful expressions like, "How goes it, cock!" "Whatyer Jock!" "Just in time ter join the picnic!"

One man with a beard was smoking a cigarette.

"Put that light out, for God's sake," said a voice that Phillip recognised as Martin's. The reply of the bearded one was to draw brightly at his fag-end, and inhale deeply. Then he said, "'Ows your gout, Percy, ol' feller?" in a mock music-hall toff's voice.

They were the Carabineers, the Dragoon Guards, Phillip heard with relief. At once he realised that they were good chaps, like Cranmer. He could feel that they were trying to be kind; and

on their best behaviour, too, like Cranmer—who had never used
guttersnipe words when with him: the very opposite of what
Father had objected to him knowing Cranmer for.

Father—he would be walking over London Bridge now, on the
way home. Home! It belonged to another world, gone for ever.

Chapter 21

MOONRISE

RICHARD was thinking, as he walked over London Bridge in the
twilight, much the same thoughts as his son, but with less
poignancy, for the world had changed since his youth. Even the
sunlight had seemed more expansive in those days, the countryside a-dance with butterflies, where in later years they seemed
to have vanished. How often had he seen a Painted Lady or
Fritillary, Marbled White or Clouded Yellow during recent
summers? Perhaps the fumes of motor cars and omnibuses, and
the drift of sulphurous fumes from ever-growing London had
something to do with it. Well, the changes he had seen coming
upon the world had certainly not turned out for the better!
Which reminded him that it was time Timmy Rat was put down:
it had developed a cough, which might very well be phthisis.
There were the two girls to be thought of.

Richard Maddison was in his fiftieth year: ten years on from
being "too old at forty", he thought with a slight self-scoff. He
was tired, he knew; ever since the outbreak of war he had
worked until seven every night at the office, and often until two
hours later. Overtime at half a crown an hour was not to be
sneezed at, of course; the war would not last for ever; the Navy
would ensure the country's protection, and its vital trade and
shipping; even so, things would never be the same again. Income
tax, already high at ninepence in the £, would probably go even
higher; while the cost of living was going up steadily. Those
damned Prussians, who had ruined the old Germany of king-
doms and principalities, the Germany of his mother, of Mozart
and Beethoven, Wagner and Goethe!

Not that Richard had read any of Goethe's works; the name
had been on his mother's lips, and later Dora had often mentioned the name.

He stopped by the parapet of the bridge, touching its cold granite, which had come from Dartmoor, that romantic region, for ever associated in his mind with the *Hound of the Baskervilles*, clear fast-running streams, and wild grey-green slopes and hills and valleys set with wind-carved tors, visited during solitary cycling holidays in the past. He looked down at the rushing swirl of waters below, the spring-tide being one of the highest of the year; then at the silhouette of the Tower Bridge spanning the tail of the Pool, dim-seen now that the lights of wharf, street, and warehouse were masked. As he gazed, he saw a smoky-red line of fire apparently upon the bridge itself, and was wondering what it was before he realised that it was the top of the moon rising beyond the Thames estuary. He stood and watched it, his spirit relieved with romantic thoughts of Swilly and Nore, of shadowy battleship and destroyer, steam-pinnace and mine-sweeper, ever on the alert to guard the shores of England.

Then, suddenly, he listened. Was it the rumble of traffic, or had the air shivered? He waited—it came again. Gunfire!

He walked on towards the station, recalling what he had read in the train that morning, of Prince Louis of Battenberg's resignation from his post as First Sea Lord of the Admiralty. It was easy to read between the lines of his letter, where he stated that his "birth and parentage impaired his usefulness in some respects". An understatement, if ever there was one! He considered that the outcry for his dismissal, led by *The Globe*, was a little unfair. After all, he was of Austrian, not German, origin. Richard had never countenanced the wild rumours of Prince Louis' confinement to the Tower, as a traitor. Well, history had certainly repeated itself in one respect!

He recalled his father telling them as children how, during the Crimean War, a crowd had waited on Tower Hill to see the Prince Consort brought there, chained hand and foot, as a traitor. The beastly mob again!

Richard had never forgotten Bloody Sunday, and his part, small as it had been, as a special constable, in limiting the riots.

In the train home, with blinds pulled against Zeppelins, which surely would follow the railway lines all leading to London's heart, he read Winston Churchill's letter to Prince Louis, accepting his resignation.

"This is no ordinary war, but a struggle between nations for life and death. It raises passions between nations of a most terrible kind. It effaces the old landmarks and frontiers of our civilisation. History will know that the first step which secured the timely concentration of the Fleet was taken by you."

It was certainly a wise act on his part, he thought as he walked over the Hill, to have removed the tell-tale name of *Lindenheim* from the bar of his gate at the outbreak of war.

The dark trees of the elms consoled him, and the night breeze coming across Kent, from the far sea he saw in his mind. Then upon the crest, between elm-row and school, he felt the night shiver, and stopping, removed his hat, the better to listen. The dull shivering rumble came again, through the air, or was it through the ground? He waited; again the deep grumble, sensed rather than heard: the guns of Flanders, where the big battle for the Channel ports was now joined!

Dark figures approached. It was Mr. Mitchell with his wife. Richard had spoken to him during occasional encounters since the outbreak of war.

"My lass and I are just out for an airing, on Hallo'e'en, Mr. Maddison. Do you hear the guns on the wind? I expect Phillip and my lads will be in the thick of it by now. Have you no' heard from Phillip? We had a letter today from Peter—the London Highlanders will be in the line by now."

On arrival home, Richard kept this information to himself.

Chapter 22

HALLO'E'EN

DULLY over the wide and open expanse of the root-field sounded the flat reports of rifles, the scoring rush of British bullets through the darkness, the crack of enemy bullets passing low overhead. The black-bearded Carabineer said the Alleyman was using explosive bullets. Phillip watched him as he removed a bullet from its brass cartridge, and pushed it back the wrong way round. If the Alleymans did, so would he, he said, with an expression on his face like that of an out-of-work man.

Night settled upon the mournful waste, with its vast human loneliness under a sky flickering incessantly with gun-fire. High above lay the uptilted constellation of the Plough, and Polaris fixed in cold but steady shining over the ring of fire breaking out of the darkness around Ypres, a fire now extending to the flooded areas behind the sand-dunes of the coast where the North Sea poured through breaches in the barrier walls. Night lay upon the battlefield, darkly gravid with the unutterable thoughts of the hosts of the lost, each one cowering within its frail shell of flesh, separated from death by secret thoughts of life that had gone, it seemed, for ever.

Away over the extending root-field, with its low layer of mist and smoke, Phillip saw a red arc moving up, dull at first, but soon clearing to a defined curve of orange as it rose clear of the earth. Almost the moon's rising was a signal, for the sky became bright with many shapes of soundless light: flashings which reached half-way to the zenith; more intense lower bulgings which merged with others, to be succeeded by wider quiverings which vanished only to be replaced by more.

The distant firing of German batteries lit the faces of men looking out of the trench, defined by parapet and parados thrown up untidily among parallel lines of turnips. Phillip saw the dim stare of faces vanish as the first droning of shells curved down the sky. With others he lay down in the trench, leaving his rifle in position on the parapet. He pressed his forearms over his head, shutting his eyes. He lay there wincing from splitting concussion upon splitting concussion, the glare of each near-dropping howitzer-shell showing through pressed eyelids. His head seemed filled with black-gold-red after each terrible detonation that out-clanged the earth. No longer was he able to control himself by thinking that each shell meant that the end of their stay in the line was nearer. He had never acquired the power to think; now he lost the power to be. He screamed until his voice seemed torn out from his throat.

"What's up, chum? Copped it, 'ave you? Got a blighty one?" the bearded Carabineer was holding his arm. He tried to get up. His legs would not move.

" 'Arf a mo', cully."

The shallow trench was filled with clods and earth; the smoking crater of a Johnson lay three yards from the parados.

"I'll soon get you on yer pins, chum."

The Carabineer lugged away lumps of clay and earth from

Phillip's legs, and helped him to his feet. Phillip's head was ringing, while a sort of snake, a black and electric zigzag flickering, ran up and down the outside of his left eye. He lay trembling against the side of the trench, until, remembering his rifle, he groped for it: to find the muzzle split wide, the bayonet twisted.

"I reckon a Alleymand explosive bullet did that."

The shells were now going beyond the road, bursting a quarter of a mile away across the ploughed field.

"They're to stop reinforcements gettin' up. Alleymans comin' over soon. Let 'em try! We'll stop the bleeders!"

"What about my rifle?" cried Phillip.

"There's lots o' buckshees. Hi there! Any spare carbines?" the fellow shouted; and scrambling into the field, went along the trench.

The moon was now clear of the earth; no longer oval, but round and yellow and casting a haze. It seemed to be floating visibly up the sky. The rows of roots were pointed with light. Waiting there, teeth riddling, Phillip heard the partridges calling from the direction of the moon. This time they made the urgent screech as when springing off the ground in alarm. He heard their wing-beats coming nearer, the *ret-ret-rettle* of throw and check of stiff pinions; then they had gone over the trench, flying strongly for the plowed field. Oh God, the Germans must have put them up!

Hardly had the covey passed, when the noise of a band playing came distinctly over the field. It was a brass band, the tune at first seeming to be echoing from elsewhere, until he realised that more than one band was playing. Then there was cheering, not like British hurrays, but shorter cheers sounding like *hoch! hoch! hoch!*

" 'Ere y'ar chum."

Phillip's new friend slithered down into the trench beside him, and held out a carbine.

"Thank you very much."

The Carabineer stared at him curiously.

"I'm very sorry to bother you again," said Phillip, "but all my cartridges are loose, and foolishly I threw away the clips. They wouldn't load into our magazines. Have you any you could lend me?"

"Blimey!" ejaculated the Carabineer. "You're posh!"

Phillip was pleased by this tribute to his gentility.

"I'm afraid I haven't any money on me——"

"That's all right, chum. Stand me a wet arterwards. 'Ere, gimme y' carbine." He took a rag from his pocket and began wiping the bolt. "Alleman'll be comin' over soon." He loaded the magazine. "Aim low, 'old yer fire till you're sure of a targit. 'Ere, fill yer pooches." He pulled a bandolier from a wooden box and waited while Phillip filled his webbing pouches.

Phillip felt suddenly elated, confident. He could hardly wait to fire the carbine. He felt outside himself now, excited and hot but also calm, as though nothing really mattered. The only thing was his hands shaking, and the electric snake flickering down his left eye.

The *pom-poom-err*, *pom-poom-err* of brass bands, the steady beating of big drums, came with a great volume of cheering and shouting from way down under the moon. Then looking round, Phillip saw a figure standing in the field behind the trench.

"Hold your fire, men!" cried the voice of Fiery Forbes. "Wait till you get the order to fire! Every round must tell."

"Come down, sir!" cried Martin's voice. "They're coming, I can see them coming, sir!"

"Hold your fire," said Captain Forbes again, shielding his eyes from the moon. Far away up the line, from northwards and the Menin Road, a crackle of rifle fire was arising, just like a dry thorn fire, thought Phillip, remembering an afternoon at Beau Brickhill when a stubbed-out hedge had been burned. Bullets began to crack overhead.

"Get down, sir!" more voices cried.

Captain Forbes slid into the trench, and taking out his case, lit a cigarette.

The crackle of musketry was sweeping louder and swifter. It seemed to rush upon the trench.

"Stand to!" Phillip heard the voice of Fiery Forbes shouting.

"Stand to, men, stand to!" echoed the anxious voice of Sergeant Henshaw, squeezing behind them along the trench.

"Don't get the wind up, chum!" said the Carabineer, as he chewed his quid of 'baccy.

When the attack was over, when the cheers and singing of the Bavarians advancing to the crest with the blare of brass-bands coming through the moon-mist had died away, then under the droning of heavy shells and the swishing of shrapnel searching the road behind, Phillip was aware of moaning in front, and repeated cries like *mutter-mutter-mutter!*, until with amazement above the sweating of his body and the ringing noise in his ears he realised that the cries of the German wounded were the same as *mother, mother, mother !* heard from the Iron Colonel's bloodless lips just before he had opened his eyes wide, and died. It was a startling thought, that the Germans felt like that, too—he hardly dare to think it. Then, wondering why the wrist of his left hand was stinging, as though the skin had been cut by a sharp knife, he stood the carbine against the trench, drew back his sleeve, and to his amazement felt a soft greasy water-blister there.

"The 'eat o' the chamber," explained the Carabineer, "boils the grease packed under the wooden cover. The barrel gits red 'ot, not as you'd notice it when you're giving the Alleyman five rounds rapid."

Five rounds! thought Phillip. He must have fired a hundred. He felt wildly exalted that the attack had failed; he wanted to laugh, to sing.

The moon of Hallo'e'en, one night away from its full shine, sailed high in the sky, so that figures of men, whether standing or lying, moving or still, complete or broken into pieces, cast the smallest shadows upon the earth.

But such quality of observation vanishes like tissue paper in flame when high explosive detonates, and a man is exposed to his own frail aloneness. Phillip leapt down into the trench when with swoop and swish German shrapnel began to crack above.

High explosive followed shrapnel. The timeless night roared on. Cries came feebly through the choking fumes; showers of sparks and fiery tongues rose from the stacks west of the road; the windmill blazed until its arms dropped to pieces with running blazing tar. The shell sunk low, while yet the farm near it was lurid with flame.

With the glare behind them, the survivors in trench and rifle pit were appalled by a sudden great burst of cheering, prolonged and repeated; and to the striking up of *Deutschland, Deutschland über Alles* the Bavarians attacked again. The rows of faces were lit by flames as they ran forward, to fall before rapid-thudding rifle fire. Phillip could hear their officers shouting; he saw one run forward, until he stumbled upon his face, sword in hand. Then from Messines came the steady *pop-pop-popple-clat-clatt!* of traversing machine-gun fire. More than one was enfilading the line of trenches. Parapet and parados, or what served for them, seemed to jerk viciously in places, sending spirts of dirt upon him. When the machine-guns stopped firing there was more shouting; another rush; some of the attacking figures leaping from side to side, but never coming really near. Others lay down, and started to fire. There were only a few flashes here and there; and as the flames behind the trench sank down, the attack seemed to be called off. Whistles were blown, shouts were heard. Phillip felt himself suddenly to be feeble.

Mr. Ogilby walked along the back of the trench, asking how they were. Any casualties? Lance-corporal Douglas reported none in his half-section; but they needed more ammunition. Sergeant Henshaw told him to detail two men to fetch boxes from the dump behind the farmhouse to the right of the burning corn-stack, now a low glowing heap of embers sometimes fluttering with lilac flames.

Douglas, tense and sharp, ordered Phillip and Martin to go. Martin, a limp figure of woe, on hearing his name, began to cough hollowly, as he held his hand to his side.

"Get back as soon as you can, boys," said Sergeant Henshaw, encouragingly. Phillip was glad to get away from the trenches. With Martin slow and silent beside him, he made for the far side of the stack ember-pile.

"We must avoid showing ourselves against the glow of the fire."

"Oh my God. I can't go on," groaned Martin.

"Come on, I say. It's not healthy here. These bullets aren't aimed anywhere, but all the same, it's no sense standing still."

"I'm not well," moaned Martin.

"The crack you hear is the air closing up behind the bullets. One of the regulars told me it was because they were explosive bullets. He said the sparks they made when hitting the road proved it, but I don't believe it. Come on, get over the road quickly!" He took Martin's arm.

"Oo are yer?" cried a voice.

"London Highlanders!"

"Pass," cried the unseen sentry.

They crossed the road.

"I hope we're relieved tonight, I can't stand much more,"

said Martin, with half-sigh, half-groan, stopping beside a hedge. He coughed hollowly, bending down, pressing his hand to his side.

"I hope so, too. What's up, a stitch?"

"Yes," gasped Martin. "I've had it ever since that shell got me in the side this morning."

Phillip thought Martin was making that an excuse to go sick, but he said nothing. "You'll be all right. Come on."

"Feel my forehead."

Phillip felt. "It feels rather hot, I must say."

"I believe I'm bleeding inside. Oh!" Martin began to sob. "I can't stick it no more, Maddison! Honestly I can't! This pain is awful, all down my side!"

"I'll carry your rifle for you. We're nearly there."

But Martin would not move. Phillip began to feel scorn for him, a Leytonstone boy indeed, with his woeful monkey-eyes. Martin was obviously putting it on. "Come on, I know it's pretty bad, but perhaps we'll be relieved tonight. That regular told me the Indian troops only had twenty-four hours in the line, then they were relieved."

"But they had lost all their officers," wept Martin. "Oh, why doesn't someone stop it?"

Phillip walked slowly beside him. They passed the dark shape of the farmhouse and went down a lane to where several shadowy figures were standing and talking in low voices. Phillip saw stretchers on the ground. Captain McTaggart the Medical Officer was kneeling by one. The orderly holding an Orlik torch beside him seemed familiar. It was Tommy Atkins.

The ammunition dump was at the other end, in an orchard. Mules with pack saddles were waiting there, their bridles held by tall transport men wearing woollen comforters. They were the Coldstreamers. Phillip asked if Sergeant Cakebread was about.

"Here I am, young Phil!" said Bertie, to his immense relief. "How's things?"

"All right, thanks." Phillip motioned to speak with him in private. "Bertie, have you heard anything about a relief?"

"Not yet. But they say a French brigade is on the way. Have you seen old Gerry? It's such a frightful schemozzle no one knows where anyone is. Like a drink?"

Hubert Cakebread offered his water-bottle. It was full of warm tea, rum in it. Phillip took a long pull. Immediately afterwards he felt it wasn't so bad, after all.

"May my pal Martin have some? I'll fetch him."

Martin was drooping, coughing hollowly, near the Medical Officer. Captain McTaggart was wiping his bloody hands on a towel. Bearers, red-cross white brassards on both arms, were arriving, folded stretchers on shoulders. They had been carrying the wounded down through the wood to the road where waggons had taken them away.

Martin spoke to Tommy Atkins, who told the Medical Officer.

"Tell him to go sick when we're out of the line," said Captain McTaggart, without looking up from what he was doing. Martin saluted, and turned away. Phillip knew what that meant: Medicine and Duty—a No. 9 pill, to clear the bowels. He touched Martin's arm, to tell him about the rum waiting for him; but Martin did not want any. He was weeping.

Carrying one wooden S.A.A. ammunition box by its rope handles between them, and Phillip dragging another partly on the ground, they set off back to the line. The boxes were heavy. They stopped frequently on the way up to the road.

Before they reached it, Martin collapsed, moaning that he could go no further.

"Hell, I can't manage more than one box by myself. Get up!"

"I can't."

"We're all in the same boat. I don't like it any more than you do. Come on, I say!"

When Martin would not, he said, "If Grannie Henshaw reports us, we'll get in a row, you know! You're a fool not to have had some of that rum, when I wangled it for you."

Martin groaned. He was trembling violently.

"Well, it's no damn good stopping here! We're right beside the road, and if they start firing, we'll cop it! Come on, get up! I know you're putting it on! Why, even those chaps wounded on stretchers didn't moan. Get up, I say!"

"I can't. I'm dying."

"Can't you even help me get this bloody weight on my shoulder? Christ, won't you even help that much? Then blast you, you Leytonstone lout!" cried Phillip, with sobbing breath, striking Martin on the head.

He tried to shoulder the box, but could not get it up. While he sat there, an outburst of shouting arose all along the front from left and right; and as rifle-fire flashed everywhere, he lay down beside Martin; then taking his bayonet off his rifle, began to break open the box, and sling the linen bandoliers over his shoulder.

"Get up, you lout! Jesus Christ, hark at them!"

The shouting had spread across the whole of the front, from Messines on the right to Wytschaete on the left. As he listened, the thin wire drawn tight within, the shouting took on an ominous note: a deeper, roaring sound, overcoming the thudding of rifle-fire at ground-level from the ground in front. There were glints in the moonlight; there were noises of running feet: isolated yells; and then a deep growling *aa-aa-ah*, like the back-wash of a wave rolling shingle down a beach.

Hearing it, Phillip was at first unable to move. He crouched low, staring towards the dreadful deep noise from which now came screams and cries. Struggling to get his voice up from his stomach, at last he managed to gasp, as he shook off the weight of linen bandoliers and tugged at Martin's arm, "It's too late! They're coming! Come on! Come on, quick! Oh, you bloody fool, you idiot!" for still Martin would not move, but lay there, face on arm.

Phillip tried once more to get him up. He pulled him by the arm, screaming at him; he beat him about the head, spraining his thumb in so doing; and then he ran, mouth open, blindly the way he had come. Behind the farmhouse, between retching attempts to get his voice, "They've broken through! Bayonet charge! They're coming over the road! Martin! Martin! Save him!"

"Control yourself, that man!" cried the authoritative voice of the Medical Officer. "Atkins, Smith, take a stretcher! You!" to Phillip. "Guide them where to go, and then rejoin your company!"

"Very good, sir," said Phillip, hoping that no one had recognised him. He realised that he had left his carbine beside Martin.

Chapter 23

REACTION

THE moon was wasted of its light, hanging pale above the five distant wooded Monts de Flandre when scattered groups of the London Highlanders, driven from L'Enfer wood, made their

way to the straight road leading to Wulverghem, a village two
miles west of Messines. Through the night-lenses of Captain
'Fiery' Forbes' binoculars Germans were visible walking
about on the ridge, apparently seeking wounded. Stray shells
whined down, twisting luridly in the unknown dark; distant
reverberations shook the dim air of dawn.

Flights of machine-gun bullets began to hiss and streak
through the semi-darkness, the traversing streams followed by
their sequences of reports. Sporadic rifle-fire opened up; it
was dangerous to group; the order was to extend, men to make
their way back to the reassembly point at Wulverghem.

Most of the inhabitants of the village remained, with many of
the houses intact, and the church. Those peasants who were
about seemed to take little interest in what was going on. Hag-
gard kilted men fell in on company markers in a field outside
the village; and having piled arms, rested.

It was known by this time that the Earl of Findhorn was
killed, with the Adjutant. Captain Forbes was in command
of the battalion.

When the roll was called one hundred and fifty men of all
ranks answered their names. Of "B" Company twenty-seven
remained, with Mr. Ogilby in command.

Captain Forbes briefly addressing the battalion survivors,
said that many of the missing would no doubt be rejoining
later.

A cavalry regiment had their lines nearby, and when from
their cooks came dixies of hot tea, Phillip learned they were the
Oxfordshire Hussars.

Later the transport waggons of the Coldstream arrived. Tins
of Maconochie were given out, as many as each man wanted.
Nobody took more than one. Phillip could not eat his.

Morning revealed a monotony of damp level fields, leafless
trees around farms with red-tiled roofs, and a dark wood about
a mile away. Dominating the landscape, frowning over all,
was Messines, looking like a mass of cracked, dark-brown crab-
shells against the sky-line. The dark-brown serrated mass was
almost sinister in distinctness with the light of early morning
behind it.

Now that day was come, and water gleaming in cart-ruts and
hoof-holes in the mud all around, Phillip felt wretched, as
though with the night something which had been his life was

gone. Almost he wanted to be back on the ridge in darkness again, among burning stacks and buildings, listening to the bird-like piping and moaning of ricochets, even the cheering and band-playing and the crashing of rifle-fire. It was terrible, and yet it was wonderful; even as the thought of ever having to go through it again was icy blackness to the mind.

What could he do, to avoid going back. If only he could get some of his ribs broken, as they said Martin had got. He had been got away just in time.

An officer of "D" Company, with a folding camera, took photographs as they stood in a loose line.

Of Baldwin he had heard no news. The stretcher-bearers knew nothing. Elliott was missing too. Phillip went to Gerry's company, to find him. Cakebread was missing, they said. Feeling heavy and hollow he hastened to the transport to see Bertie. A big red-faced Coldstreamer said the sergeant had remained during the night with his old company, hearing that all the officers had been killed. That was when the Allemans had broken through on the left, and the Highlanders had counter-attacked with the bayonet. Sergeant Cakebread had led them and had not been seen since.

"I see, thank you," said Phillip; and wondering what to do, he went to "C" Company, to see Peter Wallace, and David, and young Nimmo. It was a shock to learn that Peter had been killed, after going to the rescue of the Medical Officer, Captain McTaggart, who had been bayoneted while attending a wounded man. In the light of a burning stack Peter had run in to help, but his glasses must have dropped off, for when last seen he had been wrestling with a German, whose head he had got under his arm. Just then more Germans had appeared from the other side of the farm, and a withdrawal into the wood had been ordered. Screams of men bayoneted had been heard. If ever a man deserved the V.C., it was Peter Wallace, the dishevelled chaps of "C" Company said.

"What about David, and young Nimmo? Were they with Peter?"

Nobody seemed to know.

He wandered off by himself, thinking about Peter's bravery, and his own utter funk. It was just the same as when they had been boys in the Backfield. He had always been afraid of fighting; Peter had always been brave. There was no doubt of his own cowardice, then and now. He re-lived, with drying mouth, the scene in the trench again: the red-black-gold flash of the 5.9 bursting on the parados, his legs buried in earth, the voice of the bearded Carabineer coming from a long way away as he pulled him out. If he had not been sent back for ammunition, he would have been bayoneted with the others in the trench. He had slipped away, from behind the stretcher-bearers, as soon as they had carried off Martin. What else was there to do except clear off? Would Martin remember that he had struck him on the head? If so, he would say that he had only been trying to make him wake up to his danger, and the need to get bandoliers to the company. That was true, in a way. It *was* true. Nevertheless, or *tamen*, as the Magister would say, he had been in what Father called a blue funk.

He wandered to the road, and watched the Oxfordshire Hussars parading without their horses. Other men of the battalion were standing about there. The Hussars were Yeomanry, territorials like themselves, and going up for the first time on foot. Was there to be an attack, to try and get back the ridge? If so, they hadn't a hope, against all those German machine-guns, and in daylight, too.

Could it be true, as some of the chaps were saying, that among the Bavarians advancing to the crest, to the music of their bands floating before them in the silence of the guns, were students walking arm-in-arm because they had no rifles at all, being sustained only by the desperate singing of comrades, volunteers like themselves, who had had even less training than the youngest of the London Highlanders? And that the cries of *mutter-mutter-mutter* among the wounded were the same as *mother-mother-mother* heard from the Iron Colonel's grey lips when he had opened his eyes wide, just before dying, as he lay in the lee of the cornstack? It was a terrible thought, that the enemy was like themselves: a thought that he could not bear to think of at all, even to himself.

When the Hussars had gone, he saw a group of officers trotting up the road. They had red bands round their hats, and gold braid on the peaks. In front of them rode a Colour-sergeant, bearing a little Union Jack as a pennant. Behind him came a sturdy, white-moustached figure, which he recognised from

newspaper photographs as Field-Marshal Sir John French, the
Commander-in-Chief. Everyone saluted as he went past.

He watched the magnificent posse, as he thought of it halting
and dismounting. Sir John French spoke to several of the Highlanders. He hurried over to hear. It was surprising how short
the Commander-in-Chief was, and how kindly he spoke. He
said the battalion had done well. Their work, and the way
they had borne themselves, would never be forgotten. He asked
many questions, all in the same kindly voice, rather like Sir
Ian Hamilton's. It was a wonderful feeling, to be spoken to like
that by a Field-Marshal. He was not at all stern, like Lord
Kitchener; rather the reverse. He felt much happier. All the
staff-officers looked spotlessly clean, with gleaming brown riding
boots and belts, and shining spurs. A Rolls-Royce motor-car
with a Union Jack on its bonnet, and several mounted men,
all with sergeant's stripes, followed the group as they rode away.

With the others, Phillip was excited by the visit; but depression
returned when the order was given to fall-in on the road. He
was almost sorry to be leaving the field, muddy as it was; still,
they would be going back for a rest, and letters and parcels.

Changes were made in the company. Lance-corporal Douglas
was now full corporal, with an extra purple stripe to each sleeve
made by indelible pencil. He was in charge of the left-half
company. Collins, promoted lance-corporal, was in charge of
the section. Collins now had a determined manner, so different
from his apathetic attitude during the night bus-ride from Ypres,
long ago. Then, with a start, he realised that the bus-ride was
only last Friday night; and that today was Sunday. Sunday!
What would they be doing at home? He could not imagine his
home. Would the bell of St. Cyprian's Church be tolling for
eleven o'clock service? How unreal and far-away all that now
seemed. It was gone for ever.

After linen bandoliers of ammunition had been handed out,
the battalion moved off through the village. To his dismay
Phillip realised that they were going along the road leading to
Messines. Surely they were not going into the attack again?
Shells were bursting on the rising ground in front. There was a
lot of machine-gun fire in the distance. Why were they marching
back again? Hadn't they done their bit? He felt like crying.

They turned off the road, down a muddy lane which led to a
farm. They lined a ditch, behind a thorn hedge. They were

told not to look up, in case enemy aeroplanes saw their white
faces.

Through a gap in the hedge he watched the Hussars advancing
in open order, across the brown land which sloped almost imperceptibly down to the little brook which he had crossed with
others during the withdrawal in the darkness. Many machine-
guns were now firing, from unseen posts across the stream. Then
tiny figures of men were seen, moving down the slopes. They
were Germans. Nearer, other figures were coming back towards
the spur—the Hussars coming back.

All day the Highlanders and the Yeomanry sat or lay and
slept by the hedge. The German advance seemed to have petered
out. Phillip could not sleep; he lay back on his valise, while
recent scenes recurred again and again in his mind. The electric
snake flickered all down the left side of his head; he rubbed his
eye; it made no difference. Then as the afternoon was growing
dull other troops filed down the track, and Sergeant Furrow
told them that they were being relieved. A rumour said that
they would be returning to England, to be turned into an
Officers Training Corps. They filed away down the muddy
lane.

At first they marched fairly regularly in step down the *pavé*
road to Wulverghem; but soon fatigue, and the hard sett-stones,
made progress for each man a desperate, lonely, and unspeaking
affair. Phillip's shoes and hose, sodden from crossing the stream
the night before, soon blistered his heels. They went on
through Wulverghem, turning right-handed towards the nearest
of the low, wooded hills to the north. Darkness had come when
the first halt was called. They fell out on the right of the road,
beyond the iron rails embedded in the *pavé*.

Here the transport was waiting with hot tea and Maconochie
stew; then on again into the night, humping packs, rifles con-
tinually being shifted from shoulder to shoulder, no one speaking,
tramp tramp tramp in darkness flashing and rolling with gun-
fire along the eastern horizon.

They kept going in the hope of billets in the village below the
Mont de Kemmel; but they marched on through dark little
rows of cottages dim-seen under the embattled sky; men now
slouching along, out of step, many limping upon the uneven
pavé. Phillip was on the left of his file of fours; the *pavé* in the

middle of the road. A muddy track lay each side of it. With
clenched teeth he slogged on. They came at last to another
village. This time they halted, to lean upon muzzles of rifles,
waiting, for this was the end of the march.

As in a bad dream he followed five others into a cottage
kitchen. Their blankets had been thrown off before the advance
through the wood; no matter, this was a house, with roof to
keep out rain, and thanks be to God, said Corporal Douglas,
a stove. Shedding equipment, they lay down, but stirred to
to life once more when the post-corporal and his orderly man
brought round letters. The orderly carried an extra sack marked
Missing, in indelible pencil.

Parcels would be delivered tomorrow, said the post-corporal's
voice, heard by Phillip lying in a corner, face to the wall, precious
envelopes in breast-pocket, praying silently that all the candles
be put out—the eye-stabbing bright points of light, the jarring
voices in the room.

More of "B" company turned up in the morning. An entire
half-company of "A" arrived. Retreating with other troops after
the night of battle, they had slept elsewhere. The battalion losses
were not so heavy as had been thought; they were just under
four hundred.

For "B" company there was a foot-inspection after breakfast;
then Lance-corporal Collins marched the sick to the R.A.M.C.
post, where iodine was dabbed on Phillip's raw blisters. From
the orderly he heard that Martin was in the Casualty Clearing
Station at Locre.

Later in the morning orders came to move by 'bus. With
relief he heard they were going back to Bailleul. When they
paraded, Captain Forbes told them that he had received a
telegram from the Commander-in-Chief, offering his warmest
congratulations and thanks for the fine work they had done at
Messines. "You have given a glorious lead and example to
all Territorial troops who are going to fight in France." There
was also a letter from General Allenby, commanding the Cavalry
Corps, in which he thanked the battalion for the self-sacrificing
support given in a great emergency. "Steadiness and courage
saved a situation that was as difficult and critical to deal with
as will ever occur." If only he had known what had really
happened. Then Captain Forbes read out messages from the

2nd Battalion at Home. So the news had got to London! Ah, if only he had not run into the wood.

Yet he felt also a sort of pride as Fiery Forbes read out the messages; but upon reflection, wondered again how they could have applied to what had happened. How had the situation been *saved*? He tried to picture Father's face, when he read of it in *The Daily Trident*. He could almost hear Gran'pa on the Hill discussing it with Mr. Krebs and Mr. Bolton, in the shelter, or perhaps standing in the road outside his gate, with Mrs. Bigge looking on. Would Mrs. Neville, in her upper flat, be watching up the road as she usually did? He could imagine the serious faces, and perhaps Mrs. Neville would be crying; but not Mother. He had not seen her cry since he was a little child, though often hot spots came on her cheeks when Father bullied her, and a shine came upon her eyes.

Chapter 24

INCIDENT IN CHARLOTTE ROAD

Mrs. Neville, seated in her window with its view of the lower slopes of the grassy Hill, and all of Hillside Road, saw Mrs. Maddison walking down the pavement with what looked like Timmy Rat's box held in one hand by its strap. She knew the box well; for invariably Phillip had brought it down to show Desmond every time he had returned home for the holidays. *I just brought Timmy down to welcome Desmond home again, Mrs. Neville. His box is quite clean, really*—she could hear Phillip's voice now: at times he had such a charming, diffident manner, just like his father.

Where was Mrs. Maddison going with the box? Was she coming to see her, and perhaps ask her to take care of Phillip's white rat? Had Phillip's father decided that he would not have it in the house any longer? Surely not, while Phillip was away at the front! Well, really, whatever the reason, if Mrs. Maddison intended to ask her to look after Timmy—no, no, she must not say yes! It was unhealthy. Rats and mice—she drew the line at rats and mice. Desmond's hedgehog, that the boys had once brought home in a handkerchief, to unroll on the carpet and dip its head in milk—when, surprisingly, it unrolled

to lap up the saucer—had been able to take care of itself in the
garden—but Timmy Rat in her kitchen, never! She must be
firm!

It was shortly after eleven o'clock on the morning of Monday,
the 2nd of November. The day had started with rain, but now
it had cleared. The sun was shining in her kitchen window;
and having carried her cup of mid-morning tea to the sitting-
room, Mrs. Neville, comfortable in her chair, had worked off
her slippers, and with cup-handle ready in position for the first
slow reflective sip, had taken up the morning paper. At that
moment she caught sight of Phillip's mother; and she was about to
get up from her chair, to open the window and ask Mrs. Maddison
in for a cup of tea, when her eyes caught the headlines on the
front page of the paper lying across her knees.

LONDON HIGHLANDERS IN ACTION
BAYONET CHARGE RESTORES
BROKEN LINE SOUTH
OF YPRES

Heavy German Losses

Tears sprang from her eyes. "O my God!" she said, staring
through them. Phillip! Mrs. Cakebread's two boys! The three
Wallace brothers just down the road! They must have been
in it! O my God! poor Phillip's mother! That was it! Phillip's
father wanted to get rid of Timmy because—O, surely not!
What dreadful thoughts she was capable of! Mary, Mother of
God, forgive me!

Mrs. Neville dabbled her eyes, and rising swiftly for one so
weighty from a chair none too big for her bulk, managed to
throw up the window and call out to the familiar trim little
figure just as it was going round the corner into Charlotte Road.
Thank God, Mrs. Maddison smiled when she turned her face!
Then everything must be all right—so far, at any rate. Mrs.
Neville touched the wood of her table.

She waited while the small smiling figure crossed the road, and composed herself for the moment of speaking when Mrs. Maddison should stop by the railings at the end of the open, tiled approach to the flats. Then in her best party voice Mrs. Neville called down, sweetly,

"Do come up and have a cup of tea, dear, if you can spare the time. I've just made a pot! I'll come down and let Mazeppa out. Then Timmy will be safe in his box on the mat, behind the closed door."

Mrs. Neville, having drawn a deep breath in order to put on her shoes, hid the paper under a cushion, and went down the stairs and opened the door, Mazeppa mewing before her.

"Do come in, Mrs. Maddison. Out you go, Mazeppa now! Away with you, lazy cat! All he thinks about is his food. There now, Timmy will be safe on the mat. Go up, dear, will you? I'm such a weight, I'll follow you. You'll have a cup of tea, won't you? I've only just made it. Go up, dear, and sit down, while I fetch another cup."

"Thank you, Mrs. Neville."

"Well now, what is the latest about Phillip?" said Mrs. Neville, sweetly, having brought in her tray. "No news is good news, I always say."

"Yes, Mrs. Neville!" replied Hetty, almost gaily. "Phillip is very well, he says. They are staying in an empty convent, somewhere in France, having moved up from the railhead where they were working. He does not say, of course, what he is doing, but it is nice to think that they are in a convent, with wooden floors, too. He was always such a delicate child, and prone to catch cold."

"Well, let's hope the war will be over by Christmas, dear. I hope you don't mind me calling you 'dear'—'Mrs. Maddison' sounds so formal, for Phillip's mother, somehow." She paused, listening.

"What's that noise? Did you hear it, dear? There it is again."

"It is Timmy coughing, Mrs. Neville. He is not very well, I am afraid, nothing contagious, but he has croup, and wheezes such a lot that my husband thought that, as he was also very old, and the war, he thinks, may go on for sometime—well, perhaps it would be kinder to have Timmy put to sleep."

To her surprise she saw Mrs. Neville's eyes suddenly look staring and large, before she lowered her head and sought her

handkerchief. She too had felt almost like crying at the thought
of Phillip's pet being put to sleep—not the "put down" of Dickie,
such a harsh term. What would Phillip say when he heard?

"There now," said Mrs. Neville, looking up. "How very
silly I am, to be crying because of Timmy! Of course, dear,
Phillip's father knows best, and Timmy may have something
contagious. Why soon, like me, he'll be losing his teeth!" she
cried, with a little shriek of merriment. At once her face became
serious. "Well, it is so nice of you to come and see me—do
drop in, dear, any time you want to, won't you? I'll come
down with you and let Mazeppa in. He is quite a companion
for me, you know, now that the boys are all away from home."

At the door Hetty said goodbye, and carrying the box, went
on down Charlotte Road. She was about to turn into Dorrie's
when she saw Mr. Bolton coming out from his gate, and start
to walk up towards her, as though he wanted to say something.
He raised his bowler to her in rather less than his usual courtly
and deliberate manner; and he appeared to stagger. Could he
have been drinking? Then she realised that never before had
she seen Mr. Bolton without his pug-dog on its lead.

She smiled and nodded, and was about to go through the gate
when Mr. Bolton waved his stick, and began to walk faster than
his usual slow gait towards her. By now she knew that something
had happened; and going to meet him, saw that his face was
drawn, and tears running down his cheeks.

"Oh, Mr. Bolton, is anything the matter?"

He bowed, and lifted his hat. Holding it against his fawn covert
coat with its brown velvet collar, he looked at her with his pale
eyes and said huskily, "M'am, my boy has been killed in action."

"Oh dear, Mr. Bolton——" said Hetty, and then realised that
he was with the London Highlanders.

"Oh dear, what can I say? Oh, I am so sorry! Oh yes, of
course. Have you—have you only just heard, Mr. Bolton?"

"Not ten minutes since. Yes, it came—the War Office telegram—just as I was setting out for my walk on the Hill. Your
boy, Phillip, I trust, is all right?"

"Oh yes, we heard only this morning! He says he is billeted in
an unfinished convent."

Mr. Bolton stared at Hetty, as though striving for breath, or
words; then he said, "There has been a great battle, Mrs.
Maddison. I trust all will be well with your son."

"Oh, Mr. Bolton, have they all been in it?"

"Yes, m'am. But they saved the day, according to *The Times*."

She managed to say, "Believe me, you have my deepest sympathy in your loss." Her voice added, with a slight tremor, "These things are in the hands of God, as are all our lives, especially in these times."

Bogey the pug-dog was now to be heard and seen, barking violently, his anxious black face at one of the front windows of Mr. Bolton's house.

"Ah, the little fellow, he knows!" muttered Mr. Bolton. "Well, I must go to him." But the old man seemed loath to be left alone. "Will your father be going on the Hill this morning, do you think, Mrs. Maddison?" he muttered next.

"Oh yes, he is sure to, Mr. Bolton! He will be deeply grieved to hear of your son's—passing."

The old man drew himself up. "Well, life must go on," he said, with a ruined smile. "There's the little fellow barking for me. I shall have to go and attend to him." He went slowly back to his house.

Dorrie had not yet looked at the morning paper. Now the sisters opened it together.

"We must continue to hope, Dorrie. And to pray that God will hear our prayers."

As she was leaving, Hetty remembered Timmy Rat in his box, waiting in the hall.

"Oh no, I could not bring myself to take Phillip's pet down now, Dorrie! Certainly not! Dickie would never forgive me. Oh no! We can only hope and pray. Yes, I must wait and consult Dickie before I do anything now."

And with the box in her hand, she returned up Hillside Road, watched by Mrs. Neville, who had already heard, from Soal the greengrocer and coalman, that Mr. Bolton's son had been killed.

Later that afternoon, as, house-work done, she sat by the window sewing, she saw the telegraph boy pass on his red bicycle. The boy prepared to alight, one boot scraping on the road used as brake, while standing on the pedal with the other. Oh no, don't say that he was going to the Wallace's! Pretending to post a letter, she took an old envelope, put on a coat, and went downstairs and out to the post-box, feeling as though it were a matter of her own life and death.

She waited just inside the narrow lane, leading to the back-garden doors of the flats, until she saw the boy come out of the gate, and then moved, envelope in hand, guiltily towards the pillar box. She passed the boy as he wheeled his machine away from the curb, preparatory to mounting.

"Do you realise, I wonder," she said to the boy, with a smile, "what the sight of you stopping in a road, in these times, can mean to a mother who has a son at the front?"

"Don't blame me, m'am. I don't know what's in me tele-grams. Only sometimes, like."

"Were you the little boy who brought the telegram to Mr. Bolton's, this morning?"

"'Im what's son was killed? Yuss, I did an' all. And the lady I just bin to's 'ad three killed, all together. I wouldn't take nothin' from 'er, though she offered me a copper."

"You are a good, kind boy," said Mrs. Neville. "Now you wait here, dear, and I will bring you a nice orange."

Later in the week, Mrs. Neville heard from her charwoman that when Mrs. Cakebread went over to offer sympathy to Mrs. Wallace, and mentioned that her two boys were safe so far, though the younger one, Gerry, was wounded, Mrs. Wallace cried, "You've no right to have both alive, when I have lost all my three!"

On the same day Hetty went down to show Mrs. Neville the Field Post-card which had arrived by the eleven o'clock post, all the various laconic printed items of information crossed out in indelible pencil except *I am well*, and Phillip's signature. In her relief Mrs. Neville said gaily, "You know, dear, Phillip was always getting into scrapes, and managing to get out of them, and somehow I feel he will come through all right. He's got his wits about him, very much so, has Phillip." Then at the sight of Mr. Bolton coming out of his gate, with Bogey, to go for his walk upon the Hill, her large face started to shake, and tears streaked the powder on her cheeks.

"It's November, dear. I always get like this when the leaves fall, don't take any notice of me," she smiled. "At any rate, the London Highlanders have done their bit, and it will be some time before his battalion is used again, so that is one comfort."

"Yes," said Hetty, almost gaily. "Dorrie had a letter from

Bertie just now, apparently they have gone back to rest, and to be refitted. I am just going to post him a parcel, with a red chest-protector in it, from his grandfather, to keep out the cold."

Chapter 25

THE BROWN WOOD LINE

PHILLIP thought that Bailleul was a pleasant town. Two things made him contented: they were allowed to go into the estaminets and drink beer and *café-rhum* in the evening; and cousin Bertie had turned up, safe and sound. There was no rule about privates being seen with sergeants, so it was good to have Bertie to talk to, sometimes. Gerry was in hospital at the base with a shrapnel ball in his thigh.

Bit by bit news of the company casualties got around. Baldwin had been killed at once. Elliott had been hit by a shell as they were coming into the open out of l'Enfer wood. He had lain all doubled up, his leg and arm bones protruding out of a tattered mass of kilt and tunic. "Grannie" Henshaw had a bullet in the shoulder, in the withdrawal, and was already in England. Bertie was in high feather: he said the new Colonel of the Coldstream, with which his grandfather and great-uncles had served, had applied for him, and the C.O. had signed his papers for a commission.

From Bertie Phillip learned that the battalion was to remain at Bailleul for a large draft expected from the 2nd Battalion in England. New rifles were to be issued. Phillip had reported that his had been struck by a bullet; he said nothing about the carbine, left beside Martin as the Germans were breaking through. "I went, sir, with the others, to man the reserve line."

The Grande Place of Bailleul was filled with guns—long-toms, or naval guns from the South African war, all newly painted in blotches of decaying cabbage. Lacking ammunition, they had been withdrawn from the line, but to the troops, they were part of the reserve, which showed that things could not be too bad. The town seemed to be a centre for Territorials. The two cousins, in the bar of the Faucon d'Or, talked with some of the Honourable Artillery Company. They looked at the dining-room, where wall-mirrors had been broken by drunken Uhlan

K

officers throwing empty bottles about. There were various stories
of Uhlan atrocities. Before leaving a house in which they had
been billeted, a house owned by an old lady and her servant, some
German officers had taken out all the sheets in the linen-press,
spread them over the beds they had slept in, and then fouled
them, for a joke. In another billet they had done the same thing
upon some of the plates of a set of delicate china taken from a
glass-fronted cupboard; then they had put back the plates. And
yet, when he went into a butcher's shop to buy a piece of sausage,
Phillip learned that the Germans had paid for everything they
had asked for, though in silver marks, with the eagle on one side.
The Germans had told the butcher that the money would be
good after the war. Phillip exchanged one of his silver francs for
a German mark as a souvenir, a new word picked up from the
regulars.

The H.A.C. were very nice chaps, he thought, although somehow they did not look like soldiers, with their long lavender-
coloured greatcoats. It was the same colour as that worn by the
Officer of the Guard at the Bank of England, which he had
watched one autumn evening of the previous year, marching
through the City. He wondered if they would have to have khaki
coats before they could go into the line, lest they be mistaken for
Germans. The German coats were more grey than the H.A.C.
overcoats, judging from those he had seen on prisoners.

During the second evening out with Bertie, there was an
ominous increase in the gun-fire rolling down the wind. Another
attack was being made for Ypres. Phillip was glad to be out of it:
it was generally agreed that they had done their bit; but a shock
was coming: after dinner the next day Sergeant Furrow entered
the billet to announce company parade, full marching order, at
four o'clock, to go into the line that night.

"That's torn it," remarked Lance-corporal Collins.

"Why don't they send in the H.A.C.?" said Church. "They've
only lost two men so far, digging reserve trenches, by stray shell-
fire."

"But Sergeant!" said Phillip. "How can I go? I haven't
got my new rifle! There weren't enough to go round! I am
supposed to wait until the next issue!"

"You'll be given one before parade, from the transport
men."

Phillip followed him out of the billet.

"Please, Sergeant, may I be allowed to see the Company Commander?"

"What about?"

"I want to transfer to the transport."

"Why?"

"I like horses, Sergeant."

Sergeant Furrow looked at him from his superior height and said slowly and softly, "You'll find yourself on a piece of paper one day."

Phillip saw Church looking at him with his slightly projecting teeth showing. He never knew whether Church was smiling, or sneering, with those teeth. He had looked at him like that ever since the "Leytonstone louts" remark. He wondered, too, what was wrong in applying to go on the transport? Other chaps had said it was a good thing to be in.

Sergeant Furrow's remark recurred many times to his mind, as he rode up to Ypres by 'bus, now almost desperately missing Baldwin. So far he had not thought of Norman as dead; only a blank. Now, as with slight horror he imagined a crumpled piece of newspaper lying beside a hedge, and realised what Furrow meant, the idea of never having Norman with him again was like a blow.

Norman Baldwin dead, and gone for ever persisted as a thought, as he marched up the Menin road once more. Fresh blisters had formed under the "New Skin" on his heels, so that he padded along with a sort of lope, constantly getting out of step, to the annoyance of the man behind him. German shells were dropping both sides of the road. The rifle dished out to him was the old Mark I; it would not take the pointed ammunition clips. *You'll find yourself on a piece of paper one day!* He was that awful word, which some of the men used! Suddenly he remembered he had used it, as a joke, to describe the shag in the Free Library book. Thence to mind-pictures of Reynard's Common, Whitefoot Lane woods, bluebells everywhere in spring—trying to think of anything except Baldwin dead—and this time, perhaps——O, no, no, it could not be——

Mother—Mother——

In the darkness every 18-pounder firing blanched the road and fossilised the roadside trees with its narrow white smiting stab. They had passed beyond the gigantic moth-wing orange flashes

of up-pointing howitzers, the orange-wing flash smacking away
its shell with high corkscrewing rush diminishing into the sky.
After the 18-pounders, they were coming near the front line.
A spreading crackle of musketry was to be heard in front. Someone pointed out the château of Hooge, now in gun-light seen
half in ruins. And less than a week ago they had paraded in front
of it, for the General's inspection! Beyond the deserted château
soldiers were standing in the doorways of broken white-washed
cottages.

There had been visible a pale greenish tinge in the lower sky
as they were marching up. Now through trees on either side of
the road he saw what someone said were parachute lights rising
up to hang at the top of their arcs, and drop slowly down,
spilling wavery light like that of burning magnesium. A wood
came between them and the firing line as they turned off the
road and went along a track to a farm, which Captain Ogilby
told Sergeant Furrow was Bellewaarde. They were in reserve,
to dig support trenches and build redoubts. Phillip was one of
three men under Lance-corporal Blunden for Headquarters
guard. This meant twenty four hours respite, every two hours
out of six on sentry-go, followed by four off to sleep.

The guard-room was in a shed, next to the farmhouse kitchen,
used as the orderly-room. The shed had dry straw on its earthen
floor. He was No. 3 sentry, his first spell from ten o'clock to midnight. This meant four blessed hours sleep at once.

At ten o'clock he was awakened. It was rather fun, having two
hours before him in which to challenge all who approached, and
demand their regiment. There were many troops passing, ration
fatigues and working parties.

"Halt, who goes there?"

"Black Watch."

"Pass, Black Watch."

The flares filled the wood with mystery, so did spent bullets
flopping down. What strange German had fired into the dark?

"Halt, who goes there?"

"Camerons."

"Pass, Camerons."

They staggered past, carrying big cubes of shining tin which
glinted in the flares for ever rising beyond the black, seeming-
shifting trees.

"Halt, who goes there."

"Coldstream."

"Pass, Hotwater!"

A voice called out, "Who the pushin' hell d'ye think yeer? Harry Lauder on stilts?" in truculent Glaswegian accent.

"Fred Karno's Army."

A cat was wailing on the broken wall of a building.

"Puss! Puss! Where are you?"

"Mee-aw-iou!" cried one of the Coalies.

"Halt, who goes there?"

"Puss in pushin' boots!"

"Pass, friend!"

They went away with their biscuit boxes, talking about it, while Phillip had a quiet in-throat laugh to himself. Up the old Bloodhounds! If only he could see Cranmer again.

Bullets smacked among the trees. It was eerie with the worn-out moon adding its half-black shine to the powdery pallor of the flares.

He tramped up and down, to keep warm, to pass away time till midnight. Midnight Parade—Glinka's! He sang the song to himself, while the unseen cat mewed thinly on the broken wall. He stared, trying to see it; and was turning away when it seemed that someone had caught hold of his coat above the waist and tried to jerk it off, together with the rifle slung on his shoulder. His first thought was that the Guardsmen had attacked him for insulting their regimental name. But nothing else happened. Feeling the place of the blow, he discovered that his greatcoat was ripped across the front. A button was shattered, the webbing sling of his rifle cut. With a shaking feeling he realised that, as he had turned away, a bullet had hit the coat parallel to his body.

How welcome was the midnight relief, and a mug of hot sweet milky tea offered by gentle, dark little Blunden, who had been a messenger of the London, Liverpool, and Globe Insurance Office before the war. Then down upon the straw, with four blessed hours in which he could belong to himself.

In the morning the greatcoat was an object for wonder. Even Major Forbes, the acting C.O., came to see it. The orderly room sergeant put an extra tot of rum in his mug of tea. As he ate fried bacon sitting in the straw, he heard from the orderly room talk that they were now attached to the 1st Guards Brigade, under General Fitzclarence, a famous hero. At Bailleul, in the estaminet, there had been talk of how he had saved the day, rallying the Worcesters with a hunting horn when the line had been broken on the morning of Hallo'e'n. They were in the 1st Corps, commanded by Sir Douglas Haig, whose headquarters were the White Château just outside Ypres.

In the afternoon Phillip rejoined "B" Company in the wood while scouts went forward to Gheluvelt to find the headquarters of the battalion to which the company was now attached.

They waited, silent and tired, each one suspended in the noise of almost continuous firing.

There had been a re-arrangement in the battalion: the eight-company system had been changed to four, as among the regular battalions. "A" and "B" had been merged into No 1 Company, under Captain Ogilby. A new arrival, Second Lieutent Thorveton, was second-in-command.

While they waited, a soldier looking like an old-clo' man went by, in his hand a sheet of newspaper. He was obviously bent on retirement among the trees. It was five days old, as Phillip saw when the bearded, stumpy, muffler'd, woollen-balaclava'd, buttonless-tunic'd, mitten'd object stopped to ask for a light for his German cigar.

"Let's have a squint, mate," Phillip called to him.

The fellows crowded round, as he read out an account of the Battle for the Channel Ports. It mentioned Gheluvelt, Hooge, and other familiar names which he saw almost with a shock. To his disappointment there was nothing about Messines, although he realised that there had been no time for an account when the paper was printed.

"A newsboy here would make his fortune," said someone.

"Ta chum," said the old-clo' man, taking his paper back and wandering off, puffing the cigar.

They waited. The day dulled. The shelling increased. Wounded men began to appear, walking down among the trees. It began to drizzle. At last orders came to lead on. They filed away to the Menin Road, and marched away from the line. Cheerfulness at once returned; but soon after they turned off the road, and breaking step, followed along a yellow cart-rutted track, towards woods with the floating smoke of bombardment above them.

The track led into plantations of spruce and larch. It became a drive, with cross-drives among chestnut stoles, above which

rose standard trees of oak and ash. Occasional trees were smashed
by shell-fire. Phillip heard the crowing of cock pheasants in the
dense covert; and suddenly, as they were crossing a drive, four
invisible 18-pounders let fly, the shells scorching seemingly
overhead so close that they ducked. Yet the battery was not
visible: only fragments of cordite bags dropping in the momentary
hot air quiver of four buffeting cracks. Thank God they were
ours, he thought, seeing a notice nailed to a tree—*Het est verboden
in het bossch te gaan*—and with an interior start realising that this
was the same Belgium in which he had found the long-tailed tit's
nest outside the Ursulines convent at Wespelaer, when he and
Mother had gone there to fetch Mavis for a holiday in Brussels,
and they had all visited, Gran'pa and Uncle Joey and cousin
Petal, the Field of Waterloo, and the guide who looked and spoke
like an old sergeant called himself Captain Welsh and outlined
the plan of the battle on top of the memorial pyramid with a
malacca cane worn down almost to a stub, uttering words to
which he had not listened, they had seemed so unreal, like the
picture in the front room at home of Blücher greeting Wellington
after the battle among the dead and dying men and horses—and
now this was like the picture in the front room, with *Baldwin
dead and nearly four hundred others in the battalion.* And yet how
could it be happening to him, was it real, was it all a bad
dream?

In a moment of severed thought Phillip felt himself dissolving.
He fell, and was helped to his feet, ashen-faced, by Corporal
Douglas, who said, "I thought you were hit, Maddison. Come,
brace yourself. Let me carry your rifle."

"I can manage, thank you, Corporal," he whispered; and
helped by Douglas' kindness, clenched his teeth, struggling not
to cry out.

Twilight came; and with it a strange shifting pallor in the sky
beyond the wood. Were these star-shells he had read about?
Acceptance of the physical now enclosed him: he slogged along
with equipment and pack, hundred and fifty rounds of ammunition, fifty of them slung in bandolier, but still the clips that would
not enter the magazine of his rifle. If only he had his carbine,
if only his magazine worked properly, then—jaws working sideways on teeth—if the worst came to the worst and they were over-
run, he might shoot five Germans in eight seconds, even if they
were so near as fifteen yards from the trench. They would be

easier targets than the sparrows on the roof at home, which he
had often shot with Father's B.S.A. air-rifle.

As they approached the eastern edge of the wood dark figures
were standing about, amidst Catherine-wheels of fire from
perforated Maconochie tins of charcoal, swung on wire and
emitting crackling sparks. Others held their miniature braziers
and blew upon them, so that little coronas of flame in blue,
cerise, and yellow glowed before bearded faces, with the illusion
of home. "Wha'ch'er chum!" They wore rolled woollen
balaclavas on their heads. There was comfort in the sight of
them standing there, swinging or blowing their tiny fires of
charcoal, unconcerned by crack of bullet.

These were survivors of Mons and Le Cateau, of Marne and
Aisne, and now of Ypres, which they pronounced Ee-priss.

They were willing and ready to help the newcomers. With joy
Phillip heard they were Grenadiers. That was Cranmer's lot—
Cranmer, his old pal of Boy Scout days, the old Bloodhounds.
Might he not still be with them perhaps? He dared not ask, for
fear of seeming foolish. After all, he had not heard from Cran-
mer for nearly a year—since football days, in fact.

While they waited, he fell into reverie, thinking of those who
had been his friends: Percy Pickering, Tommy Turney (that
skellum who had stolen his birds' eggs), Peter Wallace, Desmond
Neville, Eugene, Gerry and Bertie Cakebread, *and* Cranmer.
Funny how people changed as they grew up. Gerry had once
been his favourite cousin; then, at Bailleul, he and Bertie had
suddenly become thick; yet Cranmer was, in a sense, all what
his other friends were. With Cranmer everything always happened just right. Oh, it had been fun, in the old Bloodhound
days! The thought was like one of those little glowing braziers.

"Have you a chap called Cranmer with you?"

"Yes, mate."

Almost ethereal were the rising white lines of light, the wavering, pulsating magnesium flares casting shadows of tree-trunks
and men all ways in the forest.

"Horace Cranmer?"

"That's right. 'E's dahn in the trench."

"Lead on! Pass it down! No talking!"

There was a stir of men, a clink of accoutrements, as the

whisper went down the muddy path. As they came to the edge of the wood he could see the flares rising out of what looked to be an open field in front of the wood.

"Pass it down, lead on at five paces interval! If a flare falls near you, stand quite still."

Whispered words passed from green-faced man to green-faced man, before each one moved, in a pallor of aloneness, into naked emptiness beyond the shelter of trees. With a kind of wonder Phillip saw that many dead men were lying about. The light seemed to powder them as with dry cement.

"Mind the stiffies, mate!"

Into the shining pool of the dead he began to walk, following the hazy figure in front. He felt his arm touched.

"Step down, three steps, chum."

As he slid into the trench, he saw a face in the half-blindness, and he heard himself saying, in a wonder, "Aren't you Cranmer? I'm Phillip, remember?"

"Blime, the ole Blood'ounds!"

"They said in the wood I'd find you here."

"Strike me pink! Cor, what a bit o' luck!"

It was four hours later.

"You don't 'ave to fret no more about that gas-pipe o' your'n, Phil. There's bags o' short rifles lying abaht in Noman's Land."

"How can I get one?"

"We'll crawl aht! Arst to go on listenin' patrol, see?"

"I'd like a Mauser rifle, too, if I could get it."

"Bags of 'm!"

Trained-soldier Cranmer and Private Maddison volunteered for listening patrol.

"Pass it down, patrol going out!"

"Pass it down, patrol——"

"Pass it down——"

They climbed out of the trench, and crawled slowly forward, picking their way round shell-holes and figures of the dead. Phillip coveted a German leather belt, with the brass *Gott mit uns* buckle. He wanted also a set of leather pouches with Spandau clips in them; a *pickelhaube*; a small automatic pistol; and if possible, a pair of Zeiss field-glasses. These last two objects would be very useful for shooting rabbits and watching birds respectively, when he returned home.

The German trenches were a good distance away, but snipers were well out in front, possibly this side of the barbed-wire fence, said Cranmer. So they must go slow, take a good dekko, and keep their ears washed out.

They got to the fence, which had strands of wire stapled to wooden posts. Cranmer knew a gap, under which they crawled on hands and knees. Phillip enjoyed it. With old Horace beside him, it did not feel to be dangerous; but it was an eerie feeling to be so near dead Germans. They were so still, fixed, wooden in unmovingness of face and boot and many-button'd tunic. All so still: spiked helmet, *pickelhaube* covered with khaki cloth, long boots of leather wrinkled at ankle and ending half-way to the knee. If you moved among them slowly, you felt almost one of them, except that they seemed thick, thighs tight over trousers, hands and fingers thick too.

They had been stiffies five days, Cranmer whispered. Five rounds rapid did it, every time. Each one 'it in the 'ead. That was the Bill Browns!

"If we'd had proper rifles on Messines, they wouldn't have got through our lines, Horace."

"Not likely, Phil! Up the ole Blood'ounds!"

He wanted to remain out among the cement-grey faces; he felt clear, away from the battalion. In the wavering flare-light he could see that all the pockets of the jackets and trousers of the German dead had been cut open; so had the pockets of the British dead in khaki, among them.

"Rob all my comrades," Cranmer whispered, "that's the ticket 'ere."

In the trench once more, Phillip loaded and fired his new short rifle, covered with wood to the piling-ring below the muzzle. The Mauser, too, was pleasing. It had a stiff, wooden feel, but after a few more shots he got into the way of working the bolt. They had not come across any field-glasses; but since returning Cranmer had got hold of a pair, with *Zeiss, Jena*, marked in white on them. He felt happy for the first time since leaving England. He felt that he could not be killed. This was the life!

The feeling of happiness, even enjoyment of the "picnic", remained during the first night in the trenches. The weather was fine. Sergeant Furrow gave him permission to exchange places with another man in the platoon, to be next to his "Bill

Brown friend". One territorial was spaced between two regulars.

Groups of three shared sentry duty, one hour on and two off, throughout the night. As far as Phillip could see, as he gazed around during his spells of peering and watching, the flares extended continuously from north to south; small and very low up the line, getting taller and brighter until opposite him, and then diminishing again until they disappeared in the distance.

While he stood there, smoking, and swinging his arms cabby-like for warmth, he remembered it was Guy Fawkes night. Would the street boys have their guys in soap-boxes on wheels, or would it be stopped now owing to the war? Fireworks would probably be forbidden.

The flares were really more beautiful than the Thursday night displays from the Crystal Palace, seen from the Hill. They were so pure, so lonely-looking; somehow part of romance. A strange, mysterious world; he was glad he had not missed it. How long would it last? The Russian steamroller was going on towards Berlin, so the war might be over by Christmas. Captain Ogilby said that the Germans were staking all on a last throw before Kitchener's reinforcements arrived from England. And hearing Cranmer's snores in the straw-lined snug little cubby-hole under the parapet, Phillip looked over the parapet, feeling that at last he was a real soldier.

His balaclava was rolled on his head; his scarlet chest pro-tector under shirt and vest, that had come in a parcel from home. He hoped he would soon become lousy, like the regulars. Itchy-koo they called it, after the ragtime song *Hitchy-Koo*.

He loaded the Mauser rifle. It had a wooden feel about it, but the Spandau clip sank down into the magazine as smoothly as silk, and released the clip at a press of the thumb. He would take it home, and have it converted into a shot gun. And prowl the North Downs, and the Blackwater estuary, at week-ends!

At the end of his hour, he went to rouse No. 3 in another straw-laid cave under the parapet. No. 3 refused to move. He got him out only after much tapping, prodding, and finally arm-pulling, while apologising to the old sweat for having to do it. After all, he was a hero of Mons, and like Cranmer had been in the line ever since the Retreat.

With wonder Phillip watched the hero of Mons fit a burnt matchstick into the outside edges of each eye-lid, little props to keep the eyes open. It was the only way to keep his pushin' peepers open, he said.

An hour before dawn all ranks were roused for the stand-to. The flares still rose on lily-white stalks, to bloom at the top of their curves and float down slowly; but only an occasional rifle-shot sounded flatly in the flat land of luminous mist and low shadows. Crawling out of holes, the men yawned, scratched, stamped feet; swung arms and mitten'd hands; coughed, spat. They examined rifles, worked bolts with cut-outs closed; laid them, bayonets fixed, on the parapet.

"Ere's ve ens'n, now fer'r rum," muttered Cranmer, as a young officer moved down the trench, preceded by a big red-faced sergeant carrying mess-tin and spoon. Each man, as they stopped before him, sprang with great energy to attention. Then, standing easy, he received a spoonful of the brown warming liquid. The ensign spoke in a quiet voice. Phillip observed that the men always replied with the word "Sir!"; so when he came to him, and said, "Good morning," Phillip replied "Sir!", and sprang to attention, before opening his mouth. He wanted to be a credit to Cranmer.

The rum was a spluttering firework in throat and guts: but when its effects wore off, the stand-to became dreary.

The last flare hissed up; grey light revealed the reality of the scene—rough trench, splintered trees, dirty faces, grimy hot hands and fingernails, the stubble field in front with many figures in grey lying still, visible for a long way as the field was smooth and sloped down to a lake of mist, out of which a thread of road wandered up to a village on the skyline with a church steeple prominent over red-tiled roofs.

"That's Zandvoorde," said Cranmer.

Soon the order to stand-down was given; and Cranmer said they could get into the wood and fry-up together over a fire.

"Like in the ole Blood'ound days, Phil. Cor, we 'ad some sport!"

"We damn well did! I say, what made you join the Army, Horace?"

"Well, me bruvver went for a so'jer, see, when there was no work at ve docks, then I was stood off being carter at the tannin' yards in l'il ole Berm'nsey, so I goes to ve dee-po at Caterham and signs on for seven wiv'r colours and five wiv'r reserve."

"Pretty hard life, isn't it, in peacetime?"

"Square bashin' by day an' square-pushin' by night, that's a Bill Brahn's life in peacetime."

"What's square-pushin', Horace?"

"Well, you know, Phil—wiv a tart."

"I see. Where's your brother now?"

"Pushin' up daisies on the banks of the Petty Morin."

"I'm sorry about that. When was he killed?"

"In September, on the Marne. You'll be interested to hear there was roach in the Petty Morin, Phil, like there was in the Randisbourne. Billo, mate! 'Ere's the coal-boxes arrivin'! Git yer napper dahn, boy! Into my cubby-'ole, and tuck yer tootsies in!"

Having seen Phillip well into the cubby-hole, Cranmer crouched over him, to protect him.

Chapter 26

THE BROWN WOOD LINE—*continued*

THE far sky had revolted in many places; almost immediately the stomach-liquifying down-curving and fat buzzings of 5.9 howitzer shells descended upon the wood. It looked as though an attack was coming, since the German guns had started up along the whole line, with great rolling thunder quaking the earth, beginning with a salvo upon their section of the Brown Wood Line. The sentries, one man in eight, continued to stand at the parapet, looking out; the others were ordered by a fierce, red-faced black-moustached sergeant passing down the trench to the cubby-holes under the parapet, their feet to be drawn up after them to avoid shrapnel balls.

"Where's your cubby-hole, my lad?" he demanded sharply of Cranmer. "I'll put you on a charge when we gits out!"

Phillip had already realised how terribly strict the Guards discipline was. Men on sentry were so afraid of falling asleep that they pushed open their eyes with their thumbs, and sometimes put sharpened sticks in their greatcoat collars to jab them when their heads dropped down or sideways. They hit their own faces, they struck their heads to keep awake. Some put half a matchstick to prop open their lids, so that if they did go hazy with sleep for a moment, they might still see, and recover. Cranmer said he counted bluebells, and thought of the old Bloodhound days, "second by second like", to keep himself from getting drowsy. If you did drop asleep, and were caught—the firing squad!

Most of the shrapnel seemed to be cracking down upon the wood behind, to stop supports from coming up to the front line. Phillip was indifferent to the thin little screaming rush and crack of these air-bursting shells, with their sudden ghostly blots of black smoke; even the whooping swoop of 4.2 howitzer shells was bearable; but what made him flinch and quiver, time and time again, was the coarse downward rushing droning of the Coal Boxes or Johnsons, which seemed to lift the entire earth a moment before rending apart the very air with their stupendous black brutality.

It went on and on and on; and it rang in the ears and head when it ended as abruptly as it had begun; and he was glassily aware of legs passing and someone saying, Stand to! He waited awhile before crawling out, to see men already lining the parapet.

When he looked over the parapet he had a shock.

Emerging from the low mist, hundreds, thousands, multitude upon multitude of dark figures could be seen, moving very slowly forward. Trembling, telling himself to be calm, he seized his rifle resting on the parapet, and fitted it to his left shoulder.

"Steady, lad," cried a gruff voice behind him. "Wait for it!"

He looked round, and saw the big red-faced sergeant standing beside the young Grenadier ensign, who was peering through binoculars.

The feeling of confidence they gave out calmed him. He pulled the snap-button of his pouches to open them, and waited, with fascinated fear in his loins.

"Hold your fire!" barked the voice of the sergeant. "Pass it down—no man to fire until the order!"

Phillip was not left-handed, but owing to a defective, what was called lazy right eye he had, from Bisley days with miniature .22 rifle in the school team, improvised a manner of firing from his left shoulder. When reloading he threw over the rifle at a slant and caught the nob of the bolt and jerked it back between crooked little finger and palm of his left hand, thus ejecting the empty cartridge; and in the return motion closed the bolt with thrust by base of hand, as a bad boxer hits at close quarters with open glove; and, all in the same movement, the sights were aligned and the trigger pressed—a poked shot.

Still no order to fire. The lines of little figures came on slowly, their arms and legs becoming distinct. He began to feel the calmness of the officer behind him; and greatly daring, took the Zeiss binoculars out of his haversack, focus'd them and saw, in the distance behind the extended lines, many more troops coming down the wandering, threadlike road from Zandvoorde on the sky-line.

"Hold your fire, men!" cried the sergeant.

As minute after minute passed, and no order to fire was given, Phillip began to feel agitated. The leading lines this side of the mist were now visible in his glasses as men in grey with *pickel-haube* and greatcoats rolled around their packs. Then an amazing thing happened. The attack halted, before the row of posts marking the barbed-wire fence. He could see their mous-taches under the *pickelhaube* covered with khaki cloth, as they stood still, as though on parade.

"Hold your fire, men," repeated the voice of the sergeant.

With drying mouth, Phillip watched a group of Germans coming forward, led by a very tall soldier. By his height and bearing, and because he wore gloves, he seemed to be an officer.

Later, this incident was much remarked, for two things. One, that no scouts had been sent out, before dawn, to examine the wire; the other, that, except for the officer, no one seemed to have any wire-cutters. It was unusual, too, to see an officer in front of the rank and file, for they kept well in the rear, to drive the men on, it was said.

The officer, wearing gloves, came to the wire and began to clip it. When he had cut all the strands the soldiers with him started to pull them sideways, to the next post. The officer then went beyond to a farther post, to clip there, while the men pulled up the post he had missed out. When the gap was about sixty yards wide, and the officer was about to clip once more, Phillip heard the ensign say to the sergeant, "Let him have it, Sergeant." The sergeant said "Sir!", and there was a single rifle shot.

As Phillip watched, fascinated, the German officer leaned forward, as though to look at the post from the other side. From him came a hoarse cry, then a prolonged scream, followed by another not so long but wavering and dying away. His helmet dropped off, and he remained leaning over the wire, gloved hands on arms hanging down, when all the others who had rushed together to the gap had been shot, and the only movements among the heaps of hundreds of bodies was from the ground upwards, as the wounded lay there, some kicking and twisting.

Phillip, his ears singing, became aware of a smell of fatty, burning wood. The cover of his rifle was faintly smoking, over the hot steel of the barrel. He leaned against the back of the trench, sharing the shaking feeling of relief, of comradeship, of jubilation, with the others. Men lit cigarettes. One began to sing. A captain came down the trench, his arm in a sling stained with brown, dried blood.

"Well done, men!" he said, again and again, as he went along.

As Phillip leaned against the earthen bank he saw a scared brown hen about a yard beyond the parapet appear suddenly before his eyes with skwarking open beak and jerking head, as she half-ran parallel to the parapet, among the empty bully tins thrown there. She looked at the heads in the trench anxiously, stopping now and again. He wanted to call out to the others not to shoot her, she looked so thin and lost; but when he tried to speak, he found he had no voice, his throat was a stinging rash.

He leaned against the trench, aware of the weakness of his knees, of his hands shaking, of sweat saturating his shirt. As he rested there, he saw Cranmer, with several others, jerking V-shaped fingers up and down, towards the German lines, his mouth grinning wide showing decaying teeth.

"Whatyer, Phil! Up ve ole Blood'arnds!!"

Down on the right small-arms fire had been hammering all the time; then it had died away; now it was growing again, crackling further backward, over their right shoulders, inside the wood. Had the attack got through there? An order was given to remain in a state of readiness, bayonets fixed.

A runner pushed his way down the communication trench which had been dug to the edge of the wood the previous night, with a message for the officer.

Soon afterwards the Grenadiers filed away into the wood, leaving them in the trench.

"So long, Phil!"

"Au revoir, Horace old man!"

"Don't you fret."

"Not likely!"

It was not long before "B" Company moved back through the trees, to where soldiers in khaki, breech'd and wearing puttees reversed, with leather bandoliers slung across chests, were waiting. They were Life Guards, who had galloped up from the reserve. These moustached and bearded men said the Froggies had been pushed out of their trenches by the canal, and had gone back to "Brandy Balls", otherwise Verbranden Molen. After more talk and waiting about, the Life Guards went away through the wood. Phillip felt now the safety of numbers. They were all in it together!

Rifle-firing increased. Bullets came from many directions, but chiefly from the canal. While they waited, he made a fire of green oak twigs and small branches, beside a fallen tree; and sitting there, fanned it with his glengarry. The sap was heavy in the wood. Hour after hour he kept the fire alight by fanning the hissing lengths of branch, his eyes stung with acrid smoke. Bully beef and biscuits were given out in the afternoon. He filled his water-bottle from a shell-hole; it was forbidden, but his tongue was aclack with thirst.

As he dozed on the log, while the others lay on the ground, some asleep, or dull with fatigue, a small group of Pomeranian Grenadiers, hatless and wearing only tunics, trousers, and boots, came through the wood, hands hovering over cropped heads as they hurried forward. One was bigger than the others. He had the silver-black ribbon of the Iron Cross twisted through his third button-hole. They halted, about a dozen in all with upheld hands before two British soldiers. Phillip saw one go forward to the big Pomeranian and undo the tunic button, to take the Iron Cross inside. The Pomeranian spat in his face, whereupon the other soldier upped with the butt of his rifle and caught him on the jaw. He fell backwards. While one soldier threatened the other prisoners with pointed rifle, the other knelt and ripped off the Iron Cross and put it in his pocket. After that they made the others empty their pockets. Then they went away, leaving the prisoners standing there.

Later he wondered if he had dreamed it; for when he opened his eyes again there was no one there. But when he walked

L

over, he saw the Pomeranian who had been struck lying among the wet leaves, dead.

Towards dusk the London Highlanders advanced in extended order through the trees in the direction of their old trenches by Klein Zillebeke. They were to cover the flank of the Guards Brigade when the counter-attack was made.

During the day, and the long wait in the wood, the line had been restored north of the canal; but more German attacks had driven the weary French troops back again. Dismounted Life Guards, deployed across the Verbranden Molen road, had reinforced them. The Germans had come on again; there was a *mêlée*, French, English, Germans, all mixed up; then new mass assaults had caused retirement to the reserve trenches. So the Guards were once again going into the attack at midnight; the London Highlanders, on the flank, were in support.

Wearily Phillip moved with No. 1 Company to the edge of the wood. It was cold. Flares were rising. They fixed bayonets. He looked once again to see that his magazine was loaded, then lay in line with others.

Major Forbes came along. "Bruce, will you send out a patrol to find out if the trench is held in strength? Send a corporal and two men, and warn the others not to fire."

Phillip turned his face to the leaf-mould. He hardly dared to breathe. Corporal Collins' name was called. With relief he heard two men being detailed. Then from the distance came hoarse screaming shouts, followed by a terrible racket of machine-gun fire. The Guards were attacking, poor devils. He hoped Cranmer would be all right.

The patrol came back. The trench was unoccupied. They re-occupied it without a casualty, and waited, listening to the racket down by the unseen canal. A runner came to say that the counter-attack of the Guards was successful. It was two hours after midnight.

Later, No. 1 Company was relieved by dismounted Life Guards. They filed back into the wood, to a line of bunkers which the Engineers had made, thick with sleep. The bunkers were oak branches laid on posts about three feet out of the ground, covered by two layers of sandbags, while the back, facing the enemy lines, was heaped with mounded earth. They crept in and slept.

In the morning of the yellow-tongued, thick-fingered damp grey day, Phillip saw Cranmer looking for him.

"I'm too wicked to die yet, Phil."

They went among the trees to cook breakfast together. Cranmer had a small white loaf, slightly damp and soiled, but still, it was bread. He cut it in two. Each had his ration of mixed tea and sugar, rasher of bacon, and tin of Tickler plum-and-apple jam. Plum-and-apple was by now a joke; hundreds of tins lay about unopened, with boxes of bully beef and large bright cubes of biscuits. Nobody wanted them. Fatigue parties chucked away boxes of Tickler and Fray Bentos bully.

It was like the old days in Whitefoot Lane—except that these were not the woods of Kent. Still, he and dear old Horace were together, that was the main thing. As in Bloodhound patrol days, he knelt to make a little fire, twig by twig, while Cranmer collected sticks, putting them in a heap beside the fire. Then he cut two forked sticks, stuck them in the ground, well clear of the little hut on fire, and laid a straight green stick across them, upon which to hang the canteens, as Cranmer called the mess-tins.

There was yellow-clouded water at the bottom of older shell-holes; they dipped their canteens, and hung them for boiling. Then, crouching on their heels, they fried their rashers, mopping up the fat with bread and eating every scrap hungrily. Soon the water in the canteens was pricked with bubbles, seething at the edges, swirling at the boil. In went the speckled mixture of tea and sugar; and then a fag while the "char" cooled off, a Red Hussar, of which two packets were the daily ration. The crack of a shell bursting tree-top height, followed by the rattle of its shrapnel bullets, was almost a jolly reminder of firework-night on the Hill, looking towards the Crystal Palace. Crouching behind the trunk of a big oak, Cranmer played his jew's-harp, vibrating the steel tongue against his teeth. *Swannee Ribber* followed *We all came in this world with nothing*. Phillip pretended to enjoy the music, as he thought that he and Cranmer were together again. Then Cranmer sang a song called *The Old Battalion*, a grim ballad made up, he said, by one of the Bill Browns.

"There'll be some souvenir watches and automatic pistols goin' tonight, Phil! Cor, talk about robbin' the dead, some of these 'ere blokes'd cut their muvvers' froats fer a tanner."

This information having been given, Cranmer hummed out
The Old Battalion once more on his jew's-harp.

Afterwards, they explored part of the wood. Cranmer showed
Phillip where he had a coke-bucket hidden, with a sandbag of
"black eggs", or coal *boulets*, "won" from a Keep Off Slaveys'
Bellies, who had half-inched it from a Froggie's cottage. What
was a Keep Off Slaveys' Belly? asked Phillip, to be told that it
was a K.O.S.B., otherwise King's Own Scottish Borderer. "The
name was give 'm in Dublin, you know what the Jocks is, quick
as greased lightnin', wiv them kilts," grinned Cranmer. Then,
"It's me lucky ole bucket, it's me mascot like, I wouldn't lose it
for somethink."

The black compressed eggs of coal-dust were extremely
valuable; for a fire of sticks, showing flame, was not allowed in
the trench at night. You could burn biscuits in the little old
bucket, though they made a bit of a niff until they was charred,
said Cranmer, then they turned red if you fanned 'em. A fire
was a necessity, explained Cranmer, to ward off rheumatics.
Rheumatics never yet got a bloke his ticket: no use working
rheumatics. A coke bucket give a bloke a hot cup o' char when
he come off sentry at night, a bit of all-right.

"You take it, Phil, I ain't got no kilt, you take it. Go on!"

"But how d'you know you won't need it, Horace? It's your
bucket."

"That's why I'd like you to 'ave it, Phil, straight I would.
We might go away anytime. It's a present," said Cranmer,
in his hoarse voice.

"Well, let's leave it here, Horace."

"All right, but it's yours when you want it, Phil."

"Well, thanks very much."

Having drunk their tea, they said goodbye. Phillip went
back to the trench, having marked where the fire-bucket was
concealed. It was an ordinary pail, perforated by bayonet-
stabs.

On his return, he was told off for filling sandbags for a "trained
soldier" to build up the broken parapets. The "trained soldier"
did it with almost mathematical neatness, explaining that it
was done first with a header, then with a stretcher, to tie the
bags in, like bricks.

A sniper was active in that part of the trench. Phillip heard a
Grenadier sergeant say that any guardsman hit in the head

would, after recovery in hospital, be court-martialled for unsoldierly conduct in the face of the enemy. One of the Bill Browns, not a "trained soldier", along a length of trench a couple of yards or so inside the wood was hit through the head, while sitting across a pole and winding barbed-wire on a stick; his pals swore revenge. He died; but that was not enough to wipe out the stain. They swore to go out after dark and get the sniper, who was thought to be lying out in front, behind some stiffies this side of the wire. Someone had seen the flash. They would bring him in, and after interrogation before the officer, they would take him into the wood and brain him with entrenching tool handles.

Phillip was surprised, and a little abashed, by the dark bitter anger in the pre-war soldiers: the dark compression of peace-time urban destitution, the low mind-strata of starvation in slums, when the taunt of *soldier* was an insult on a level with street-walkers. But the abashment was momentary; the warm and comradely strength, and the security it gave to be among the regulars, was what kept him going.

Three of the Bill Browns went out that night, after the whispered word was passed round, "No firing—listening patrol out." They did not get the sniper; but they did get several sandbags of loot, including watches, small black automatic pistols, Iron Crosses, cigar cases, money, brandy flasks, and about a dozen gold rings, cut off the fingers of the dead. Phillip tried to buy a pistol, offering five francs and a ten-shilling note, all the money he had on him; but the guardsman, wrapping the automatic in his red bandana handkerchief, said he would not sell under fifty francs.

There were still hares in the wood; and the grating *koch-karr*, followed by wing-flutters, of crowing cock pheasants sometimes answered the whistle and crack of a shrapnel shell. Cranmer stalked a cock, and shot it, early one morning; the problem was, how to cook it? Phillip suggested spitting it on a green stick, and turning it over a fire; Cranmer did this, for a surprise, while Phillip was "up" at sentry; and when Phillip went into the wood, along the little track to the place where the fire-bucket was hidden, there was Cranmer regarding a blackened object, with burned head and claws, tied with wire to a stick.

"Why didn't you pluck it first, Horace?"

"Cor, I knew there was suthin' I forgot, Phil!"

However, it was voted a very good meal by Phillip, to Cranmer's anxious satisfaction.

"Blime, like th' ole Blood'ound days, when we roasted a 'edge'og, 'n it went pop in th' middle, remember, Phil?"

Phillip's wish to be lousy was fulfilled. He wore, as part of active-service equipment of the British infantryman, a cholera or body belt. This was a closely knitted woollen band enclosing kidneys and belly, about three inches wide. It was supposed to protect against chill; but in practice it became a trap for the small grey parasites, their centres blood-pointed after feeding and black-pointed during relaxation.

After scratching for two days, he burned the cholera belt on Cranmer's coke-bucket at night, causing various remarks to be made down the trench where the smoke drifted.

The guardsmen exterminated lice in the crutches of their trousers, and the tails of their grey shirts, by an interesting method. A man sat on the trench floor, trousers down for inspection around the crutch; and when he spotted an itchy-koo, he touched one end of a thin yellow stalk of cordite, got by opening a cartridge, on the burning tobacco of his pipe, and charred the louse with the fizzing end.

Phillip opened a German cartridge: it was full of black glittering grains. He opened an English round, and burned one of the thin sticks, like doll's-house macaroni, watching it fizzing with a small dull yellow flame. He learned, too, that one of the ways to work your ticket was to chew cordite. It gave you symptoms of heart disease, making the beats irregular, and a temperature. But it did not pay to go sick in war-time; all a bloke got was a No. 9 pill, and duty. Another way was to eat soap, to give you dysentery; but this could be detected in hospital, if they wiped your forehead with a hot flannel, when a lather came. Then you would get a court-martial, and jankers— up to twenty years if you didn't get the death penalty for coward- ice in face of the enemy.

"Twenty years' hard labour? My God!"

"Yus, and you stops in the line when your company goes in support, and gits Field Punishment No. 1 when the company is in billets. Then, after the war, you serves the rest o' your time in the Glass House."

"What's the Glass House?"

"Jankers, the so'jer's prison."

"And what is Field Punishment No. 1?"

"You parades in full marching order wiv defaulters every hour, buttons clean, boots polished sole an' all, khaki blanco on equipment. Then for two hours a day they tie you to a transport waggon wheel by your wrists, yer toes just off'r ground, a'rter which back to the old spud-'ole, and all sanitary fatigues, as well as defaulters."

"What's a spud-hole?"

"Guard room."

"Good lord! How long do you get Field Punishment for?"

"Thirty days, per'aps."

"Good God! What a way to serve a Mons hero!"

Phillip was shocked. How different everything was from what people at home thought it was!

"That's nuffink," said Cranmer. "There wor a bloke on the Aisne what fell out wi' blisters and tiredness, in another lot, not our'n, and the Froggies cotched 'im and 'anded 'im over to our lot, and they give 'im a court-martial and shot 'im next mornin', and what's more I know where they buried 'im, in a orchard what the Alleymans cut the trees round like, you know, they cut the bark and the trees die, for the sap of a tree is its blood, like."

"What did the Alleyman want to hurt the trees for?"

"Devilment, so's the ole ooman what lived in the 'ouse wouldn't 'ave no more apples. They're proper sods, the Alleymans, they shoot at kids and ole people, as you might shoot a dog."

"I wouldn't shoot a dog, would you?"

"Not bleedin' likely, but in a manner o' speaking, like a dog is treated sometimes, suthin' cruel, see?"

"Yes, I know what you mean, Horace. The world's a funny place, in my opinion. For instance, there was a chap in the old 'H' Company, of our lot, who reported sick, with pains in his guts, and was given a No. 9 pill, and sent back to duty. He was carried to hospital the next night; and died of peritonitis the next day, in the Field Hospital at Dickebusch, from a burst appendix."

"Go hon!" said Cranmer, awed by the educated words.

Then, to change an awkward subject, "R bart a lit'l' old toon, Phil? I'll say the words fust-like." Whereupon Cranmer crooned,

> "We all come in vis worl'
> Viv nothin', no cloes to wear.
> All your life, bear in mind
> All your money you must leave be'ind,
> Finish up, wivout the slightest doubt
> The same as you began, for
> We all come in vis worl' viv nothin'
> And we can't take anyfing aht."

"Jolly good, Horace," said Phillip, when the little concert was over. He thought he would buy a jew's-harp when he had the chance.

When the Grenadiers handed over, to go where fighting was severe, north of the Menin Road, the London Highlanders held their line of trenches with one man about every six yards.

By night and by day working parties, fatigues, digging, carrying, revetting. There was no time, no energy, for letter-writing. Sleep, sleep, sleep. Shells fell in the trench; digging was continuous. Snipers out in front. Even a spade-end copped it. *Crack!* dirt-spirt, ringing ear-drums, ragged iron hole. But the worst sniping came from a fixed rifle enfilading the communication trench. *Crack !* and a man was lying on his back, mouth open, snoring, piteous rough hair, bright red blood trilling, trilling, trilling.

By now he was indifferent to lack of latrine. The custom was to use empty Maconochie tins and chuck them over the parapet, present for the Alleyman.

Every night, and again before each dawn, there were attacks to right and left of the canal, judging by the roar and racket of small-arms fire.

One morning the Germans came over on the left of the Highlanders' front, in broad daylight. There they were, crossing a space in the plantations where tobacco had been grown. Rows of tarred wooden shelters stood there, long brown tobacco leaves hanging inside. And there the attack stopped. Survivors tried to hide, until shrapnel smashed the wooden shelters and they ran out, and were bowled over like rabbits.

"If the Germans planned this war, they did it damned inefficiently," said Slade, the red-faced, imperturbable bank-clerk.

Phillip was puzzled by the way the Germans attacked, always bunched up together, shouting—some said, singing—presenting targets that nobody could miss. None ever came as far as the new barbed-wire fence, two hundred yards away.

This fence was hung with empty bully-beef tins to give warning of wire-clipping at night. Then it seemed that the Germans were firing at the strands, to cut them. Or was it at the empty tins strung along the wire? *Ping*—they sent a tin dancing, again and again.

"They're nearly all seventeen-year-old volunteers over there," Phillip heard Captain Ogilby say. "Their best troops may have been transferred to the Russian front."

The rumour went round that the Germans were given ether to drink before an attack; then that they had bombs in their pockets, to blow up their captors if they were captured. Certainly, now and again, a dead German lying out in front gave out a little puff of smoke when the body was hit by a bullet. Later, it was said that they had come over with jam-pot grenades; and it was these that were detonated by the bullets.

Someone had a newspaper. There were photographs of the Grand Duke Nicholas, Russian Commander-in-Chief, whose armies were well into East Prussia. Perhaps after all there would be peace by Christmas. Phillip held to the hope, as did all the soldiery of the line, in the dead weight and dark inertia of the night.

O, when would peace come?

Chapter 27

AT THE GUILDHALL

"THE GERMANS," said the Prime Minister that night, in his peroration at the Lord Mayor's Banquet, "the Germans have retired baulked and frustrated by the immovable steadfastness and valour of the Allies!"

Cheers of the assembled guests beat down in waves from the rafters. The flags of the Allies moved with the heated air arising with perspiration. The French and Russian Ambassadors beat their hands on the cloth of the high table, causing extra bubbles to rise in champagne glasses standing on slim stems on either side of the big silver-gilt Loving Cup.

"But that is not enough!" cried the Prime Minister with controlled emphasis. "We shall never sheathe the sword, which we have not lightly drawn, until Belgium recovers in full measure all, and more than all, that she has sacrificed——"

Cheers swept up again; and Thomas Turney looked to the gallery where the wooden effigies of Gog and Magog seemed to stare down upon the assembly of uniforms in many styles and colours, on the ladies with their scintillating jewelry.

"—until France is adequately secured against the menace of aggression——"

The French Ambassador bowed his head, as once again massed cheering, odorous of turtle soup—the only course served hot at the banquet—roast beef carved from barons in temporary pulpits at each side of the Hall, mince-pies, ice-cream, and vintage champagne—interrupted the speaker.

"—until the rights of the smaller nationalities of Europe are placed upon an unassailable foundation, and until the military domination of Prussia is wholly and finally destroyed!"

Thomas Turney, sitting with an acquaintance of the shelter on the Hill, patted the table with one hand and pulled down the black waistcoat of his evening suit with the other. He had come, not as the invited Chairman of Mallard, Carter & Turney, Ltd., Printers & Wholesale Stationers of Sparhawk Street, High Holborn, as once before in the reign of Edward VII, but on a spare Press ticket. He found the place extremely hot, the applause raucous, as he thought of his friend Bolton. He had drunk modestly of the wine, having regard for his digestion.

"That is a great task worthy of a great nation! It needs for its accomplishment that every man among us, old or young, rich or poor, busy or leisurely, learned or simple, should give what he has and do what he can."

Amidst a furore of applause the Right Honourable H. H. Asquith sat down.

Ah, for the pen of a Pepys, thought Thomas Turney, to do justice to the scene. Then, what a pity Hetty was not there with him to see it. He could have arranged an invitation for the two of them. Of all the historic scenes the Guildhall had seen, none could have been more important to European civilisation than the one he was witnessing. The thing that had moved him about Asquith's speech was the news of the great battle for Ypres—the Germans "retiring baulked and frustrated", his very words. They would bring comfort to Hetty and Dorrie.

"What is the uniform Asquith is wearing, can ye tell me? He looks like an Admiral, don't he?" he asked his neighbour and companion, of *The Morning Post*, seeing that he had finished his short-hand notes. "What, are you writing in German?"

"Oh no, it's an old system I learned long ago—Taylors. The P.M. is wearing the uniform of the Elder Brethren of Trinity House. Well, if you will excuse me, I must go to catch the late country edition. Wonderful sight, isn't it? The ladies' jewels alone would pay for the Expeditionary Force in France for a week! As for the City plate, shining so magnificently behind the chair of my Lord Mayor, what wouldn't Asquith's opposite number Theobald von Bethmann Hollweg give to get his hands on it! Well, I'll be calling for you in about three-quarters of an hour's time: but if by any chance I am delayed, you will find me at the *Post*. Are you sure that you won't be too tired, in the meanwhile?"

"Never felt better!" replied Thomas Turney. It was his second visit to the City that day. He had come up with Hetty that morning, to see the Lord Mayor's Show, mainly a khaki parade, giving Londoners their first sight of Dominion troops, strapping young fellows from Canada, Newfoundland, Australia and New Zealand.

But what had remained in his mind was the sight of kerbside hawkers offering German Iron Crosses for sale—"Kaiser Bill's Iron Crosses—anyone can wear 'em—or stamp on 'em if he likes!"

They had come up by tram, on the twopenny midday ticket. Thomas Turney's second visit, however, had been by taxicab: as homewards he and his Fleet Street acquaintance of the Hill were going that night.

The City streets at eleven o'clock were dark, shadowy, chill, after the brilliant scene within the Guildhall. Most of the street-lamps were out. Those alight were masked by dark blue paint, so that a small square of light shone down upon pavement and gutter. No clocks struck behind unlighted dials. Big Ben of Westminster Palace was silent for the duration. A romantic scene, he remarked, as the cab's steel-studded rear tyres made their regular scoring sound against the wooden blocks of the Embankment; a scene worthy of a Whistler with the mind of Rembrandt. Then the starry sky was pierced by thin sword-like beams of searchlights, reflected upon the tide of London river below the bridge.

Chapter 28

THE BROWN WOOD LINE—*continued*

DURING the misty Flemish night a deserter came across, crying out, "Do not shoot, Mister Herr Englander, do not shoot!" Rumour said that when he was taken to battalion headquarters in the wood, he told there was to be a great attack the next morning led by the Garde du Corps Prusse, the dreaded Prussian Guard, who never surrendered, and never took prisoners. The deserter said he had seen them in billets at Werwick and Komines. They had been brought from the French front at Arras.

The rumour came from the signallers' bunker. Corporal Douglas said it was true.

The night, the chloral darkness tainted with the sweetness of decaying flesh, nauseating and thick as licorice-powder, the timeless blackness sprouting white lilies of corruption, was passed by Phillip in intermittent control of his death-fear. The Prussian Guard! It was a relief when, shortly after five o'clock, in the stand-to before dawn, the flares from the German trenches stopped rising, and a hurricane shrapnel shelling whistled and rattled down upon the wood.

Nothing fell near the Brown Wood Line at first. He knew that the shelling was to prevent supports coming up: his thoughts made him shake. Why had the Grenadiers gone away? *Cranmer,* he cried in his mind, as he fought annihilating truth.

Limp and palpitating, he pressed himself into the damp straw, hands over face to stop the red-gold-black steel-fragmentation roars of five-nines now falling upon the Line, crashes breaking apart his head, to scatter brains through eyes and ears and mouth. He held the crucifix, next to the brown *papier-mâché* identity disc: but no words of prayer would form in his mind. Every time a word-thought came it was broken in rending flame-crash, golloped with saliva of black electric zig-zagging snakes scintillating out of retching saccharine brown stench of decaying flesh falling into the trench with lumps of clay and jagged ends of wood. He was sick, and became feeble.

Men were shouting. He was pulled violently by the collar. The black beard and black bitter eyes of Corporal Douglas stared at him. He got up and heard screaming; swaying he saw a man lying face up, his fixed eyes in green face bulging, his kilt in tatters by the stumps of blown-off legs.

He fumbled at the toeless sock covering rifle bolt against mud, and stared, mouth and head greasy-rotten, yellow with un-digested bully beef in sour stomach, into dim dirty dark beyond cratered parapet and heard rapid short cheers, *Hoch-hoch-hoch!* in the distance. A calm-seeming figure appeared. Captain Ogilly, brass pistol in hand, stood ready to fire into the air.

Two Vèry pistols had been issued to the battalion the previous day. The flares were poor, half as bright as the Germans': when they burned, *if* they burned, they soon dropped sizzling upon the ground. They had no parachutes, they were useless.

Why weren't the Vickers guns firing? Two, purchased privately before the war, had at last come up with the trans-port. They were supposed to be sited on either flank of the battalion front, to give protecting cross fire. Why weren't they firing?

With reports of his rifle ringing in ears, he fired into the gloom. Then, in the ghastly clear of dawn, he saw them, line behind line, moving slowly in regular order. Bloody thousands of them! Now it was started, he found himself aiming and firing steadily: squeeze trigger, reload, aim sights in line, squeeze again, conscious of other reddish-black gashes thumping on either side of him. Why weren't the Vickers guns firing? Surely tripods had been set-up in sand-bag emplacements in the parapet the previous night; they had not fired, of course, to conceal their whereabouts until the attack. The only Vickers guns in the entire British Expeditionary Force! Yet they were not firing.

What was so terrifying, what the Magister would call awe-full, was the way the Prussians seemed to be coming forward at a jog trot, rifles at the porte. They were all big men, made taller by the brass spikes on their helmets. There was none of the running and jumping sideways of the Bavarians coming up to the road

at Messines, after the singing. These came on in line, shoulder
to shoulder, as though it were the battle of Waterloo. When
they came nearer, he could see that they were in full marching
order, with overcoats rolled around their packs. This made them
look very big, massive. Nothing could stop them. *Peter Wallace
bayonetted, with Captain McTaggart.* O Christ!

Panic gave way to a swearing rage, to hot anger of firing, reloading, shaking hands pressing in clips, hair on back of head
twitching. Other men were swearing, too; but he did not know
this. The Prussians advanced on the right, though many tumbled
in front. He could see the brown bullock hair on the outside of a
square leather pack when one stumbled, shot.

There were shouts on the right.

"Back into the wood! Withdraw! Withdraw!"

They had over-run No. 3 Company, on the right. Sergeant
Furrow was shouting to get out, over the open ground at the
double, lie down inside the wood, give covering fire while the
other half-section withdrew.

"Steady now, boys!"

Gibbering, wetting himself with fear, he scrambled out. Filled
with leaden aching, he ran for the trees. He got there somehow,
found himself behind a thick trunk, firing across the front, while
the half-section ran hare-eyed, open-mouthed.

Calmer, still trembling, he went with them to the support
position, a shallow trench hardly more than an outline. They lay
down, facing the flank, until shouts and shots told them of the
counter-attack. His shirt was cold with sweat. What a game it
was, what a game.

In the afternoon they were relieved by French troops, whose
blue overcoats and red trousers were covered with mud. The
French had been fighting by the canal to the south. Meanwhile
rumours had told how Fiery Forbes had led the counter-attack,
with the acting-Adjutant and Headquarters staff, and stragglers
of No. 2 Company which had been over-run on the right. They
had cleared the Germans out of the wood with the bayonet, and
taken some prisoners.

These came past the company sitting by the reserve line. Unarmed, the prisoners were marched back by their feld-webel who,
seeing the Adjutant, halted his men and gave him a terrific
salute. The Adjutant told one of the Orderly Room clerks, little
Kirk of the tent party at Bleak Hill, to take them away to the

cage behind the Menin Road. So Kirk set off, walking beside the feld-webel, looking as though he had not the least idea where he was going. However, he said later, on his return, the German sergeant-major had been very helpful, handing him a nominal roll of his men to give the Military Police at the barbed-wire cage.

The French soldiers looked ill, with sunken eyes, and yellow hollow cheeks. Phillip felt dull, too. They were leaving the Bill Brown Line. Cranmer's lucky fire-bucket was lost, left in the trench. The thought of Cranmer gone brought tears. Others were crying—overcome by the unendurable power of high explosive, the cold emptiness of life, the negation of the broken tangled wood, the thought of being lost for ever, belonging to death, life but heavy movement without purpose and death the end.

He slouched away with the remnants of No. 1 Company, hose over spats mud-balled, one among others straggling in loose order, slowly following the shambler in front, just able to keep himself from staggering wide, his eyes on the back of the shambler in front, vaguely aware that they were returning to the Menin Road, with its *pavé* hurtful to the feet; and rest.

But why had they turned not towards Ypres, but back to the line again? Not again, O Christ, not *again*? There was nothing to do but follow the shambler in front, one step forward after another since there was nothing to do about it.

The Menin road was crowded with traffic, going both ways. Red-cross motor ambulances, horse-drawn waggons, limbers, shell-caissons, walking wounded, some with *pickelhauben* slung on shoulders, arms and shoulders red-white bandages, convict-hair-cropped German prisoners in muddy leather boots, tunics cut away and hanging loose with blood-dripping arms, jaws bullet-skewed, dead mules and horses lying legs-up all along the road-side, limbers, waggons, field-guns, all broken by shell-fire. And ominous sight, most disheartening—heavy howitzers were trundling down towards Ypres.

Nobody spoke. They stopped, moved on, halted again. Marching was shuffling and loose: automatic movements of men with wills no longer active. The remaining coherencies of their minds were fixed upon the next step onwards; men moving from a moment of chaos into a moment of chaos.

Chapter 29

PAUSE

DURING the past few days and nights the London Highlanders had been lent to the Brigade holding what officially was known as the Brown Wood Line, but, among the troops, the Bill Brown Line. Now they were returning to their own Brigade, in the woods north-west of Gheluvelt. Here the fighting had been the most severe. At half-past nine in the morning, after four hours intensive shelling, fresh battalions of the Garde du Corps had made their first tremendous onslaught through the fog, piercing the line north and south of Gheluvelt in their original rush, and penetrating the Nonne Bosschen, the Nuns' Wood.

Vorwärts Preussen, immer vorwärts! The Kaiser had addressed the senior officers of twenty-three Deutschland divisions—nearly a quarter of a million men—the day before: the war would be won if they took Ypres, which was the way to the sea, to the Pax Germanica, to a place in the sun! There were only nine *Entente* divisions between them and victory! Vorwärts!

The Kaiser made no reference then, or later—nor had he ever done so before—to "walking over the contemptible little British Army." That supposed Order of the Day, alleged to have come from the All Highest's General Headquarters at Aix-la-Chapelle during the previous August, had been faked in its entirety by a staff-officer at the London War Office named Frederick Maurice —later made a Knight of the Cross of St. Michael and St. George. The idea of the faking had been to give heart to tired British troops in retreat from Mons and Le Cateau.

Richard Maddison, when he read of the protest made by the young and pacifist-socialist Marquess of Tavistock, heir to the dukedom of Bedford, of his public protest that the Kaiser never uttered such a remark, almost shouted to Hetty, at the breakfast table with his silent daughters, that the fellow was a traitor, and should go to the Tower!

The Old Contemptibles, as *The Daily Trident* and other newspapers were calling the defenders of Ypres, had been continuously in the line for nearly twelve weeks. On the front of Sir Douglas Haig's 1st Corps the Prussians, by midday of November

11, had broken through to a depth of two and a half miles. In one place they got to within a hundred yards of a battery of howitzers, and a battery of field-guns. Rifle fire of mixed cooks, headquarter clerks and others, stopped them.

At half-past three in the afternoon of that dull and misty day the Garde du Corps came on again, marching between two enfilade fires, from north-east and south-west. So accurate was the rapid fire of the peace-time trained British soldiers that the attack wilted. The Oxfordshire Light Infantry and the Northamptons charged the survivors with the bayonet.

Farman biplanes, the "Longhorns" of the Royal Flying Corps, Union Jack painted large under each lower wing, reported more German troops coming up the long straight poplar'd road from Menin, through Gheluwe, and lesser lanes and tracks to Terhand, Kruiseecke, Zuidhoek, Malenhoek, all leading from the plain of Flanders to the great woods dark upon the least of slopes above Ypres, the holding of which town meant eventual victory to one side, as its loss meant eventual defeat.

So the attacks continued, until many of the battalions of the British Expeditionary Force, the red little, dying little Army, were decimated. Scottish Borderers and Irish Rifles, Gordons and Cheshires, men of the level lands of Bedfordshire and Lincolnshire, the Northumberland Fusiliers and the Duke of Wellington's —the bullets flailed, the shells spouted; while Crown Prince Rupprecht of Bavaria, and the Duke of Würtemberg—the one in command south-east of Ypres, the other commanding the armies of the north-east—were ordered again, and again, and yet again, to break the thin British line. The 1st Guards Brigade, originally mustering four thousand men, now had four officers and about three hundred men. The situation, in the reserved language of Corps and Army commanders, was critical.

Reserves had already been brought up from the 4th Guards Brigade, from the Brown Wood Line, and were being expended. The last battalion, the London Highlanders, was now on its way. Cranmer had arrived before Phillip.

Do vibrations, thoughts, acts of hate (or lost love) exist or continue together with gestures of love, of goodwill, in the ethereal or spiritual life of the world? The bullet breaks the body, and falls spent; does thought continue? In the multitude of

the cries of the Battle of Ypres, let one little fragmentary hope
of London be remembered—*Up the ole Blood'ounds!*

When the London Highlanders arrived, in the sombre light of
that wet November afternoon, fighting was still going on in the
woods. Remnants of British and German battalions were mixed
up, firing in little groups among the trees. On the ground lay
many more dead and dying, in field grey and khaki, than moved
on feet behind trees and crouched, rifles supported on elbows, in
the clearings or rides.

To the last arrivals, some of the walking wounded by a first-
aid post were full of tales of disaster. Others were optimistic,
that they would soon be out of it, safe with Blighty ones. Many
stories came from the men in charge of the Brigade ammunition
dump where No. 1 Company under Captain Ogilby halted to
draw extra linen bandoliers.

The Royal Fusiliers had been cut-up to a man, Phillip heard
the Regimental Sergeant-Major, in charge of ammunition, tell
Captain Ogilby. Their Commanding Officer had been killed.
The Worcesters had been cut to pieces, so had the South Lancs,
and the Wilts, and the Irish Rifles.

"A trying day for British Arms, sir!" remarked that peace-
time mass of beer, beef and duty, the R.S.M., now reduced to
duty, duty, duty.

The fifteenth Brigade had caught it too. "Still, when it's all
over, it will be pleasant to get back to real soldiering, sir!" was the
remark by which the R.S.M. was remembered after he was killed.

The cockney slinging out bandoliers had a different attitude
to that of the old Coldstreamer.

"I never sin anyfink like it, in all Christ's creation, straight I
never! Them pushin' squar'eads come on agin an' agin, like
they was square-bashin'! The whole pushin' woods was lousy
wiv'm, straight they was!" He had a bandage round his left
hand. "Cut me 'and to the bone when I took 'old er th' bynit
er one pushin' great sod of a Prewshun what wor goin' ter stick
me. Me! Ju Jitsu champion of the rig'm'nt what took five pun
off'r 'Ackenschmidt when 'e couldn't lay me aht in five pushin'
minutes at the 'Olborn Empire when 'e challenged all comers!
Me, the pushin' Prewshun makes for to stick *me*!

"What 'appened? I dunno, arst me! Shall I tell you? Right
mate! Look, I'm dahn, see, on me knees like, and the great

soddin' bastard's runnin' at me. So I seize 'is bynit wiv me 'and,
see, stick it in ver grarnd, gives a jerk wiv me uvver 'and at the
butt, pulls 'im forrard, tips 'im arse over tip flat on 'is back and
me pal what played for the 'Spurs kicks 'is brains aht. That's
what 'appened, since you arst me. Thought at first I got a Blighty
one, but not this trip."

"How did you get this job?" asked someone.

"I found it, mate! Life's what you make it, in this world, an'
the next! You swing the drippin', or you get it swung on you,
see? Anymore for anymore? The Old Firm, the old sweaty sox,
water-proof all through, what is butter only grease?"

His eyes were dark and hard all the time he spoke; he never
smiled; he was greasy in face and neck and hands, and greasy all
over chest, ribs and thighs, too; his quiff was plastered down on
his forehead in a curl, looking as though he had just combed and
pressed it there; as he had; with butter, from a tin he had taken
from the ration dump. Grease kept out the cold from Jabez Wolfe
when he swam the Channel; and as the storeman said, what was
butter only grease?

The rain, which had been intermittent since mid-day, began
to fall steadily. From in front and from all sides of the wood came
the continuous rattle and crackle of rifle fire, crossing and re-
crossing, and now, ominously near, the hammering of machine-
guns. Phillip knew by the almost deliberate slowness that they
were German. He had heard them before; he had seen a captured
Spandau brought back by the Grenadiers from the counter-
attack. It fired, not on a tripod like the Maxim, but on sleds. It
was slower, as it was heavier.

While they rested there, he got up and wandered off. There
was a sense of freedom in being alone. He went among the trees,
with his last folded sheet of precious newspaper.

The brief meditation over, he strolled among the dead, peering
at their faces, wondering how they had felt at the moment of
death, and trying to think what had happened to the thoughts
in their heads. Did thoughts leave the brain at the moment of
death, as separate things, or did they cease with life? How could
thoughts, which were mostly eye-pictures, each one taken at a
certain moment in living, and stored in grey matter like soft
herring roe, but looser and greyer, which was the brain, how
could thoughts exist outside their cells? Could a camera, broken,

influence the negatives it had once taken? The positives existed apart from the camera. But it was too difficult to puzzle out. If there was a God, however, why did He permit such terrible things to happen?

He filled his water-bottle with clay-stained water at the bottom of a new shell-hole, and drank his fill behind a tree. Then stooping down, he watched the water running into the blue enamelled neck again, while a paralysing cold thought came that he would perhaps never drink from it again. But if he did come out all right, the water might give him typhoid. If so, he would get to hospital, and out of this hell. Even if he was a wreck after the fever, it would be better than being killed.

He returned to his company. Many of the fellows were crouching or sitting back to back on the ground, holding to their upright rifle barrels, heads bowed in sleep. He sat beside them.

How long he was asleep he did not know; but when he looked up again, conscious of the stale, thick, fatty taste of bully beef on tongue and in throat, he saw multitudes of heavy drops of rain jumping with little splashes on the brown and black fallen leaves, and on the sodden coats and caps and muddy hose around him. But how, he wondered, were they shouting, when they were asleep.

"They're coming! Thousands of 'em! They've broken through!"

He tried to get to his feet without falling over, so heavy was equipment, rifle, overcoat. Corporal Douglas was kicking the others, to waken them. As they extended among the trees, he saw the lashing cold drops of the storm bouncing, spray-shattered, off sprawled grey and khaki lying fixed upon the ground in terribly untidy groups. He could hardly see, but did not care, it did not matter that water was running down his cap-comforter into his eyes, dripping down his neck, trickling cold on his stomach. Nothing mattered. Nothing had ever mattered. God, what a world! Nothing was fair. Let the bullets hit him, he did not care. Punishment, punishment, punishment! Cry, cry, cry, cry! Let his tears stream into the earth with the rain, and wash all life away. Hey, Baldwin?

Men were pointing, shouting, crouching down to fix bayonets. His bayonet would not lock; it was muddy. He began to gibber to himself. The Prussian Guards were coming through the trees.

He shouted to himself, "Shut your bloody mouth!" He screamed at himself, scratching his face. "Liar! Liar! I did not tell Milton the Arithmetic answers!" Then, "Oh! Oh!" as he tried again to lock the bayonet on the locking clip. He managed to click it on, despite the mud in the ring. Other soldiers passed by, in little groups, their eyes staring. Among them was a wild, mad-looking grey-moustached officer, with red tabs and gold braid on his tunic collar buttoned to his neck. He put a copper hunting horn at the side of his mouth, and blew it, then taking off his cap with his other hand scooped the air with it like the huntsmen did to otter hounds at Lynmouth, to urge them on. *Yaa-oi! Yaa-oi! C'arn'yer!* Then going forward again he blew more notes on the horn and gave another wild screaming cheer.

"Up Guards, and at 'em!" cried Phillip, stumbling forward. Men were shouting hoarsely all along the line. One passed close by Phillip, swearing continuously in teeth-snarling voice, all the gutter-words, filth and muck of the gutters rushing with dirty rain-water to a drain. He began to swear like the regulars. He heard his own voice, very thin, coming out of a little thrill. He was one of them, he was not afraid, he was going forward! They were all like Cranmer, with their hard set faces, their glaring eyes, their bared teeth. Some were hatless; others wore balaclavas over chins, only eyes and noses and open mouths showing. The clean looking things about them were the new light-brown cloth bandoliers of ammunition across their chests.

Phillip went forward through the trees, light head on automatic body. It was wonderful not to care any more. All fear had gone with the upsurging heat of his body. The dull ache of his limbs was gone. He went forward among British Grenadiers, Irish Guardsmen, Coalies, Jocks, Odds and Sods, passing from tree to tree, only partly conscious of the great slant of rain. He thought he saw Cranmer yelling among the others, and wondered if the rest of the Brigade had come up. There were shrieks and cries and roared out oaths in the rain, men were falling, writhing, sudden loud shots ringing in his ears; with detached amazement he saw Germans running about much like themselves among the trees just in front, others in spiked helmets on heads standing, showing teeth open-mouthed above many-button'd grey tunics, yelling amidst the thin plate-breaking clash of bayonets. A khaki sergeant, whooping and yaaring, pushed past him. The Germans were going down. They were screaming. They were holding up their hands. They were surrendering! He felt a savage delight, a thrilling terror, a magnification of the feeling he had had when he set fire to the long dry grass of the Backfield in summer, as he saw them trying to push away the bayonets with their hands. "A-a-ah!" It was all over!

But it was not all over. They had surrendered, and they were being killed. They were rolling on the ground, bloody heads and faces, bodies hunching up, faces in hands, kicking, clinging; bayonet stabs, shots, butts bashing heads, screams, shouts, thuds.

More Germans, big men, were coming up. The Prussian Guards! "A-a-ah!" he shouted, and raised his rifle to fire at them again and again, cursing the harshness of the steel-harsh hot bolt. Then something went off right in his face, brassy bright speckles. His knees gave way; he banged his lip on the back-sight of his rifle as he sat down. The rain leapt everywhere in a drenching downpour. The noise receded.

When he felt steadier, he got up and walked among the men on the ground, Germans and British, some doubled up and crying out, clutching their stomachs, some moaning, beating their arms, kicking with their feet. *Water! Wasser! Water! Wasser!* Why were they so thirsty? Some stared at him, with eyes bulged like those of rabbits caught by ferrets, bulging from straining. He saw them rising up with the ground, very slowly. He clutched at the ground, to stop it going away; but it went away.

The night came on; the rain fell.

He felt very sick when he opened his eyes, feeling instant terror. Mother, mother!

Gradually he remembered where he was. He was very cold. His head ached. His eye was speckly with the electric snake, his mouth had the sour, yellow taste of bully beef. He managed to sit up, to look about him. Stretcher-bearers were carrying back wounded men. Had he been hit? He could move his arms and legs. He felt his face. There was a bump on his forehead, but no hole there. He rolled over, got on his knees, managed to push himself to his feet. His shoes and hose and slipped-down spats were sodden weights. He wanted to lie down, to go to sleep again; but it was too cold, too wet.

He picked up his rifle. A burst brass case was in the breach. It must have exploded there. It had gone off in his face. The breach was marked by the explosion. Twice like that, what an escape. Then there was the bullet that had cut his coat. Ah, the crucifix! He felt it safe under his shirt.

He threw down the rifle, then, seeing Tommy Atkins and another man with a stretcher, picked it up again and went to speak to them. Tommy Atkins, red-cheeked and determined as ever, but face thinner and more serious, said, "We looked at you, just now, Maddison, and thought you had concussion."

"Christ, what a life!" he sobbed.

"Talking like that won't help matters, Maddison."

Carrying his damaged rifle, tears smudging his dirty face, Phillip went back to find the Colour-sergeant. On the way he stopped to look at a party of men beside two stretcher bearers. They were carrying the body of the grey-moustached General, who had blown the horn, on a stretcher. He had been shot through the neck during the night. Later, Phillip heard that he was General Fitzclarence, who had rallied the troops at Gheluvelt a fortnight before, and led a counter-attack that had prevented the break-through. Everyone said he was a wonderful officer. He had won the Victoria Cross three times during the South African war.

For the next four nights and days the London Highlanders remained in the woods, in support: making bunkers, wiring the reserve line of watery shallow trenches, working as carrying parties, while by day and by night rain fell intermittently through the pine and beech trees.

It was the end of the autumn fighting weather. Winter was now settling upon the brown landscape, with its soil sandy-yellow in places. Soon the springs would break, the water-table rise to within eighteen inches of the surface. Wet and cold were now the things to be dreaded, to be endured.

Among trees splintered and gashed, where still an occasional cock pheasant was heard to crow, and an odd hare seen to race upon the fallen leaves, the shell-holes began to fill with misty grey water, which rose to within a foot of their crumbling craters. Water seeped up into new reserve trenches as they were being dug, being trodden into marn. Yellow clay clung to the blades of shovels with greater tenacity than the force of the diggers. Digging went on slowly, at least it gave temporary warmth to bodies in sodden uniforms. Phillip dreamed as he shivered, when

digging was done, of glaring August roads, of the great heats of
the march from London when the dust floated over those happy
days gone now for ever.

Sandbags, laid header-stretcher on tarred felt covering the
rough timbered frames of bunker roofs, had broken the tarred
felt in places. Here water dripped, on greatcoats and kilts already
saturated with the rains outside.

There was little time for sleep. Long hours were spent winding
off barbed wire, from heavy rolls on to sticks; each to be borne,
at night, upon the shoulders of two men, to the line. Out in
front, under the hiss and pop and quiver of flares, both German
and British wiring parties were working. Such work was justly
called a fatigue. There were fatigues for carrying steel-loophole
plates, bundles of sand-bags, and spades; ammunition fatigues;
rations fatigues; fatigue parties under the Royal Engineers,
starting from battalion dumps near the front line. Wooden
crates filled with cigarettes and air-tight tins of tobacco began
to arrive—cursed by the fatigue parties. Worst of all was a new
sort of entanglement made under surveillance of the Royal
Engineers at their dump beside the Menin Road—loops of wire,
like concertinas pressed flat, fixed between two sets of wooden
trestles. These had to be hauled and handled right into noman's-land, slip, slosh, gash; out among the dead swelling under
upheaved and broken trees, while traversing machine-guns sent
chips and flakes of wood flying.

If a machine-gun started to traverse when a flare was falling
you must stand still, in a glaring shade of luminous dust that
seemed to take away all shape and cover all with an intangible
cement powder of light. Gone was romantic feeling about the
lily-white stalks of flares, whose going out meant utter darkness
without sense of uprightness so that often you found yourself flat
in sudden mud on your face, or the back of your head. Life had
the actuality of nightmare, thick with tiredness in a slow, dragging
world; a deadness of living only just endurable from moment to
moment by the thought of relief. The news that the aged Field-
Marshal Lord Roberts had died of a chill at St. Omer, after
inspecting troops, came like a whisper across the mud and
desolation, through the weight and inertia of the night.

Chapter 30

REST

AT THE beginning of the third week of November the Guards Brigade was relieved.

Despite exhaustion, hope upheld the territorials, and discipline the regulars, on the march down the Menin Road, to the Grande Place of Ypres, where the Cloth Hall, the Cathedral of St. Martin, and many of the other buildings were as yet unshelled.

But there was to be no rest there. They went on through the wide and cobbled square, leaving the town by the Rue du Beurre. The column crossed railway line and canal, and continued along a tree-lined road. The men did not know their destination. Not to know was part of the mental torture, though none thought of mental torture, for so long had it been accepted as life itself. No whistling or singing; each man trudged, among others near yet remote, in desperate aloneness.

Several of the Highlanders, including Phillip, had lost shoes in the mud of the woods. They made the march unshod.

After nine days of fighting the London Highlanders numbered less than three hundred all told; even so, the battalion was almost as long, in columns of fours, as the rest of the brigade. The Coldstream had lost all their officers, and had a hundred and fifty other ranks. The Scots Guard had one captain and sixty-nine other ranks. The Black Watch mustered one lieutenant and a hundred and nine other ranks. The Cameron Highlanders had three officers and a hundred and forty other ranks.

Despite constant grinding nervous thought that with his lacerated bare feet he could never continue after each ten-minute halt at every hour, Phillip did not fall out. Towards the end of the march, when all except the Guards had lost step and line, he was light-headed, feeling that he could keep on quite a bit yet. He carried Lance-Corporal Blunden's rifle for the last two hours, or nine kilometres. Blunden, kind little modest Blunden, small dark Suffolk man, was also bare-foot.

The march lasted, with halts, over eight hours.

That night and all the next day and night they slept on billet floors. On the second morning came the reaction. Phillip was rather surprised to see so many of the stronger-looking men in the sick-parade with him. Among them was Sergeant Furrow, who went to hospital. In his place Douglas acted as platoon commander. Phillip's feet were not bad enough to get him to hospital; but he was excused duty, after they had been painted with iodine. He lay all the rest of the day in his billet, mourning in a dull void world, sometimes crying to himself, face turned to the wall. He tried to write a letter to his mother; it was put away unfinished. There was too much to say; there was nothing to say.

It was only at night that he learned of the London Rifles' arrival from St. Omer that afternoon on their way up the line; and he realised that he had missed his cousin Willie. The next morning, when he hobbled to the centre of the town, wearing a pair of wooden *sabots* borrowed from the old man of his billet, he heard that the Rifles had already marched out. He sat in the Rossignol estaminet, but it was lonely there, among unknown faces, so he went back to his billet, as snow began to fall.

When the draft from the 2nd Battalion arrived, there were many new faces in No. 1 Company; but he made no new friend. Instead, he became the centre of four or five of the newcomers in his billet, all ready to defer to one of the original battalion, the man with the greatcoat ripped horizontally across the breast by a Spandau bullet. They sat together in the Rossignol at night. Almost an evening fixture there was an old soldier of the A.S.C., who owned a crown-and-anchor board, and took their money. "Come on, my lucky lads, try your fancy! Here we are again, Box and Cox, the Army bankers! The Old Sweaty Sox! Often bent, but never broke! Back your fancy, my lucky lads! You comes here in rags and you rides away in moticars! If you don't speculate you can't accumulate!" Rattle of dice, the throw-down. "Up she comes, the old mood-'ook!" as the anchor turned up among the Major (crown), the Curse (diamond), Shovel (spade), Shamrock (club), and Heart.

The immediate past receded into the dark region of the inner mind: shut away in moments of the day—parades, drills, route marches, football: hidden in the bright lights of smoky estaminet when songs were sung, and there was always the patter of the "rough and tough, the old and bold" soldier of Ally Sloper's Cavalry, said to be worth fifty thousand francs, sitting at his board on the table by the wall, the bloody old skrimshanking thief. This was the life!

"Where you lay, I pay! I touch the money, but I never touch the dice! Any more for the lucky old mud-'ook? Are you all done, gentlemen? Are you all done? You lay, I pay! Copper to copper, silver to silver, *and gold to gold.* Here she goes" (rattle of dice)—"and out she comes—the lucky heart, the Curse, and the Major." He took in more francs than he paid out; for the odds were 6 to 1 against. But the patter went on and on, with the rattle, the throw, the chink of silver francs.

One of the main subjects of talk in the estaminets at that time was commissions. Almost daily men were leaving the battalion for England, to assume the coveted star and braid upon the tunic cuff. There was a look in their eyes as they came out of the orderly room, already temporary second-lieutenants of the New Armies, ordered to report the next morning for their passes HOME. The estaminets frequented by the Bleak Hill Boys became very noisy at night, as old friends had their final "wets" together, before going back to billets in the frosty nights hung with glittering stars that remained, despite the flashing of the guns.

Hoch der Kaiser!
Donner und Blitzen!
Salmon and Gluckstein!
BAA-AA-AH!!

"Where you lay, I pay! I touch the money, but I never touch the dice!"

This was the life!

Among the remaining survivors of the company, Phillip heard rumours that the battalion was to become an Officers Training Corps. There was not much doubt about what was the best service to be commissioned in. Quite a number of fellows had already applied for the Army Service Corps, Mechanical Transport section, for not only were A.S.C. officers paid more than any other branches—even a lorry-driver private, enlisted since the war, got six shillings a day, more than a junior officer of infantry —but the A.S.C. lived in comfort in rear areas, they could sleep once every twenty-four hours, and *in a bed.* For that reason alone there were no more vacancies in the A.S.C.

One of the fortunate ones going home had been gazetted to the Royal Garrison Artillery, whose heavy howitzers were normally miles behind the front line. The Royal Engineers came next for comfort; they worked up the line, but they went back to permanent billets where they could sleep dry.

Next in order of desirability was the Royal Field Artillery, the 18-pounders. They were about a mile back; they ate at a table under cover; above all, they could sleep out of the rain. All second-lieutenants of the branches behind the actual trenches were paid more than infantry second-lieutenants, who got five shillings and sixpence a day.

This seemed riches to Phillip; but he knew he would not stand the ghost of a chance if he applied for a commission. Nor would he ever dare to approach Douglas to ask the new Company Sergeant-Major to take him before Captain Ogilby. In any case, the new Colonel was not forwarding any more applications, as so many men had already left the battalion: and if all who were eligible were recommended, the battalion would scarcely muster more than a platoon. And in that platoon, of course, would be himself, the original Elastic Highlander. Still, what did it matter —this was the life!

He had gone to the estaminet in the first place for its name, *Au Rossignol*, which brought back the bluebell woods of Kent. One night while he was sitting there with the usual four of the new draft someone sang a Kipling song, *Gentlemen Rankers*, that made him feel he was glad to be staying on, a *café-rhum* drinking lad, one of the old Bleak Hill b'hoys, don't you know, who had fought in shoes and spats—Gentlemen-rankers out on the spree, Damned from here to Eternity, God ha' mercy on such as we —Bah! Yah!! BAA-AA-AH!!!

In shouted chorus, in the warmth and smoke of the Nightingale with its grey marble counter, rows of bottles on shelf of mirror'd wall, Marie leaning over the counter and smiling, madame's china coffee pots with big ornamentated curved spouts and handles on the stove behind. This was the life!

"Have a drink, you chaps? Cinq café-rhums, Marie!"

"Oui, m'sieu."

"Cheer-ho, you chaps!"

Downham in the office used to say Cheer-ho, and Phillip had said Cheer-ho ever since. People like the Leytonstone men said Cheer-o.

Phillip the veteran with the gaping tear across his greatcoat went back with the four new chaps to the billet at nine o'clock, when the estaminets were out of bounds to soldiers, telling himself that it was the only life. His letters home were cheery, dashed off usually in the early afternoon, after the route march of the morning and with dinner inside him. This was the life!

And this the death—broken sleep upon billet floor; phantoms in the silence of the night, the snorings of Church, mutterings and teeth-grindings of Collins which went on and on until the sudden shout broke from him, the cry of exploding nerves. Silence again, but not for long; movements in the straw; the shut dark hung with snore and mutter, scenes, faces, flinchings, terrors—the childhood "battle of the brain" come again, to be thrust away, pressed back, hands clenched, knees drawn up against cries ever imminent, groans to be blanket-muffled lest the new chaps in the straw discover his real self, his donkey-boy cowardice, as Peter Wallace had done, and Father, Magister, Martin, Furrow, and others whose faces swirled about him, distorting past his mental sight, passing through his eyes with faces of wax melting in flames of blazing stack and windmill, dripping under shadows of broken trees in the death-pallor of flares and skeleton roofs of farms under which thousands of more or less donkey-boys in khaki lay dead, with tens of thousands of donkey-boys in *feld grau*, while the moon looked down in frozen grief.

Mutter—mutter—mother—mother—the rain was beating on the window pane.

Chapter 31

PRIE DIEU

HOLDING his umbrella over himself and Hetty, Thomas Turney stood on the Thames Embankment, watching the funeral procession of Lord Roberts on its way to the crypt of St. Paul's Cathedral. Drifting rain had dispelled the slight fog of the late November morning, which began in doubtful grey, so they had come well wrapped up, Thomas Turney with soft brown canvas gaiters around his trousers below the knee.

As the gun-carriage passed, he removed his black square hat and saw upon the coffin, draped with Union Jack, the sword and baton, the medals and orders and decorations, together with the service cap of the dead Field-Marshal. Behind the gun-carriage a groom led a black charger, bearing large black full-dress riding-boots reversed in the irons.

Among the twelve pall-bearers, six in single file on either side of the gun-carriage, he recognised Lord Kitchener, Sir Evelyn Wood, both Field-Marshals, and Admiral Lord Charles Beresford. It was remarkable that not one of the twelve appeared to be in step with the muffled drum-beats, the band playing *Dead March in Saul* in slow time which the Guards, rifles reversed, paced out with legs rigid and boot-toes pointed. No, the high and mighty seemed to be doing a step of their own forward, each in a different time, while white feathers in cocked hats undulated to the movements.

Rain swayed with the gusts of wind; a sparrow flew, a plane-tree leaf fell; the drum muffled in *crêpe* beat out hollow thuds to music seeming to sob with the finality of death, all glory done, yet all to do again, from one generation to another, anguish and hope, dust to dust.

"We'll take the tram, Hetty, and get a cab from Blackfriars before the street is closed, if we're so fortunate."

So they caught up with the procession and passed it, leaving behind the bump and blare, the out-of-step elderly skipping, the rigidity of slow-marching guardsmen.

"I hope you won't catch cold, Papa——"

"No, my girl, I'm well wrapped up. I put on my chest-protector, as a precaution. I hope Phillip is wearing his, you can't be too careful in this weather."

"He is well away from the trenches now, he writes this morning, Papa. They are getting up football teams among the companies. He thinks they may soon be training to be officers."

"I see the scale of officer's pay has been raised, Hetty, according to *The Telegraph*. And the messing is not to be so expensive, as it was before the war. Income tax, d'ye see how it's gone up? Lloyd George has doubled it in the War Budget, in this morning's paper, to one and sixpence. The un-earned tax, I see, is up fivepence to one and eightpence in the pound. We shall all have to practise stricter economy now—d'ye see they've put an extra threepence on a pound of tea?"

"Yes, Papa, Dickie told me this morning."

They managed to get a cab to St. Paul's, and walked up the steps where pigeons, descendants of wild rock doves, were strutting with the sparrows, as much a part of the London scene as the look of shut-away thought on the faces of the people.

They entered the Cathedral, and were in vast gloom beaded by remote candle-points. They sat down on one side of the nave; and kneeling, prayed for their wishes: Thomas Turney that his children and grandchildren would be preserved in all trials and tribulations ahead, particularly his three grandsons, and that a successful end to the war be forthcoming before all business, on which the welfare of the nation depended, was dislocated irreparably. Almighty God, he thought in supplication, would understand his meaning, clumsily expressed as it might be—Amen.

Hetty prayed for her son to be brought safely through the war, and for all sons of mothers: would Dear God answer their prayers, and bring peace upon earth once more, in the name of the Lord Jesus, to whom all sorrows were known, and by Mary the Blessed Mother of God, who had stood by and seen the Agony of Love for the World denied as it was denied now, O God, in the dreadful war because men's hearts were hardened against Thy Word. I beseech thee, O God, to hear my prayer, and to bring my son Phillip through all dangers and trials. He is a good boy, Dear God, and when he has come to thy Word, his goodness will be a light, Thy Light, O Lord, among men.

She sat up, her eyes gleaming in the candles that burned for the dead in that cavernous stillness of marble and stone, murmurous with the remote traffic of the city, the dull thudding of a drum, its aisles whispering with the feet of the bereaved coming to their seats, and the flutters of a solitary rock-dove high up in the dome, lost within vast space, seeking a way to freedom.

August 1953—*February* 1954
Devon.

HENRY WILLIAMSON

The Dark Lantern

The courtship and marriage of Richard Maddison and Hetty Turney.

"There is a magic about this book. . . . This expedition into a late Victorian suburb and merchant materialism is unexpected and it is as genuine and affectionate as it is accomplished."—JOHN BETJEMAN (*Daily Telegraph*). "So engrossing and so delightful that I deliberately rationed my reading of it, laying it aside to spin out the pleasure as long as possible."—JAMES HANLEY (*Recorder*).

Donkey Boy

Phillip Maddison—the first years.

"A multi-coloured portrait vibrant with light and shade. Mr Williamson's study of a sensitive child, yearning for love and understanding, is a masterly piece of work."—FRED URQUHART (*Time and Tide*). "A fine novel."—PAMELA HANSFORD JOHNSON (*John O'London's*).

Young Phillip Maddison

"There is a loving detail about the record of the boy Phillip in the years before 1914 that makes an ordinary existence of hopes and frustrations, youthful joys and fears, remarkably interesting."—R. C. CHURCHILL (*Birmingham Post*). "One breathes here genuine country air combined with acute human observation."—*Glasgow Evening News*.